STAR WARS®

HEIR TO THE EMPIRE

20TH ANNIVERSARY EDITION

STAR WARS®

HEIR TO THE EMPIRE

20TH ANNIVERSARY EDITION

TIMOTHY ZAHN

 BALLANTINE BOOKS · NEW YORK

Published in the United States by Del Rey, an imprint of The Random House Publishing Group, a division of Random House, Inc., New York.
DEL REY is a registered trademark and the Del Rey colophon is a trademark of Random House, Inc.

An earlier edition of this work was published in different form in hardcover in 1991 and in mass market paperback in 1992 in the United States by Spectra, an imprint of The Random House Publishing Group, a division of Random House, Inc.

ISBN 978-0-345-52829-2
eISBN 978-0-345-53000-4

Printed in the United States of America on acid-free paper

www.starwars.com
www.delreybooks.com

9 8 7 6 5 4 3 2 1

20th Anniversary Edition

Book design by Christopher M. Zucker

To all the fans of the *Star Wars* Expanded Universe:

Thanks for letting me be a part of your lives these past two decades. I hope you've enjoyed it as much as I have.

THE STAR WARS NOVELS TIMELINE

OLD REPUBLIC
5000–33 YEARS BEFORE
STAR WARS: A New Hope

*Lost Tribe of the Sith**
Precipice
Skyborn
Paragon
Savior
Purgatory
Sentinel

3650 YEARS BEFORE STAR WARS: A New Hope

The Old Republic
Deceived
Fatal Alliance

Red Harvest

*Lost Tribe of the Sith**
Pantheon**
Secrets**

1032 YEARS BEFORE STAR WARS: A New Hope

Knight Errant

Darth Bane: Path of Destruction
Darth Bane: Rule of Two
Darth Bane: Dynasty of Evil

RISE OF THE EMPIRE
33–0 YEARS BEFORE
STAR WARS: A New Hope

Darth Maul: Saboteur*
Cloak of Deception
Darth Maul: Shadow Hunter

32 YEARS BEFORE STAR WARS: A New Hope

STAR WARS: EPISODE I
THE PHANTOM MENACE

Rogue Planet
Outbound Flight
The Approaching Storm

22 YEARS BEFORE STAR WARS: A New Hope

STAR WARS: EPISODE II
ATTACK OF THE CLONES

22–19 YEARS BEFORE STAR WARS: A New Hope

The Clone Wars
The Clone Wars: Wild Space
The Clone Wars: No Prisoners

Clone Wars Gambit
Stealth
Siege

Republic Commando
Hard Contact
Triple Zero
True Colors
Order 66

Shatterpoint
The Cestus Deception
The Hive*
MedStar I: Battle Surgeons
MedStar II: Jedi Healer
Jedi Trial
Yoda: Dark Rendezvous
Labyrinth of Evil

19 YEARS BEFORE STAR WARS: A New Hope

STAR WARS: EPISODE III
REVENGE OF THE SITH

Dark Lord: The Rise of Darth Vader

Coruscant Nights
Jedi Twilight
Street of Shadows
Patterns of Force

Imperial Commando
501st

The Han Solo Trilogy
The Paradise Snare
The Hutt Gambit
Rebel Dawn

The Adventures of Lando Calrissian
The Han Solo Adventures
The Force Unleashed
The Force Unleashed II
Death Troopers

*An eBook novella
**Forthcoming

REBELLION
0–5 YEARS AFTER
STAR WARS: A New Hope

Death Star
Shadow Games

0

STAR WARS: EPISODE IV
A NEW HOPE

Tales from the Mos Eisley Cantina
Allegiance
Choices of One
Galaxies: The Ruins of Dantooine
Splinter of the Mind's Eye

3 YEARS AFTER STAR WARS: A New Hope

STAR WARS: EPISODE V
THE EMPIRE STRIKES BACK

Tales of the Bounty Hunters
Shadows of the Empire

4 YEARS AFTER STAR WARS: A New Hope

STAR WARS: EPISODE VI
RETURN OF THE JEDI

Tales from Jabba's Palace
Tales from the Empire
Tales from the New Republic

The Bounty Hunter Wars
  The Mandalorian Armor
  Slave Ship
  Hard Merchandise

The Truce at Bakura
Luke Skywalker and the Shadows of
  Mindor

NEW REPUBLIC
5–25 YEARS AFTER
STAR WARS: A New Hope

X-Wing
  Rogue Squadron
  Wedge's Gamble
  The Krytos Trap
  The Bacta War
  Wraith Squadron
  Iron Fist
  Solo Command

The Courtship of Princess Leia
A Forest Apart*
Tatooine Ghost

The Thrawn Trilogy
  Heir to the Empire
  Dark Force Rising
  The Last Command

X-Wing: Isard's Revenge

The Jedi Academy Trilogy
  Jedi Search
  Dark Apprentice
  Champions of the Force

I, Jedi
Children of the Jedi
Darksaber
Planet of Twilight
X-Wing: Starfighters of Adumar
The Crystal Star

The Black Fleet Crisis Trilogy
  Before the Storm
  Shield of Lies
  Tyrant's Test

The New Rebellion

The Corellian Trilogy
  Ambush at Corellia
  Assault at Selonia
  Showdown at Centerpoint

The Hand of Thrawn Duology
  Specter of the Past
  Vision of the Future

Fool's Bargain*
Survivor's Quest

*An eBook novella
**Forthcoming

THE STAR WARS NOVELS TIMELINE

NEW JEDI ORDER
25–40 YEARS AFTER
STAR WARS: A New Hope

Boba Fett: A Practical Man*

The New Jedi Order
Vector Prime
Dark Tide I: Onslaught
Dark Tide II: Ruin
Agents of Chaos I: Hero's Trial
Agents of Chaos II: Jedi Eclipse
Balance Point
Recovery*
Edge of Victory I: Conquest
Edge of Victory II: Rebirth
Star by Star
Dark Journey
Enemy Lines I: Rebel Dream
Enemy Lines II: Rebel Stand
Traitor
Destiny's Way
Ylesia*
Force Heretic I: Remnant
Force Heretic II: Refugee
Force Heretic III: Reunion
The Final Prophecy
The Unifying Force

35   *YEARS AFTER STAR WARS: A New Hope*

The Dark Nest Trilogy
The Joiner King
The Unseen Queen
The Swarm War

LEGACY
40+ YEARS AFTER
STAR WARS: A New Hope

Legacy of the Force
Betrayal
Bloodlines
Tempest
Exile
Sacrifice
Inferno
Fury
Revelation
Invincible

Crosscurrent
Riptide
Millennium Falcon

43   *YEARS AFTER STAR WARS: A New Hope*

Fate of the Jedi
Outcast
Omen
Abyss
Backlash
Allies
Vortex
Conviction
Ascension**
Apocalypse**

*An eBook novella
**Forthcoming

FOREWORD

AT A TIME WHEN *Star Wars* is so firmly entrenched in our culture and so seemingly ubiquitous, it's hard to imagine a moment when it had all but disappeared from sight.

But that was exactly the time we faced back in the late eighties.

Star Wars had a phenomenal run during the release of the original trilogy. The films broke all box-office records. The toys sold like hotcakes. Younger incarnations of us boogied to *Star Wars* disco music. And then it all stopped. George stopped making the films. The boys who bought the toys moved on to sports and girls, and the disco ducks hunkered down to begin their careers. The world moved on.

By 1986, acting on the sage advice of our sole shareholder and resident Yoda, Lucas Licensing decided it was time to give *Star Wars* a rest. A few years later, with no new films on the horizon, we timidly started to think about what products might now be of interest to *Star Wars* fans. The first thing we realized was that our fan base had grown a bit older. The kids who bought the toys were now in college. Fans who had been teens or adults when the films first came out were probably starting careers or families. Where could we take *Star Wars* that would be relevant to their lives?

It was clear to us that simply revisiting the past would be of marginal interest. It was too early for a nostalgia play and, frankly, not very stimulating. We needed to give fans something new, something that appealed to a more mature sensibility. And, we reasoned, because *Star Wars* is all about story, the natural ground to explore was books—books that could expand the story, starting with the characters and situations so vividly established in the films and taking them to places never before imagined.

I was the head of Licensing, and back then I had a tiny staff. My finance director, Lucy Autrey Wilson, had been one of the company's first employees. Back in 1974, Lucy actually worked in George's house and helped type the scripts for *Star Wars: A New Hope.* She was a good finance person, but she was a restless soul and had a passion for publishing. She had implored me for years to give her the chance to make new publishing deals for *Star Wars.* And for years I had responded to her not unlike the way that Han responds to Luke when he says, "And who's gonna fly it, kid? You?"

Fortunately for Lucy—and for all of us—by 1989 there was a convergence in the Force. I was persuaded that it was time to restart our adult fiction publishing program and seriously explore new stories in the *Star Wars* universe. And I was willing to give Lucy the chance to find a publisher who shared our vision. But before we could do that, there was one last hurdle. If we were to play in this particular sandbox, we needed to consult the owner of the sandbox. So I went to George Lucas and humbly requested permission to expand his universe. He was appropriately skeptical (I seem to recall a response along the lines of, "No one is going to buy this") but supportive enough to give me the opportunity to fail. We established some very basic guidelines: The stories would have to take place after *Return of the Jedi;* events prior to *A New Hope* were off limits because if George were ever to make more *Star Wars* films, that was where he would go; and no major characters could be killed. Other than that, George made it clear that he would be hands-off. It seemed so simple and straightforward. I don't think George or I had any idea what we were getting ourselves into.

Lucy went out and pitched the concept of a new series of *Star Wars* spin-off books. She approached a number of publishers who felt that *Star Wars* was a dead issue and passed on the opportunity. But to our great relief, one publisher—Bantam Books—understood the vision: new *Star Wars* stories written by great writers could really mobilize the fans. Lucy made the deal and Bantam brought us a great writer—Tim Zahn. And Tim delivered.

I'll never forget the day that Lucy came into my office in 1991 to tell me the news that Tim's *Heir to the Empire* had premiered at number one on the *New York Times* hardcover bestseller list. It was an emotional moment. In a single stroke we knew that our instinct had been right. And even better, we knew that the flame of passion among our fans hadn't died after all. It needed only the right spark at the right time for it to burn anew—and more strongly than ever!

—HOWARD ROFFMAN
President, Lucas Licensing

INTRODUCTION

**A long time ago in a galaxy far,
far away. . . .**

WELL, ACTUALLY, IT WAS Illinois.

But it *was* a long time ago.

It was Monday, November 6, 1989, to be exact, at about four o'clock in the afternoon. I was sitting in my home office in Champaign, Illinois, working on a novel I'd just sold to Bantam Books called *Angelmass,* when I got an unexpected call from my agent, Russell Galen. After the usual pleasantries, he dropped what would be, for me, the understatement of the decade:

"Tim, we have a very interesting offer here."

As I stood there staring out a window in growing amazement, he went on to relate how, a year earlier, the head of Bantam Spectra, Lou Aronica, had written to Lucasfilm with an idea about restarting the *Star Wars* saga. Lou's plan was to create a three-book saga that would pick up the story after *Return of the Jedi,* an era in which no author had ever been permitted to write.

As fate (or the Force) would have it, that letter had arrived just as Howard Roffman and the team at Lucasfilm had decided to restart their adult publishing program.

That would have been awesome enough. What raised it to flabbergastable level was that Bantam and Lucasfilm were offering *me* the books.

I'd been a *Star Wars* fan as long as anyone else on the planet. (Well, okay, maybe not *everyone* else. I didn't make it to the theater until the second night.) Back in the early 1980s, when I was trying to forge a career for myself in the field, the *Star Wars* movie soundtracks were among my favorite records to listen to as I wrote. So much so that I distinctly remember thinking at the time that if George Lucas could come out of essentially nowhere to make a success of himself, maybe I could, too.

And now I was being invited to play in the universe he had created.

Anyway, Russ and I discussed it for forty minutes or so, and I told him I would think about it overnight and give him my answer in the morning. We said good-bye, and then I hung up the phone . . . and spent the next couple of hours panicking.

At issue was the fact that this offer was very much a two-edged sword. I had the chance to jump-start my career in a way I could never have anticipated or even hoped. I also had the chance to fail spectacularly in front of a potential audience of millions.

Because I was going to have to write *Star Wars*. Not something science-fictiony or space-operatic with the name *Star Wars* on it. I was going to have to write *Star Wars*. I would have to somehow capture the scope and feel of the universe; the faces and voices of the main characters; the ebb and flow and rhythm of the movies. The readers had to hear Mark Hamill's and Carrie Fisher's and Harrison Ford's voices inside my quotation marks. The people flipping through those pages needed to be able to hear John Williams's music in the backs of their minds.

If I couldn't do that, or at least get close, it wouldn't be *Star Wars*. It would be *An Adventure of Two Guys Named Han and Luke*. And that would be a waste of everyone's time.

There was more. Not only did I have to get the feel of the universe right, I also had to come up with a story—a three-book-long story, in fact—that wasn't simply a rehash of what George had already done. I would have to age the movie characters believably, and create new characters that would fit seamlessly into the mix.

By the next morning I still didn't know if I could pull all that off. But I did know that I very much wanted to try. So I told Russ I was on board and got to work.

The first part was easy enough. By Thanksgiving, a little over two weeks later, I had a forty-page preliminary outline for the trilogy, and had had some conversations with Betsy Mitchell, my editor on the project.

We then hit an unexpected snag (unexpected to me, anyway): the Bantam and Lucasfilm lawyers were still hammering out their contract. Until they had a contract, I couldn't get a contract with Bantam to write the books, and until I had my contract, Lucasfilm wouldn't look at my outline (for legal reasons that I certainly understood). And until they approved my outline, it was pointless for me to start writing.

Between the lawyers and the back-and-forth LFL approval process it was a solid six months before I was finally able to get to work. (As it is, I jumped the gun by about a week, figuring that whatever final changes LFL might want probably wouldn't affect the first two or three chapters that much.) Along the way there were problems to be ironed out, disagreements to be discussed, compromises to be made, and occasionally capitulation (on my part) to be graciously made.

I groused some about the latter. We authors usually grouse when we don't get our way. But as I look back, I can honestly say that the book is much better because of the suggestions and changes that I sometimes only grudgingly accepted.

I mailed the book to Betsy on November 2, 1990 (yes, we still mailed paper manuscripts back then), a bit less than six months after I'd started and almost exactly a year after I was offered the project. For me, at that time, six months was phenomenally fast, though in the past twenty years I've gotten considerably faster. (For instance, my most recent *Star Wars* book, *Choices of One,* took only three months to write.) As with the outline, the finished manuscript went through an approval/change process with Bantam and Lucasfilm, and after a lot of (mostly minor) changes it was finally declared finished. Cover art was commissioned, other editorial stuff was done, the promotional and ad campaigns were arranged, and all was ready to go.

Except for one question, the question that had been hanging over the project since the very beginning.

Namely, would anyone actually buy the book?

Lou had been convinced from the start that the audience was out there. But even he was taking it mostly on faith. After all, *Return of the Jedi* was eight years in the past and the *Star Wars* fans were quiet.

There were hints, of course. A couple of months before *Heir* came out I went to talk to a class of fourth-graders, and took a copy of the cover to show them. These kids, who'd barely been alive when the last *Star Wars* movie came out, gazed excitedly at the cover art, pointing out Han and Luke and Chewie to one another. Through the magic of VCR tape, they were fully up to speed with everything *Star Wars*.

But hints are only hints. So Bantam and Lucasfilm hedged their bets. They set the price of the book at fifteen dollars, considerably below market standard for hardcovers. The sales staff worked hard to drum up enthusiasm among booksellers, with mixed results. They bought print ads and put out an actual radio ad. (I'd never before had a radio ad for one of my books. Nor, I think, have I had once since.)

After that, there was nothing to do but sit back and cross our fingers.

May 1991.

It's been said by some that the Thrawn Trilogy restarted *Star Wars*. That sounds very impressive, but it's not really true. A more accurate statement would be that I was the first person since *Jedi* who was permitted to stick a fork into the piecrust to see if there was still any steam underneath.

There was steam. *Man*, was there steam.

The first run of seventy thousand copies was gone within two weeks, and Bantam was scrambling to get more printed. (Semi-useless fact: the printer ran out of blue cover stock after the third printing, so the fourth printing was on a tan cover stock. Even today, if I see one of those come across my autographing table I'll do a whole Force "I know what printing this is" routine.) I was told by some bookstore clerks that they were selling *Heir* right out of the box, that they would be putting the books on the rack and someone would catch sight of *Star Wars* on the cover, grab one, and head to checkout.

The book made it to number one on the *New York Times* list, the authors' Holy Grail. (It actually beat out John Grisham's *The Firm*. He later sent me a copy of his book with an autograph and a very nice, very tongue-in-cheek request for me to get out of his way.)

Heir went through multiple printings—I don't remember how many. In fact, Bantam was still printing new hardcovers *after* the paperback came out, which Russ told me almost never happens. (As I recall, his actual comment had a bit more French in it—he was as astonished as anyone else.)

The book actually made it into a *Jeopardy!* question, which is beyond even *New York Times* Holy Grail status. ("Timothy Zahn's bestselling novel *Heir to the Empire* is a sequel to this movie trilogy." I still have that episode on tape somewhere.)

The *Star Wars* fans were out there, all right. And after three new movies, the hit *Clone Wars* TV show, and numerous books and comics, they and *Star Wars* are still going strong.

Reading *Heir* again after all these years has been an interesting and slightly unsettling experience. On the one hand, I see all the stylistic things I would change if I were writing it today—some of the sentence and paragraph structure, bits and pieces of writing technique, maybe some of the pacing. But on the other hand, the story still holds up well. Maybe even a little better than I'd expected it to.

So I invite you now to join Betsy and me on a journey down memory lane. Twenty years is a long time, but we'll do my best to remember how it all happened.

—TIMOTHY ZAHN

STAR WARS®

HEIR TO THE EMPIRE

20TH ANNIVERSARY EDITION

CHAPTER 1

"CAPTAIN PELLAEON?" a voice called down the portside crew pit through the hum of background conversation. "Message from the sentry line: the scoutships have just come out of lightspeed."

Pellaeon, leaning over the shoulder of the man at the *Chimaera's*[1] bridge engineering monitor, ignored the shout. "Trace this line for me," he ordered, tapping a light pen at the schematic on the display.

The engineer threw a questioning glance up at him. "Sir . . . ?"

"I heard him," Pellaeon said. "You have an order, Lieutenant."

"Yes, sir," the other said carefully, and keyed for the trace.

"Captain Pellaeon?" the voice repeated, closer this time. Keeping his eyes on the engineering display, Pellaeon waited until he could hear the sound of the approaching footsteps. Then, with all the regal weight that fifty years

1. Each of the three classic *Star Wars* movies includes a Star Destroyer in its opening scene. All of my Rebellion-era books do the same.

—TIMOTHY ZAHN

spent in the Imperial Fleet gave to a man, he straightened up and turned.

The young duty officer's brisk walk faltered; came to an abrupt halt. "Uh, sir—" He looked into Pellaeon's eyes and his voice faded away.

Pellaeon let the silence hang in the air for a handful of heartbeats, long enough for those nearest to notice. "This is not a cattle market in Shaum Hii, Lieutenant Tschel," he said at last, keeping his voice calm but icy cold. "This is the bridge of an Imperial Star Destroyer. Routine information is not—repeat, *not*—simply shouted in the general direction of its intended recipient. Is that clear?"

Tschel[2] swallowed. "Yes, sir."

Pellaeon held his eyes a few seconds longer, then lowered his head in a slight nod. "Now. Report."

"Yes, sir." Tschel swallowed again. "We've just received word from the sentry ships, sir: the scouts have returned from their scan raid on the Obroa-skai system."

"Very good." Pellaeon nodded. "Did they have any trouble?"

"Only a little, sir—the natives apparently took exception to them pulling a dump of their central library system. The wing commander said there was some attempt at pursuit, but that he lost them."

"I hope so," Pellaeon said grimly. Obroa-skai held a strategic position in the borderland regions, and intelligence reports indicated that the New Republic was making a strong bid for its membership and support. If they'd had armed emissary ships there at the time of the raid. . . .

Well, he'd know soon enough. "Have the wing commander report to the bridge ready room with his report as soon as the ships are aboard," he told Tschel. "And have the sentry line go to yellow alert. Dismissed."

"Yes, sir." Spinning around with a reasonably good imitation of a proper military turn, the lieutenant headed back toward the communications console.

The *young* lieutenant . . . which was, Pellaeon thought

2. I wanted to set up the Fleet as having suffered during the chaos and retreat of the years since Endor, slipping back from the generally efficient war machine shown in the movies to something less polished. Lieutenant Tschel was an example of the eager but inexperienced crewers that the Empire now had to whip into fighting shape, contrasting with the old-school competence and tradition of Captain Pellaeon.

—TZ

with a trace of old bitterness, where the problem really lay. In the old days—at the height of the Empire's power—it would have been inconceivable for a man as young as Tschel to serve as a bridge officer aboard a ship like the *Chimaera*. Now—

He looked down at the equally young man at the engineering monitor. Now, in contrast, the *Chimaera* had virtually no one aboard except young men and women.

Slowly, Pellaeon let his eyes sweep across the bridge, feeling the echoes of old anger and hatred twist through his stomach. There had been many commanders in the Fleet, he knew, who had seen the Emperor's original Death Star as a blatant attempt to bring the Empire's vast military power more tightly under his direct control, just as he'd already done with the Empire's political power.[3] The fact that he'd ignored the battle station's proven vulnerability and gone ahead with a second Death Star had merely reinforced that suspicion. There would have been few in the Fleet's upper echelons who would have genuinely mourned its loss . . . if it hadn't, in its death throes, taken the Super Star Destroyer *Executor* with it.

Even after five years Pellaeon couldn't help but wince at the memory of that image: the *Executor,* out of control, colliding with the unfinished Death Star and then disintegrating completely in the battle station's massive explosion. The loss of the ship itself had been bad enough; but the fact that it was the *Executor* had made it far worse. That particular Super Star Destroyer had been Darth Vader's personal ship, and despite the Dark Lord's legendary—and often lethal—capriciousness, serving aboard it had long been perceived as the quick line to promotion.

Which meant that when the *Executor* died, so also did a disproportionate fraction of the best young and midlevel officers and crewers.[4]

The Fleet had never recovered from that fiasco. With the *Executor*'s leadership gone, the battle had quickly turned into a confused rout, with several other Star De-

3. The Grand Admirals were to be part of this same overall plan: an extra layer put in at the top of the military command, its members appointed by and answerable only to the Emperor.

—TZ

4. Later, after the 501st Legion fan group began, it was also established that Vader similarly liked to grab the Empire's best stormtroopers and add them to his personal legion. I got to play with that idea a bit in later books.

—TZ

5. When *Heir* first came out, I got a few questions about how this fit with the celebrations we saw at the end of *Return of the Jedi*. My answer was that those were spontaneous shows of relief and defiance by the galaxy's ordinary citizens, but that the Empire's military was far from defeated. In fact, it would be ten more years of *Star Wars* time until *Vision of the Future*, when the war with the Empire would finally end.

—TZ

6. I don't see Thrawn as the type to use unwilling conscripts. Clearly, this was something other Imperial leaders had initiated before his return.

—TZ

7. I wanted *Heir*'s villain to be a military leader, as opposed to a governor, Moff, or Sith. But a normal admiral seemed too commonplace. Hence, the Grand Admirals.

I first ran across the title, by the way, in connection with the German navy in William L. Shirer's *The Rise and Fall of the Third Reich*.

—TZ

stroyers being lost before the order to withdraw had finally been given. Pellaeon himself, taking command when the *Chimaera*'s former captain was killed, had done what he could to hold things together; but despite his best efforts, they had never regained the initiative against the Rebels. Instead, they had been steadily pushed back . . . until they were here.

Here, in what had once been the backwater of the Empire, with barely a quarter of its former systems still under nominal Imperial control.[5] Here, aboard a Star Destroyer manned almost entirely by painstakingly trained but badly inexperienced young people, many of them conscripted from their home worlds by force or threat of force.[6]

Here, under the command of possibly the greatest military mind the Empire had ever seen.

Pellaeon smiled—a tight, wolfish smile—as he again looked around his bridge. No, the end of the Empire was not yet. As the arrogantly self-proclaimed New Republic would soon discover.

He glanced at his watch. Two-fifteen. Grand Admiral Thrawn[7] would be meditating in his command room now . . . and if Imperial procedure frowned on shouting across the bridge, it frowned even harder on interrupting a Grand Admiral's meditation by intercom. One spoke to him in person, or one did not speak to him at all. "Continue tracing those lines," Pellaeon ordered the engineering lieutenant as he headed for the door. "I'll be back shortly."

The Grand Admiral's new command room was two levels below the bridge, in a space that had once housed the former commander's luxury entertainment suite. When Pellaeon had found Thrawn—or rather, when the Grand Admiral had found him—one of his first acts had been to take over the suite and convert it into what was essentially a secondary bridge.

A secondary bridge, meditation room . . . and perhaps more. It was no secret aboard the *Chimaera* that since the recent refitting had been completed the Grand Admiral had been spending a great deal of his time here. What *was* secret was what exactly he did during those long hours.

Stepping to the door, Pellaeon straightened his tunic and braced himself. Perhaps he was about to find out. "Captain Pellaeon to see Grand Admiral Thrawn," he announced. "I have informa—"

The door slid open before he'd finished speaking. Mentally preparing himself, Pellaeon stepped into the dimly lit entry room. He glanced around, saw nothing of interest, and started for the door to the main chamber, five paces ahead.

A touch of air on the back of his neck was his only warning. "Captain Pellaeon," a deep, gravelly, catlike voice mewed into his ear.

Pellaeon jumped and spun around, cursing both himself and the short, wiry creature standing less than half a meter away. "Blast it, Rukh," he snarled. "What do you think you're doing?"

For a long moment Rukh just looked up at him, and Pellaeon felt a drop of sweat trickle down his back. With his large dark eyes, protruding jaw, and glistening needle teeth,[8] Rukh was even more of a nightmare in the dimness than he was in normal lighting.

Especially to someone like Pellaeon, who knew what Thrawn used Rukh and his fellow Noghri for.[9]

"I'm doing my job," Rukh said at last. He stretched his thin arm almost casually out toward the inner door, and Pellaeon caught just a glimpse of the slender assassin's knife before it vanished somehow into the Noghri's sleeve. His hand closed, then opened again, steel-wire muscles moving visibly beneath his dark gray skin.[10] "You may enter."

"*Thank* you," Pellaeon growled. Straightening his tunic again, he turned back to the door. It opened at his approach, and he stepped through—

Into a softly lit art museum.

8. With none of Vader's backstory available at the time, and having just invented the Noghri species for this story, I came up with the idea that Vader might have designed his mask to look like a stylized version of a Noghri face, the better to facilitate his command of the death commando squads. (At the time, of course, I didn't know that it would be revealed in RotS that Palpatine had provided the mask.) I wasn't allowed to explicitly make the mask/Noghri connection in *Heir*, but I thought I might be permitted to do so later in the trilogy, so I went ahead and designed the aliens' faces with that resemblance in mind.

Of course, we know now that the mask (which had originally been based on Ralph McQuarrie's preproduction drawings) *was* provided by Palpatine, based on his own twisted, evil Sith specs, and had nothing whatsoever to do with the Noghri.

Just as well that LFL hadn't let me run with this one. Yet another instance where their caution about letting my imagination stray too far saved me from future embarrassment.

—TZ

9. Originally, I had Rukh and his fellows being Sith, keying off Vader's title *Lord of the Sith*. Since at that point the term hadn't been defined, I figured I was safe. But Lucasfilm was concerned that George *would* want to use the Sith at some future date (which, as we all know, he did) and told me to pick some other term for them.

I fumed about that for a while, but of course I'm very grateful now that they ordered me to make that change.

—TZ

10. My original idea was that Noghri skin started out a pale gray in childhood and gradually darkened to black as the Noghri grew to adulthood. But there were concerns about possible racial questions (even though the Noghri were eminently honorable and would eventually become New Republic allies), so I changed the skin to gray.

—TZ

11. We never saw a command chair in any of the movies. The Star Destroyer bridge seemed to be modeled on the old sailing ship design, where the officers stood or paced as they observed the deck

He stopped short, just inside the room, and looked around in astonishment. The walls and domed ceiling were covered with flat paintings and planics, a few of them vaguely human-looking but most of distinctly alien origin. Various sculptures were scattered around, some freestanding, others on pedestals. In the center of the room was a double circle of repeater displays, the outer ring slightly higher than the inner ring. Both sets of displays, at least from what little Pellaeon could see, also seemed to be devoted to pictures of artwork.

And in the center of the double circle, seated in a duplicate of the Admiral's Chair on the bridge,[11] was Grand Admiral Thrawn.

He sat motionlessly, his shimmery blue-black hair glinting in the dim light, his pale blue skin looking cool and subdued and very alien on his otherwise human frame. His eyes were nearly closed as he leaned back against the headrest, only a glint of red showing between the lids.

Pellaeon licked his lips, suddenly unsure of the wisdom of having invaded Thrawn's sanctum like this. If the Grand Admiral decided to be annoyed . . .

"Come in, Captain," Thrawn said, his quietly modulated voice cutting through Pellaeon's thoughts. Eyes still closed to slits, he waved a hand in a small and precisely measured motion. "What do you think?"

"It's . . . very interesting, sir," was all Pellaeon could come up with as he walked over to the outer display circle.

"All holographic, of course," Thrawn said, and Pellaeon thought he could hear a note of regret in the other's voice. "The sculptures and flats both. Some of them are lost; many of the others are on planets now occupied by the Rebellion."

"Yes, sir." Pellaeon nodded. "I thought you'd want to know, Admiral, that the scouts have returned from the Obroa-skai system. The wing commander will be ready for debriefing in a few minutes."

Thrawn nodded. "Were they able to tap into the central library system?"

"They got at least a partial dump," Pellaeon told him. "I don't know yet if they were able to complete it—apparently, there was some attempt at pursuit. The wing commander thinks he lost them, though."

For a moment Thrawn was silent. "No," he said. "No, I don't believe he has. Particularly not if the pursuers were from the Rebellion." Taking a deep breath, he straightened in his chair and, for the first time since Pellaeon had entered, opened his glowing red eyes.

Pellaeon returned the other's gaze without flinching, feeling a small flicker of pride at the achievement. Many of the Emperor's top commanders and courtiers had never learned to feel comfortable with those eyes. Or with Thrawn himself, for that matter. Which was probably why the Grand Admiral had spent so much of his career out in the Unknown Regions, working to bring those still-barbaric sections of the galaxy under Imperial control.[12] His brilliant successes had won him the title of Warlord[13] and the right to wear the white uniform of Grand Admiral—the only nonhuman ever granted that honor by the Emperor.

Ironically, it had also made him all the more indispensable to the frontier campaigns. Pellaeon had often wondered how the Battle of Endor would have ended if Thrawn, not Vader, had been commanding the *Executor*. "Yes, sir," he said. "I've ordered the sentry line onto yellow alert. Shall we go to red?"

"Not yet," Thrawn said. "We should still have a few minutes. Tell me, Captain, do you know anything about art?"

"Ah . . . not very much," Pellaeon managed, thrown a little by the sudden change of subject. "I've never really had much time to devote to it."

"You should make the time." Thrawn gestured to a part of the inner display circle to his right. "Saffa paintings," he identified them. "Circa 1550 to 2200, Pre-Empire Date.

(cont.) and rigging and gave orders. But it seemed to me that Thrawn would spend a lot of time up there, and to minimize the distractions of fatigue would arrange to have a chair.

Also, of course, ringing the chair with repeater displays would allow him to keep a closer eye on what was happening aboard his ship.

—TZ

12. Thrawn's—and Palpatine's—real agendas for the Unknown Regions campaigns were fairly vague here. The background for all of that would be slowly developed and revealed in future books.

—TZ

13. *Heir to the Empire* wasn't my original title for the book, but was suggested by Lou Aronica at Bantam. My choices were *Wild Card* (which was vetoed because Bantam was also doing the Wild Cards superhero anthology series) and *Warlord's Gambit*. Though we ultimately went with *Heir*, there are still bits of setup—such as here—for that other title.

—TZ

Note how the style changes—right here—at the first contact with the Thennqora. Over there"—he pointed to the left-hand wall—"are examples of Paonidd extrassa art. Note the similarities with the early Saffa work, and also the mid-eighteenth-century Pre-Em Vaathkree flatsculp."

"Yes, I see," Pellaeon said, not entirely truthfully. "Admiral, shouldn't we be—?"

He broke off as a shrill whistle split the air. "Bridge to Grand Admiral Thrawn," Lieutenant Tschel's taut voice called over the intercom. "Sir, we're under attack!"

Thrawn tapped the intercom switch. "This is Thrawn," he said evenly. "Go to red alert, and tell me what we've got. Calmly, if possible."

"Yes, sir." The muted alert lights began flashing, and Pellaeon could hear the sound of the klaxons baying faintly outside the room. "Sensors are picking up four New Republic Assault Frigates,"[14] Tschel continued, his voice tense but under noticeably better control. "Plus at least three wings of X-wing fighters. Symmetric cloud-vee formation, coming in on our scoutships' vector."

Pellaeon swore under his breath. A single Star Destroyer, with a largely inexperienced crew, against four Assault Frigates and their accompanying fighters . . . "Run engines to full power," he called toward the intercom. "Prepare to make the jump to lightspeed." He took a step toward the door—

"Belay that jump order, Lieutenant," Thrawn said, still glacially calm. "TIE fighter crews to their stations; activate deflector shields."

Pellaeon spun back to him. "Admiral—"

Thrawn cut him off with an upraised hand. "Come here, Captain," the Grand Admiral ordered. "Let's take a look, shall we?"

He touched a switch; and abruptly, the art show was gone. Instead, the room had become a miniature bridge monitor, with helm, engine, and weapons readouts on the walls and double display circle. The open space had become a holographic tactical display; in one corner a flash-

14. Assault Frigates were modified Dreadnoughts, a little more than a third the size of a Star Destroyer. They were older ships—Clone Wars era—but still packed a hefty punch.
  Both Assault Frigates and Dreadnoughts came by way of West End Games (WEG) and their *Star Wars* role-playing games sourcebooks.
  More about WEG later.
                    —TZ

ing sphere indicated the invaders. The wall display nearest to it gave an ETA estimate of twelve minutes.

"Fortunately, the scoutships have enough of a lead not to be in danger themselves," Thrawn commented. "So. Let's see what exactly we're dealing with. Bridge: order the three nearest sentry ships to attack."

"Yes, sir."

Across the room, three blue dots shifted out of the sentry line onto intercept vectors. From the corner of his eye Pellaeon saw Thrawn lean forward in his seat as the Assault Frigates and accompanying X-wings shifted in response. One of the blue dots winked out—

"Excellent," Thrawn said, leaning back in his seat. "That will do, Lieutenant. Pull the other two sentry ships back, and order the Sector Four line to scramble out of the invaders' vector."

"Yes, sir," Tschel said, sounding more than a little confused.

A confusion Pellaeon could well understand. "Shouldn't we at least signal the rest of the Fleet?" he suggested, hearing the tightness in his voice. "The *Death's Head* could be here in twenty minutes, most of the others in less than an hour."

"The last thing we want to do right now is bring in more of our ships, Captain," Thrawn said. He looked up at Pellaeon, and a faint smile touched his lips. "After all, there *may* be survivors, and we wouldn't want the Rebellion learning about us. Would we?"

He turned back to his displays. "Bridge: I want a twenty-degree port yaw rotation—bring us flat to the invaders' vector, superstructure pointing at them.[15] As soon as they're within the outer perimeter, the Sector Four sentry line is to re-form behind them and jam all transmissions."

"Y-yes, sir. Sir—?"

"You don't have to understand, Lieutenant," Thrawn said, his voice abruptly cold. "Just obey."

"Yes, sir."

Pellaeon took a careful breath as the displays showed

15. One reason we proposed Tim to Lucasfilm as the author of the new *Star Wars* trilogy was his background in writing military science fiction. His previous novels—including the Cobra series and *Black-collar*—were excellent examples of the craft.
—BETSY MITCHELL

16. One of the criticisms often thrown at *Star Wars* is that X-wings fly like atmosphere fighters, banking and turning when the vacuum of space shouldn't allow that. However, the movies posited S-Foils (which at the time I interpreted as "spacefoils," as opposed to airfoils), which I also assumed were "pressing" against the universe's vacuum energy (sometimes called zero-point energy). In that same vein, I created the etheric rudder, also interacting with the vacuum energy, to give steering capability.

The term never caught on, though, and has since quietly been dropped. But I think the principle still stands.

—TZ

17. One of the coolest parts of writing *Star Wars* books is when you occasionally see something you've done borrowed for use in another part of the vast Lucasfilm universe. In this case, it was the "Storm Over Ryloth" episode of the *Clone Wars* TV series, where the Marg Sabl maneuver is used against a Trade Federation blockade.

What's even cooler is that the featurette of that episode on the DVD specifically credits the

the *Chimaera* rotating as per orders. "I'm afraid I don't understand, either, Admiral," he said. "Turning our superstructure toward them—"

Again, Thrawn stopped him with an upraised hand. "Watch and learn, Captain. That's fine, bridge: stop rotation and hold position here. Drop docking bay deflector shields, boost power to all others. TIE fighter squadrons: launch when ready. Head directly away from the *Chimaera* for two kilometers, then sweep around in open cluster formation. Backfire speed, zonal attack pattern."

He got an acknowledgment, then looked up at Pellaeon. "Do you understand now, Captain?"

Pellaeon pursed his lips. "I'm afraid not," he admitted. "I see now that the reason you turned the ship was to give the fighters some exit cover, but the rest is nothing but a classic Marg Sabl closure maneuver. They're not going to fall for anything that simple."

"On the contrary," Thrawn corrected coolly. "Not only will they fall for it, they'll be utterly destroyed by it. Watch, Captain. And learn."

The TIE fighters launched, accelerating away from the *Chimaera* and then leaning hard into etheric rudders to sweep back around it like the spray of some exotic fountain.[16] The invading ships spotted the attackers and shifted vectors—

Pellaeon blinked. "What in the Empire are they *doing?*"

"They're trying the only defense they know of against a Marg Sabl,"[17] Thrawn said, and there was no mistaking the satisfaction in his voice. "Or, to be more precise, the only defense they are psychologically capable of attempting." He nodded toward the flashing sphere. "You see, Captain, there's an Elom commanding that force ... and Elomin simply cannot handle the unstructured attack profile of a properly executed Marg Sabl."

Pellaeon stared at the invaders, still shifting into their utterly useless defense stance ... and slowly it dawned on him what Thrawn had just done. "That sentry ship attack a few minutes ago," he said. "You were able to tell from *that* that those were Elomin ships?"

"Learn about art, Captain," Thrawn said, his voice almost dreamy. "When you understand a species' art, you understand that species."[18]

He straightened in his chair. "Bridge: bring us to flank speed. Prepare to join the attack."

An hour later, it was all over.[19]

The ready room door slid shut behind the wing commander, and Pellaeon gazed back at the map still on the display. "Sounds like Obroa-skai is a dead end," he said regretfully. "There's no way we'll be able to spare the manpower that much pacification would cost."

"For now, perhaps," Thrawn agreed. "But only for now."

Pellaeon frowned across the table at him. Thrawn was fiddling with a data card, rubbing it absently between finger and thumb, as he stared out the view port at the stars. A strange smile played about his lips. "Admiral?" he asked carefully.

Thrawn turned his head, those glowing eyes coming to rest on Pellaeon. "It's the second piece of the puzzle, Captain," he said softly, holding up the data card. "The piece I've been searching for now for over a year."

Abruptly, he turned to the intercom, jabbed it on. "Bridge, this is Grand Admiral Thrawn. Signal the *Death's Head;* inform Captain Harbid we'll be temporarily leaving the Fleet. He's to continue making tactical surveys of the local systems and pulling data dumps wherever possible. Then set course for a planet called Myrkr—the nav computer has its location."

The bridge acknowledged, and Thrawn turned back to Pellaeon. "You seem lost, Captain," he suggested. "I take it you've never heard of Myrkr."

Pellaeon shook his head, trying without success to read the Grand Admiral's expression. "Should I have?"

(cont.) maneuver to *Heir.* Thrawn would have been pleased.

—TZ

18. I'm often asked where the whole art-as-tactical-insight idea came from. Sadly, I have no particular epiphany or historical reference I can point to. It's just something that popped into my mind during the Thrawn development process.

—TZ

19. One of the questions I'm most frequently asked is how I came up with the idea and person of Grand Admiral Thrawn.

The *Star Wars* movies revolved around villains who led by coercion and fear. That may work for short-range operation (Vader's crew certainly put their hearts into their work), but it's not so good long-range or long-term.

So I decided to do something different to try to create a commander who could lead by loyalty.

What qualities does such a commander have to have? The first, obviously, is strategic and tactical skill. His troops must believe that any operation they're going into has a good chance of success, with as few casualties on their side as possible.

There will be many other

examples of Thrawn's tactical skill throughout the book, but here's the first: he defeats an entire New Republic task force without, apparently, ever even bothering to leave his meditation room.

There are a few other qualities that I came up with when mulling over Thrawn's character. I'll comment more on those as we go along.

—TZ

"Probably not. Most of those who have been smugglers, malcontents, and otherwise useless dregs of the galaxy."

He paused, taking a measured sip from the mug at his elbow—a strong Forvish ale, from the smell of it—and Pellaeon forced himself to remain silent. Whatever the Grand Admiral was going to tell him, he was obviously going to tell it in his own way and time. "I ran across an offhand reference to it some seven years ago," Thrawn continued, setting his mug back down. "What caught my attention was the fact that, although the planet had been populated for at least three hundred years, both the Old Republic and the Jedi of that time had always left it strictly alone." He cocked one blue-black eyebrow slightly. "What would you infer from that, Captain?"

Pellaeon shrugged. "That it's a frontier planet, somewhere too far away for anyone to care about."

"Very good, Captain. That was my first assumption, too . . . except that it's not. Myrkr is, in fact, no more than a hundred fifty light-years from here—close to our border with the Rebellion and well within the Old Republic's boundaries." Thrawn dropped his eyes to the data card still in his hand. "No, the actual explanation is far more interesting. And far more useful."

Pellaeon looked at the data card, too. "And that explanation became the first piece of this puzzle of yours?"

Thrawn smiled at him. "Again, Captain, very good. Yes. Myrkr—or more precisely, one of its indigenous animals—was the first piece. The second is on a world called Wayland." He waved the data card. "A world for which, thanks to the Obroans, I finally have a location."

20. Thrawn never did accept the legitimacy of the New Republic. Later, as I've filled in more of his backstory, I've tried to give some of the reasons for his stubbornness on this point.

—TZ

"I congratulate you," Pellaeon said, suddenly tired of this game. "May I ask just what exactly this puzzle is?"

Thrawn smiled—a smile that sent a shiver up Pellaeon's back. "Why, the only puzzle worth solving, of course," the Grand Admiral said softly. "The complete, total, and utter destruction of the Rebellion."[20]

CHAPTER 2

"LUKE?"

The voice came softly but insistently. Pausing amid the familiar landscape of Tatooine—familiar, yet oddly distorted—Luke Skywalker turned to look.

An equally familiar figure stood there watching him. "Hello, Ben," Luke said, his voice sounding sluggish in his ears. "Been a long time."

"It has indeed," Obi-wan Kenobi said gravely. "And I'm afraid that it will be longer still until the next time. I've come to say good-bye, Luke."

The landscape seemed to tremble; and abruptly, a small part of Luke's mind remembered that he was asleep. Asleep in his suite in the Imperial Palace, and dreaming of Ben Kenobi.[1]

"No, I'm not a dream," Ben assured him, answering Luke's unspoken thought. "But the distances separating us have become too great for me to appear to you in any other way. Now, even this last path is being closed to me."

1. Having Ben show up in a dream was to be an echo of Luke's vision of Ben (possibly his first *visual* contact) in his near-unconscious state in the swirling snow of the Hoth night.

On Hoth, I've assumed the timing and circumstances of the vision were mostly factors of Luke's inexperience and lack of strength in the Force, requiring that borderline state of mind and body for Ben to make his appearance. Here, conversely, it's Ben's weakness or distance that dictates the means of contact.

—TZ

"No," Luke heard himself say. "You can't leave us, Ben. We need you."

Ben's eyebrows lifted slightly, and a hint of his old smile touched his lips. "You don't need me, Luke. You are a Jedi, strong in the Force." The smile faded, and for a moment his eyes seemed to focus on something Luke couldn't see. "At any rate," he added quietly, "the decision is not mine to make. I have lingered too long already, and can no longer postpone my journey from this life to what lies beyond."

A memory stirred: Yoda on his deathbed, and Luke pleading with him not to die. *Strong am I in the Force,* the Jedi Master had told him softly. *But not that strong.*[2]

"It is the pattern of all life to move on," Ben reminded him. "You, too, will face this same journey one day." Again, his attention drifted away, then returned. "You are strong in the Force, Luke, and with perseverance and discipline you will grow stronger still." His gaze hardened. "But you must never relax your guard. The Emperor is gone, but the dark side is still powerful. Never forget that."

"I won't," Luke promised.

Ben's face softened, and again he smiled. "You will yet face great dangers, Luke," he said. "But you will also find new allies, at times and places where you expect them least."

"New allies?" Luke echoed. "Who are they?"

The vision seemed to waver and become fainter. "And now, farewell," Ben said, as if he hadn't heard the question. "I loved you as a son, and as a student, and as a friend. Until we meet again, may the Force be with you."

"Ben—!"

But Ben turned, and the image faded . . . and in the dream, Luke knew he was gone. *Then I am alone,* he told himself. *I am the last of the Jedi.*

He seemed to hear Ben's voice, faint and indistinct, as if from a great distance. "Not the last of the old Jedi, Luke. The first of the new."[3]

The voice trailed off into silence, and was gone . . . and Luke woke up.

---

2. I used a fair number of movie quotes in these books, not just to remind readers of those scenes (like any of us *Star Wars* fans really *needed* reminders), but also because important or traumatic events in a person's life tend to remain vivid for years to come. Luke's last conversation with Yoda would be one of those events, and something he would never forget.

—TZ

3. One of the parameters I wanted to set for the trilogy was that Luke would be entirely on his own as a Jedi, with no one he could call on for help or advice.

And though I didn't know it at the time, the line about "the first of the new Jedi" nicely sets up Kevin J. Anderson's Jedi Academy Trilogy, as well as many other future books.

—TZ

For a moment he just lay there, staring at the dim lights of the Imperial City playing across the ceiling above his bed and struggling through the sleep-induced disorientation. The disorientation, and an immense weight of sadness that seemed to fill the core of his being. First Uncle Owen and Aunt Beru had been murdered; then Darth Vader, his real father, had sacrificed his own life for Luke's; and now even Ben Kenobi's spirit had been taken away.

For the third time, he'd been orphaned.[4]

With a sigh, he slid out from under the blankets and pulled on his robe and slippers. His suite contained a small kitchenette, and it took only a few minutes to fix himself a drink, a particularly exotic concoction Lando had introduced him to on his last visit to Coruscant. Then, attaching his lightsaber to his robe sash, he headed up to the roof.

He had argued strongly against moving the center of the New Republic here to Coruscant,[5] had argued even more strongly against[6] setting up their fledgling government in the old Imperial Palace. The symbolism was all wrong, for one thing, particularly for a group which—in his opinion—already had a tendency to pay too much attention to symbols.

But despite all its drawbacks, he had to admit that the view from the top of the Palace was spectacular.

For a few minutes he stood at the roof's edge, leaning against the chest-high wrought stone railing and letting the cool night breeze ruffle his hair. Even in the middle of the night the Imperial City was a bustle of activity, with the lights of vehicles and streets intertwining to form a sort of flowing work of art. Overhead, lit by both the city lights and those of occasional airspeeders flitting through them, the low-lying clouds were a dim sculptured ceiling stretching in all directions, with the same apparent endlessness as the city itself. Far to the south, he could just make out the Manarai Mountains, their snow-covered peaks illuminated, like the clouds, largely by reflected light from the city.[7]

4. In the frenetic, life-and-death challenges of the movies, it's easy to forget that Luke's really had a pretty hard life. It's the kind of thing that comes back most depressingly in the darkness and silence at three in the morning.
—TZ

5. Before *Heir*, the Empire's capital was referred to as *Imperial Center*. My take on that was that the planet must have had a history previous to the Republic and Empire, and would have therefore had some other name. (After all, most Earth capitals were already thriving or at least up-and-coming cities before they became capitals—Washington, DC, being a notable exception.)

Since a largely urbanized world would probably sparkle wonderfully in the sunlight (as well as glittering with its own lights on its dark side), I gave the planet the name *Coruscant*, which means "glittering."

At that point I had no idea that the prequel movies would ever be made. I had even less idea that George might actually use *Coruscant* as the name of the Republic capital.

But they were, and he did.

(cont.)
When *The Phantom Menace* came out, the one promotional toy I made absolutely sure to get hold of was the Coruscant globe from Pizza Hut. It currently sits proudly in my office amid my collection of *Star Wars* ship models.

—TZ

6. One of the things I wanted to set up early in the book was that Force guidance didn't always come as flashes of knowledge or the ability to block blaster shots. It can also come in more subtle ways, under circumstances where Luke himself might not understand the reason or even recognize that the nudge was coming from the Force. By the end of the Thrawn trilogy, it will become clear that Luke's uneasiness about setting up shop here had good, solid reason behind it.

—TZ

7. At the time I knew that Coruscant was a planetwide city, but I assumed that there would still be a few areas of wilderness (maybe called *parks* by the inhabitants) that would have no buildings on them. Mountains, for one thing, would probably not be cost-effective to knock down.

He was gazing at the mountains when, twenty meters behind him, the door into the Palace was quietly opened.

Automatically, his hand moved toward his lightsaber; but the motion had barely begun before it stopped. The sense of the creature coming through the doorway . . . "I'm over here, Threepio," he called.

He turned to see C-3PO shuffling his way across the roof toward him, radiating the droid's usual mixture of relief and concern. "Hello, Master Luke," he said, tilting his head to look at the cup in Luke's hand. "I'm terribly sorry to disturb you."

"That's all right," Luke told him. "I just wanted some fresh air, that's all."

"Are you certain?" Threepio asked. "Though of course I don't mean to pry."

Despite his mood, Luke couldn't help but smile. Threepio's attempts to be simultaneously helpful, inquisitive, and polite never quite came off. Not without looking vaguely comical, anyway. "I'm just a little depressed, I guess," he told the droid, turning back to gaze out over the city again. "Putting together a real, functioning government is a lot harder than I expected. Harder than most of the Council members expected,[8] too." He hesitated. "Mostly, I guess I'm missing Ben tonight."

For a moment Threepio was silent. "He was always very kind to me," he said at last. "And also to Artoo, of course."

Luke raised his cup to his lips, hiding another smile behind it. "You have a unique perspective on the universe, Threepio," he said.

From the corner of his eye, he saw Threepio stiffen. "I hope I didn't offend you, sir," the droid said anxiously. "That was certainly not my intent."

"You didn't offend me," Luke assured him. "As a matter of fact, you might have just delivered Ben's last lesson to me."

"I beg your pardon?"

Luke sipped at his drink. "Governments and entire planets are important, Threepio. But when you sift everything down, they're all just made up of people."

There was a brief pause. "Oh," Threepio said.

"In other words," Luke amplified, "a Jedi can't get so caught up in matters of galactic importance that it interferes with his concern for individual people." He looked at Threepio and smiled. "Or for individual droids."

"Oh. I see, sir." Threepio cocked his head toward Luke's cup. "Forgive me, sir . . . but may I ask what that is that you're drinking?"

"This?" Luke glanced down at his cup. "It's just something Lando taught me how to make a while back."

"Lando?" Threepio echoed, and there was no missing the disapproval in his voice. Programmed politeness or not, the droid had never really much cared for Lando.

Which wasn't very surprising, given the circumstances of their first meeting. "Yes, but in spite of such a shady origin, it's really quite good," Luke told him. "It's called hot chocolate."[9]

"Oh. I see." The droid straightened up. "Well, then, sir. If you are indeed all right, I expect I should be on my way."

"Sure. By the way, what made you come up here in the first place?"

"Princess Leia sent me, of course," Threepio answered, clearly surprised that Luke would have to ask. "She said you were in some kind of distress."

Luke smiled and shook his head. Leave it to Leia to find a way to cheer him up when he needed it. "Show-off," he murmured.

"I beg your pardon, sir?"

Luke waved a hand. "Leia's showing off her new Jedi skills, that's all. Proving that even in the middle of the night she can pick up on my mood."

Threepio's head tilted. "She really *did* seem concerned about you, sir."

(cont.)
Besides, the rich and powerful always want some nature-type areas left open where they can build their private country retreats.

—TZ

8. Work-related problems are another of those cheery thought categories that usually hit about 3 A.M.

—TZ

9. This was one of those odd thoughts that came out of the blue and struck me as both clever and logical. Hot chocolate wouldn't be something desert people would naturally gravitate toward. (There are cold desserts, of course, but with two suns I always assumed Tatooine is mostly pretty warm. Now, of course, the *Star Wars Essential Atlas* and other official material backs up that assumption.)

I also caught way more grief for this than I ever expected. Quite a few people took me to task for putting an Earth-based drink into the *Star Wars* universe.

Of course, those same people apparently weren't bothered by the Millennium *Falcon,* or lightsabers. It was, though,

(cont.)
a reminder that you never know what word or image might jolt someone out of their suspension of disbelief.

Anyway, why would anyone want to live in that Galaxy Far, Far Away if they don't have chocolate? Inconceivable . . .

—TZ

10. C-3PO always seems about three steps behind everyone else, on pretty much everything. One of his many charms, and a lot of fun to write.

—TZ

11. When this book was being written, no one involved had a glimmer that one day one of Leia's unborn children would someday turn to the dark side. Perhaps her time in the Imperial Palace was a contributor to that event . . .

—BM

"I know," Luke said. "I'm just joking."

"Oh." Threepio seemed to think about that. "Shall I tell her you're all right, then?"[10]

"Sure." Luke nodded. "And while you're down there, tell her that she should quit worrying about me and get herself back to sleep. Those bouts of morning sickness she still gets are bad enough when she *isn't* worn-out tired."

"I'll deliver the message, sir," Threepio said.

"And," Luke added quietly, "tell her I love her."

"Yes, sir. Good night, Master Luke."

"Good night, Threepio."

He watched the droid go, a fresh flow of depression threatening again to drag him down. Threepio wouldn't understand, of course—no one on the Provisional Council had understood, either. But for Leia, just over three months pregnant, to be spending the bulk of her time here . . .[11]

He shivered, and not from the cool night air. *This place is strong with the dark side.* Yoda had said that of the cave on Dagobah—the cave where Luke had gone on to fight a lightsaber duel with a Darth Vader who had turned out to be Luke himself. For weeks afterward the memory of the sheer power and presence of the dark side had haunted his thoughts; only much later had he finally realized that Yoda's primary reason for the exercise had been to show him how far he still had to go.

Still, he'd often wondered how the cave had come to be the way it had. Wondered whether perhaps someone or something strong in the dark side had once lived there.

As the Emperor had once lived here . . .

He shivered again. The really maddening part of it was that he *couldn't* sense any such concentration of evil in the Palace. The Council had made a point of asking him about that, in fact, when they'd first considered moving operations here to the Imperial City. He'd had to grit his teeth and tell them that, no, there seemed to be no residual effects of the Emperor's stay.

But just because he couldn't sense it didn't necessarily mean it wasn't there.[12]

He shook his head. *Stop it,* he ordered himself firmly. Jumping at shadows wasn't going to gain him anything but paranoia. His recent nightmares and poor sleep were probably nothing more than the stresses of watching Leia and the others struggling to turn a military-oriented rebellion into a civilian-based government. Certainly Leia would never have agreed to come anywhere near this place if she'd had any doubts herself about it.

Leia.

With an effort, Luke forced his mind to relax and let his Jedi senses reach outward. Halfway across the palace's upper section he could feel Leia's drowsy presence. Her presence, and that of the twins she carried within her.[13]

For a moment he held the partial contact, keeping it light enough to hopefully not wake her any further, marveling again at the strange feel of the unborn children within her. The Skywalker heritage was indeed with them; the fact that he could sense them at all implied they must be tremendously strong in the Force.

At least, he assumed that was what it meant. It had been something he'd hoped he would someday have a chance to ask Ben about.

And now that chance was gone.

Fighting back sudden tears, he broke the contact. His mug felt cold against his hand; swallowing the rest of the chocolate, he took one last look around. At the city, at the clouds . . . and, in his mind's eye, at the stars that lay beyond them. Stars, around which revolved planets, upon which lived people. Billions of people. Many of them still waiting for the freedom and light the New Republic had promised them.

He closed his eyes against the bright lights and the equally bright hopes. There was, he thought wearily, no magic wand that could make everything better.

Not even for a Jedi.

12. As we'll see in *Dark Force Rising*, the place where the Emperor died *is* heavy with residual effects of his presence there.

—TZ

13. Did Obi-Wan and Anakin have any of this same sense of Luke and Leia when Padmé was carrying them? An intriguing question, and one I'm not sure we ever had an answer for.

—TZ

Threepio shuffled his way out of the room, and with a tired sigh Leia Organa Solo settled back against the pillows. *Half a victory is better than none,* the old saying crossed her mind.

The old saying she'd never believed for a minute. Half a victory, to her way of thinking, was also half a defeat.

She sighed again, feeling the touch of Luke's mind. His encounter with Threepio had lightened his dark mood, as she'd hoped it would; but with the droid gone, the depression was threatening to overtake him again.

Perhaps she should go to him herself. See if she could get him to talk through whatever it was that had been bothering him for the past few weeks.

Her stomach twisted, just noticeably. "It's all right," she soothed, rubbing her hand gently across her belly. "It's all right. I'm just worried about your Uncle Luke, that's all."

Slowly, the twisting eased. Picking up the half-filled glass on the nightstand, Leia drank it down, trying not to make a face. Warm milk was pretty far down on her list of favorite drinks, but it had proved to be one of the fastest ways to soothe these periodic twinges from her digestive tract. The doctors had told her that the worst of her stomach troubles should begin disappearing any day now. She hoped rather fervently that they were right.

Faintly, from the next room, came the sound of footsteps. Quickly, Leia slapped the glass back on the nightstand with one hand as she hauled the blankets up to her chin with the other. The bedside light was still glowing, and she reached out with the Force to try to turn it off.

The lamp didn't even flicker. Gritting her teeth, she tried again; again, it didn't work. Still not enough fine control over the Force, obviously, for something as small as a light switch. Untangling herself from the blankets, she tried to make a lunge for it.

Across the room, the side door opened to reveal a tall

woman in a dressing robe. "Your Highness?" she called softly, brushing her shimmering white hair back from her eyes. "Are you all right?"

Leia sighed and gave up. "Come on in, Winter. How long have you been listening at the door?"

"I haven't been listening," Winter said as she glided into the room, sounding almost offended that Leia would even suggest such a thing of her. "I saw the light coming from under your door and thought you might need something."

"I'm fine," Leia assured her, wondering if this woman would ever cease to amaze her. Awakened in the middle of the night, dressed in an old robe with her hair in total disarray, Winter still looked more regal than Leia herself could manage on her best days. She'd lost track of the number of times when, as children together on Alderaan, some visitor to the Viceroy's court had automatically assumed Winter was, in fact, the Princess Leia.[14]

Winter had probably not lost track, of course. Anyone who could remember whole conversations verbatim should certainly be able to reconstruct the number of times she'd been mistaken for a royal princess.

Leia had often wondered what the rest of the Provisional Council members would think if they knew that the silent assistant sitting beside her at official meetings or standing beside her at unofficial corridor conversations was effectively recording every word they said. Some of them, she suspected, wouldn't like it at all.

"Can I get you some more milk, Your Highness?" Winter asked. "Or some crackers?"

"No, thank you." Leia shook her head. "My stomach isn't really bothering me at the moment. It's . . . well, you know. It's Luke."

Winter nodded. "Same thing that's been bothering him for the past nine weeks?"

Leia frowned. "Has it been that long?"

Winter shrugged. "You've been busy," she said with her usual knack for diplomacy.

14. One of the best parts about writing *Heir* was the opportunity to create new characters and fit them into the *Star Wars* universe. Winter was the first person I introduced into the "good guy" side of the equation.

Aside from her general usefulness as a character, she also gave me the opportunity to express my opinion that Leia always seemed too tomboyish to fit comfortably into the role of a soft, pampered member of the aristocracy.

Which, given that we now know her mother was the feisty, down-in-the-dirt Padmé, isn't all that surprising.

—TZ

"Tell me about it," Leia said dryly. "I don't know, Winter—I really don't. He told Threepio that he misses Ben Kenobi, but I can tell that's not all of it."

"Perhaps it has something to do with your pregnancy," Winter suggested. "Nine weeks ago would put it just about right."

"Yes, I know," Leia agreed. "But that's also about the time Mon Mothma and Admiral Ackbar were pushing to move the government seat here to Coruscant. Also about the time we started getting those reports from the borderlands about some mysterious tactical genius having taken command of the Imperial Fleet." She held her hands out, palms upward. "Take your pick."

"I suppose you'll just have to wait until he's ready to talk to you." Winter considered. "Perhaps Captain Solo will be able to draw him out when he returns."

Leia squeezed thumb and forefinger together, a wave of anger-filled loneliness sweeping over her. For Han to have gone out on yet another of these stupid contact missions, leaving her all alone—

The flash of anger disappeared, dissolving into guilt. Yes, Han was gone again; but even when he was here it seemed sometimes like they hardly saw each other. With more and more of her time being eaten up by the enormous task of setting up a new government, there were days when she barely had time to eat, let alone see her husband.

But that's my job, she reminded herself firmly; and it was a job that, unfortunately, only she could do. Unlike virtually all the others in the Alliance hierarchy, she had had extensive training in both the theory and the more practical aspects of politics. She'd grown up in the Royal House of Alderaan, learning about systemwide rule from her foster father—learning it so well that while still in her teens she was already representing him in the Imperial Senate. Without her expertise, this whole thing could easily collapse, particularly in these critical early stages of the New Republic's development. A few more months—just a few more months—and she'd be able to ease off a little. She'd make it all up to Han then.

The guilt faded. But the loneliness remained.[15]

"Maybe," she told Winter. "In the meantime, we'd better both get some sleep. We have a busy day tomorrow."

Winter arched her eyebrows slightly. "There's another kind?" she asked with a touch of Leia's earlier dryness.

"Now, now," Leia admonished, mock-seriously. "You're far too young to become a cynic. I mean it, now—off to bed with you."

"You're sure you don't need anything first?"

"I'm sure. Go on, scat."

"All right. Good night, Your Highness."

She glided out, closing the door behind her. Sliding down flat onto the bed, Leia readjusted the blankets over her and shifted the pillows into a more or less comfortable position. "Good night to you two, too," she said softly to her babies, giving her belly another gentle rub. Han had suggested more than once that anyone who talked to her own stomach was slightly nuts. But then, she suspected that Han secretly believed *everyone* was slightly nuts.

She missed him terribly.

With a sigh, she reached over to the nightstand and turned off the light. Eventually, she fell asleep.

A quarter of the way across the galaxy,[16] Han Solo sipped at his mug and surveyed the semiorganized chaos flowing all around him. *Didn't we,* he quoted to himself, *just leave this party?*

Still, it was nice to know that, in a galaxy busily turning itself upside down, there were some things that never changed. The band playing off in the corner was different, and the upholstery in the booth was noticeably less comfortable; but apart from that, the Mos Eisley cantina looked exactly the same as it always had. The same as it had looked the day he'd first met Luke Skywalker and Obi-wan Kenobi.

15. Siblings, even twins, usually have vastly different personalities. But given the way Luke and Leia had approached their Rebellion duties, I figured that they would both have similar tendencies to occasionally feel overwhelmed by the tasks still facing them. Especially since both would likely feel that they were the only ones who could handle their particular jobs.

—TZ

16. As no official map of the *Star Wars* galaxy existed at this time (and wouldn't for many years to come), any positional relationship between Coruscant and Tatooine was pure guesswork.

—TZ

It felt like a dozen lifetimes ago.

Beside him, Chewbacca growled softly. "Don't worry, he'll be here," Han told him. "It's just Dravis. I don't think he's ever been on time for anything in his whole life."

Slowly, he let his eyes drift over the crowd. No, he amended to himself, there *was* one other thing different about the cantina: virtually none of the other smugglers who had once frequented the place were anywhere to be seen. Whoever had taken over what was left of Jabba the Hutt's organization must have moved operations off Tatooine. Turning to peer toward the cantina's back door, he made a mental note to ask Dravis about it.

He was still gazing off to the side when a shadow fell across the table. "Hello, Solo," a snickering voice said.

Han gave himself a three-count before turning casually to face the voice. "Well, hello, Dravis." He nodded. "Long time no see. Have a seat."

"Sure," Dravis said with a grin. "Soon as you and Chewie both put your hands on the table."[17]

Han gave him an injured look. "Oh, come *on*," he said, reaching up to cradle his mug with both hands. "You think I'd invite you all the way here just to shoot at you? We're old buddies, remember?"

"Sure we are," Dravis said, throwing Chewbacca an appraising glance as he sat down. "Or at least we used to be. But I hear you've gone respectable."

Han shrugged eloquently. "*Respectable*'s such a vague word."

Dravis cocked an eyebrow. "Oh, well, then let's be specific," he said sardonically. "I hear you joined the Rebel Alliance, got made a general, married a former Alderaanian princess, and got yourself a set of twins on the way."

Han waved a self-deprecating hand. "Actually, I resigned the general part a few months back."

Dravis snorted. "Forgive me. So what's all this about? Some kind of warning?"

Han frowned. "What do you mean?"

17. The lesson of Greedo's carelessness is apparently still remembered in these parts.

—TZ

"Don't play innocent, Solo," Dravis said, the banter gone from his tone. "New Republic replaces Empire—all fine and sweet and dandy, but you know as well as I do that it's all the same to smugglers. So if this is an official invitation to cease and desist our business activities, let me laugh in your face and get out of here." He started to get up.

"It's nothing like that," Han told him. "As a matter of fact, I was hoping to hire you."

Dravis froze, halfway up. "What?" he asked warily.

"You heard right," Han said. "We're looking to hire smugglers."

Slowly, Dravis sat back down. "Is this something to do with your fight with the Empire?" he demanded. "Because if it is—"

"It isn't," Han assured him. "There's a whole spiel that goes along with this, but what it boils down to is that the New Republic is short of cargo ships at the moment, not to mention experienced cargo ship pilots.[18] If you're looking to earn some quick and honest money, this would be a good time to do it."

"Uh-*huh.*" Dravis leaned back in his chair, draping an arm over the seat back as he eyed Han suspiciously. "So what's the catch?"

Han shook his head. "No catch. We need ships and pilots to get interstellar trade going again. You've got 'em. That's all there is to it."

Dravis seemed to think it over. "So why work for you and your pittance directly?" he demanded. "Why can't we just smuggle the stuff and make more per trip?"

"You could do that," Han conceded. "But only if your customers had to pay the kind of tariffs that would make hiring smugglers worthwhile. In this case"—he smiled—"they won't."

Dravis glared at him. "Oh, come *on,* Solo. A brand-new government, hard-pressed like crazy for cash—and you want me to believe they won't be piling tariffs on top of each other?"

18. This was one of those little things that probably never even occurred to some of the Alliance leaders in the heat of the Rebellion: that all the ships they were converting to fighters or using—and often losing—as transports would translate to severely lowered carrying capacity once they tried to get the New Republic up and running.

There would be myriad such details, and I certainly couldn't go into all of them in the book. But I wanted to give a flavor of why Leia is feeling such weight on her shoulders.

—TZ

"Believe anything you want," Han said, letting his own tone go frosty. "Go ahead and try it, too. But when you're convinced, give me a call."[19]

Dravis chewed at the inside of his cheek, his eyes never leaving Han's. "You know, Solo," he said thoughtfully, "I wouldn't have come if I didn't trust you. Well, maybe I was curious, too, to see what scam you were pulling. And I might be willing to believe you on this, at least enough to check it out myself. But I'll tell you right up front that a lot of others in my group won't."

"Why not?"

"Because you've gone respectable, that's why. Oh, don't give me that hurt look—the simple fact is that you've been out of the business too long to even remember what it's like. Profits are what drives a smuggler, Solo. Profits and excitement."

"So what are you going to do instead, operate in the Imperial sectors?" Han countered, trying hard to remember all those lessons in diplomacy that Leia had given him.

Dravis shrugged. "It pays," he said simply.

"For now, maybe," Han reminded him. "But their territory's been shrinking for five years straight, and it's going to keep getting smaller. We're just about evenly gunned now, you know, and our people are more motivated and a lot better trained than theirs."

"Maybe." Dravis cocked an eyebrow. "But maybe not. I hear rumors that there's someone new in charge out there. Someone who's been giving you a lot of trouble—like in the Obroa-skai system, for instance? I hear you lost an Elomin task force out there just a little while ago. Awfully sloppy, losing a whole task force like that."

Han gritted his teeth. "Just remember that anybody who gives *us* trouble is going to give *you* trouble, too." He leveled a finger at the other. "And if you think the New Republic is hungry for cash, think of how hungry the Empire must be right now."

"It's certainly an adventure," Dravis agreed easily, getting to his feet. "Well, it really was nice seeing you again, Solo, but I gotta go. Say hi to your princess for me."

Han sighed. "Just give your people our offer, okay?"

"Oh, I will. Might even be some who'll take you up on it. You never can tell."

Han nodded. It was, really, all he could have expected out of this meeting. "One other thing, Dravis. Who exactly is the big fish in the pond now that Jabba's gone?"

Dravis eyed him thoughtfully. "Well . . . I guess it's not really a secret," he decided. "Mind you, there aren't any really official numbers. But if I were betting, I'd put my money on Talon Karrde."

Han frowned. He'd heard of Karrde, of course, but never with any hint that his organization was even in the top ten, let alone the one on top. Either Dravis was wrong, or Karrde was the type who believed in keeping a low profile. "Where can I find him?"

Dravis smiled slyly. "You'd like to know that, wouldn't you? Maybe someday I'll tell you."

"Dravis—"

"Gotta go. See you around, Chewie."

He started to turn; paused. "Oh, by the way. You might tell your pal over there that he's got to be the worst excuse for a backup man I've ever seen. Just thought you'd like to know." With another grin, he turned again and headed back into the crowd.

Han grimaced as he watched him go. Still, at least Dravis had been willing to turn his back on them as he left. Some of the other smugglers he'd contacted hadn't even trusted him that far. Progress, sort of.[20]

Beside him, Chewbacca growled something derogatory. "Well, what do you expect with Admiral Ackbar sitting on the Council?" Han shrugged. "The Calamarians were death on smugglers even before the war, and everyone knows it. Don't worry, they'll come around. Some of them, anyway. Dravis can blather all he wants about profit and excitement; but you offer them secure maintenance facili-

20. Though this clearly is a job that only Han can do, and though he may grouse about it, there's none of Luke's or Leia's angst over the burden. That's just not the kind of guy Han is.

—TZ

ties, no Jabba-style skimming, and no one shooting at them, and they'll get interested. Come on, let's get going."

He slid out of the booth and headed for the cantina and the exit just visible beyond it. Halfway across, he stopped at one of the other booths and looked down at its lone occupant. "I've got a message for you," he announced. "I'm supposed to tell you that you're the worst excuse for a backup man that Dravis has ever seen."

Wedge Antilles grinned up at him as he slid out from behind the table. "I thought that was the whole idea," he said, running his fingers through his black hair.

"Yes, but Dravis didn't." Though privately, Han would be the first to admit that Dravis had a point. As far as he was concerned, the only times Wedge *didn't* stick out like a lump on plate glass was when he was sitting in the cockpit of an X-wing blasting TIE fighters into dust. "So where's Page, anyway?" he asked, glancing around.

"Right here, sir," a quiet voice said at his shoulder.

Han turned. Beside them had appeared a medium-height, medium-build, totally nondescript-looking man. The kind of man no one would really notice; the kind who could blend invisibly into almost any surroundings.

Which had, again, been the whole idea. "You see anything suspicious?" Han asked him.

Page shook his head. "No backup troops; no weapons other than his blaster. This guy must have genuinely trusted you."

"Yeah. Progress." Han took one last look around. "Let's get going. We're going to be late enough back to Coruscant as it is. And I want to swing through the Obroa-skai system on the way."

"That missing Elomin task force?" Wedge asked.

"Yeah," Han said grimly. "I want to see if they've figured out what happened to it yet. And if we're lucky, maybe get some idea of who did it to them."

CHAPTER 3

THE FOLD-OUT TABLE in his private office was set, the food was ready to serve, and Talon Karrde was just pouring the wine when the tap came on his door. As always, his timing was perfect. "Mara?" he called.

"Yes," the young woman's voice confirmed through the door. "You asked me to join you for dinner."

"Yes. Please come in."

The door slid open, and with her usual catlike grace Mara Jade walked into the room. "You didn't say what"—her green eyes flicked to the elaborately set table—"this was all about," she finished, her tone just noticeably different. The green eyes came back to him, cool and measuring.

"No, it's not what you're thinking," Karrde assured her, motioning her to the chair opposite his. "This is a business meal—no more, no less."

From behind his desk came a sound halfway between a cackle and a purr. "That's right, Drang—a business meal," Karrde said, turning toward the sound. "Come on, out with you."

The vornskr peered out from around the edge of the desk, its front paws gripping the carpet, its muzzle close to the floor as if on the hunt. "I said out with you," Karrde repeated firmly, pointing toward the open door behind Mara. "Come on, your dish has been set up in the kitchen. Sturm's[1] already there—chances are he's eaten half your supper by now."

Reluctantly, Drang slunk out from behind the desk, cackle/purring forlornly to himself as he padded toward the door. "Don't give me that poor-little-me act," Karrde chided, picking a piece of braised bruallki from the serving dish. "Here—this should cheer you up."

He tossed the food in the general direction of the doorway. Drang's lethargy vanished in a single coiled-spring leap as he snagged the mouthful in midair. "There," Karrde called after him. "Now go and enjoy your supper."

The vornskr trotted out.[2] "All right," Karrde said, shifting his attention back to Mara. "Where were we?"

"You were telling me this was a business meal," she said, her voice still a little cool as she slid into the seat across from his and surveyed the table. "It's certainly the nicest business meal I've had in quite a while."

"Well, that's the point, really," Karrde told her, sitting down and reaching over to the serving tray. "I think it's occasionally good for us to remember that being a smuggler doesn't necessarily require one to be a barbarian, too."

"Ah." She nodded, sipping at her wine. "And I'm sure most of your people are so very grateful for that reminder."

Karrde smiled. So much, he thought, for the unusual setting and scenario throwing her off balance. He should have known that particular gambit wouldn't work on someone like Mara. "It *does* often make for an interesting evening," he agreed. "Particularly"—he eyed her—"when discussing a promotion."

A flicker of surprise, almost too fast to see, crossed her face. "A promotion?" she echoed carefully.

1. "Sturm und Drang" (storm and stress) was an eighteenth-century German romantic literary movement emphasizing struggles of the individual against society. I thought those names would appeal to Karrde, whom I saw as being an educated, pun-loving sort.

This one didn't get me nearly as much grief as the hot chocolate reference. My assumption is that those who caught the reference were more amused than annoyed by it.

—TZ

2. I wrote this scene long before we had any cats of our own. Little did I know just how true-to-life it was.

—TZ

"Yes," he said, scooping a serving of bruallki onto her plate and setting it in front of her. "Yours, to be precise."

The wary look was back in her eyes. "I've only been with the group for six months, you know."

"Five and a half, actually," he corrected her. "But time has never been as important to the universe as ability and results . . . and your ability and results have been quite impressive."

She shrugged, her red-gold hair shimmering with the movement. "I've been lucky," she said.

"Luck is certainly part of it," he agreed. "On the other hand, I've found that what most people call luck is often little more than raw talent combined with the ability to make the most of opportunities."

He turned back to the bruallki, dished some onto his own plate. "Then there's your talent for starship piloting, your ability to both give and accept orders"—he smiled slightly, gesturing to the table—"and your ability to adapt to unusual and unexpected situations. All highly useful talents for a smuggler."

He paused, but she remained silent. Evidently, somewhere in her past she'd also learned when not to ask questions. Another useful talent. "The bottom line, Mara, is that you're simply too valuable to waste as a backup or even as a line operator," he concluded. "What I'd like to do is to start grooming you toward eventually becoming my second in command."

There was no chance of mistaking her surprise this time. The green eyes went momentarily wide, and then narrowed. "What exactly would my new duties consist of?" she asked.

"Traveling with me, mostly," he said, taking a sip of wine. "Watching me set up new business, meeting with some of our long-term customers so that they can get to know you—that sort of thing."

She was still suspicious—he could tell that from her eyes. Suspicious that the offer was a smoke screen to mask some more personal request or demand on his part. "You don't have to answer now," he told her. "Think about it, or talk to some of the others who've been with the organization longer." He looked her straight in the eye. "They'll tell you that I don't lie to my people."[3]

Her lip twisted. "So I've heard," she said, her voice going noncommittal again. "But bear in mind that if you give me that kind of authority, I *am* going to use it. There's some revamping of the whole organizational structure—"

She broke off as the intercom on his desk warbled. "Yes?" Karrde called toward it.

"It's Aves," a voice said. "Thought you'd like to know we've got company: an Imperial Star Destroyer just made orbit."

Karrde glanced at Mara as he got to his feet. "Any make on it yet?" he asked, dropping his napkin beside his plate and stepping around the desk to where he could see the screen.

"They're not exactly broadcasting ID sigs these days." Aves shook his head. "The lettering on the side is hard to read at this distance, but Torve's best guess is that it's the *Chimaera*."[4]

"Interesting," Karrde murmured. Grand Admiral Thrawn himself. "Have they made any transmissions?"

"None that we've picked up—wait a minute. Looks like . . . yes—they're launching a shuttle. Make that two shuttles. Projected landing point . . ." Aves frowned at something offscreen for a moment. "Projected landing point somewhere here in the forest."

Out of the corner of his eyes, Karrde saw Mara stiffen a bit. "Not in any of the cities around the edge?" he asked Aves.

"No, it's definitely the forest. No more than fifty kilometers from here, either."

Karrde rubbed his forefinger gently across his lower lip, considering the possibilities. "Still only two shuttles?"

3. In some ways, Karrde is my vision of how Han might have ended up if he hadn't dropped into the Mos Eisley cantina that afternoon for a quiet drink. Both men have a code of honor, especially toward their friends, and both are willing to be part of a larger group, though Han admittedly dragged his feet a long time before getting to that place.

—TZ

4. Not sure Imperial ships (or Rebel ships, for that matter) had their names or operating numbers anywhere on their hulls. Still, it *is* something most Earth navies do, so I figured it was reasonable here, too.

—TZ

"That's all so far." Aves was starting to look a little nervous. "Should I call an alert?"

"On the contrary. Let's see if they need any help. Give me a hailing channel."

Aves opened his mouth; closed it again. "Okay," he said, taking a deep breath and tapping something offscreen. "You have hailing."

"Thank you. Imperial Star Destroyer *Chimaera*, this is Talon Karrde. May I be of any assistance to you?"

"No response," Aves muttered. "You think maybe they didn't want to be noticed?"

"If you don't want to be noticed, you don't use a Star Destroyer," Karrde pointed out. "No, they're most likely busy running my name through ship's records. Be interesting to see someday just what they have on me. If anything." He cleared his throat. "Star Destroyer *Chimaera*, this is—"

Abruptly, Aves's face was replaced by that of a middle-aged man wearing a captain's insignia. "This is Captain Pellaeon of the *Chimaera*," he said brusquely. "What is it you want?"

"Merely to be neighborly," Karrde told him evenly. "We track two of your shuttles coming down, and wondered if you or Grand Admiral Thrawn might require any assistance."

The skin around Pellaeon's eyes tightened, just a bit. "Who?"

"Ah." Karrde nodded, allowing a slight smile. "Of course. I haven't heard of Grand Admiral Thrawn, either. Certainly not in connection with the *Chimaera*. Or with some intriguing information raids on several systems in the Paonnid/Obroa-skai region, either."

The eyes tightened a little more. "You're very well informed, Mr. Karrde,"[5] Pellaeon said, his voice silky but with menace lurking beneath it. "One might wonder how a lowly smuggler would come by such information."

5. At the time of *Heir*, we had no idea what the common honorific was in the *Star Wars* universe. C-3PO called Luke *master*, but that might have been a droid thing. Other people were typically addressed by rank or title.

Still, I think this is the only time I used *Mr.* in the book. Even Karrde is later referred to as *captain*, though I'm not sure that's really accurate. (He owns and runs ships, but doesn't usually captain them.)

Now, thanks to the prequels, we know that *master* is indeed the universal term.

—TZ

Karrde shrugged. "My people hear stories and rumors; I take the pieces and put them together. Much the same way your own intelligence units operate, I imagine. Incidentally, if your shuttles are planning to put down in the forest, you need to warn the crews to be careful. There are several dangerous predator species living here, and the high metal content of the vegetation makes sensor readings unreliable at best."

"Thank you for the advice," Pellaeon said, his voice still frosty. "But they won't be staying long."

"Ah." Karrde nodded, running the possibilities through his mind. There were, fortunately, not all that many of them. "Doing a little hunting, are they?"

Pellaeon favored him with a slightly indulgent smile. "Information on Imperial activities is very expensive. I'd have thought a man in your line of work would know that."

"Indeed," Karrde agreed, watching the other closely. "But occasionally one finds bargains. It's the ysalamiri you're after, isn't it?"

The other's smile froze. "There are no bargains to be had here, Karrde," he said after a moment, his voice very soft. "And *expensive* can also mean *costly.*"

"True," Karrde said. "Unless, of course, it's traded for something equally valuable. I presume you're already familiar with the ysalamiri's rather unique characteristics—otherwise, you wouldn't be here. Can I assume you're also familiar with the somewhat esoteric art of safely getting them off their tree branches?"

Pellaeon studied him, suspicion all over his face. "I was under the impression that ysalamiri were no more than fifty centimeters long and not predatory."

"I wasn't referring to *your* safety, Captain," Karrde told him. "I meant theirs. You can't just pull them off their branches, not without killing them. An ysalamir in this stage is sessile—its claws have elongated to the point where they've essentially grown directly into the core of the branch it inhabits."[6]

"And you, I suppose, know the proper way to do it?"

"Some of my people do, yes," Karrde told him. "If you'd like, I could send one of them to rendezvous with your shuttles. The technique involved isn't especially difficult, but it really *does* have to be demonstrated."

"Of course," Pellaeon said, heavily sardonic. "And the fee for this esoteric demonstration . . . ?"

"No fee, Captain. As I said earlier, we're just being neighborly."

Pellaeon cocked his head slightly to one side. "Your generosity will be remembered." For a moment he held Karrde's gaze; and there was no mistaking the twin-edged meaning to the words. If Karrde was planning some sort of betrayal, it too would be remembered. "I'll signal my shuttles to expect your expert."

"He'll be there. Good-bye, Captain."

Pellaeon reached for something off-camera, and once again Aves's face replaced his on the screen. "You get all that?" Karrde asked the other.

Aves nodded. "Dankin and Chin are already warming up one of the Skiprays."

"Good. Have them leave an open transmission; and I'll want to see them as soon as they're back."

"Right." The display clicked off.

Karrde stepped away from the desk, glanced once at Mara, and reseated himself at the table. "Sorry for the interruption," he said conversationally, watching her out of the corner of his eye as he poured himself some more wine.

Slowly, the green eyes came back from infinity; and as she looked at him, the muscles of her face eased from their deathlike rigidness. "You're really not going to charge them for this?" she asked, reaching a slightly unsteady hand for her own wine. "They'd certainly make *you* pay if you

6. One of the tricky things about writing *Star Wars* (or any other shared media work) is to not only keep track of what was done in the movies, but also keep track of what *wasn't* done. If something that could have been useful wasn't done, it means there must have been a good reason why not.

The ysalamiri are a good example. A creature that can block Jedi abilities should have been used all over the place throughout the movies by anti-Jedi forces . . . *unless* they were unreliable, difficult to find, difficult to use, et cetera. To be on the safe side, I invoked two of those limiting parameters: the creatures are relatively unknown (the Jedi would hardly broadcast their existence, after all), and they're hard to get off their trees without killing them.

—TZ

wanted something. That's about all the Empire really cares about these days, money."

He shrugged. "We get to have our people watching them from the moment they set down to the moment they lift off. That seems an adequate fee to me."[7]

7. Early on, I set up Karrde to be more than just a smuggler, but also a seeker of information. That would turn out to have useful ramifications here as well as in several other books down the line.

—TZ

She studied him. "You don't believe they're here just to pick up ysalamiri, do you?"

"Not really." Karrde took a bite of his bruallki. "At least, not unless there's a use for the things that we don't know about. Coming all the way out here to collect ysalamiri is a bit of an overkill to use against a single Jedi."

Mara's eyes again drifted away. "Maybe it's not Sky-walker they're after," she murmured. "Maybe they've found some more Jedi."

"Seems unlikely," Karrde said, watching her closely. The emotion in her voice when she'd said Luke Skywalker's name . . . "The Emperor supposedly made a clean sweep of them in the early days of the New Order. Unless," he added as another thought occurred to him, "they've per-haps found Darth Vader."

"Vader died on the Death Star," Mara said. "Along with the Emperor."

"That's the story, certainly—"

"He died there," Mara cut him off, her voice suddenly sharp.

"Of course." Karrde nodded. It had taken him five months of close observation, but he'd finally pinned down the handful of subjects guaranteed to trigger strong re-sponses from the woman. The late Emperor was among them, as was the pre-Endor Empire.

And at the opposite end of the emotional spectrum was Luke Skywalker. "Still," he continued thoughtfully, "if a Grand Admiral thinks he has a good reason to carry ysa-lamiri aboard his ships, we might do well to follow his lead."

Abruptly, Mara's eyes focused on him again. "What for?" she demanded.

"A simple precaution," Karrde said. "Why so vehement?"

He watched as she fought a brief internal battle. "It seems like a waste of time," she said. "Thrawn's probably just jumping at shadows. Anyway, how are you going to keep ysalamiri alive on a ship without transplanting some trees along with them?"

"I'm sure Thrawn has some ideas as to the mechanics of it," Karrde assured her. "Dankin and Chin will know how to poke around for details."

Her eyes seemed strangely hooded. "Yes," she muttered, her voice conceding defeat. "I'm sure they will."

"And in the meantime," Karrde said, pretending not to notice, "we still have business to discuss. As I recall, you were going to list some improvements you would make in the organization."

"Yes." Mara took another deep breath, closing her eyes . . . and when she opened them again she was back to her usual cool self. "Yes. Well—"

Slowly at first, but with ever-increasing confidence, she launched into a detailed and generally insightful compendium of his group's shortcomings. Karrde listened closely as he ate, wondering again at the hidden talents of this woman. Someday, he promised himself silently, he was going to find a way to dig the details of her past out from under the cloak of secrecy she'd so carefully shrouded it with. To find out where she'd come from, and who and what she was.

And to learn exactly what it was Luke Skywalker had done to make her so desperately hate him.[8]

8. Karrde's not alone here—there are many readers who also want to learn Mara's backstory.

On the other hand, there are also many readers who want that backstory to remain shrouded in mystery. Whatever I end up doing on this one, I'm going to be in trouble with somebody.

Still, there are a few things we *do* know about Mara's past. We'll get to those in a bit. . . .

—TZ

CHAPTER 4

IT TOOK THE *CHIMAERA* nearly five days at its Point Four[1] cruising speed to cover the three hundred fifty light-years between Myrkr and Wayland. But that was all right, because it took the engineers nearly that long to come up with a portable frame that would both support and nourish the ysalamiri.

"I'm still not convinced this is really necessary," Pellaeon grumbled, eyeing with distaste the thick curved pipe and the fur-scaled, salamander-like creature attached to it. The pipe and its attached frame were blasted heavy, and the creature itself didn't smell all that good. "If this Guardian you're expecting was put on Wayland by the Emperor in the first place, then I don't see why we should have any problems with him."

"Call it a precaution, Captain," Thrawn said, settling into the shuttle's copilot seat and fastening his own straps. "It's conceivable we could have trouble convincing him of who we are. Or even that we still serve the Empire." He

1. I had a whole hyperdrive system worked out, modeled on the time-dilation formula from Relativistic physics, with a range of possible light-speed numbers that ran exponentially from zero (dead stop) to one (infinite speed). It was elegant, looked very cool, and allowed me to actually use some of my college physics.

Alas, later on, when I wasn't looking, Lucasfilm and/or West End Games came up with an entirely different system. Still, it was fun while it lasted.

—TZ

sent a casual glance across the displays and nodded to the pilot. "Go."

There was a muffled *clank*, and with a slight jolt the shuttle dropped from the *Chimaera*'s docking bay and started its descent toward the planet surface. "We might have had an easier time convincing him with a squad of stormtroopers along," Pellaeon muttered, watching the repeater display beside his seat.

"We might also have irritated him," Thrawn pointed out. "A Dark Jedi's[2] pride and sensibilities are not to be taken lightly, Captain. Besides—" he looked over his shoulder "—that's what Rukh is for. Any close associate of the Emperor ought to be familiar with the glorious role the Noghri have played over the years."

Pellaeon glanced at the silent nightmare figure seated across the aisle. "You seem certain, sir, that the Guardian will be a Dark Jedi."

"Who else would the Emperor have chosen to protect his personal storehouse?" Thrawn countered. "A legion of stormtroopers, perhaps, equipped with AT-ATs and the kind of advanced weaponry and technology you could detect from orbit with your eyes closed?"

Pellaeon grimaced. That, at least, was something they wouldn't have to worry about. The *Chimaera*'s scanners had picked up nothing beyond bow-and-arrow stage anywhere on Wayland's surface. It wasn't all that much comfort. "I'm just wondering whether the Emperor might have pulled him off Wayland to help against the Rebellion."

Thrawn shrugged. "We'll know soon enough."

The gentle roar of atmospheric friction against the shuttle's hull was growing louder now, and on Pellaeon's repeater display details of the planet's surface were becoming visible. Much of the area directly beneath them appeared to be forest, spotted here and there with large, grassy plains. Ahead, occasionally visible through the haze

2. With the official definition of *Sith* still a few years in the future, I had to come up with a label for a Jedi who has fallen to the dark side. I chose the descriptive if not very original term *Dark Jedi*.

The definition is unfortunately a bit squishy, referring nowadays to both a fallen Jedi and also a Force-user who never underwent proper training, but perhaps learned under the tutelage of another Dark Jedi.

For this reason (and probably a few others), the term is somewhat discouraged. At the time, though, it was the best any of us had to work with.

—TZ

of clouds, a single mountain rose above the landscape. "Is that Mount Tantiss?"[3] he asked the pilot.

"Yes, sir," the other confirmed. "The city ought to be visible soon."

"Right." Reaching surreptitiously to his right thigh, Pellaeon adjusted his blaster in its holster. Thrawn could be as confident as he liked, both in the ysalamiri and in his own logic. For his part, Pellaeon still wished they had more firepower.

The city nestled against the southwestern base of Mount Tantiss was larger than it had looked from orbit, with many of its squat buildings extending deep under the cover of the surrounding trees. Thrawn had the pilot circle the area twice, and then put down in the center of what appeared to be the main city square, facing a large and impressively regal-looking building.

"Interesting," Thrawn commented, looking out the viewports as he settled his ysalamir backpack onto his shoulders. "There are at least three styles of architecture out there—human plus two different alien species. It's not often you see such diversity in the same planetary region, let alone side by side in the same city. In fact, that palace thing in front of us has itself incorporated elements from all three styles."

"Yes," Pellaeon agreed absently, peering out the viewports himself. At the moment, the buildings were of far less interest to him than the people the life-form sensors said were hiding behind and inside them. "Any idea whether those alien species are hostile toward strangers?"

"Probably," Thrawn said, stepping to the shuttle's exit ramp, where Rukh was already waiting. "Most alien species are. Shall we go?"

The ramp lowered with a hiss of released gases. Gritting his teeth, Pellaeon joined the other two. With Rukh in the lead, they headed down.

No one shot at them as they reached the ground and

3. Tantiss was named after Tantalus, a son of Zeus who was admitted to the company of the gods—and then abused the privilege. (The stories about how he did so are many and varied.) That seemed to fit the Emperor—he had the gift of the Jedi, but had abused his power to enslave the galaxy.

The Sith philosophy, we know now, isn't quite that simple. But it still involves the use and abuse of power.

—TZ

took a few steps away from the shuttle. Nor did anyone scream, call out, or make any appearance at all. "Shy, aren't they?" Pellaeon murmured, keeping his hand on his blaster as he looked around.

"Understandably," Thrawn said, pulling a megaphone disk from his belt. "Let's see if we can persuade them to be hospitable."

Cupping the disk in his hand, he raised it to his lips. "I seek the Guardian of the mountain," his voice boomed across the square, the last syllable echoing from the surrounding buildings. "Who will take me to him?"

The last echo died away into silence. Thrawn lowered the disk and waited; but the seconds ticked by without any response. "Maybe they don't understand Basic," Pellaeon suggested doubtfully.

"No, they understand," Thrawn said coldly. "The humans do, at any rate. Perhaps they need more motivation." He raised the megaphone again. "I seek the Guardian of the mountain," he repeated. "If no one will take me to him, this entire city will suffer."

The words were barely out of his mouth when, without warning, an arrow flashed toward them from the right. It struck Thrawn in the side, barely missing the ysalamir tube wrapped around his shoulders and back, and bounced harmlessly off the body armor hidden beneath the white uniform.[4] "Hold," Thrawn ordered as Rukh leaped to his side, blaster at the ready. "You have the location?"

"Yes," the Noghri grated, his blaster pointed at a squat two-story structure a quarter of the way around the square from the palace.

"Good." Thrawn raised the megaphone again. "One of your people just shot at us. Observe the consequences." Lowering the disk again, he nodded to Rukh. "Now."

And with a tight grin of his needle teeth, Rukh proceeded—quickly, carefully, and scientifically—to demolish the building.

4. One might ask why Thrawn didn't routinely wear body armor, given that this shows he had it available.

The answer is that body armor tends to be heavy and uncomfortable, and Thrawn would normally not bother with it unless he expected to be going into danger.

—TZ

He took out the windows and doors first, putting perhaps a dozen shots through them to discourage any further attack. Then he switched to the lower-floor walls. By the twentieth shot, the building was visibly trembling on its foundations. A handful of shots into the upper-floor walls, a few more into the lower—

And with a thunderous crash, the building collapsed in on itself.

Thrawn waited until the sound of crunching masonry had died away before raising the megaphone again. "Those are the consequences of defying me," he called. "I ask once more: who will take me to the Guardian of the mountain?"

"I will," a voice said from their left.

Pellaeon spun around. The man standing in front of the palace building was tall and thin, with unkempt gray hair and a beard that reached almost to the middle of his chest. He was dressed in shin-laced sandals and an old brown robe, with a glittering medallion of some sort half hidden behind the beard. His face was dark and lined and regal to the point of arrogance as he studied them, his eyes holding a mixture of curiosity and disdain. "You are strangers," he said, the same mixture in his voice. "Strangers"—he glanced up at the shuttle towering over them—"from offworld."

"Yes, we are," Thrawn acknowledged. "And you?"

The old man's eyes flicked to the smoking rubble Rukh had just created. "You destroyed one of my buildings," he said. "There was no need for that."

"We were attacked," Thrawn told him coolly. "Were you its landlord?"

The stranger's eyes might have flashed; at the distance, Pellaeon couldn't say for certain. "I rule," he said, his voice quiet but with menace beneath it. "All that is here is mine."

For a handful of heartbeats he and Thrawn locked eyes. Thrawn broke the silence first. "I am Grand Admiral Thrawn, Warlord of the Empire, servant of the Emperor. I seek the Guardian of the mountain."

The old man bowed his head slightly. "I will take you to him."

Turning, he started back toward the palace. "Stay close together," Thrawn murmured to the others as he moved to follow. "Be alert for a trap."

No more arrows came as they crossed the square and walked under the carved keystone archway framing the palace's double doors. "I would have thought the Guardian would be living in the mountain," Thrawn said as their guide pulled open the doors. They came easily; the old man, Pellaeon decided, must be stronger than he looked.

"He did, once," the other said over his shoulder. "When I began my rule, the people of Wayland built this for him." He crossed to the center of the ornate foyer room, halfway to another set of double doors, and stopped. "Leave us," he called.

For a split second Pellaeon thought the old man was talking to him. He was just opening his mouth to refuse when two flanking sections of wall swung open and a pair of scrawny men stepped out of hidden guard niches. Glowering silently at the Imperials, they shouldered their crossbows and left the building. The old man waited until they were gone, then continued on to the second set of double doors. "Come," he said, gesturing to the doors, an odd glitter in his eyes. "The Emperor's Guardian awaits you."

Silently, the doors swung open, revealing the light of what looked to be several hundred candles filling a huge room. Pellaeon glanced once at the old man standing beside the doors, a sudden premonition of dread sending a shiver up his back. Taking a deep breath, he followed Thrawn and Rukh inside.

Into a crypt.

There was no doubt as to what it was. Aside from the flickering candles, there was nothing else in the room but a large rectangular block of dark stone in the center.

"I see," Thrawn said quietly. "So he is dead."

"He is dead," the old man confirmed from behind them. "Do you see all the candles, Grand Admiral Thrawn?"

"I see them." Thrawn nodded. "The people must have honored him greatly."

"Honored him?" The old man snorted gently. "Hardly. Those candles mark the graves of offworlders who have come here since his death."

Pellaeon twisted to face him, instinctively drawing his blaster as he did so. Thrawn waited another few heartbeats before slowly turning around himself. "How did they die?" he asked.

The old man smiled faintly. "I killed them, of course. Just as I killed the Guardian." He raised his empty hands in front of him, palms upward. "Just as I now kill you."

Without warning, blue lightning bolts flashed from his fingertips—

And vanished without a trace a meter away from each of them.

It all happened so fast that Pellaeon had no chance to even flinch, let alone fire. Now, belatedly, he raised his blaster, the scalding hot air from the bolts washing over his hand—

"Hold," Thrawn said calmly into the silence. "However, as you can see, Guardian, we are not ordinary offworlders."

"The Guardian is dead!" the old man snapped, the last word almost swallowed up by the crackle of more lightning. Again, the bolts vanished into nothingness before even coming close.

"Yes, the old Guardian is dead," Thrawn agreed, shouting to be heard over the crackling thunder. "You are the Guardian now. It is you who protects the Emperor's mountain."[5]

"I serve no Emperor!" the old man retorted, unleashing a third useless salvo. "My power is for myself alone."

As suddenly as it had started, the attack ceased. The old man stared at Thrawn, his hands still raised, a puzzled and

5. My original reasoning was just what's laid out here: that whomever Palpatine had left to guard his storehouse had been killed by Joruus C'baoth when he somehow stumbled on the place.

　To my mild surprise, speculation quickly arose that C'baoth *was* the original guardian, and it was merely because of his insanity that he thought he'd killed someone and taken his place.

　Such speculation is wrong, of course.

　I think . . .

　　　　　—TZ

oddly petulant expression on his face. "You are not Jedi. How do you do this?"

"Join us and learn," Thrawn suggested.

The other drew himself up to his full height. "I am a Jedi Master,"[6] he ground out. "I join no one."

"I see." Thrawn nodded. "In that case, permit *us* to join *you*." His glowing red eyes bored into the old man's face. "And permit us to show you how you can have more power than you've ever imagined. All the power even a Jedi Master could desire."

For a long moment the old man continued to stare at Thrawn, a dozen strange expressions flicking in quick succession across his face. "Very well," he said at last. "Come. We will talk."

"Thank you," Thrawn said, inclining his head slightly. "May I ask who we have the honor of addressing?"

"Of course." The old man's face was abruptly regal again, and when he spoke his voice rang out in the silence of the crypt. "I am the Jedi Master Joruus C'baoth."[7]

Pellaeon inhaled sharply, a cold shiver running up his back. "Joruus C'baoth?" he breathed. "But—"

He broke off. C'baoth looked at him, much as Pellaeon himself might look at a junior officer who has spoken out of turn. "Come," he repeated, turning back to Thrawn. "We will talk."

He led the way out of the crypt and back into the sunshine. Several small knots of people had gathered in the square in their absence, huddling well back from both the crypt and the shuttle as they whispered nervously together.

With one exception. Standing directly in their path a few meters away was one of the two guards C'baoth had ordered out of the crypt. On his face was an expression of barely controlled fury; in his hands, cocked and ready, was his crossbow. "You destroyed his home," C'baoth said, almost conversationally. "Doubtless he would like to exact vengeance."

The words were barely out of his mouth when the guard

6. A Jedi Master like no other! George Lucas's first three films gave us Obi-Wan, Yoda, and Darth Vader. The concept of someone wielding Jedi powers whose grip on reality is, shall we say, tenuous, was entirely new.
—BM

7. In my first outline this character was an insane clone of Obi-Wan Kenobi, created before the Clone Wars by the Emperor and put here to guard the storehouse. That would have given me a very interesting dynamic to work with, especially when Luke faces him in *Dark Force Rising*. At that point, with his own emotions running high, Luke would have to determine whether this was a trick, or in fact a reincarnation of his old friend and Master.

Lucasfilm vetoed the idea. I lobbied very hard to keep it, modifying it six ways from Sunday to try to make sure I didn't step on George's yet-to-be-written prequel toes. But it was to no avail. Reluctantly, grouchily, I rewrote the part for C'baoth instead.

Now, as is the case with so many of the strictures and boundaries Lucasfilm put on me, I'm glad they reined me in. Not only is C'baoth an interesting character in his own right,

(cont.)

but my subsequent *Out-bound Flight* novel would have had to be drastically different.

C'baoth, incidentally, is pronounced *SA-bay-oth*, with the first vowel pronounced like the *a* in has. If I'd realized how hard it was going to be for everyone else to figure out, I would have changed the spelling.

To be fair, part of the problem was also that when the audio adaptations of the books came out, several of the names and words were a bit mangled, leaving a lingering confusion in the minds of everyone who heard them.

It wasn't just my stuff, either. Anthony Daniels, who did one of the readings, later told me the pronunciation sheet he was given had Tatooine wrong, too.

—TZ

8. Thrawn doesn't show this kind of emotion very often. It's likely some of this is the distant memories of his encounter years earlier with the original, nonclone C'baoth.

Of course, I didn't know that until years later when I wrote *Outbound Flight*. An

suddenly snapped the crossbow up and fired. Instinctively, Pellaeon ducked, raising his blaster—

And three meters from the Imperials the bolt came to an abrupt halt in midair.

Pellaeon stared at the hovering piece of wood and metal, his brain only slowly catching up with what had just happened. "They are our guests," C'baoth told the guard in a voice clearly intended to reach everyone in the square. "They will be treated accordingly."

With a crackle of splintering wood, the crossbow bolt shattered, the pieces dropping to the ground. Slowly, reluctantly, the guard lowered his crossbow, his eyes still burning with a now impotent rage. Thrawn let him stand there another second like that, then gestured to Rukh. The Noghri raised his blaster and fired—

And in a blur of motion almost too fast to see, a flat stone detached itself from the ground and hurled itself directly into the path of the shot, shattering spectacularly as the blast hit it.

Thrawn spun to face C'baoth, his face a mirror of surprise and anger.[8] "C'baoth—!"

"These are *my* people, Grand Admiral Thrawn," the other cut him off, his voice forged from quiet steel. "Not yours; mine. If there is punishment to be dealt out, *I* will do it."

For a long moment the two men again locked eyes.[9] Then, with an obvious effort, Thrawn regained his composure. "Of course, Master C'baoth," he said. "Forgive me."

C'baoth nodded. "Better. Much better." He looked past Thrawn, dismissed the guard with a nod. "Come," he said, looking back at the Grand Admiral. "We will talk."

"You will now tell me," C'baoth said, gesturing them to low cushions, "how it was you defeated my attack."

"Let me first explain our offer," Thrawn said, throwing

a casual glance around the room before easing carefully down on one of the cushions. Probably, Pellaeon thought, the Grand Admiral was examining the bits of artwork scattered around. "I believe you'll find it—"

"You will now tell me how it was you defeated my attack," C'baoth repeated.

A slight grimace, quickly suppressed, touched Thrawn's lips. "It's quite simple, actually." He looked up at the ysalamir wrapped around his shoulders, reaching a finger over to gently stroke its long neck. "These creatures you see on our backs are called ysalamiri. They're sessile tree-dwelling creatures from a distant, third-rate planet, and they have an interesting and possibly unique ability—they push back the Force."

C'baoth frowned. "What do you mean, push it back?"

"They push its presence out away from themselves," Thrawn explained. "Much the same way a bubble is created by air pushing outward against water. A single ysalamir can occasionally create a bubble as large as ten meters across; a whole group of them reinforcing one another can create much larger ones."[10]

"I've never heard of such a thing," C'baoth said, staring at Thrawn's ysalamir with an almost childlike intensity. "How could such a creature have come about?"

"I really don't know," Thrawn conceded. "I assume the talent has some survival value, but what that would be I can't imagine." He cocked an eyebrow. "Not that it matters. For the moment, the ability itself is sufficient for my purpose."

C'baoth's face darkened. "That purpose being to defeat my power?"

Thrawn shrugged. "We were expecting to find the Emperor's Guardian here. I needed to make certain he would allow us to identify ourselves and explain our mission." He reached up again to stroke the ysalamir's neck. "Though as it happens, protecting us from the Guardian was really

(cont.) other case of being able to fit pieces into a puzzle that at the time I didn't even know I was making.

—TZ

9. This scene sets up a balance of two kinds of power that will affect the next three books: Thrawn's military command and tactics-oriented mind versus C'baoth's Force abilities and the danger of his completely unpredictable thought processes.

—BM

10. I caught more grief for this one than even the hot chocolate incident. The complaints mostly focused on the idea that the Force is created by living beings, and that it can't be "pushed back" in the way I described, certainly not from other living beings.

Note, though, that I didn't say that was the case. Thrawn did, and contrary to popular belief Thrawn doesn't know everything.

What's actually happening—and we'll see it in action later—is that ysalamiri simply suppress the level of the Force to something below the threshold that

Jedi can access. It's a fine distinction, but an important one.

Still, the bottom line for Jedi—and more important for C'baoth—is basically the same. Thrawn can therefore be excused for perhaps oversimplifying his explanation.

—TZ

11. Actually, we know from *The Empire Strikes Back* that the cloaking shield was at least marginally functional at that time.

But the rumors may not have reached Thrawn, out in the Unknown Regions, until closer to Endor.

—TZ

only an extra bonus. I have something far more interesting in mind for our little pets."

"That being . . . ?"

Thrawn smiled. "All in good time, Master C'baoth. *And* only after we've had a chance to examine the Emperor's storehouse in Mount Tantiss."

C'baoth's lip twisted. "So the mountain is all you really want."

"I need the mountain, certainly," Thrawn acknowledged. "Or rather, what I hope to find within it."

"And that is . . . ?"

Thrawn studied him for a moment. "There were rumors, just before the Battle of Endor, that the Emperor's researchers had finally developed a genuinely practical cloaking shield.[11] I want it. Also," he added, almost as an afterthought, "another small—almost trivial—bit of technology."

"And you think to find one of these cloaking shields in the mountain?"

"I expect to find either a working model or at least a complete set of schematics," Thrawn said. "One of the Emperor's purposes in setting up this storehouse was to make sure that interesting and potentially useful technology didn't get lost."

"That, and collecting endless mementos of his glorious conquests." C'baoth snorted. "There are rooms and rooms of that sort of cackling self-congratulation."

Pellaeon sat up a bit straighter. "You've been inside the mountain?" he asked. Somehow, he'd expected the storehouse to be sealed with all sorts of locks and barriers.

C'baoth sent him a scornfully patient look. "Of course I've been inside. I killed the Guardian, remember?" He looked back at Thrawn. "So. You want the Emperor's little toys; and now you know you can just walk into the mountain, with or without my help. Why are you still sitting here?"

"Because the mountain is only part of what I need,"

Thrawn told him. "I also require the partnership of a Jedi Master like yourself."

C'baoth settled back into his cushion, a cynical smile showing through his beard. "Ah, we finally get down to it. This, I take it, is where you offer me all the power even a Jedi Master could desire?"

Thrawn smiled back. "It is indeed. Tell me, Master C'baoth: are you familiar with the Imperial Fleet's disastrous defeat at the Battle of Endor five years ago?"

"I've heard rumors. One of the offworlders who came here spoke about it." C'baoth's gaze drifted to the window, to the palace/crypt visible across the square. "Though only briefly."

Pellaeon swallowed. Thrawn himself didn't seem to notice the implication. "Then you must have wondered how a few dozen Rebel ships could possibly rout an Imperial force that outgunned it by at least ten to one."

"I didn't spend much time with such wonderings," C'baoth said dryly. "I assumed that the Rebels were simply better warriors."

"In a sense, that's true," Thrawn agreed. "The Rebels did indeed fight better, but not because of any special abilities or training. They fought better than the Fleet because the Emperor was dead."

He turned to look at Pellaeon. "You were there, Captain—you must have noticed it. The sudden loss of coordination between crew members and ships; the loss of efficiency and discipline. The loss, in short, of that elusive quality we call fighting spirit."

"There was some confusion, yes," Pellaeon said stiffly. He was starting to see where Thrawn was going with this, and he didn't like it a bit. "But nothing that can't be explained by the normal stresses of battle."

One blue-black eyebrow went up, just slightly. "Really? The loss of the *Executor*—the sudden, last-minute TIE fighter incompetence that brought about the destruction of the Death Star itself—the loss of six other Star Destroyers in engagements that none of them should have had trouble with? *All* of that nothing but normal battle stress?"

"The Emperor was not directing the battle," Pellaeon snapped with a fire that startled him. "Not in any way. I was there, Admiral—*I* know."

"Yes, Captain, you were there," Thrawn said, his voice abruptly hard. "And it's time you gave up your blindfold and faced the truth, no matter how bitter you find it. You had no real fighting spirit of your own anymore—none of you in the Imperial Fleet did. It was the Emperor's will that drove you; the Emperor's mind that provided you with strength and resolve and efficiency. You were as dependent on that presence as if you were all borg-implanted into a combat computer."[12]

"That's not true," Pellaeon shot back, stomach twisting painfully within him. "It can't be. We fought on after his death."

"Yes," Thrawn said, his voice quiet and contemptuous. "You fought on. Like cadets."

C'baoth snorted. "So is *this* what you want me for, Grand Admiral Thrawn?" he asked scornfully. "To turn your ships into puppets for you?"

"Not at all, Master C'baoth," Thrawn told him, his voice perfectly calm again. "My analogy with combat borg implants was a carefully considered one. The Emperor's fatal error was in seeking to control the entire Imperial Fleet personally, as completely and constantly as possible. That, over the long run, is what did the damage. My wish is merely to have you enhance the coordination between ships and task forces—and then only at critical times and in carefully selected combat situations."

C'baoth threw a look at Pellaeon. "To what end?" he rumbled.

"To the end we've already discussed," Thrawn said. "Power."[13]

"What sort of power?"

12. I borrowed this from Sauron's driving of his forces in *The Lord of the Rings*. Much as I sympathize with the Alliance, I felt there had to be something going on beneath the surface to explain their victory at Endor.

It's also, I think, consistent with Palpatine's pride and nature. Endor was to be *his* victory over the Rebellion, and he would have made sure he could claim it as such.

Logic aside, of course, I also needed this ability for C'baoth to use later in the books.

—TZ

13. Thrawn had spent years observing Palpatine, watching how he used his power, seeing what his goals and desires were. From that analysis, he would naturally have concluded that all Dark Jedi would want the same kind of power over people and worlds.

—TZ

For the first time since landing, Thrawn seemed taken aback. "The conquering of worlds, of course. The final defeat of the Rebellion. The reestablishment of the glory that was once the Empire's New Order."

C'baoth shook his head. "You don't understand power, Grand Admiral Thrawn. Conquering worlds you'll never even visit again isn't power. Neither is destroying ships and people and rebellions you haven't looked at face-to-face." He waved his hands in a sweeping gesture around him, his eyes glittering with an eerie fire. "*This*, Grand Admiral Thrawn, is power. This city—this planet—these people. Every human, Psadan, and Myneyrsh who live here are mine. *Mine.*" His gaze drifted to the window again. "I teach them. I command them. I punish them. Their lives, and their deaths, are in *my* hands."

"Which is precisely what I offer you," Thrawn said. "Millions of lives—billions, if you wish. All those lives to do with as you please."

"It isn't the same," C'baoth said, a note of paternal patience in his voice. "I have no desire to hold distant power over faceless lives."

"You could have just a single city to rule, then," Thrawn persisted. "As large or as small as you wish."

"I rule a city now."

Thrawn's eyes narrowed. "I need your assistance, Master C'baoth. Name your price."

C'baoth smiled. "My price? The price for my service?" Abruptly, the smile vanished. "I'm a Jedi Master, Grand Admiral Thrawn," he said, his voice simmering with menace. "Not a mercenary for hire like your Noghri."

He threw a contemptuous look at Rukh, sitting silently off to one side. "Oh, yes, Noghri—I know what you and your people are. The Emperor's private Death Commandos; killing and dying at the whim of ambitious men like Darth Vader and the Grand Admiral here."

"Lord Vader served the Emperor and the Empire," Rukh

grated, his dark eyes staring unblinkingly at C'baoth. "As do we."

"Perhaps." C'baoth turned back to Thrawn. "I have all I want or need, Grand Admiral Thrawn. You will leave Wayland now."

Thrawn didn't move. "I need your assistance, Master C'baoth," he repeated quietly. "And I will have it."

"Or you'll do what?" C'baoth sneered. "Have your Noghri try to kill me? It would almost be amusing to watch." He looked at Pellaeon. "Or perhaps you'll have your brave Star Destroyer captain try to level my city from orbit. Except that you can't risk damaging the mountain, can you?"

"My gunners could destroy this city without even singeing the grass on Mount Tantiss," Pellaeon retorted. "If you need a demonstration—"

"Peace, Captain," Thrawn cut him off calmly. "So it's the personal, face-to-face sort of power you prefer, Master C'baoth? Yes, I can certainly understand that. Not that there can be much challenge left in it—not anymore. Of course," he added reflectively, glancing out the window, "that may be the whole idea. I expect that even Jedi Masters eventually get too old to be interested in anything except to sit out in the sun."

C'baoth's forehead darkened. "Have a care, Grand Admiral Thrawn," he warned. "Or perhaps I'll seek challenge in your destruction."

"That would hardly be a challenge for a man of your skill and power," Thrawn countered with a shrug. "But then, you probably already have other Jedi here under your command."

C'baoth frowned, obviously thrown by the sudden change in subject. "Other Jedi?" he echoed.

"Of course. Surely it's only fitting that a Jedi Master have lesser Jedi serving beneath him. Jedi whom he may teach and command and punish at will."

Something like a shadow crossed C'baoth's face. "There

are no Jedi left," he murmured. "The Emperor and Vader hunted them down and destroyed them."

"Not all of them," Thrawn told him softly. "Two new Jedi have arisen in the past five years: Luke Skywalker and his sister, Leia Organa Solo."

"And what is that to me?"

"I can deliver them to you."

For a long minute C'baoth stared at him, disbelief and desire struggling for supremacy on his face. The desire won. "Both of them?"

"Both of them." Thrawn nodded. "Consider what a man of your skill could do with brand-new Jedi. Mold them, change them, re-create them in any image you choose." He cocked an eyebrow. "And with them would come a very special bonus . . . because Leia Organa Solo is pregnant. With twins."

C'baoth inhaled sharply. "*Jedi* twins?" he hissed.

"They have the potential, or so my sources tell me." Thrawn smiled. "Of course, what they ultimately became would be entirely up to you."

C'baoth's eyes darted to Pellaeon; back to Thrawn. Slowly, deliberately, he stood up. "Very well, Grand Admiral Thrawn," he said. "In return for the Jedi, I will assist your forces. Take me to your ship."

"In time, Master C'baoth," Thrawn said, getting to his feet himself. "First we must go into the Emperor's mountain. This bargain is dependent on whether I find what I'm looking for there."

"Of course." C'baoth's eyes flashed. "Let us both hope," he said warningly, "that you do."

It took seven hours of searching, through a mountain fortress much larger than Pellaeon had expected. But in the end, they did indeed find the treasures Thrawn had hoped for. The cloaking shield . . . and that other small, almost trivial, bit of technology.

The door to the Grand Admiral's command room slid open; settling himself, Pellaeon stepped inside. "A word with you, Admiral?"

"Certainly, Captain," Thrawn said from his seat in the center of the double display circle. "Come in. Has there been any update from the Imperial Palace?"

"No, sir, not since yesterday's," Pellaeon said as he walked to the edge of the outer circle, silently rehearsing one last time how he was going to say this. "I can request one, if you'd like."

"Probably unnecessary." Thrawn shook his head. "It looks like the details of the Bimmisaari trip have been more or less settled. All we have to do is alert one of the commando groups—Team Eight, I think—and we'll have our Jedi."

"Yes, sir," Pellaeon braced himself. "Admiral . . . I have to tell you that I'm not convinced dealing with C'baoth is a good idea. To be perfectly honest, I don't think he's entirely sane."

Thrawn cocked an eyebrow. "Of course he's not sane. But then, he's not Joruus C'baoth, either."

Pellaeon felt his mouth fall open. "What?"

"Joruus C'baoth is dead," Thrawn said. "He was one of the six Jedi Masters aboard the Old Republic's Outbound Flight project.[14] I don't know if you were highly enough placed back then to have known about it."

"I heard rumors," Pellaeon frowned, thinking back. "Some sort of grand effort to extend the Old Republic's authority outside the galaxy, as I recall, launched just before the Clone Wars broke out. I never heard anything more about it."

"That's because there wasn't anything more to be heard," Thrawn said evenly. "It was intercepted by a task force outside Old Republic space and destroyed."

Pellaeon stared at him, a shiver running up his back. "How do you know?"

Thrawn raised his eyebrows. "Because I was the force's

14. Outbound Flight was essentially a throwaway line, a way to confirm that this C'baoth was indeed a clone, as well as to underline Thrawn's military capabilities.

But it didn't stay a throwaway for long. I ended up working out a few more details in *Specter of the Past* and *Vision of the Future,* and ultimately did an entire novel, *Outbound Flight.*

I wish I'd known at the time that the project was going to grow to that size. I would have given it a much cooler name.

—TZ

commander. Even at that early date the Emperor recognized that the Jedi had to be exterminated. Six Jedi Masters aboard the same ship was too good an opportunity to pass up."

Pellaeon licked his lips. "But then . . . ?"

"Who is it we've brought aboard the *Chimaera*?" Thrawn finished the question for him. "I should have thought that obvious. Joruus C'baoth—note the telltale mispronunciation of the name *Jorus*—is a clone."

Pellaeon stared at him. "A *clone*?"

"Certainly," Thrawn said. "Created from a tissue sample, probably sometime just before the real C'baoth's death."

"Early in the war, in other words," Pellaeon said, swallowing hard. The early clones—or at least those the fleet had faced[15]—had been highly unstable, both mentally and emotionally. Sometimes spectacularly so . . . "And you deliberately brought this thing aboard my ship?" he demanded.

"Would you rather we have brought back a full-fledged Dark Jedi?" Thrawn asked coldly. "A second Darth Vader, perhaps, with the sort of ambitions and power that might easily lead him to take over your ship? Count your blessings, Captain."

"At least a Dark Jedi would have been predictable," Pellaeon countered.

"C'baoth is predictable enough," Thrawn assured him. "And for those times when he isn't—" He waved a hand at the half dozen frameworks encircling his command center. "That's what the ysalamiri are for."

Pellaeon grimaced. "I still don't like it, Admiral. We can hardly protect the ship from him while at the same time having him coordinate the fleet's attacks."

"There's a degree of risk involved," Thrawn agreed. "But risk has always been an inescapable part of warfare. In this case, the potential benefits far outweigh the potential dangers."

15. Again, my assumptions about the Clone Wars were exactly backward: I assumed the clones would be fighting *against* the Republic instead of being on their side. (Nice twist, George!)
 Fortunately, *facing* doesn't necessarily mean *fighting*. My choice of words here was pure luck, but it helped me avoid a retroactive gaffe.
                                                —TZ

Reluctantly, Pellaeon nodded. He didn't like it—was fairly certain he would never like it—but it was clear that Thrawn had made up his mind. "Yes, sir," he muttered. "You mentioned a message to Team Eight. Will you be wanting me to transmit that?"

"No, I'll handle it myself." Thrawn smiled sardonically. "Their glorious leader, and all that—you know how Noghri are. If there's nothing more . . . ?"

It was, clearly, a dismissal. "No, sir," Pellaeon said. "I'll be on the bridge if you require me." He turned to go.

"It will bring us victory, Captain," the Grand Admiral called softly after him. "Quiet your fears, and concentrate on that."

If it doesn't kill us all. "Yes, sir," Pellaeon said aloud, and left the room.

CHAPTER 5

HAN FINISHED HIS REPORT, sat back, and waited for the criticism to start.

It was a very short wait. "So once again your smuggler friends refuse to commit themselves," Admiral Ackbar said, sounding more than a little disgusted. His high-domed head bobbed twice in some indecipherable Calamarian gesture, his huge eyes blinking in time with the head movements. "You'll recall that I disagreed with this idea all along," he added, waving a webbed hand toward Han's report case.

Han glanced across the table at Leia. "It's not a matter of commitment, Admiral," he told the other. "It's a matter that most of them just don't see any real gain in switching from their current activities to straight shipping."

"Or else it's a lack of trust," a melodic alien voice put in. "Could that be it?"

Han grimaced before he could stop himself. "It's possible," he said, forcing himself to look at Borsk Fey'lya.

"Possible?" Fey'lya's violet eyes widened, the fine cream-colored fur covering his body rippling slightly with the motion. It was a Bothan gesture of polite surprise, one which Fey'lya seemed to use a lot.[1] "You said *possible*, Captain Solo?"

Han sighed quietly and gave up. Fey'lya would only maneuver him into saying it some other way if he didn't. "Some of the groups I've talked to don't trust us," he conceded. "They think the offer might be some sort of trap to bring them out into the open."

"Because of me, of course," Ackbar growled, his normal salmon color turning a little darker. "Haven't you tired of retaking this same territory, Councilor Fey'lya?"

Fey'lya's eyes widened again, and for a moment he gazed silently at Ackbar as the tension around the table quickly rose to the level of thick paste. They had never liked each other, Han knew, not from the day Fey'lya had first brought his sizable faction of the Bothan race into the Alliance after the Battle of Yavin. Right from the start Fey'lya had been jockeying for position and power, cutting deals wherever and whenever he could and making it abundantly clear that he expected to be given a high position in the fledgling political system Mon Mothma was putting together. Ackbar had considered such ambitions to be a dangerous waste of time and effort, particularly given the bleak situation the Alliance was facing at the time, and with typical bluntness had made no effort to conceal that opinion.

Given Ackbar's reputation and subsequent successes, Han had little doubt that Fey'lya would ultimately have been shunted off to some relatively unimportant government post in the New Republic . . . if it hadn't happened that the spies who discovered the existence and location of the Emperor's new Death Star had been a group of Fey'lya's Bothans.

Preoccupied at the time with more urgent matters, Han had never learned the details of how Fey'lya had managed to parlay that serendipity into his current position on the

1. In *Return of the Jedi*, Mon Mothma said that Bothan spies had learned the new Death Star's location and an Imperial code that would allow a surreptitious Rebel approach. Even though all that turned out to be a trap, I figured the Bothans would probably use that to work themselves into a good position in the fledgling New Republic hierarchy.

Especially if I gave them a high level of smooth political maneuvering skills. The result of that train of thought was Borsk Fey'lya.

But even beyond that, I wanted to show the New Republic as being a somewhat uneasy patchwork of differing political views, motivations, and goals. We have this conflict in any group of humans of any size—surely among different types of aliens the effect would be even more pronounced.

So, again, Borsk Fey'lya. For all the frustration and trouble he causes, he's not a "villain" in the usual sense. He and his people simply have different ways of achieving their political goals. The fact that his approach causes chaos and possible destruction is apparently never a concern to him. It's the way

Council. And to be perfectly honest, he wasn't sure he wanted to.

"I merely seek to clarify the situation in my own mind, Admiral," Fey'lya said at last into the heavy silence. "It's hardly worthwhile for us to continue sending a valuable man like Captain Solo out on these contact missions if each is predoomed to failure."

"They're *not* predoomed to failure," Han cut in. Out of the corner of his eye he saw Leia give him a warning look. He ignored it. "The kind of smugglers we're looking for are conservative businesspeople—they don't just jump into something new without thinking it through first. They'll come around."

Fey'lya shrugged, his fur again rippling. "And meanwhile, we expend a great deal of time and effort with nothing to show for it."

"Look, you can't build up any—"

A gentle, almost diffident tap of a hammer from the head of the table cut off the argument. "What the smugglers are waiting for," Mon Mothma said quietly, her stern gaze touching each of the others at the table in turn, "is the same thing the rest of the galaxy is waiting for: the formal reestablishment of the principles and law of the Old Republic. *That* is our first and primary task, Councilors. To become the New Republic in fact as well as in name."

Han caught Leia's eye, and this time he was the one who sent out the warning look. She grimaced, but nodded slightly and kept quiet.

Mon Mothma let the silence linger a moment longer, again sending her gaze around the table. Han found himself studying her, noting the deepening lines in her face, the streaks of gray in her dark hair, the thinness rather than slenderness of her neck. She'd aged a lot since he'd first met her, back when the Alliance was trying to find a way out from under the shadow of the Empire's second Death Star.[2] Ever since then, Mon Mothma had been right

(cont.)
Bothans have always done things, and he—and they—see no reason to change.

—TZ

2. This seems to imply that Han first met Mon Mothma in *Return of the Jedi,* around the time of the Endor operation briefing. However, in *Allegiance* I have them meeting shortly after the Battle of Yavin, nearly four years earlier.

Does that make this line a goof? Well . . . maybe not. In a much later story, "The Tale of the 'Tonika Sisters,'" from *Tales from the Star Wars Cantina,* I have a Rebel agent getting hold of a segment of the second Death Star's prototype superlaser. Ergo, as far back as Yavin, rumors of a second Death Star would already be swirling around the Empire. Ergo, the line in *Allegiance* isn't really a mistake.

Note that among other things, that bit of retrofitting implies that it took the Rebellion those same four years to track those rumors down. No wonder the Bothans came in for high praise when they brought the name *Endor* to Alliance attention.

Still, don't let all these clever explanations give

(cont.)
you the impression that I had this whole immense thing mapped out in advance. Right now, I'm using the Indiana Jones approach, and making it up (more or less) as I go.
—TZ

in the middle of this horrendous task of setting up a viable government, and the strain had clearly told on her.

But despite what the years were doing to her face, her eyes still held the same quiet fire they'd possessed then— the same fire, or so the stories went, that had been there since her historic break with the Emperor's New Order and her founding of the Rebel Alliance. She was tough, and smart, and fully in control. And everyone present knew it.

Her eyes finished their sweep and came to rest on Han. "Captain Solo, we thank you for your report; and, too, for your efforts. And with the Captain's report, this meeting is adjourned."

She tapped the hammer again and stood up. Han closed his report case and worked his way through the general confusion around to the other side of the table. "So," he said quietly, coming up behind Leia as she collected her own things. "Are we out of here?"

"The sooner the better," she muttered back. "I just have to give these things to Winter."

Han glanced around and lowered his voice a notch. "I take it things were going a little rough before they called me in?"

"No more than usual," she told him. "Fey'lya and Ackbar had one of their polite little dogfights, this one over the fiasco at Obroa-skai—that lost Elomin force—with some more of Fey'lya's veiled suggestions that the job of Commander in Chief is too much for Ackbar to handle. And then, of course, Mon Mothma—"

"A word with you, Leia?" Mon Mothma's voice came from over Han's shoulder.

Han turned to face her, sensing Leia tense a little beside him as she did likewise. "Yes?"

"I forgot to ask you earlier if you'd talked to Luke about going with you to Bimmisaari," Mon Mothma said. "Did he agree?"

"Yes." Leia nodded, throwing an apologetic look at Han.

"I'm sorry, Han; I didn't get a chance to tell you. The Bimms sent a message yesterday asking that Luke be there with me for the talks."

"They did, huh?" A year ago, Han reflected, he would probably have been furious at having a painstakingly crafted schedule flipped at the last minute like this. Leia's diplomatic patience must be starting to rub off on him.

Either that, or he was just getting soft. "They give any reasons?"

"The Bimms are rather hero-oriented," Mon Mothma said before Leia could answer, her eyes searching Han's face. Probably trying to figure out just how mad he was about the change in plans. "And Luke's part in the Battle of Endor *is* rather well known."

"Yeah, I'd heard that," Han said, trying not to be too sarcastic. He had no particular quarrel with Luke's position in the New Republic's pantheon of heroes—the kid had certainly earned it. But if having Jedi around to brag about was so important to Mon Mothma, then she ought to be letting Leia get on with her own studies instead of foisting all this extra diplomatic work on her. As it was, he would bet on an ambitious snail to make full Jedi before she did.[3]

Leia found his hand, squeezed it. He squeezed back, to show that he wasn't mad. Though she probably already knew that. "We'd better get going," she told Mon Mothma, using her grip on Han's hand to start steering him away from the table. "We still have to collect our droids before we leave."

"Have a good trip," Mon Mothma said gravely. "And good luck."

"The droids are already on the *Falcon*," Han told Leia as they wove their way around the various conversations that had sprung up between the Councilors and staff members. "Chewie got them aboard while I came here."

"I know," Leia murmured.

"Right," Han said, and left it at that.

3. And Mon Mothma undoubtedly recognizes the problem and conflict: future dividends of Leia as a Jedi versus present dividends of Leia as diplomat. Present versus future: a decision we all have to make from time to time.

And that's one of the reasons the *Star Wars* movies were so successful. They portrayed real people—with real, timeless, human problems and challenges—against the backdrop of a wondrous universe.

—TZ

She squeezed his hand again. "It'll be all right, Han. You, me, and Luke together again—it'll be just like old times."

"Sure," Han said. Sitting around with a group of half-furred, half-size aliens, listening to Threepio's precise voice all day as he translated back and forth, trying to penetrate yet another alien psychology to figure out what exactly it would take to get them to join the New Republic— "Sure," he repeated with a sigh. "Just exactly like old times."[4]

4. "Just exactly like old times" perfectly calls to mind various scenes in the original *Star Wars:* Luke practicing his new-found Force abilities, Chewie and R2-D2 playing dejarik, Han and Leia sniping at each other. Therefore there's no need to spell out what occurs between the end of this chapter and the beginning of chapter 6. Tim simply announces that the *Falcon* has arrived at Bimmisaari.

—BM

CHAPTER 6

THE WAVING ALIEN TREES shied back like some sort of huge tentacles from the landing area, and with the barest of bumps Han set the *Millennium Falcon* down on the uneven ground. "Well, here we are," he announced to no one in particular. "Bimmisaari. Fur and moving plants a specialty."[1]

"None of that," Leia warned him, unstrapping from the seat behind him and running through the Jedi relaxation techniques Luke had taught her. Political dealings with people she knew were relatively easy for her. Diplomatic missions with unfamiliar alien races were something else entirely.

"You'll do fine," Luke said from beside her, reaching over to squeeze her arm.

Han half turned. "I wish you two wouldn't do that," he complained. "It's like listening to half a conversation."

"Sorry," Luke apologized, climbing out of his seat and stooping to peer out the *Falcon*'s nose window. "Looks like

1. One of the subtle tricks George used in the *Star Wars* movies was to show us only a few different planets, but to then use throwaway mentions of others along the way, thus giving us a feel for a much larger galaxy than we were actually seeing.

I wanted to continue that technique by throwing in short visits to lots of different worlds such as Bimmisaari.

—TZ

our reception committee coming. I'll go get Threepio ready."

"We'll be there in a minute," Leia called after him. "You ready, Han?"

"Yeah," Han told her, adjusting his blaster in its holster. "Last chance to change your mind, Chewie."

Leia strained her ears as Chewbacca growled out a curt reply. Even after all these years she still couldn't understand him nearly as well as Han could—some subtle level of harmonics in the Wookiee's voice, apparently, that she had trouble picking up.

But if some of the words were less than distinct, the overall meaning came through crystal clear. "Oh, come on," Han urged. "You've been fawned over before— remember that big awards thing back at the Yavin base? I didn't hear you complaining *then*."

"It's all right, Han," Leia put in over Chewbacca's response. "If he wants to stay aboard with Artoo and work on the stabilizers, that's fine. The Bimms won't be offended."

Han looked out the nose window at the approaching delegation. "I wasn't worried about offending them," he muttered. "I just thought it'd be nice to have a little extra backup along. Just in case."

Leia smiled and patted his arm. "The Bimms are very friendly people," she assured him. "There won't be any trouble."

"I've heard *that* before," Han said dryly, pulling a comlink from a small storage compartment beside his seat. He started to clip it to his belt; changed direction in midmotion and fastened it to his collar instead.

"Looks good there," Leia said. "Are you going to put your old general's insignia on your belt now?"

He made a face at her. "Very funny. With the comlink here, all I have to do is casually switch it on and I'll be able to talk to Chewie without being obvious about it."

"Ah." Leia nodded. It *was* a good idea, at that. "Sounds

like you've been spending too much time with Lieutenant Page and his commandos."

"I've been spending too much time sitting in on Council meetings," he countered, sliding out of his seat and standing up. "After four years of watching political infighting, you learn the occasional value of subtlety. Come on, Chewie—we'll need you to lock up behind us."

Luke and Threepio were waiting when they got to the hatchway. "Ready?" Luke asked.

"Ready," Leia said, taking a deep breath. With a hiss of released airseal the hatchway opened, and together they walked down the ramp to where the yellow-clad, half-furred creatures waited.

The arrival ceremony was short and, for the most part, unintelligible, though Threepio did his best to keep up a running translation of the five-part harmony the whole thing seemed to have been written in. The song/welcome ended and two of the Bimms stepped forward, one of them continuing the melody while the other held up a small electronic device. "He offers greetings to Distinguished Visitor Councilor Leia Organa Solo," Threepio said, "and hopes your discussions with the Law Elders will be fruitful. He also requests that Captain Solo return his weapon to the ship."

The droid said it so matter-of-factly that it took a second for the words to penetrate. "What was that last?" Leia asked.

"Captain Solo must leave his weapon aboard the ship," Threepio repeated. "Weapons of violence are not permitted within the city. There are no exceptions."

"Terrific," Han murmured into her ear. "You didn't tell me this one was coming."

"I didn't *know* this one was coming," Leia countered quietly, giving the two Bimms a reassuring smile. "Doesn't look like we've got any choice."

"Diplomacy," Han growled, making a curse out of the word. Unfastening his gun belt, he wrapped it carefully around the holstered blaster and set the package up inside the hatchway. "Happy?"

"Aren't I always?" Leia nodded to Threepio. "Tell them we're ready."

The droid translated. Stepping aside, the two Bimms gestured back the way they'd come.

They were perhaps twenty meters from the *Falcon*, with the sounds of Chewbacca sealing the hatchway coming from behind them, when something abruptly occurred to Leia. "Luke?" she murmured.

"Yes, I know," he murmured back. "Maybe they figure it's just part of the proper Jedi's outfit."

"Or else their weapons detector doesn't read lightsabers," Han put in quietly from Leia's other side. "Either way, what they don't know won't hurt them."

"I hope so," Leia said, forcing down her reflexive diplomatic misgivings. After all, if the Bimms themselves hadn't objected to it . . . "Good skies, would you look at that crowd?"

They were waiting where the path exited the trees—hundreds of Bimms, standing perhaps twenty deep on both sides of the way, all clothed in the same tooled yellow. The official reception committee shifted to single file and started down the gauntlet without giving the crowd a second glance; bracing herself, Leia followed.

It was a little strange, but not nearly as uncomfortable as she'd feared it would be. Each Bimm reached out a hand as she passed, touching her with a feathery lightness on shoulder or head or arm or back. It was all done in complete silence, and complete order, with the aura of perfect civilization about it.

Still, she was glad that Chewbacca had decided not to come. He hated—rather violently—being pawed by strangers.

They passed through the crowd, and the Bimm walking nearest Leia sang something. "He says the Tower of Law is just ahead," Threepio translated. "It's the location of their planetary council."

Leia peered over the heads of the leading Bimms. There, obviously, was the Tower of Law. And next to it . . . "Threepio, ask what that thing is beside it," she instructed the droid. "That building that looks like a three-level dome with the sides and most of the roof cut away."

The droid sang, and the Bimm replied. "It's the city's main marketplace," Threepio told her. "He says they prefer the open air whenever possible."

"That roof probably stretches to cover more of the dome framework when the weather's bad," Han added from behind her. "I've seen that design in a few other places."

"He says that perhaps you can be given a tour of the facility before you leave," Threepio added.

"Sounds great," Han said. "Wonderful place to pick up souvenirs."

"Quiet," Leia warned. "Or you can wait in the *Falcon* with Chewie."

The Bimmisaari Tower of Law was fairly modest, as planetary council meeting places went, topping the three-level marketplace beside it by only a couple of floors. Inside, they were led to a large room on the ground floor where, framed by huge tapestries covering the walls, another group of Bimms waited. Three of them stood and sang as Leia entered.

"They add their greetings to those given you at the landing area, Princess Leia," Threepio translated. "They apologize, however, for the fact that the talks will not be able to begin quite yet. It appears that their chief negotiator became ill just moments ago."

"Oh," Leia said, taken slightly aback. "Please express our sympathies, and ask if there's anything we can do to help."

"They thank you," Threepio said after another exchange of songs. "But they assure you that will not be necessary.

There is no danger to him, merely inconvenience." The droid hesitated. "I really don't think you should inquire further, Your Highness," he added, a bit delicately. "The complaint appears to be of a rather personal nature."

"I understand," Leia said gravely, suppressing a smile at the prim tone of the droid's voice. "Well, in that case, I suppose we might as well return to the *Falcon* until he feels ready to continue."

The droid translated, and one of their escort stepped forward and sang something in reply. "He offers an alternative, Your Highness: that he would be eager to conduct you on a tour of the marketplace while you wait."

Leia glanced at Han and Luke. "Any objections?"

The Bimm sang something else. "He further suggests that Master Luke and Captain Solo might find something to interest them in the Tower's upper chambers," Threepio said. "Apparently, there are relics there dating from the middle era of the Old Republic."

A quiet alarm went off in the back of Leia's mind. Were the Bimms trying to split them up? "Luke and Han might like the market, too," she said cautiously.

There was another exchange of arias. "He says they would find it excessively dull," Threepio told her. "Frankly, if it's anything like marketplaces I've seen—"

"I like marketplaces," Han cut him off brusquely, his voice dark with suspicion. "I like 'em a lot."[2]

Leia looked at her brother. "What do you think?"

Luke's eyes swept the Bimms; measuring them, she knew, with all of his Jedi insight. "I don't see what danger they could be," he said slowly. "I don't sense any real duplicity in them. Nothing beyond that of normal politics, anyway."

Leia nodded, her tension easing a little. Normal politics—yes, that was probably all it was. The Bimm probably just wanted the chance to privately bend her ear on behalf of his particular viewpoint before the talks got started in earnest. "In that case," she said, inclining her head to the Bimm, "we accept."

"The marketplace has been in this same spot for over two hundred years," Threepio translated as Han and Leia followed their host up the gentle ramp between the second and third levels of the open dome structure. "Though not in this exact form, of course. The Tower of Law, in fact, was built here precisely because it was already a common crossroads."

"Hasn't changed much, has it?" Han commented, pressing close to Leia to keep them from getting run down by a particularly determined batch of shoppers. He'd seen a lot of marketplaces on a lot of different planets, but seldom one so crowded.

Crowded with more than just locals, too. Scattered throughout the sea of yellow-clad Bimms—*don't they ever wear any other color?*—he could see several other humans, a pair of Baradas, an Ishi Tib, a group of Yuzzumi, and something that looked vaguely like a Paonnid.[3]

"You can see why this place is worth getting into the New Republic," Leia murmured to him.

"I guess so," Han conceded, stepping to one of the booths and looking at the metalware displayed there. The owner/operator sang something toward him, gesturing to a set of carving knives. "No, thanks," Han told him, moving back. The Bimm continued to jabber at him, his gestures becoming sharper— "Threepio, will you have our host tell him that we're not interested?" he called to the droid.

There was no response. "Threepio?" he repeated, looking around.

Threepio was staring off into the crowd. "Hey, Goldenrod," he snapped. "I'm talking to you."

Threepio spun back. "I'm terribly sorry, Captain Solo," he apologized. "But our host seems to have disappeared."

3. As with extra planets, I can easily throw lots of different aliens into the background scenes.

One of the advantages books have over movies—my costume and makeup departments don't take up much space.

—TZ

"What do you mean, disappeared?" Han demanded, looking around. Their particular Bimm, he remembered, had worn a set of shiny pins on his shoulders.

Pins that were nowhere to be seen. "How could he just disappear?"

Beside him, Leia gripped his hand. "I've got a bad feeling about this," she said tightly. "Let's get back to the Tower."

"Yeah," Han agreed. "Come on, Threepio. Don't get lost." Shifting his grip on Leia's hand, he turned—

And froze. A few meters away, islands in the churning sea of yellow, three aliens stood facing them. Short aliens, not much taller than the Bimms, with steel-gray skin, large dark eyes, and protruding jaws.

And, held ready in their hands, stokhli sticks.

"We've got trouble," he murmured to Leia, turning his head slowly to look around, hoping desperately that those three were all there were.

They weren't. There were at least eight more, arrayed in a rough circle ten meters across. A circle with Han, Leia, and Threepio at its center.

"Han!" Leia said urgently.

"I see them," he muttered. "We're in trouble, sweetheart."

He sensed her glance behind them. "Who are they?" she breathed.

"I don't know—never seen anything like them before. But they're not kidding around. Those things are called stokhli sticks—shoot a spraynet mist two hundred meters, with enough shockstun juice to take down a good-sized Gundark." Abruptly, Han noticed that he and Leia had moved, instinctively backing away from the nearest part of the aliens' circle. He glanced over his shoulder— "They're herding us toward the down ramp," he told her. "Must be trying to take us without stirring up the crowd."

"We're doomed," Threepio moaned.

Leia gripped Han's hand. "What are we going to do?"

"Let's see how closely they're paying attention." Trying to watch all the aliens at once, Han casually reached his free hand toward the comlink attached to his collar.

The nearest alien lifted his stokhli stick warningly. Han froze, slowly lowered the hand again. "So much for that idea," he muttered. "I think it's time to pull in the welcome mat. Better give Luke a shout."

"He can't help us."

Han glanced down at her; at her glazed eyes and pinched face. "Why not?" he demanded, stomach tightening.

She sighed, just audibly. "They've got him, too."

CHAPTER 7

IT WAS MORE A FEELING than anything approaching an actual word, but it echoed through Luke's mind as clearly as if he'd heard it shouted.

Help!

He spun around, the ancient tapestry he'd been studying forgotten as his Jedi senses flared into combat readiness. Around him, the large top-floor Tower room was as it had been a minute earlier: deserted except for a handful of Bimms strolling among the huge wall tapestries and relic cases. No danger here, at least nothing immediate. *What is it?* he sent back, starting for the next room and the staircase leading down.

He caught a quick vision from Leia's mind, a picture of alien figures and a vivid impression of a contracting noose. *Hang on,* he told her. *I'm coming.* All but running now, he ducked through the doorway to the staircase room, grabbing the jamb to help with his turn—

And braked to an abrupt halt. Standing between him

and the stairway was a loose semicircle of seven silent gray figures.

Luke froze, his hand still uselessly gripping the doorjamb, half a galaxy away from the lightsaber on his belt. He had no idea what the sticks were his assailants were pointing at him, but he had no desire to find out the hard way. Not unless he absolutely had to. "What do you want?" he asked aloud.

The alien in the center of the semicircle—the leader, Luke guessed—gestured with his stick. Luke glanced over his shoulder into the room he'd just left. "You want me to go back in there?" he asked.

The leader gestured again . . . and this time Luke saw it. The small, almost insignificant tactical error. "All right," he said, as soothingly as possible. "No problem." Keeping his eyes on the aliens and his hands away from his lightsaber, he began to back up.

They herded him steadily back across the room toward another archway and a room he hadn't gotten to before Leia's emergency call had come. "If you'd just tell me what you want, I'm sure we could come to some sort of agreement," Luke suggested as he walked. Faint scuffling sounds told him that there were still some Bimms wandering around, presumably the reason the aliens hadn't already attacked. "I would hope we could at least talk about it. There's no particular reason why any of you has to be hurt."

Reflexively, the leader's left thumb moved. Not much, but Luke was watching, and it was enough. A thumb trigger, then. "If you have some business with me, I'm willing to talk," he continued. "You don't need my friends in the marketplace for that."

He was almost to the archway now. A couple more steps to go. If they'd just hold off shooting him that long . . .

And then he was there, with the carved stone looming over him. "Now where?" he asked, forcing his muscles to relax. This was it.

Again, the leader gestured with his stick . . . and midway through the motion, for a single instant, the weapon was pointed not at Luke but at two of his own companions.

And reaching out through the Force, Luke triggered the thumb switch. There was a loud, sharp hiss as the stick bucked in its owner's hands and what looked like a fine spray shot out the end.

Luke didn't wait to see what exactly the spray did. The maneuver had bought him maybe a half second of confusion, and he couldn't afford to waste any of it. Throwing himself back and to the side, he did a flip into the room behind him, angling to get to the slight protection afforded by the wall beside the doorway.

He just barely made it. Even as he cleared the archway there was a stuttering salvo of sharp hisses, and as he flipped back to his feet he saw that the doorjamb had grown strange semisolid tendrils of some thin, translucent material. Another tendril shot through the doorway as he hastily backed farther away, sweeping in a spiral curve that seemed to turn from fine mist to liquid stream to solid cylinder even as it curved.

His lightsaber was in his hand now, igniting with a *snap-hiss*[1] of its own. They'd be through that doorway in seconds, he knew, all efforts at subtlety abandoned. And when they came—

He clenched his teeth, a memory of his brief skiff-battle encounter with Boba Fett flashing through his mind. Wrapped in the bounty hunter's smart-rope,[2] he'd escaped only by snapping the cable with a deflected blaster shot. But here there would be no blasters to try that trick with.

For that matter, he wasn't absolutely sure what his lightsaber could do directly against the sprays. It would be like trying to cut through a rope that was continually re-creating itself.

---

1. I thought long and hard about how to write the sound of an igniting lightsaber. I finally went with *snap-hiss.*

—TZ

2. This gadget is now called a *fibercord whip,* but at the time it either hadn't been named or I'd failed to find the right reference. (I suspect the former, since Lucasfilm didn't correct it in the manuscript.)

On the other hand, as with many things *Star Wars,* it's quite possible the weapon had several names. Maybe *Fibercord Whip* was once a trademarked name that has now fallen into common usage, while *smart-rope* was the generic name.

Back in my physics days, we used to call this procedure *hand-waving.* I'll be using more of it as we go along.

—TZ

Or rather, like trying to cut seven such ropes.[3]

He could hear their footsteps now, sprinting toward his room even as the spiraling tendril sweeping the doorway made sure he stayed too far back to ambush them as they came through it. A standard military technique, played out with the kind of precision that showed he wasn't dealing with amateurs.

He raised the lightsaber to en garde position, risking a quick look around. The room was decorated like all the others he'd seen on this floor, with ancient wall tapestries and other relics—no real cover anywhere. His eyes flicked across the walls, searching for the exit that by implication had to be here somewhere. But the action was so much useless reflex. Wherever the exit was, it was almost certainly too far away to do him any good.

The hiss of the spray stopped; and he turned back just in time to see the aliens charge into the room. They spotted him, spun around to bring their weapons to bear—

And reaching up with the Force, Luke ripped one of the tapestries from the wall beside him and brought it down on top of them.

It was a trick that only a Jedi could have pulled off, and it was a trick that, by all rights, ought to have worked. All seven of the aliens were in the room by the time he got the tapestry loose, and all seven were beneath it as it began its fall. But by the time it landed in a huge wrinkled pile on the floor, all seven had somehow managed to back completely out of its way.

From behind the heap came the sharp hiss of their weapons, and Luke ducked back involuntarily before he realized the webbing sprays weren't coming anywhere near him. Instead, the misty tendrils were sweeping outward, shooting around and past the downed tapestry to crisscross the walls.

His first thought was that the weapons must have gone off accidentally, jostled or bumped as the aliens tried to get

3. As I mentioned in the foreword, one of my goals in writing *Heir* was to do something that was *Star Wars* but which didn't just cover the same territory as the movies. Part of that challenge was to come up with new problems and weapons for our heroes to face.

Lightsabers are great for blocking blaster bolts and cutting through AT-AT armor, but what about something semiliquid?

Of course, once I've gotten Luke into this situation, I also have to come up with a way to get him out of it. . . .

—TZ

out from under the falling tapestry. But a split second later he realized the truth: that they were deliberately webbing the other tapestries into place on the walls to prevent him from trying the same trick twice. Belatedly, Luke tugged at the heaped tapestry, hoping to sweep them back with it, and found that it, too, was now solidly webbed in place.[4]

The spraying ceased, and a single dark eye poked cautiously around the tapestry mountain . . . and with a strange sort of sadness, Luke realized that he no longer had any choices left. There was, now, only one way to end this if Han and Leia were to be saved.

He locked his lightsaber on and let his mind relax, reaching out with Jedi senses toward the seven figures, forming their image in his mind's eye. The alien watching him brought his weapon around the edge of the tapestry—

And, reaching back over his left shoulder, Luke hurled his lightsaber with all his strength.

The blade scythed toward the edge of the tapestry, spinning through the air like some strange and fiery predator. The alien saw it, reflexively ducked back—

And died as the lightsaber sliced through the tapestry and cut him in half.

The others must have realized in that instant that they, too, were dead; but even then they didn't give up. Howling a strangely chilling wail, they attacked: four throwing themselves around the sides of the barrier, the other two actually leaping straight up to try to shoot over it.

It made no difference. Guided by the Force, the spinning lightsaber cut through their ranks in a twisting curve, striking each of them in turn.

A heartbeat later, it was all over.

Luke took a shuddering breath. He'd done it. Not the way he'd wanted to, but he'd done it. Now, he could only hope he'd done it in time. Calling the lightsaber back to his hand on a dead run, he sprinted past the crumpled

4. A writer absolutely has to make his villains clever and competent. It's no fun—and no challenge—for the heroes to get out of trouble without sweating about it first.

—TZ

alien bodies and stretched out again through the Force. *Leia?*

The decorative columns flanking the downward ramp were visible just beyond the next row of booths when, beside him, Han felt Leia twitch. "He's free," she said. "He's on his way."

"Great," Han muttered. "Great. Let's hope our pals don't find out before he gets here."

The words were barely out of his mouth when, in what looked like complete unison, the circle of aliens raised their stokhli sticks and started pushing their way through the milling crowd of Bimms. "Too late," Han gritted. "Here they come."

Leia gripped his arm. "Should I try to take their weapons away from them?"

"You'll never get all eleven," Han told her, looking around desperately for inspiration.

His eyes fell on a nearby table loaded with jewelry display boxes . . . and he had it. Maybe. "Leia—that jewelry over there? Grab some of it."

He sensed her throw a startled look up at him. "What—?"

"Just do it!" he hissed, watching the approaching aliens. "Grab it and throw it to me."

Out of the corner of his eye he saw one of the smaller display boxes stir as she strained to establish a grip on it. Then, with a sudden lurch, it leaped toward him, slapping into his hands and scattering small neckpieces to the ground before he managed to get hold of the rest.

And abruptly the raucous conversational hum of the marketplace was split by a piercing shriek. Han turned toward it, just in time to see the owner of the pilfered merchandise stabbing two fingers toward him. "Han!" he heard Leia shout over the scream.

"Get ready to duck!" he shouted back—

And was literally bowled off his feet as a yellow wave of enraged Bimms leaped atop him, knocking the accused shoplifter to the ground.

And with their bodies forming a barrier between him and the stokhli sticks, he dropped the jewelry and grabbed for his comlink. "Chewie!" he bellowed over the din.

Luke heard the shriek even from the top Tower floor; and from the sudden turmoil in Leia's mind, it was instantly clear that he would never make it to the marketplace in time.

He skidded to a halt, mind racing. Across the room a large open window faced the open-domed structure; but five floors was too far for even a Jedi to safely leap. He glanced back to the room he'd just left, searching for possibilities . . . and his eye fell on the end of one of the aliens' weapons, just visible through the archway.

It was a long shot, but it was as good a chance as he was going to get. Reaching out through the Force, he called the weapon flying to his hand, studying its controls as he ran to the window. They were simple enough: spray profile and pressure, plus the thumb trigger. Setting for the narrowest spray and the highest pressure, he braced himself against the side of the window, aimed for the marketplace's partial dome covering, and fired.

The stick kicked harder against his shoulder than he'd expected it to as the spray shot out, but the results were all he could have hoped for. The front end of the arching tendril struck the roof, forming a leisurely sort of pile as more of the semisolid spray pushed forward to join it. Luke held the switch down for a count of five, then eased up, keeping a firm Force grip on the near end of the tendril to prevent it from falling away from the stick. He gave it a few seconds to harden before touching it tentatively with a finger, gave it a few seconds more to make sure it was solidly attached to the marketplace roof. Then, taking a deep breath, he grabbed his makeshift rope with both hands and jumped.[5]

A tornado of air blew at him, tugging at his hair and clothes as he swung down and across. Below and partway across the top level he could see the mass of yellow-clad Bimms and the handful of gray figures struggling to get past them to Han and Leia. There was a flicker of light, visible even in the bright sunshine, and one of the Bimms slumped to the ground—stunned or dead, Luke couldn't tell which. The floor was rushing up at him—he braced himself to land—

And with a roar that must have rattled windows for blocks around, the *Millennium Falcon* screamed by overhead.

The shock wave threw Luke's landing off, sending him sprawling across the floor and into two of the Bimms. But even as he rolled back up to his feet, he realized that Chewbacca's arrival couldn't have been better timed. Barely ten meters away, the two alien attackers nearest him had turned their attention upward, their weapons poised to ensnare the *Falcon* when it returned. Snatching his lightsaber from his belt, Luke leaped over a half dozen bystanding Bimms, cutting both attackers down before they even knew he was there.

From overhead came another roar; but this time Chewbacca didn't simply fly the *Falcon* past the marketplace. Instead, forward maneuvering jets blasting, he brought it to a hard stop. Hovering directly over his beleaguered companions, swivel blaster extended from the ship's underside, he opened fire.

The Bimms weren't stupid. Whatever Han and Leia had done to stir up the hornet's nest, the hornets themselves clearly had no desire to get shot at from the sky. In an instant the roiling yellow mass dissolved, the Bimms abandoning their attack and streaming away in terror from the *Falcon*. Forcing his way through the crowd, using the

5. From the *Star Wars* movies, it's clear that George loves a good, swashbuckling, Errol Flynn-type rope swing. Luckily, so do I.

—TZ

Bimms for visual cover as much as he could, Luke started around the attackers' circle.

Between his lightsaber and the *Falcon*'s swivel blaster, they made a very fast, very clean sweep of it.

"You," Luke said with a shake of his head, "are a mess."

"I'm sorry, Master Luke," Threepio apologized, his voice almost inaudible beneath the layers of hardened spraynet that covered much of his upper body like some bizarre sort of gift wrapping. "I seem to always be causing you trouble."

"That's not true, and you know it," Luke soothed him, considering the small collection of solvents arrayed in front of him on the *Falcon*'s lounge table. So far none of the ones he'd tried had been even marginally effective against the webbing. "You've been a great help to all of us over the years. You just have to learn when to duck."

Beside Luke, Artoo twittered something. "No, Captain Solo did *not* tell me to duck," Threepio told the squat droid stiffly. "What he said was, 'Get ready to duck.' I should think the difference would be apparent even to you."

Artoo beeped something else. Threepio ignored it. "Well, let's try this one," Luke suggested, picking up the next solvent in line. He was hunting for a clean cloth among his pile of rejects when Leia came into the lounge.

"How is he?" she asked, walking over and peering at Threepio.

"He'll be all right," Luke assured her. "He may have to stay like this until we get back to Coruscant, though. Han told me these stokhli sticks are used mostly by big-game hunters on out-of-the-way planets, and the spraynet they use is a pretty exotic mixture." He indicated the discarded solvent bottles.

"Maybe the Bimms can suggest something," Leia said, picking up one of the bottles and looking at its label. "We'll ask them when we get back down."

Luke frowned at her. "We're going back down?"

She frowned at him in turn. "We have to, Luke—you know that. This is a diplomatic mission, not a pleasure cruise. It's considered bad form to pull out right after one of your ships has just shot up a major local marketplace."

"I would think the Bimms would consider themselves lucky that none of their people got killed in the process," Luke pointed out. "Particularly when what happened was at least partly their fault."

"You can't blame a whole society for the actions of a few individuals," Leia said—rather severely, Luke thought. "Especially not when a single political maverick has simply made a bad decision."

"A bad *decision?*" Luke snorted. "Is *that* what they're calling it?"

"That's what they're calling it." Leia nodded. "Apparently, the Bimm who led us into the marketplace trap was bribed to take us there. He had no idea what was going to happen, though."

"And I suppose he had no idea what the stuff he gave the chief negotiator would do, either?"

Leia shrugged. "Actually, there's still no hard evidence that he or anyone else poisoned the negotiator," she said. "Though under the circumstances, they're willing to concede that that's a possibility."

Luke made a face. "Generous of them. What does Han have to say about us putting back down?"

"Han doesn't have any choice in the matter," Leia said firmly. "This is *my* mission, not his."

"That's right," Han agreed, stepping into the lounge. "Your mission. But *my* ship."

Leia stared at him, a look of disbelief on her face. "You didn't," she breathed.

"I sure did," he told her calmly, dropping into one of the seats across the lounge. "We made the jump to lightspeed about two minutes ago. Next stop, Coruscant."

"Han!" she flared, as angry as Luke had ever seen her. "I told the Bimms we were coming right back down."

"And I told them there'd be a short delay," Han countered. "Like long enough for us to collect a squadron of X-wings or maybe a Star Cruiser to bring back with us."

"And what if you've offended them?" Leia snapped. "Do you have any *idea* how much groundwork went into this mission?"

"Yeah, as it happens, I do," Han said, his voice hardening. "I also have a pretty good idea what could happen if our late pals with the stokhli sticks brought friends with them."

For a long minute Leia stared at him, and Luke sensed the momentary anger fading from her mind. "You still shouldn't have left without consulting me first," she said.

"You're right," Han conceded. "But I didn't want to take the time. If they *did* have friends, those friends probably had a ship." He tried a tentative smile. "There wasn't time to discuss it in committee."

Leia smiled lopsidedly in return. "I am *not* a committee," she said wryly.[6]

And with that, the brief storm passed and the tension was gone. Someday, Luke promised himself, he would get around to asking one of them just what that particular private joke of theirs referred to. "Speaking of our pals," he said, "did either of you happen to ask the Bimms who or what they were?"

"The Bimms didn't know," Leia said, shaking her head. "I've certainly never seen anything like them before."

"We can check the Imperial archives when we get back to Coruscant," Han said, feeling gingerly at one cheek where a bruise was already becoming visible. "There'll be a record of them somewhere."

"Unless," Leia said quietly, "they're something the Empire found out in the Unknown Regions."

Luke looked at her. "You think the Empire was behind this?"

6. Along with things like the hot chocolate, one of the major complaints I received was that I'd used too many of the movie lines in the book. The accusation was that I was simply trying to connect to the movies to add legitimacy to my books.

I disagreed, and this particular quote is a good example of what I was actually trying to do. Every family, over their years together, develops a collection of private words and phrases that evoke incidents in their past—a kind of shorthand to their shared memories. In this case, Han's comment is a reminder of the asteroid field incident, when his snap judgment (or so Leia thought at the time) proved to be the correct action. Leia's response, again echoing that time, is her admission that he was right in that case and, yes, he's probably right in this one, too.

—TZ

"Who else could it have been?" she said. "The only question is why."

"Well, whatever the reason, they're going to be disappointed," Han told her, getting to his feet. "I'm going back to the cockpit, see if I can muddle our course a little more. No point in taking chances."

A memory flashed through Luke's mind: Han and the *Falcon*, sweeping right through the middle of that first Death Star battle to shoot Darth Vader's fighters off his back. "Hard to imagine Han Solo not wanting to take chances," he commented.

Han leveled a finger at him. "Yeah, well, before you get cocky, try to remember that the people I'm protecting are you, your sister, your niece, and your nephew. That make any difference?"

Luke smiled. "Touché," he admitted, saluting with an imaginary lightsaber.

"And speaking of that," Han added, "isn't it about time Leia had a lightsaber of her own?"

Luke shrugged. "I can make her one anytime she's ready," he said, looking at his sister. "Leia?"

Leia hesitated. "I don't know," she confessed. "I've never really felt comfortable with the thing." She looked at Han. "But I suppose I ought to make the effort."

"I think you should," Luke agreed. "Your talents may lie along a different direction, but you should still learn all the basics. As far as I can tell, nearly all the Jedi of the Old Republic carried lightsabers, even those who were primarily healers or teachers."[7]

She nodded. "All right," she said. "As soon as my work load lightens up a little."

"*Before* your work load lightens," Han insisted. "I mean that, Leia. All these wonderful diplomacy skills of yours aren't going to do you or anyone else any good if the Empire locks you away in an interrogation room somewhere."

Reluctantly, Leia nodded again. "I suppose you're right. As soon as we get back, I'll tell Mon Mothma she's just

7. Even Yoda carried one, as we know now from the prequels.

—TZ

going to have to cut down on my assignments." She smiled at Luke. "I guess semester break's over, Teacher."

"I guess so," Luke said, trying to hide the sudden lump in his throat.

Leia noticed it anyway; and, for a wonder, misinterpreted it. "Oh, come on," she chided gently. "I'm not *that* bad a student. Anyway, look on it as good practice—after all, someday you'll have to teach all this to the twins, too."

"I know," Luke said softly.

"Good," Han said. "That's settled, then. I'm heading up; see you later."

"'Bye," Leia said. "Now—" She turned to give Threepio a critical look. "Let's see what we can do about all this goop."

Leaning back in his seat, Luke watched her tackle the hardened webbing, a familiar hollow pain in the pit of his stomach. *I took it upon myself,* Ben Kenobi had said about Darth Vader, *to train him as a Jedi. I thought that I could instruct him just as well as Yoda.*

I was wrong.

The words echoed through Luke's mind, all the way back to Coruscant.

CHAPTER 8

FOR A LONG MINUTE Grand Admiral Thrawn sat in his chair, surrounded by his holographic works of art, and said nothing. Pellaeon kept himself at a motionless attention, watching the other's expressionless face and glowing red eyes and trying not to think about the fate couriers of bad news had often suffered at the hands of Lord Vader. "All died but the coordinator, then?" Thrawn asked at last.

"Yes, sir," Pellaeon confirmed. He glanced across the room, to where C'baoth stood studying one of the wall displays, and lowered his voice a bit. "We're still not entirely sure what went wrong."

"Instruct Central to give the coordinator a thorough debriefing," Thrawn said. "What report from Wayland?"

Pellaeon had thought they'd been talking too quietly for C'baoth to hear them. He was wrong. "Is that it, then?" C'baoth demanded, turning away from the display and striding over to tower over Thrawn's command chair. "Your Noghri have failed; so too bad, and on to more pressing business? You promised me Jedi, Grand Admiral Thrawn."[1]

1. *Admiral* would be the normal shipboard form of address (*Grand Admiral* is awkwardly long for casual conversation), but C'baoth almost invariably uses the entire rank. Not as a form of respect, of course, but as a form of sarcasm.

–TZ

Thrawn gazed coolly up at him. "I promised you Jedi," he acknowledged. "And I will deliver them." Deliberately, he turned back to Pellaeon. "What report from Wayland?" he repeated.

Pellaeon swallowed, trying hard to remember that with ysalamiri scattered all through the command room, C'baoth had no power whatsoever. At least for the moment. "The engineering team has finished its analysis, sir," he told Thrawn. "They report that the cloaking shield schematics seem complete, but that to actually build one will take some time. It'll also be highly expensive, at least for a ship the size of the *Chimaera*."

"Fortunately, they won't have to start with anything nearly this big," Thrawn said, handing Pellaeon a data card. "Here are the specs for what we'll need at Sluis Van."

"The shipyards?" Pellaeon frowned, taking the data card. The Grand Admiral had so far been very secretive about both his goals and the strategy for that attack.

"Yes. Oh, and we're also going to need some advanced mining machines—mole miners, I believe they're informally called. Have Intelligence start a records search; we'll need a minimum of forty."

"Yes, sir." Pellaeon made a note on his data pad. "One other thing, sir." He threw a quick glance at C'baoth. "The engineers also report that nearly eighty percent of the Spaarti cylinders we'll need are functional or can be restored to working order with relative ease."

"Spaarti cylinders?" C'baoth frowned. "What are those?"

"Just that other little bit of technology I was hoping to find in the mountain," Thrawn soothed him, throwing a quick warning look in Pellaeon's direction. An unnecessary precaution; Pellaeon had already decided that discussing Spaarti cylinders with C'baoth would not be a smart thing to do. "So. Eighty percent. That's excellent, Captain. Excellent." A gleam came into those glowing eyes. "How very thoughtful of the Emperor to have left such fine equipment for us to rebuild his Empire with. What about the mountain's power and defense systems?"

"Also operational, for the most part," Pellaeon said. "Three of the four reactors have already been brought on line. Some of the more esoteric defenses seem to have decayed, but what's left should defend the storehouse more than adequately."

"Again, excellent." Thrawn nodded. The brief flicker of emotion was gone, and he was all cool business again. "Instruct them to begin bringing the cylinders to full operational status. The *Death's Head* should arrive within two or three days with the extra specialists and two hundred ysalamiri they'll need to get things started. At that point"— he smiled faintly—"we'll be ready to begin the operation in earnest. Beginning with the Sluis Van shipyards."

"Yes, sir." Pellaeon glanced at C'baoth again. "And about Skywalker and his sister?"

"We'll use Team Four next," the Grand Admiral said. "Transmit a message telling them to withdraw from their current assignment and stand ready for further orders."

"You want *me* to transmit the message, sir?" Pellaeon asked. "Not that I'm questioning the order," he added hastily. "But in the past you've usually preferred to contact them yourself."

Thrawn's eyebrows lifted slightly. "Team Eight failed me," he said softly. "Sending the message through you will let the others know how displeased I am."

"And when Team Four also fails you?" C'baoth put in. "They will, you know. Will you be merely *displeased* with them, too? Or will you admit your professional killing machines simply can't handle a Jedi?"

"They've never yet met any foe they can't handle, Master C'baoth," Thrawn said coolly. "One group or another will succeed. Until then—" He shrugged. "A few Noghri, more or less, won't seriously drain our resources."

Pellaeon winced, throwing a reflexive glance at the

chamber door. Rukh, he suspected, wouldn't be nearly that phlegmatic about the casually proposed deaths of some of his people. "On the other hand, Admiral, this attempt will have put them on their guard," he pointed out.

"He's right," C'baoth said, jabbing a finger in Pellaeon's direction. "You can't fool a Jedi twice with the same trick."

"Perhaps," Thrawn said, the word polite but his tone not conceding anything. "What alternative do you suggest? That we concentrate on his sister and leave him alone?"

"That *you* concentrate on his sister, yes," C'baoth agreed loftily. "I think it best.that I deal with the young Jedi myself."

Again, the eyebrows went up. "And how would you propose to do that?"

C'baoth smiled. "He is a Jedi; I am a Jedi. If I call, he will come to me."

For a long moment Thrawn looked up at him. "I need you with my fleet," he said at last. "Preparations for the assault on the Rebellion's Sluis Van space dock facilities have already begun. Some of the preliminaries to that assault will require a Jedi Master's coordination."

C'baoth drew himself up to his full height. "My assistance was promised only upon *your* promise to deliver my Jedi to me. I will have them, Grand Admiral Thrawn."

Thrawn's glowing eyes bored into C'baoth's. "Does a Jedi Master go back on his word, then? You knew that obtaining Skywalker for you might take some time."

"All the more reason for me to begin now," C'baoth shot back.

"Why can't we do both?" Pellaeon cut in.

Both looked at him. "Explain, Captain," Thrawn ordered, a hint of threat audible in his tone.

Pellaeon gritted his teeth, but it was too late to back out now. "We could begin by starting rumors of your presence somewhere, Master C'baoth," he said. "Some sparsely populated world where you might have lived for years without anyone really noticing. Rumors of that sort would be certain to make their way back to the New Rep— to the Rebellion," he corrected, glancing at Thrawn. "Particularly with the name Joruus C'baoth attached to them."

C'baoth snorted. "And you think that on the strength of an idle rumor he'll rush foolishly to find me?"

"Let him be as cautious as he likes," Thrawn said thoughtfully, the threat gone from his voice. "Let him bring half the Rebellion's forces with him, if he chooses. There will be nothing there to connect you to us."

Pellaeon nodded. "And while we find a suitable planet and start the rumors into motion, you can remain here to assist with the Sluis Van preliminaries. Hopefully, their response to our activities will keep Skywalker too busy to check out the stories until after the Sluis Van part is over."

"And if not," Thrawn added, "we'll know when he makes his move, and in plenty of time to get you there ahead of him."

"Hmm," C'baoth murmured, stroking his long beard, his gaze drifting off to infinity. Pellaeon held his breath . . . and after a minute the other abruptly nodded. "Very well," he said. "The plan is sound. I will go to my chambers now, Grand Admiral Thrawn, and choose a world from which to make my appearance." With an almost regal nod to each of them, he strode out.

"Congratulations, Captain," Thrawn said, eyeing Pellaeon coolly. "Your idea seems to have caught Master C'baoth's fancy."

Pellaeon forced himself to meet that gaze. "I apologize, Admiral, if I spoke out of turn."

Thrawn smiled faintly. "You served too long under Lord Vader, Captain," he said. "I have no qualms about accepting a useful idea merely because it wasn't my own. My position and ego are not at stake here."[2]

Except, perhaps, when dealing with C'baoth . . . "Yes, sir," Pellaeon said aloud. "With your permission, Admiral, I'll

2. The second quality of a good commander: the ability to hear, evaluate, and adopt good ideas even if—perhaps *especially* if—they come from those who are technically his inferiors.

—TZ

go prepare those transmissions to the Wayland and Noghri teams."

"At your convenience, Captain. And continue to monitor the preparations for the Sluis Van operation." Thrawn's glowing eyes seemed to bore into his. "Monitor them closely, Captain. With Mount Tantiss and Sluis Van both, the long path to victory over the Rebellion will have begun. With, or even without, our Jedi Master."

In theory, Inner Council meetings were supposed to be a quieter, more casual sort of encounter than the more formal Provisional Council[3] things. In actual practice, Han had long ago found out, an Inner Council grilling could be just as rough as being raked over the fires by the larger group.

"Let me get this straight, then, Captain Solo," Borsk Fey'lya said with his usual oily politeness. "You, alone, and without consultation with anyone in official authority, made the decision to cancel the Bimmisaari mission."

"I've already said that," Han told him. He felt like suggesting to the Bothan that he pay better attention. "I've also stated my reasons for doing so."

"Which, in my opinion, were good and proper ones," Admiral Ackbar's gravelly voice interjected in Han's support. "Captain Solo's duty at that point was abundantly clear: to protect the ambassador in his charge and to return safely to alert us."

"Alert us to what?" Fey'lya countered. "Forgive me, Admiral, but I don't understand what exactly this threat is we're supposedly facing. Whoever these gray-skinned beings were, they clearly weren't considered important enough by the Old Senate to even be included in the records. I doubt a race that insignificant is likely to be capable of mounting a major offensive against us."

"We don't *know* that that's the reason they aren't in the

3. At the time I was writing *Heir,* all we knew about the Old Republic's political system was that it had included a Senate. Rather than try to guess at any other details, I settled on giving the New Republic a provisional form of government, with the implication that it would be changed at some point in the future.

That way, if I got more details along the way as to how things were supposed to be done, I could have Leia and Mon Mothma revamp the whole thing.

—TZ

records," Leia put in. "It could simply be an oversight or gap damage."

"Or else a deliberate erasure," Luke said.

Fey'lya's fur rippled, indicating polite disbelief. "And why would the Imperial Senate want to erase the records of an entire race's existence?"

"I didn't say it was necessarily the Senate's idea," Luke said. "Maybe the aliens themselves destroyed their records."

Fey'lya sniffed. "Far-fetched. Even if it was possible, why would anyone want to do it?"[4]

"Perhaps Councilor Organa Solo can answer that," Mon Mothma interjected calmly, looking at Leia. "You were more involved in the information side of the Imperial Senate than I was, Leia. Would such a manipulation have been possible?"

"I really don't know," Leia said, shaking her head. "I never got all that deeply into the actual mechanics of how the Senate's records were handled. Common wisdom, though, would suggest that it's impossible to create a security system that can't be broken by someone determined enough to do it."

"That still doesn't answer the question of why these aliens of yours would be that determined," Fey'lya sniffed.

"Maybe they saw the Old Republic's coming demise," Leia told him, her voice starting to sound a little irritated. "They might have erased all references to themselves and their world in hopes the rising Empire might not notice them."

Fey'lya was fast, all right; Han had to give him that. "In that case," the Bothan smoothly switched gears, "perhaps a fear of rediscovery was all that motivated *this* attack, as well." He looked at Ackbar. "Regardless, I see no reason to make a full-fledged military operation out of this. To reduce our glorious forces to the level of a mere diplomatic entourage is an insult to their courage and their fighting spirit."

4. I generally dislike writing characters who deliberately distort, misinterpret, or ignore facts for their own political ends the way Fey'lya does here. Probably because I dislike seeing that done in real life.

But sometimes the requirements of the story mean you just have to take a deep breath and do it.

—TZ

"You can dispense with the speeches, Councilor," Ackbar rumbled. "None of our 'glorious forces' are here to be impressed by them."

"I say only what I feel, Admiral," Fey'lya said, with that air of wounded pride he did so well.

Ackbar's eyes swiveled toward Fey'lya— "I wonder," Leia spoke up quickly, "if we could get back to the original subject here. I presume it hasn't escaped anyone's notice that, whatever their motivation, the aliens were ready and waiting for us when we reached Bimmisaari."

"We're going to need tighter security for these missions, obviously," Ackbar said. "At both ends—your attackers *did* suborn a local Bimm politician, after all."

"All of which will cost that much more time and effort," Fey'lya murmured, a section of his fur rippling.

"It can't be helped," Mon Mothma said firmly. "If we don't protect our negotiators, the New Republic will stagnate and wither. Accordingly"—she looked at Ackbar—"you will detail a force to accompany Councilor Organa Solo on her trip back to Bimmisaari tomorrow."

Tomorrow? Han threw a sharp look at Leia, got an equally surprised look in return. "Excuse me," he said, raising a finger. "Tomorrow?"

Mon Mothma looked at him, an expression of mild surprise on her face. "Yes, tomorrow. The Bimms are still waiting, Captain."

"I know, but—"

"What Han is trying to say," Leia jumped in, "is that I had intended at this meeting to ask for a brief leave of absence from my diplomatic duties."

"I'm afraid that's impossible," Mon Mothma said with a slight frown. "There's far too much work to be done."

"We're not talking about a vacation here," Han told her, trying to remember his diplomatic manners. "Leia needs more time to concentrate on her Jedi training."

Mon Mothma pursed her lips, throwing glances at Ackbar and Fey'lya. "I'm sorry," she said, shaking her head. "I, of all people, recognize the need to add new Jedi to our ranks. But for now there are simply too many urgent demands on our time." She looked at Fey'lya again—almost, Han thought sourly, as if seeking his permission. "In another year—possibly sooner," she added, glancing at Leia's stomach, "we'll have enough experienced diplomats for you to devote the bulk of your time to your studies. But right now I'm afraid we need you here."

For a long, awkward moment the room was silent. Ackbar spoke first. "If you'll excuse me, I'll go and have that escort force prepared."

"Of course." Mon Mothma nodded. "Unless there's something more, we stand adjourned."

And that was that. Jaw clenched tightly, Han began collecting his data cards together. "You all right?" Leia asked quietly from beside him.

"You know, it was a lot easier back when we were just taking on the Empire," he growled. He threw a glare across the table at Fey'lya. "At least *then* we knew who our enemies were."[5]

Leia squeezed his arm. "Come on," she said. "Let's go see if they've gotten Threepio cleaned up yet."

5. Han Solo: master of tact. You gotta love him.
—TZ

CHAPTER 9

THE TACTICAL OFFICER STEPPED up to the *Chimaera*'s bridge command station, bringing his heels smartly together. "All units signal ready, Admiral," he reported.

"Excellent," Thrawn said, his voice glacially calm. "Prepare for lightspeed."

Pellaeon threw a glance at the Grand Admiral, then returned his attention to the bank of tactical and status readouts facing him. To the readouts, and to the blackness outside that seemed to have swallowed up the rest of Pellaeon's five-ship task force. Three-thousandths of a light-year away, the Bpfassh system's sun was a mere pinprick, indistinguishable from the other stars blazing all around them. Conventional military wisdom frowned on this business of picking a spot just outside the target system as a jumping-off point—it was considered dangerously easy for one or more ships to get lost on the way to such a rendezvous, and it was difficult to make an accurate hyperspace jump over so short a distance. He and Thrawn, in fact, had had a long and barely civilized argument over the idea the first time the Grand Admiral had included it in one of his attack plans. Now, after nearly a year of practice, the procedure had become almost routine.

Perhaps, Pellaeon thought, the *Chimaera*'s crew wasn't as inexperienced as their ignorance of proper military protocol sometimes made them seem.[1]

"Captain? Is my flagship ready?"

Pellaeon brought his mind back to the business at hand. All ship defenses showed ready; the TIE fighters in their bays were manned and poised. "The *Chimaera* is fully at your command, Admiral," he said, the formal question and response a ghostly remembrance of the days when proper military protocol was the order of the day throughout the galaxy.

"Excellent," Thrawn said. He swiveled in his chair to face the figure seated near the rear of the bridge. "Master C'baoth." He nodded. "Are my other two task forces ready?"

"They are," C'baoth said gravely. "They await merely my command."

Pellaeon winced and threw another glance at Thrawn. But the Grand Admiral had apparently decided to let the comment pass. "Then command them," he told C'baoth, reaching up to stroke the ysalamir draped across the framework fastened to his chair. "Captain: begin the count."

"Yes, sir." Pellaeon reached to his board, touched the timer switch. Scattered around them, the other ships would be locking onto that signal, all of them counting down together . . .

The timer went to zero, and with a flare of starlines through the forward ports, the *Chimaera* jumped.

Ahead, the starlines faded into the mottling of hyperspace. "Speed, Point Three," the helmsman in the crew pit below called out, confirming the readout on the displays.

"Acknowledged," Pellaeon said, flexing his fingers once and settling his mind into combat mode as he watched the

1. The third quality of a good commander: the ability to see what is most valuable in his troops. Competence and the ability to learn are more important than the trappings of pomp and pageantry.
Though Pellaeon clearly still misses that pomp, at least a little.

—TZ

timer now counting up from zero. Seventy seconds; seventy-four, seventy-five, seventy-six—

The starlines flared again through the mottled sky, and shrank back into stars, and the *Chimaera* had arrived.

"All fighters: launch," Pellaeon called, throwing a quick look at the tactical holo floating over his display bank. They had come out of hyperspace exactly as planned, within easy striking range of the double planet[2] of Bpfassh and its complicated system of moons. "Response?" he called to the tactical officer.

"Defending fighters launching from the third moon," the other reported. "Nothing larger visible as yet."

"Get a location on that fighter base," Thrawn ordered, "and detail the *Inexorable* to move in and destroy it."

"Yes, sir."

Pellaeon could see the fighters now, coming at them like a swarm of angry insects. Off on the *Chimaera*'s starboard flank, the Star Destroyer *Inexorable* was moving toward their base, its TIE fighter wedge sweeping ahead of it to engage the defenders.[3] "Change course to the farther of the twin planets," he ordered the helmsman. "TIE fighters to set up an advance screen. The *Judicator* will take the other planet." He looked at Thrawn. "Any special orders, Admiral?"

Thrawn was gazing at a mid-distance scan of the twin planets. "Stay with the program for now, Captain," he said. "Our preliminary data appear to have been adequate; you may choose targets at will. Remind your gunners once again that the plan is to hurt and frighten, not obliterate."

"Relay that." Pellaeon nodded toward the communications station. "Have TIE fighters so reminded, as well."

Out of the corner of his eye, he saw Thrawn turn. "Master C'baoth?" he said. "What's the status of the attacks in the other two systems?"

"They proceed."

Frowning, Pellaeon swiveled around. It had been

2. I have another double planet, Poln Major and Poln Minor, as the centerpiece of my latest *Star Wars* book, *Choices of One*. There must be something about double planets I really like.

—TZ

3. Once again one would think, from this description of tactics, that Tim has a military background. He does not!

—BM

C'baoth's voice, but so throaty and strained as to be nearly unrecognizable.

As was, indeed, his appearance.

For a long moment Pellaeon stared at him, a cold feeling in the pit of his stomach. C'baoth sat with unnatural stiffness, his eyes closed but visibly and rapidly moving behind the lids. His hands gripped the arms of his chair, and his lips were pressed so tightly together that the veins and cords in his neck stood out. "Are you all right, Master C'baoth?" he asked.

"Save your concern, Captain," Thrawn told him coldly. "He's doing what he enjoys most: controlling people."

C'baoth made a sound somewhere between a snort and a derisive chuckle. "I told you once, Grand Admiral Thrawn, that this is not true power."

"So you've said," Thrawn said, his tone neutral. "Can you tell what sort of resistance they're facing?"

C'baoth's frowning face frowned harder. "Not precisely. But neither force is in danger. That much I can feel in their minds."

"Good. Then have the *Nemesis* break off from the rest of its group and report back to the rendezvous to await us."

Pellaeon frowned at the Grand Admiral. "Sir—?"

Thrawn turned to him, a warning gleam in his glowing eyes. "Attend to your duties, Captain," he said.

—and with a sudden flash of insight, Pellaeon realized that this multiedged attack on New Republic territory was more than simply part of the setup for the Sluis Van raid. It was, in addition, a test. A test of C'baoth's abilities, yes; but also a test of his willingness to accept orders.[4] "Yes, Admiral," Pellaeon murmured, and turned back to his displays.

The *Chimaera* was in range now, and tiny sparks started to appear on the tactical holo as the ship's huge turbolaser batteries began firing. Communications stations flared

4. The fourth quality of a good commander: he plans ahead as much as possible.

—TZ

and went black; planetside industrial targets flared, went dark, then flared again as secondary fires were ignited. A pair of old *Carrack*-class light cruisers[5] swept in from starboard, the *Chimaera*'s TIE fighter screen breaking formation to engage them. Off in the distance, the *Stormhawk*'s batteries were blazing against an orbiting defense platform; and even as Pellaeon watched, the station flared into vapor. The battle seemed to be going well.

Remarkably well, in fact . . .

An unpleasant feeling began to stir in the pit of Pellaeon's stomach as he checked his board's real-time status readout. Thus far the Imperial forces had lost only three TIE fighters and sustained superficial damage to the Star Destroyers, compared to eight of the enemy's line ships and eighteen of its fighters gone. Granted, the Imperials vastly outgunned the defenders. But still . . .

Slowly, reluctantly, Pellaeon reached to his board. A few weeks back he'd made up a statistical composite of the *Chimaera*'s battle profiles for the past year. He called it up, superimposed it over the current analysis.

There was no mistake. In every single category and subcategory of speed, coordination, efficiency, and accuracy, the *Chimaera* and its crew were running no less than 40 percent more effective than usual.

He turned to look at C'baoth's strained face, an icy shiver running up his back. He'd never really bought into Thrawn's theory as to how and why the Fleet had lost the Battle of Endor. Certainly he'd never *wanted* to believe it. But now, suddenly, the issue was no longer open to argument.

And with the bulk of his attention and power on the task of mentally communicating with two other task forces nearly four light-years away, C'baoth still had enough left to do all this.

Pellaeon had wondered, with a certain private contempt, just what had given the old man the right to add the word *Master* to his title. Now, he knew.

5. I was just a couple of weeks into *Heir* when I received a big box containing some of the sourcebooks and game modules that West End Games had created over the years for the *Star Wars* role-playing game. Along with the books came instructions from Lucasfilm that I was to coordinate *Heir* with the WEG material.

As usual, I groused a little about that. But once I actually started digging into the books I realized the WEG folks had put together a boatload of really awesome stuff, including lists of aliens, equipment, ground vehicles, and ship types.

So as it turned out, not only was the WEG material easy to coordinate with, but it saved me the work of having to invent all my own technology as I went along.

—TZ

"Getting another set of transmissions," the communications officer reported. "A new group of midrange planetary cruisers launching."

"Have the *Stormhawk* move to intercept," Thrawn ordered.

"Yes, sir. We've now also pinpointed the location of their distress transmissions, Admiral."

Shaking away his musings, Pellaeon glanced across the holo. The newly flashing circle was on the farthest of the system's moons. "Order Squadron Four to move in and destroy it," he ordered.

"Belay that," Thrawn said. "We'll be long gone before any reinforcements can arrive. We might as well let the Rebellion waste its resources rushing useless forces to the rescue. In fact"—the Grand Admiral consulted his watch—"I believe it's time for us to take our leave. Order fighters back to their ships; all ships to lightspeed as soon as their fighters are aboard."

Pellaeon tapped keys at his station, giving the *Chimaera*'s status a quick prelightspeed check. Another bit of conventional military wisdom was that Star Destroyers should play the role of mobile siege stations in this kind of full-planet engagement; that to employ them in hit-and-fade[6] operations was both wasteful and potentially dangerous.

But then, proponents of such theories had obviously never watched someone like Grand Admiral Thrawn in action.

"Order the other two forces to break off their attacks, as well," Thrawn told C'baoth. "I presume you are in close enough contact to do that?"

"You question me too much, Grand Admiral Thrawn," C'baoth said, his voice even huskier than it had been earlier. "Far too much."

"I question all that is not yet familiar to me," Thrawn countered, swiveling back around again. "Call them back to the rendezvous point."

"As you command," the other hissed.

6. Another of the challenges of writing *Heir* was to come up with phrases that are familiar and are properly descriptive, but aren't *quite* the way we would normally say them. Thus *hit-and-run* becomes *hit-and-fade*.

—TZ

Pellaeon glanced back at C'baoth. Testing the other's abilities under combat conditions was all good and proper. But there was such a thing as pushing too far.

"He must learn who's in command here," Thrawn said quietly, as if reading Pellaeon's thoughts.

"Yes, sir." Pellaeon nodded, forcing his voice to remain steady. Thrawn had proved time and again that he knew what he was doing. Still, Pellaeon couldn't help but wonder uneasily if the Grand Admiral recognized the extent of the power he'd awakened from its sleep on Wayland.

Thrawn nodded. "Good. Have there been any further leads on those mole miners I asked for?"

"Ah—no, sir." A year ago, too, he would have found a strange unreality in conversing about less than urgent matters while in the middle of a combat situation. "At least not in anything like the numbers you want. I think the Athega system's still our best bet. Or it will be if we can find a way around the problems of the sunlight intensity there."

"The problems will be minimal," Thrawn said with easy confidence. "If the jump is done with sufficient accuracy, the *Judicator* will be in direct sunlight for only a few minutes each way. Its hull can certainly handle that much. We'll simply need to take a few days first to shield the viewports and remove external sensors and communications equipment."

Pellaeon nodded, swallowing his next question. There would, of course, be none of the difficulties that would normally arise from blinding and deafening a Star Destroyer in that way. Not as long as C'baoth was with them.

"Grand Admiral Thrawn?"

Thrawn turned around. "Yes, Master C'baoth?"

"Where are my Jedi, Grand Admiral Thrawn? You promised me that your tame Noghri would bring me my Jedi."

Out of the corner of his eye, Pellaeon saw Rukh stir. "Patience, Master C'baoth," Thrawn told him. "Their preparations took time, but they're now complete. They await merely the proper time to act."

"That time had best be soon," C'baoth warned him. "I grow tired of waiting."

Thrawn threw a glance at Pellaeon, a quietly smoldering look in his glowing red eyes. "As do we all," he said quietly.

Far ahead of the freighter *Wild Karrde,*[7] one of the Imperial Star Destroyers centered in the cockpit's forward viewport gave a flicker of pseudomotion and disappeared. "They're leaving," Mara announced.

"What, already?" Karrde said from behind her, his voice frowning.

"Already," she confirmed, keying the helm display for tactical. "One of the Star Destroyers just went to lightspeed; the others are breaking off and starting prelightspeed maneuvering."

"Interesting," Karrde murmured, coming up to look out the viewport over her shoulder. "A hit-and-fade attack—and with Star Destroyers, yet. Not something you see every day."

"I heard about something like that happening over at the Draukyze system a couple of months back," the co-pilot, a bulky man named Lachton, offered. "Same kind of hit-and-fade, except there was only one Star Destroyer on that one."

"At a guess, I'd say we're seeing Grand Admiral Thrawn's influence on Imperial strategy," Karrde said, his tone thoughtful with just a hint of concern mixed in. "Strange, though. He seems to be taking an inordinate amount of risk for the potential benefits involved. I wonder what exactly he's up to."

"Whatever it is, it'll be something complicated," Mara told him, hearing the bitterness in her voice. "Thrawn was never one to do things simply. Even back in the old days

7. All of Karrde's ship names involve puns or some other kind of wordplay—*Wild Karrde* (wild card), *Starry Ice* (starry eyes), *Etherway* (either way), and so on.

—TZ

when the Empire was capable of style or subtlety, he stood out above the rest."

"You can't afford to be simple when your territory's shrinking the way the Empire's has been." Karrde paused, and Mara could feel him gazing down at her. "You seem to know something about the Grand Admiral."

"I know something about a lot of things," she countered evenly. "That's why you're grooming me to be your lieutenant, remember?"

"Touché," he said easily. "—there goes another one."

Mara looked out the viewport in time to see a third Star Destroyer go to lightspeed. One more to go. "Shouldn't we get moving?" she asked Karrde. "That last one will be gone in a minute."

"Oh, we're scratching the delivery," he told her. "I just thought it might be instructive to watch the battle, as long as we happened to be here at the right time."

Mara frowned up at him. "What do you mean, we're scratching the delivery? They're expecting us."

"Yes, they are." He nodded. "Unfortunately, as of right now, the whole system is also expecting a small hornet's nest of New Republic ships. Hardly the sort of atmosphere one would like to fly into with a shipload of contraband materials."

"What makes you think they'll come?" Mara demanded. "They're not going to be in time to do anything."

"No, but that's not really the point of such a show," Karrde said. "The point is to score domestic political gains by bustling around, presenting a comforting display of force, and otherwise convincing the locals that something like this can never happen again."

"And promising to help clean up the wreckage," Lachton put in.

"That goes without saying," Karrde agreed dryly. "Regardless, it's not a situation we really want to fly into. We'll send a transmission from our next stop telling them we'll try to make delivery again in a week."

"I still don't like it," Mara insisted. "We promised them we'd do it. We *promised.*"[8]

There was a short pause. "It's standard procedure," Karrde told her, a touch of curiosity almost hidden beneath the usual urbane smoothness of his voice. "I'm sure they'd prefer late delivery to losing the entire shipment."

With an effort, Mara forced the black haze of memory away. Promises . . . "I suppose so," she conceded, blinking her attention back to the control board. While they'd been talking, the last Star Destroyer had apparently gone to lightspeed, leaving nothing behind but enraged and impotent defenders and mass destruction. A mess for the New Republic's politicians and military people to clean up.

For a moment she gazed out at the distant planets. Wondering if Luke Skywalker might be among those the New Republic would send to help clean up that mess.

"Whenever you're ready, Mara."

With an effort, she shook away the thought. "Yes, sir," she said, reaching for the board. *Not yet,* she told herself silently. *Not yet. But soon. Very, very soon.*

The remote swooped; hesitated; swooped again; hesitated again; swooped once more and fired. Leia, swinging her new lightsaber in an overlarge arc, was just a shade too slow. "Gah!" she grunted, taking a step backward.

"You're not giving the Force enough control," Luke told her. "You have to— Wait a minute."

Reaching out with the Force, he put the remote on pause. He remembered vividly that first practice session on the *Falcon,* when he'd had to concentrate on Ben Kenobi's instructions while at the same time keeping a wary eye on the remote. Doing both together hadn't been easy.

But perhaps that had been the whole idea. Perhaps a lesson learned under stress was learned better.

He wished he knew.[9]

"I'm giving it all the control I can," Leia said, rubbing

8. Like Karrde, Mara has an ethical core that doesn't take kindly to broken promises or bent loyalty.

—TZ

9. Over the years I've slowly gotten better at the art of teaching, but I can strongly identify with Luke's concerns over his own ability in that area. Especially when all I had to do was teach elementary physics, and he has to train a Jedi.

—TZ

her arm where the remote's stinger blast had caught her. "I just don't have the proper techniques down yet." She impaled him with a look. "Or else I just wasn't cut out for this sort of fighting."

"You can learn it," Luke said firmly. "*I* learned it, and I never had any of that self-defense training you got when you were growing up on Alderaan."

"Maybe that's the problem," Leia said. "Maybe all those old fighting reflexes are getting in my way."

"I suppose that's possible," Luke admitted, wishing he knew that, too. "In that case, the sooner you start unlearning them, the better. Now: ready—"

The door buzzed. "It's Han," Leia said, stepping away from the remote and closing down her lightsaber. "Come in," she called.

"Hi," Han said as he walked into the room, glancing in turn at Leia and Luke. He wasn't smiling. "How's the lesson going?"

"Not bad," Luke said.

"Don't ask," Leia countered, frowning at her husband. "What's wrong?"

"The Imperials," Han said sourly. "They just pulled a three-prong hit-and-fade on three systems in the Sluis sector. Some place called Bpfassh and two unpronounceable ones."[10]

Luke whistled softly. "Three at once. Getting pretty cocky, aren't they?"

"That seems par for them these days." Leia shook her head, the skin around her eyes tight with concentration. "They're up to something, Han—I can feel it. Something big; something dangerous." She waved her hands helplessly. "But I can't for the life of me figure out what it could be."

"Yeah, Ackbar's been saying the same thing." Han nodded. "Problem is he's got nothing to back it up. Except for the style and tactics, this is all pretty much the same rearguard harassment the Empire's been pulling for probably the last year and a half."

10. For some reason, Han not lumping Bpfassh in with the "unpronounceable" ones strikes me as both funny and very Han.

—TZ

"I know," Leia gritted. "But don't sell Ackbar short—he's got good military instincts. No matter what certain other people say."

Han cocked an eyebrow. "Hey, sweetheart, I'm on *your* side. Remember?"

She smiled wanly. "Sorry. How bad was the damage?"

Han shrugged. "Not nearly as bad as it could have been. Especially considering that they hit each place with four Star Destroyers. But all three systems are pretty shook up."

"I can imagine." Leia sighed. "Let me guess: Mon Mothma wants me to go out there and assure them that the New Republic really *is* able and willing to protect them."

"How'd you guess?" Han growled. "Chewie's getting the *Falcon* prepped now."

"You're not going alone, are you?" Luke asked. "After Bimmisaari—"

"Oh, don't worry," Han said, throwing him a tight smile. "We're not going to be sitting ducks this time. There's a twenty-ship convoy going out to assess the damage, plus Wedge and Rogue Squadron.[11] It'll be safe enough."

"That's what we said about Bimmisaari, too," Luke pointed out. "I'd better come along."

Han looked at Leia. "Well, actually . . . you can't."

Luke frowned at him. "Why not?"

"Because," Leia answered quietly, "the Bpfasshi don't like Jedi."

Han's lip twisted. "The story is that some of their Jedi went bad during the Clone Wars and really mangled things before they were stopped. Or so Mon Mothma says."

"She's right." Leia nodded. "We were still getting echoes of the whole fiasco in the Imperial Senate when I was serving there. It wasn't just Bpfassh, either—some of those Dark Jedi escaped and made trouble all throughout the Sluis sector. One of them even got as far as Dagobah before he was caught."

11. Rogue Squadron was half convenience and half a throwaway line—a unit I could move around wherever I needed it, with Wedge in command because anyone who can survive three *Star Wars* movies is welcome in my book any day.

I would never in my wildest dreams have guessed how well and how far Mike Stackpole and, later, Aaron Allston would run with the whole idea.

—TZ

Luke felt a jolt run through him. *Dagobah?* "When was that?" he asked as casually as possible.

"Thirty, thirty-five years ago,"[12] Leia said, her forehead creased slightly as she studied his face. "Why?"

Luke shook his head. Yoda had never mentioned a Dark Jedi ever being on Dagobah. "No reason," he murmured.

"Come on, we ·can discuss history later," Han put in. "The sooner we get going, the sooner we can get this over with."

"Right," Leia agreed, latching her lightsaber to her belt and heading for the door. "I'll get my travel bag and give Winter some instructions. Meet you at the ship."

Luke watched her leave; turned back to find Han eyeing him. "I don't like it," he told the other.

"Don't worry—she'll be safe," Han assured him. "Look, I know how protective you're feeling toward her these days. But she can't always have her big brother standing over her."

"Actually, we've never figured out which of us is older," Luke murmured.

"Whatever," Han waved the detail away. "The best thing you can do for her right now is what you're already doing. You make her a Jedi, and she'll be able to handle anything the Imperials can throw at her."

Luke's stomach tightened. "I suppose so."

"As long as Chewie and me are with her, that is," Han amended, heading for the door. "See you when we get back."

"Be careful," Luke called after him.

Han turned, one of those hurt/innocent expressions on his face. "Hey," he said. "It's *me.*"

He left, and Luke was alone.

For a few moments he wandered around the room, fighting against the heavy weight of responsibility that seemed sometimes on the verge of smothering him. Risking his own life was one thing, but to have Leia's future in

12. One of the more subtle goofs in *Heir* is in the dating. At the time, George hadn't settled on the final time line, and we were told that the Clone Wars took place thirty-five years before *A New Hope*.

However, from the prequels we now know that the Clone Wars ended only nineteen years before *ANH*. All the dates in *Heir* are therefore off by those sixteen years.

Personally, I put it down to the chaos of information loss during the Empire, and sloppy work on the part of post-Empire historians. These things happen . . .

—TZ

his hands was something else entirely. "I'm not a teacher," he called aloud into the empty room.

The only response was a flicker of movement from the still-paused remote. On sudden impulse, Luke kicked the device to life again, snatching his lightsaber from his belt as it moved to the attack. A dozen stinger blasts shot out in quick succession as the remote swooped like a crazed insect; effortlessly, Luke blocked each in turn, swinging the lightsaber in a flashing arc that seemed to engulf him, a strange exultation flowing through mind and body. *This* was something he could fight—not distant and shadowy like his private fears, but something solid and tangible. The remote fired again and again, each shot ricocheting harmlessly from the lightsaber blade—

With a sudden beep the remote stopped. Luke stared at it in confusion, wondering what had happened . . . and abruptly realized he was breathing heavily. Breathing heavily, and sweating. The remote had a twenty-minute time limit built in, and he'd just come to the end of it.

He closed down the lightsaber and returned it to his belt, feeling a little eerie about what had just happened. It wasn't the first time he'd lost track of time like that, but always before it had been during quiet meditation. The only times it had happened in anything like a combat situation were back on Dagobah, under Yoda's supervision.

On Dagobah . . .

Wiping the sweat out of his eyes with his sleeve, he walked over to the comm desk in the corner and punched up the spaceport. "This is Skywalker," he identified himself. "I'd like my X-wing prepped for launch in one hour."

"Yes, sir," the young maintenance officer said briskly. "We'll need you to send over your astromech unit first."

"Right." Luke nodded. He'd refused to let them wipe the X-wing's computer every few months, as per standard procedure. The inevitable result was that the computer had effectively molded itself around Artoo's unique personality, so much so that the relationship was almost up to true droid counterpart level. It made for excellent operational speed and efficiency; unfortunately, it also meant that none of the maintenance computers could talk to the X-wing anymore. "I'll have him there in a few minutes."

"Yes, sir."

Luke keyed off and straightened up, wondering vaguely why he was doing this. Surely Yoda's presence would no longer be there on Dagobah for him to talk to or ask questions of.

But then, perhaps it would.

CHAPTER 10

"AS YOU CAN SEE," Wedge said, his voice grimly conversational as he crunched through plastic and ceramic underfoot, "the place is something of a mess."

"That's for sure," Leia agreed, feeling a little sick as she looked around at the flat-bottomed, rubble-strewn crater. A handful of other Republic representatives from her party were wandering around the area, too, holding quiet conversations with their Bpfasshi escorts and occasionally pausing to pick through the pieces of what had once been a major power plant. "How many people died in the attack?" she asked, not at all sure she wanted to hear the answer.

"In this system, a few hundred," Wedge told her, consulting a data pad. "Not too bad, really."

"No." Involuntarily, Leia glanced up at the deep blue-green sky above them. Not bad, indeed. Especially considering that there had been no fewer than four Star Destroyers raining destruction down on them. "A lot of damage, though."

"Yeah." Wedge nodded. "But not nearly as much as there could have been."

"I wonder why," Han muttered.

"So does everyone else," Wedge agreed. "It's been the second most popular question around here these days."

"What's the first?" Leia asked.

"Let me guess," Han put in before Wedge could answer. "The first is, why did they bother pounding on Bpfassh in the first place."

"You got it." Wedge nodded again. "It's not like they didn't have any better targets to choose from. You've got the Sluis Van[1] shipyards about thirty light-years away, for starters—a hundred ships there at any given time, not to mention the docking facilities themselves. Then there's the Praesitlyn communications station at just under sixty, and four or five major trade centers within a hundred. An extra day of travel each way, tops, at Star Destroyer cruising speeds. So why Bpfassh?"

Leia thought it over. It *was* a good question. "Sluis Van itself is pretty heavily defended," she pointed out. "Between our Star Cruisers and the Sluissi's own permanent battle stations, any Imperial leader with a gram of sense would think twice before tackling it. And those other systems are all a lot deeper into New Republic space than Bpfassh. Maybe they didn't want to push their luck that far."

"While they tested their new transmission system under combat conditions?" Han suggested darkly.

"We don't *know* that they've got a new system," Wedge cautioned him. "Coordinated simultaneous attacks have been done before."

"No." Han shook his head, looking around. "No, they've got something new. Some kind of booster that lets them punch subspace transmissions through deflector shields and battle debris."

"I don't think it's a booster," Leia said, a shiver running up her back. Something was starting to tingle, way back at

---

the edge of her mind. "No one in any of the three systems picked up any transmissions."

Han frowned down at her. "You okay?" he asked quietly.

"Yes," she murmured, shivering again. "I was just re-membering that when—well, when Darth Vader was hav-ing us tortured on Bespin, Luke knew it was happening from wherever he was at the time. And there were rumors that the Emperor and Vader could do that, too."[2]

"Yeah, but they're both dead," Han reminded her. "Luke said so."

"I know," she said. The tingling at the edge of her mind was getting stronger . . . "But what if the Imperials have found another Dark Jedi?"

Wedge had gotten ahead of them, but now he turned back. "You talking about C'baoth?"

"What?" Leia frowned.

"Joruus C'baoth," Wedge said. "I thought I heard you mention Jedi."

"I did," Leia said. "Who's Joruus C'baoth?"

"He was one of the major Jedi Masters back in pre-Empire days," Wedge said. "Supposed to have disappeared before the Clone Wars started. I heard a rumor a couple of days ago that he's surfaced again and set up shop on some minor world named Jomark."[3]

"Right." Han snorted. "And he was just sitting around doing nothing during the Rebellion?"

Wedge shrugged. "I just report 'em, General. I don't make 'em up."

"We can ask Luke," Leia said. "Maybe he knows some-thing. Are we ready to move on?"

"Sure," Wedge said. "The airspeeders are over this way—"

And in a sudden rush of sensation, the tingling in Leia's mind abruptly exploded into certain knowledge. "Han, Wedge—*duck!*"

—and at the rim of the crater a handful of well-remembered gray-skinned aliens appeared.

2. In fact, as we all know, Luke knew about the tor-ture *before* it actually happened. But under the circumstances Leia may have been a little fuzzy on the details.
Luke may also have fudged those same details a bit to keep Leia and the others from knowing how far away he'd been. Later, we'll learn that he's still keeping Dagobah's signifi-cance a secret.
—TZ

3. Another Tuckerization: Mark Jones of Tampa. For-tunately, Mark never took offense that Jomark was only a *minor* world.
—TZ

"Cover!" Han shouted to the other Republic reps in the crater as the aliens opened up with blasters. Grabbing Leia's wrist, he dived for the limited protection of a huge but badly twisted plate of shielding metal that had somehow gotten itself dug halfway into the ground. Wedge was right behind them, slamming hard into Leia as he reached cover.

"Sorry," he panted in apology, yanking out his blaster and turning to throw a cautious look around the edge of their shelter. One look was all he got before a blaster bolt spattered metal near his face and sent him jerking back. "I'm not sure," he said, "but I think we've got trouble."

"I think you're right," Han agreed grimly. Leia turned to see him, blaster drawn, returning his comlink to his belt with his free hand. "They've learned. This time they're jamming our communications."

Leia felt cold all over. Way out here, without comlinks, they were as good as helpless. Totally cut off from any possibility of help . . .

Her hand, reaching automatically for her stomach, brushed her new lightsaber instead. She pulled it free, a fresh determination pushing past the fear. Jedi or not, experienced or not, she wasn't going to give up without a fight.

"Sounds like you've run into these guys before," Wedge said, reaching around the barrier to squeeze off a couple of blind shots in the general direction of their attackers.

"We've met," Han grunted back, trying to get into position for a clear shot. "Haven't really figured out what they want, though."

Leia reached for her lightsaber's control stud, wondering if she had enough skill yet to block blaster fire . . . and paused. Over the noise of blasters and crackling metal she could hear a new sound. A very familiar sound . . . "Han!"

"I hear it," Han said. "Way to go, Chewie."

"What?" Wedge asked.

"That whine you hear is the *Falcon*," Han told him,

leaning back to look over their shelter. "Probably discovered they were jamming us and put two and two together. Here he comes."

With a screaming roar the familiar shape of the *Millennium Falcon* swooped by overhead. It circled once, ignoring the ineffectual blasts ricocheting from its underside, and dropped to a bumpy landing directly between them and their attackers. Peering cautiously around their barrier, Leia saw the ramp lower toward them.

"Great," Han said, looking past her shoulder. "Okay. I'll go first and cover you from the bottom of the ramp. Leia, you're next; Wedge, you bring up the rear. Stay sharp—they may try to flank us."

"Got it." Wedge nodded. "Ready when you are."

"Okay." Han got his feet under him—

"Wait a minute," Leia said suddenly, gripping his arm. "There's something wrong."

"Right—we're getting shot at," Wedge put in.

"I'm serious," Leia snapped. "Something here's not right."

"Like what?" Han asked, frowning at her. "Come on, Leia, we can't sit here all day."

Leia gritted her teeth, trying to chase down the feeling tingling through her. It was still so nebulous . . . and then suddenly she had it. "It's Chewie," she told them. "I can't feel his presence on the ship."

"He's probably just too far away," Wedge said, a distinct note of impatience in his voice. "Come on—he's going to get the ship shot out from under him if we don't get going."

"Hang on a minute," Han growled, still frowning at Leia. "He's okay for now—all they're using is hand blasters. Anyway, if things get too hot, he can always use the—"

He broke off, a strange look on his face. A second later, Leia got it, too. "The underside swivel blaster,"[4] she said. "Why isn't he using it?"

"Good question," Han said grimly. He leaned out again,

4. In various sources this weapon is identified as a "Taim & Bak auto blaster cannon," a "BlasTech Ax-108 'Ground Buzzer' surface-defense blaster cannon," and simply as "concealed blaster cannon."

I figure that my term, *underside swivel blaster,* is probably a generic term for all such handy gadgets.

—TZ

taking a hard look this time . . . and when he ducked back under cover there was a sardonic half-grin on his face. "Simple answer: that's not the *Falcon.*"

"What?" Wedge asked, his jaw dropping a couple of centimeters.

"It's a fake," Han told him. "I can't believe it—these guys actually dug up another working YT-1300 freighter somewhere."[5]

Wedge whistled softly. "Boy, they must really want you bad."

"Yeah, I'm starting to get that impression myself," Han said. "Got any good ideas?"

Wedge glanced around the edge of the barrier. "I don't suppose running for it qualifies."

"Not with them sitting out there at the edge of the crater waiting to pick us off," Leia told him.

"Yeah," Han agreed. "And as soon as they realize we're not going to just walk into their decoy, it'll probably get worse."

"Is there any way we can at least disable that ship?" Leia asked him. "Keep it from taking off and attacking us from above?"

"There are lots of ways," he grunted. "The problem is you have to be inside for most of them. The outside shielding isn't great, but it blocks hand blasters just fine."

"Will it block a lightsaber?"

He threw a suspicious frown at her. "You're not suggesting . . . ?"

"I don't think we've got any choice," she told him. "Do we?"

"I suppose not," he grimaced. "All right—but *I'll* go."

Leia shook her head. "We all go," she said. "We know they want at least one of us alive—otherwise, they'd just have flown by overhead and blasted us. If we all go together, they won't be able to fire. We'll head straight in as if we're going aboard, then split off to the sides at the last second and take cover behind the ramp. Wedge and I can

---

5. The West End Games material gave me the model designation for the *Falcon.* Unfortunately, it didn't mention that the ships were pretty common throughout the galaxy. Ergo, digging one up wouldn't have been nearly as hard as Han implied here.

Probably what Han meant wasn't that they'd found another YT-1300, but that they'd found one with the same quirks and add-ons as the *Falcon.* Sure—that's what he meant.

—TZ

fire up and inside to keep them busy while you take the lightsaber and disable them."

"I don't know," Han muttered. "I think just Wedge and me should go."

"No, it has to be all of us," Leia insisted. "That's the only way to guarantee they won't shoot."

Han looked at Wedge. "What do you think?"

"I think it's the best chance we're going to get," the other said. "But if we do it, we'd better do it fast."

"Yeah." Han took a deep breath and handed Leia his blaster. "All right. Give me the lightsaber. Okay; ready...*go.*"

He ducked out from cover and charged for the ship, crouching down as he ran to avoid the blaster fire criss-crossing the crater—the other Republic reps, Leia noted as she and Wedge followed, doing a good job of keeping the rim attackers busy. Inside the ship she could see a hint of movement, and she gripped Han's blaster a little tighter. A half second in the lead, Han reached the ramp; and swerving suddenly to the side ducked under the hull.

The aliens must have realized instantly that their trap had failed. Even as Leia and Wedge skidded to a halt at opposite sides of the ramp, they were greeted by a burst of blaster fire from the open hatch. Dropping to the ground, Leia squirmed as far back as she could under the ramp, firing blindly into the hatch to discourage those inside from coming down after them. Across the ramp, Wedge was also firing; somewhere behind her, she could hear a faint scrabbling across the ground as Han got into position for whatever sabotage he was planning. A shot blazed past from above, narrowly missing her left shoulder, and she tried to back a little farther into the ramp's shadow. Behind her, clearly audible through the blaster fire, she heard a *snap-hiss* as Han ignited her lightsaber. Gritting her teeth, she braced herself, not knowing quite why—

And with a blast and shock wave that knocked her flat against the ground, the whole ship bounced a meter in the air and then slammed back down again.

Through the ringing in her ears, she heard someone give a war whoop. The firing from the hatch had abruptly stopped, and in the silence she could hear a strange hissing roar coming from above her. Cautiously, she eased away from the ramp and crawled a little ways out of concealment.

She'd been prepared to see the freighter leaking something as a result of Han's sabotage. She wasn't prepared for the huge white gaseous plume that was shooting skyward like the venting of a ruptured volcano.

"You like it?" Han asked, easing over beside her and glancing up to admire his handiwork.

"That probably depends on whether the ship's about to blow up," Leia countered. "What did you *do?*"

"Cut through the coolant lines to the main drive," he told her, retrieving his blaster and handing back her lightsaber. "That's all their pressurized korfaise gas floating away."

"I thought coolant gases were dangerous to breathe," Leia said, looking warily at the billowing cloud.

"They are," Han agreed. "But korfaise is lighter than air, so we won't have any trouble down here. *Inside* the ship is another matter. I hope."

Abruptly, Leia became aware of the silence around them. "They've stopped shooting," she said.

Han listened. "You're right. Not just the ones inside the ship, either."

"I wonder what they're up to," Leia murmured, tightening her grip on the lightsaber.

A second later she got her answer. A violent thunderclap came from above them, flattening her to the ground with the shock wave. For a horrifying second she thought the aliens had set the ship to self-destruct; but the sound faded away, and the ramp beside her was still intact. "What was *that?*"

"That, sweetheart," Han said, pulling himself to his feet,

"was the sound of an escape pod being jettisoned." He eased cautiously away from the relative protection of the ramp, scanning the sky. "Probably modified for atmospheric maneuvering. Never realized before how loud those things were."

"They usually take off in vacuum," Leia reminded him, standing up herself. "So. Now what?"

"Now"—Han pointed—"we collect our escort and get out of here."

"Our escort?" Leia frowned. "What esc—?"

Her question was cut off by the roar of engines as three X-wings shot overhead, wings in attack position and clearly primed for trouble. She looked up at the white tower of korfaise gas . . . and suddenly understood. "You did that deliberately, didn't you?"

"Well, sure," Han said, looking innocent. "Why just disable a ship when you can disable it *and* send up a distress signal at the same time?" He gazed up at the cloud. "You know," he said thoughtfully, "sometimes I still amaze myself."[6]

"I can assure you, Captain Solo," Admiral Ackbar's gravelly voice came over the *Falcon*'s speaker, "that we are doing everything in our power to find out how this happened."

"That's what you said four days ago," Han reminded him, trying hard to be civil. It wasn't easy. He'd long since gotten used to being shot at himself, but having Leia under the hammer with him was something else entirely. "Come on—there can't be all *that* many people who knew we were coming to Bpfassh."

"You might be surprised," Ackbar said. "Between the Council members, their staffs, the prep crews at the spaceport, and various security and support personnel, there may be up to two hundred people who had direct access to your itinerary. And that doesn't count friends

6. A couple of weeks after I finished *Heir* and sent it in, my editor, Betsy Mitchell, called to chat about the manuscript. In the course of the conversation she asked if I liked Han best of all the movie characters.

I assured her that I liked them all, and asked why she would think I liked Han best. She said, "Because you gave him all the best lines."

She may have been right. But in all fairness, as far as giving Han good lines is concerned, George got there a long time before I did.

—TZ

and colleagues any of those two hundred might have mentioned it to. Tracking through all of them is going to take time."

Han grimaced. "That's great. May I ask what you suggest we do in the meantime?"

"You have your escort."

"We had them four days ago, too," Han countered. "It didn't do us a lot of good. Commander Antilles and Rogue Squadron are fine in a space battle, but this kind of stuff isn't exactly their area of expertise. We'd do better with Lieutenant Page[7] and some of his commandos."

"Unfortunately, they're all out on assignment," Ackbar said. "Under the circumstances, perhaps it would be best if you simply brought Councilor Organa Solo back here where she can be properly protected."

"I'd love to," Han said. "The question is whether she'll be any safer on Coruscant than she is here."

There was a long moment of silence, and Han could imagine Ackbar's huge eyes swiveling in their sockets. "I'm not sure I appreciate the tone of that question, Captain."

"I don't much like it either, Admiral," Han told him. "But face it: if the Imperials are getting information *out* of the Palace, they might just as easily be able to get their agents *in*."

"I think that highly unlikely," Ackbar said, and there was no missing the frostiness in his tone. "The security arrangements I've set up on Coruscant are quite capable of handling anything the Imperials might try."

"I'm sure they are, Admiral." Han sighed. "I only meant—"

"We'll let you know when we have further information, Captain," Ackbar said. "Until then, do whatever you feel is necessary. Coruscant out."

The faint hum of the carrier cut off. "Right," Han muttered under his breath. "Bpfassh out, too."

For a minute he just sat there in the *Falcon*'s cockpit,

7. Like Rogue Squadron, Page was another mostly background character whom other authors later picked up and ran with.

Ran with in both directions, in fact, as he was retroactively added into the Rebellion era.

Or at least his name was. There were certainly Rebel commandos running around making trouble for Palpatine's Empire—it was only after *Heir* was published that Page was associated by name with some of those operations.

—TZ

thinking evil thoughts about politics in general and Ackbar in particular. In front of him the displays that normally monitored ship's status were showing views of the
landing field around them, with special emphasis on the
areas just outside the hatch. The underside swivel blaster
was extended and ready, the deflector shields set for hair-
trigger activation, despite the fact that the things weren't
all that effective inside an atmosphere.

Han shook his head, a mixture of frustration and disgust in his mouth. *Who'd ever have thought,* he marveled
to himself, *that the day would come when I was actually
paranoid?*

From the rear of the cockpit came the sound of a soft
footstep. Han turned, hand automatically dropping to his
blaster—

"It's just me," Leia assured him, coming forward and
glancing at the displays. She looked tired. "You finished
talking with Ackbar already?"

"It wasn't much of a conversation," Han told her sourly.
"I asked what they were doing to find out how our pals
with the blasters knew we were coming here, he assured
me they were doing everything possible to find out, I managed to step on his toes, and he signed off in a huff. Pretty
much like usual with Ackbar these days."

Leia gave him a wry smile. "You *do* have a way with people, don't you?"

"This one's not my fault," Han objected. "All I did was
suggest that his security people *might* not be up to keeping
these guys out of the Imperial Palace. *He's* the one who
overreacted."

"I know." Leia nodded, dropping wearily into the copilot's seat. "For all his military genius, Ackbar just doesn't
have the polish to be a good politician. And with Fey'lya
nipping at his heels . . ." She shrugged uncomfortably. "He
just gets more and more overprotective of his territory."

"Yeah, well, if he's trying to keep Fey'lya away from the

military, he's got the wrong end of the blaster," Han growled. "Half of them are already convinced that Fey'lya's the guy to listen to."

"Unfortunately, he often is," Leia conceded. "Charisma and ambition. Dangerous combination."

Han frowned. There had been something in her voice just then . . . "What do you mean, dangerous?"

"Nothing," she said, a guilty look flicking across her face. "Sorry—talking out of turn."

"Leia, if you know something—"

"I don't *know* anything," she said, in a tone that warned him to drop it. "It's just a feeling I have. A sense that Fey'lya has his eye on more than just Ackbar's job as supreme commander. But it's just a feeling."

Like the feeling she had that the Empire was up to something big? "Okay," he said soothingly. "I understand. So. You all done here?"

"As done as I can be," she said, the tiredness back in her voice. "The rebuilding's going to take some time, but the organization for that will have to be handled from Coruscant." She leaned back in her seat and closed her eyes. "Convoys of replacement equipment, consultants and maybe extra workers—you know the sort of thing."

"Yeah," Han said. "And I suppose you're anxious to get right back and start the ball rolling."

She opened her eyes and gave him a curious look. "You sound like you're not."

Han gave the outside displays a thoughtful scan. "Well, it's what everyone's going to expect you to do," he pointed out. "So maybe we ought to do something else."

"Such as?"

"I don't know. Find somewhere no one would think to look for you, I guess."

"And then . . . ?" she asked, her voice ominous.

Unconsciously, Han braced himself. "And then hole up there for a while."

"You know I can't do that," she said, her tone just about

what he'd expected. "I have commitments back on Coruscant."

"You've got commitments to yourself, too," he countered. "Not to mention to the twins."

She glared at him. "That's not fair."

"Isn't it?"

She turned away from him, an unreadable expression on her face. "I can't be out of touch, Han," she said quietly. "I just can't. There's too much happening back there for me to bury myself away."

Han gritted his teeth. They seemed to be running over this same territory a lot lately. "Well, if all you need right now is to keep in touch, how about if we go someplace that has a diplomatic station? You'd at least be able to get official Coruscant news there."

"And how do we make sure the local ambassador doesn't give us away?" She shook her head. "I can't believe I'm talking like this," she muttered. "It's like we're back being the Rebellion again, not the legitimate government."

"Who says the ambassador has to know?" Han asked. "We've got a diplomatic receiver on the *Falcon*—we can tap into the transmission on our own."

"Only if we can get hold of the station's encrypt scheme," she reminded him. "*And* then plug it into our receiver. That may not be possible."

"We can find a way," Han insisted. "At least it would buy Ackbar some time to track down the leak."

"True." Leia considered, slowly shook her head. "I don't know. The New Republic's encrypt codes are nearly impossible to break."

Han snorted. "I hate to disillusion you, sweetheart, but there are slicers[8] running around loose who eat government encrypt codes for breakfast. All we have to do is find one of them."

"And pay him enormous sums of money?" Leia said dryly.

"Something like that," Han agreed, thinking hard. "On

8. Again, a word that echoes a familiar term—hacker—but is different enough to fit comfortably into the *Star Wars* universe.

—TZ

the other hand, even slicers occasionally owe other people favors."

"Oh?" Leia threw him a sideways look. "I don't suppose you'd know any of them."

"As a matter of fact, I do." Han pursed his lips. "Trouble is, if the Imperials have done their homework, they probably know all about it and have someone watching him."

"Meaning . . . ?"

"Meaning we're going to have to find someone who's got his own list of slicer contacts." He reached over to the console and tapped the *Falcon*'s comm switch. "Antilles, this is Solo. You copy?"

"Right here, General," Wedge's voice came back promptly.

"We're leaving Bpfassh, Wedge," Han told him. "That's not official yet—you're in charge of telling the rest of the delegation about it once we're off the ground."

"I understand," Wedge said. "You want me to assign you an escort, or would you rather slip out quietly? I've got a couple of people I'd trust all the way to the end of the galaxy."

Han sent Leia a lopsided smile. Wedge understood, all right. "Thanks, but we wouldn't want the rest of the delegation to feel unprotected."

"Whatever you want. I can handle anything that needs doing at this end. See you back at Coruscant."

"Right." Han cut off the comm. "Eventually," he added under his breath as he keyed for intercom. "Chewie? We ready to fly?"

The Wookiee growled an affirmative. "Okay. Make sure everything's bolted down and then come on up. Better bring Threepio, too—we might have to talk to Bpfasshi Control on the way out."

"Do I get to know where we're going?" Leia asked as he started the prelaunch sequence.

"I already told you," Han said. "We need to find someone we can trust who has his own list of illegals."

A suspicious glint came into her eye. "You don't mean . . . Lando?"

"Who else?" Han said innocently. "Upstanding citizen, former war hero, honest businessman. Of *course* he'll have slicer contacts."

Leia rolled her eyes skyward. "Why," she murmured, "do I suddenly have a bad feeling about this?"

CHAPTER 11

"HANG ON, ARTOO," Luke called as the first gusts of atmospheric turbulence began to bounce the X-wing around. "We're coming in. Scanners all working okay?"

There was an affirmative twitter from the rear, the translation appearing across his computer scope. "Good," Luke said, and turned his attention back to the cloud-shrouded planet rushing up to meet them. It was odd, he thought, how it had only been on that first trip in to Dagobah that the sensors had so totally failed on approach.

Or perhaps not so odd. Perhaps that had been Yoda, deliberately suppressing his instruments so as to be able to guide him unsuspectingly to the proper landing site.[1]

And now Yoda was gone . . .

Firmly, Luke put the thought out of his mind. Mourning the loss of a friend and teacher was both fitting and honorable, but to dwell unnecessarily on that loss was to give the past too much power over the present.

1. Luke's actually wrong here—Yoda couldn't have affected his X-wing's systems at that distance. (Otherwise, Ben wouldn't have had to physically go to the tractor beam station on the Death Star.)

But Yoda *could* have affected Luke's perception at the critical time.

—TZ

The X-wing dropped into the lower atmosphere, and within seconds was completely enveloped by thick white clouds. Luke watched the instruments, taking the approach slow and easy. The last time he'd come here, just before the Battle of Endor, he'd made the landing without incident; but just the same, he had no intention of pushing his luck. The landing sensors had Yoda's old homestead pinpointed now. "Artoo?" he called. "Find me a good level spot to set down, will you?"

In response, a red rectangle appeared on the forward scope, a ways east of the house but within walking distance of it. "Thanks," Luke told the droid, and keyed in the landing cycle. A moment later, with one last mad flurry of displaced tree branches, they were down.

Slipping off his helmet, Luke popped the canopy. The rich odors of the Dagobah swamp flooded in on him, a strange combination of sweet and decay that sent a hundred memories flashing through his mind. That slow twitch of Yoda's ears—the strange but tasty stew he'd often made—the way that wispy hair of his had tickled Luke's ears whenever he rode on Luke's back during training. The training itself: the long hours, the physical and mental fatigue, the gradually increasing sense of and confidence in the Force, the cave and its dark side images—

The cave?

Abruptly, Luke stood up in the cockpit, hand going reflexively to his lightsaber as he peered through the haze. Surely he hadn't brought his X-wing down by the cave.

He had. There, no more than fifty meters away, was the tree that grew from just above that evil place, its huge blackened shape jutting upward through the surrounding trees. Beneath and between its tangled roots, just visible through the mists and shorter vegetation, he could see the dark entrance to the cave itself.[2]

"Wonderful," he muttered. "Just wonderful."

From behind him came an interrogative set of beeps.

2. I'd always been a little confused about this. In *The Empire Strikes Back*, it appears that Luke is going into a cave; yet on the soundtrack that scene is listed as "The Magic Tree."

Fortunately, I was able to work the description so that I could sort of have it both ways.

—TZ

"Never mind, Artoo," he called over his shoulder, dropping his helmet back onto the seat. "It's all right. Why don't you stay here, and I'll—"

The X-wing rocked, just a bit, and he looked back to find Artoo already out of his socket and working his way gingerly forward. "Or if you'd rather, you can come along," he added wryly.

Artoo beeped again—not a cheerful beep, exactly, but one that definitely sounded relieved. The little droid hated being left alone. "Hang on," Luke directed him. "I'll get down and give you a hand."

He jumped down. The ground felt a little squishy beneath his feet, but it was easily firm enough to support the X-wing's weight. Satisfied, he reached out with the Force to lift Artoo from his perch and lower the droid to the ground beside him. "There you go," he said.

From off in the distance came the long, trilling wail of one of Dagobah's birds. Luke listened as it ran down the scale, eyes searching the swamp around him and wondering why exactly he'd come here. Back on Coruscant it had seemed important—even vital—that he do so. But now that he was actually standing here it all seemed hazy. Hazy, and more than a little silly.

Beside him, Artoo beeped questioningly. With an effort, Luke shook off the uncertainties. "I thought Yoda might have left something behind that we could use," he told the droid, choosing the most easily verbalized of his reasons. "The house should be"—he glanced around to get his bearings—"that way. Let's go."

The distance wasn't great, but the trip took longer than Luke had anticipated. Partly it was the general terrain and vegetation—he'd forgotten just how difficult it was to get from one place to another through the Dagobah swamps. But there was something else, too: a low-level but persistent pressure at the back of his mind that seemed to press inward, clouding his ability to think.

But at last they arrived . . . to find the house effectively gone.

For a long minute Luke just stood there, gazing at the mass of vegetation occupying the spot where the house had been, a freshly renewed sense of loss struggling against the embarrassing realization that he'd been a fool. Growing up in the deserts of Tatooine, where an abandoned structure could last for half a century or more, it had somehow never even occurred to him to consider what would happen to that same structure after five years in a swamp.

Beside him, Artoo twittered a question. "I thought Yoda might have left some tapes or books behind," Luke explained. "Something that would tell me more about the methods of Jedi training. Not much left, though, is there?"

In response, Artoo extended his little sensor plate. "Never mind," Luke told him, starting forward. "As long as we're here, I guess we might as well take a look."

It took only a few minutes to cut a path through the bushes and vines with his lightsaber and to reach what was left of the house's outer walls. For the most part they were rubble, reaching only to his waist at their highest, and covered with a crisscrossing of tiny vines. Inside was more vegetation, pushing up against, and in some places through, the old stone hearth. Half buried in the mud were Yoda's old iron pots, covered with a strange-looking moss.

Behind him, Artoo gave a quiet whistle. "No, I don't think we're going to find anything useful," Luke agreed, squatting down to pull one of the pots out of the ground. A small lizard darted out as he did so, and disappeared into the reedy grass. "Artoo, see if you can find anything electronic around here, will you? I never saw him use anything like that, but . . ." He shrugged.

The droid obediently raised his sensor plate again. Luke watched as it tracked back and forth . . . and suddenly stopped. "Find something?" Luke asked.

Artoo twittered excitedly, his dome swiveling to look back the way they'd come. "Back that way?" Luke frowned. He looked down at the debris around him. "Not here?"

Artoo beeped again and turned around, rolling with some difficulty across the uneven surface. Pausing, he swiveled his dome back toward Luke and made a series of sounds that could only have been a question. "Okay, I'm coming." Luke sighed, forcing back the odd sense of dread that had suddenly seized him. "Lead the way."

The sunlight filtering through the leafy canopy overhead had become noticeably dimmer by the time they came within sight of the X-wing. "Now where?" Luke asked Artoo. "I hope you're not going to tell me that all you were picking up was our own ship."

Artoo swiveled his dome back around, trilling a decid-edly indignant denial. His sensor plate turned slightly—

To point directly at the cave.

Luke swallowed hard. "You're sure?"

The droid trilled again. "You're sure," Luke said.

For a minute he just looked across through the mists at the cave, indecision swirling through his mind. There was no genuine need for him to go in there—of that much he was certain. Whatever it was Artoo had detected, it would not be anything Yoda had left behind. Not in there.

But then what was it? Leia had referred to a Bpfasshi Dark Jedi who'd come here. Could it be something of his?

Luke gritted his teeth. "Stay here, Artoo," he instructed the droid as he started across to the cave. "I'll be back as soon as I can."

Fear and anger, Yoda had often warned him, were the slaves of the dark side. Vaguely, Luke wondered which side curiosity served.[3]

Up close, the tree straddling the cave looked as evil as he remembered it: twisted, dark, and vaguely brooding, as if it was itself alive with the dark side of the Force. Perhaps it

3. Depending on the moti-vation and the object of the curiosity, I suspect it can serve either side.

—TZ

was. Luke couldn't tell for sure, not with the overwhelm-
ing emanations of the cave flooding his senses. It was,
clearly, the source of the low-level pressure he'd felt ever
since his arrival on Dagobah, and for a moment he wondered why the effect had never been this strong before.

Perhaps because Yoda had always been here before, his
presence shielding Luke from the true strength of the
cave's power.

But now Yoda was gone ... and Luke was facing the
cave alone.

He took a deep breath. *I am a Jedi,* he reminded himself
firmly. Slipping his comlink from his belt, he thumbed it
on. "Artoo? You copy?"

The comlink trilled back. "Okay. I'm starting in. Give
me a signal when I get close to whatever it is you're picking
up."

He got an affirmative-sounding beep. Returning the
comlink to his belt, he drew his lightsaber. Taking another
deep breath, he ducked under the gnarled tree roots and
stepped into the cave.

This, too, was as bad as he remembered it. Dark, dank,
alive with skittering insects and slimy plants, it was generally as unpleasant a place as Luke had ever been in. The
footing seemed more treacherous than it had been before,
and twice in the first dozen steps he nearly fell on his face
as the ground gave way beneath his weight; not badly, but
enough to throw him off balance. Through the mists
ahead a well-remembered spot loomed, and he found
himself gripping his lightsaber all the more tightly as he
neared it. On this spot, once, he'd fought a nightmare battle with a shadowy, unreal Darth Vader....

He reached the place and stopped, fighting back the fear
and memories. But this time, to his relief, nothing happened. No hissing breath came from the shadows; no Dark
Lord glided forward to confront him. Nothing.

Luke licked his lips and pulled the comlink off his belt.
No; of course there would be nothing. He had already

faced that crisis—had faced it and conquered it. With Vader redeemed and gone, the cave had nothing further to threaten him with except nameless and unreal fears, and those only if he allowed them to have power over him. He should have realized that from the start. "Artoo?" he called. "You still there?"

The little droid buzzed in reply. "All right," Luke said, starting forward again. "How far do I have to—?"

And right in the middle of his sentence—practically in the middle of a step—the haze of the cave abruptly coalesced around him into a flickering, surreal vision . . .

He was on a small, open-air ground vehicle, hovering low over some sort of pit. The ground itself was indistinct, but he could feel a terrible heat rising all around him from it. Something poked hard in his back, urging him forward onto a narrow board protruding horizontally from the vehicle's side—

Luke caught his breath, the scene suddenly coming clear. He was back on Jabba the Hutt's skiff, being prepared for his execution in the Great Pit of Carkoon—

Ahead, he could see the shape of Jabba's Sail Barge now, drifting a bit closer as the courtiers jostled one another for a better view of the coming spectacle. Many of the barge's details were indistinct through the dream mists, but he could see clearly the small, dome-topped figure of Artoo at the top of the ship. Awaiting Luke's signal . . .

"I'm not going to play this game," Luke called out toward the vision. "I'm not. I've faced this crisis, too, and I've defeated it."

But his words seemed dead even in his own ears . . . and even as he spoke them, he could feel the jab of the guard's spear in his back, and could feel himself drop off the end of the plank. In midair he twisted around, grabbing the end of the board and flipping high over the guards' heads—

He landed and turned back toward the Sail Barge, hand

extended for the lightsaber Artoo had just sent arcing toward him.

It never reached him. Even as he stood there waiting for it, the weapon changed direction, curving back toward the other end of the Sail Barge. Frantically, Luke reached out for it with the Force; but to no avail. The lightsaber continued its flight—

And came to rest in the hand of a slender woman standing alone at the top of the barge.

Luke stared at her, a feeling of horror surging through him. In the mists, with the sun behind her, he could see no details of her face . . . but the lightsaber she now held aloft like a prize told him all he needed to know. She had the power of the Force . . . and had just condemned him and his friends to death.

And as the spears pushed him again onto the plank he heard, clearly through the dream mists, her mocking laughter . . .

"No!" Luke shouted; and as suddenly as it had appeared, the vision vanished. He was back in the cave on Dagobah, his forehead and tunic soaked with sweat, a frantic electronic beeping coming from the comlink in his hand.

He took a shuddering breath, squeezing his lightsaber hard to reassure himself that he did indeed still have it. "It's—" He worked moisture into a dry throat and tried again. "It's okay, Artoo," he reassured the droid. "I'm all right. Uh . . ." He paused, fighting through the disorientation to try to remember what he was doing here. "Are you still picking up that electronic signal?"

Artoo beeped affirmatively. "Is it still ahead of me?"

Another affirmative beep. "Okay," Luke said. Shifting the lightsaber in his hand, he wiped more of the sweat from his forehead and started cautiously forward, trying to watch all directions at once.

But the cave had apparently done its worst. No more visions rose to challenge his way as he continued deeper in . . . and at last, Artoo signaled that he was there.

The device, once he'd finally pried it out of the mud and moss, was a distinct disappointment: a small, somewhat flattened cylinder a little longer than his hand, with five triangular, rust-encrusted keys on one side and some flowing alien script engraved on the other. "This is it?" Luke asked, not sure he liked the idea of having come all the way in here just for something so totally nondescript. "There's nothing else?"

Artoo beeped affirmatively, and gave a whistle that could only be a question. "I don't know what it is," Luke told the droid. "Maybe you'll recognize it. Hang on; I'm coming out."

The return trip was unpleasant but also uneventful, and a short time later he emerged from under the tree roots with a sigh of relief into the relatively fresh air of the swamp.

It had grown dark while he'd been inside, he noted to his mild surprise; that twisted vision of the past must have lasted longer than it had seemed. Artoo had the X-wing's landing lights on; the beams were visible as hazy cones in the air. Wading his way through the ground vegetation, Luke headed toward the X-wing.

Artoo was waiting for him, beeping quietly to himself. The beeping became a relieved whistle as Luke came into the light, the little droid rocking back and forth like a nervous child. "Relax, Artoo, I'm all right," Luke assured him, squatting down and pulling the flattened cylinder out of his side pocket. "What do you think?"

The droid chirped[4] thoughtfully, his dome swiveling around to examine the object from a couple of different directions. Then, abruptly, the chirping exploded into an excited electronic jabbering. "What?" Luke asked, trying to read the flurry of sounds and wondering wryly why Threepio was never around when you needed him. "Slow down, Artoo. I can't—never mind," he interrupted himself, getting to his feet and glancing around in the gathering dark-

4. One of the challenges I faced was to find a way to describe R2-D2's sounds without having Skywalker Sound to draw on.

I also didn't want to simply say "he beeped" every time he said something, since that could get boring. So I made up a small note card with alternatives and kept it handy.

Hence, at various spots throughout the book, Artoo warbles, chirps, twitters, grunts, gurgles, jabbers, beeps, and probably a few others that I've forgotten.

Amazing what an hour with a thesaurus can accomplish.

—TZ

ness. "I don't think there's any point in hanging around here anymore, anyway."

He looked back at the cave, now almost swallowed up by the deepening gloom, and shivered. No, there was no reason to stay ... and at least one very good reason to leave. So much, he thought glumly, for finding any kind of enlightenment here. He should have known better. "Come on," he told the droid. "Let's get you back in your socket. You can tell me all about it on the way home."

Artoo's report on the cylinder was, it turned out, fairly short and decidedly negative. The little droid did not recognize the design, could not decipher its function from what his general-purpose scanners could pick up, and didn't even know what language the script on the side was written in, let alone what it said. Luke was beginning to wonder what all the droid's earlier excitement had been about ... until the last sentence scrolled across his computer scope.

"Lando?" Luke frowned, reading the sentence again. "I don't remember ever seeing Lando with anything like this."

More words scrolled across the scope. "Yes, I realize I was busy at the time," Luke agreed, unconsciously flexing the fingers of his artificial right hand.[5] "Getting fitted with a new hand will do that. So did he give it to General Madine, or was he just showing it to him?"

Another sentence appeared. "That's okay," Luke assured the droid. "I imagine you were busy, too."

He looked into his rear display, at the crescent of Dagobah growing ever smaller behind him. He had intended to go straight back to Coruscant and wait for Leia and Han to return from Bpfassh. But from what he'd heard, their mission there could run a couple of weeks or even more. And Lando had invited him more than once to

5. One of the rules of fantasy and SF writing (and of mysteries, for that matter) is to make sure to give the readers all the bits and pieces of information that you'll be using later—it's unfair to suddenly spring something on them just when you need it to get out of the corner you've painted yourself into.

Nearly every reader will remember that Luke has a mechanical right hand, and most will assume I'm just putting this in as another link to the movies. But of course, it's also going to turn out to be very important down the road. . . .

—TZ

visit his new rare-ore mining operation on the superhot planet of Nkllon.[6]

"Change in plans, Artoo," he announced, keying in a new course. "We're going to swing over to the Athega system and see Lando. Maybe he can tell us what this thing is."

And on the way, he'd have time to think about that disturbing dream or vision or whatever it was he'd had in the cave. And to decide whether it had been, in fact, nothing more than a dream.

6. Another Tuckerism: longtime Athens, Georgia, fan Klon Newell, one of the most enthusiastic supporters of my original Cobra series way back in the eighties.

—TZ

CHAPTER 12

"NO, I DON'T HAVE a transit permit for Nkllon," Han said patiently into the *Falcon*'s transmitter, glaring across at the modified B-wing running beside them. "I also don't have any accounts here. I'm trying to reach Lando Calrissian."

From the seat behind him came a sound that might have been a stifled laugh. "You say something?" he asked over his shoulder.

"No," Leia said innocently. "Just remembering the past."

"Right," Han growled. He remembered, too; and Bespin wasn't on his list of fond memories. "Look, just give Lando a call, will you?" he suggested to the B-wing. "Tell him that an old friend is here, and thought we might play a hand of sabacc for my choice of his stock. Lando will understand."

"We want to *what?*" Leia asked, leaning forward around his chair to give him a startled look.

Han muted the transmitter. "The Imperials might have spies here, too," he reminded her. "If they do, announcing our names to the whole Athega system wouldn't be very smart."

"Point," Leia conceded reluctantly. "That's a pretty strange message, though."

"Not to Lando," Han assured her. "He'll know it's me—provided that middle-level button pusher[1] out there loosens up and sends it in."

Beside him, Chewbacca growled a warning: something big was approaching from aft-starboard. "Any make on it?" Han asked, craning his neck to try to get a look.

The transmitter crackled back to life before the Wookiee could answer. "Unidentified ship, General Calrissian has authorized a special transit waiver for you," the B-wing said, his tone sounding a little disappointed. He'd probably been looking forward to personally kicking the troublemakers out of his system. "Your escort is moving to intercept; hold your current position until he arrives."

"Acknowledged," Han said, not quite able to bring himself to thank the man.

"Escort?" Leia asked cautiously. "Why an escort?"

"That's what you get for going off and doing politics stuff when Lando drops by the Palace for a visit," Han admonished her, still craning his neck. There it was . . . "Nkllon's a superhot planet—way too close to its sun for any normal ship to get to without getting part of its hull peeled off. Hence"—he waved Leia's attention to the right—"the escort."

There was a sharp intake of air from behind him, and even Han, who'd seen Lando's holos of these things, had to admit it was an impressive sight. More than anything else the shieldship resembled a monstrous flying umbrella, a curved dish fully half as big across as an Imperial Star Destroyer. The underside of the dish was ridged with tubes and fins—pumping and storage equipment for the coolant that helped keep the dish from burning up during the trip inward. Where the umbrella's handle would have been was a thick cylindrical pylon, reaching half as far back as

1. There apparently is no paper in the *Star Wars* universe, so the term *paper pusher* is again one of those that needs a little tweaking.

—TZ

the umbrella dish was wide, its far end bristling with huge radiator fins. In the center of the pylon, looking almost like an afterthought, was the tug ship that drove the thing.

"Good skies," Leia murmured, sounding stunned. "And it actually *flies?*"

"Yeah, but not easily," Han told her, watching with a slight trickle of apprehension as the monstrosity moved ever closer to his ship. It didn't have to move all *that* close—the *Falcon* was considerably smaller than the huge container ships the shieldships normally escorted. "Lando told me they had all sorts of trouble getting the things designed properly in the first place, and almost as much trouble teaching people how to fly them."

Leia nodded. "I believe it."

The transmitter crackled again. "Unidentified ship, this is Shieldship Nine. Ready to lock; please transmit your slave circuit code."

"Right," Han muttered under his breath, touching the transmit switch. "Shieldship Nine, we don't have a slave circuit. Just give me your course and we'll stay with you."

There was a moment of silence. "Very well, unidentified ship," the voice said at last—reluctantly, Han thought. "Set your course at two-eight-four; speed, point six sublight."

Without waiting for an acknowledgment, the huge umbrella began to drift off. "Stay with him, Chewie," Han told the copilot. Not that that would be a problem; the *Falcon* was faster and infinitely more maneuverable than anything that size. "Shieldship Nine, what's our ETA for Nkllon?"

"You in a hurry, unidentified ship?"

"How could we be in a hurry, with this wonderful view?" Han asked sarcastically, looking at the underside of the dish that filled pretty much the entire sky. "Yeah, we're in kind of a hurry."

"Sorry to hear that," the other said. "You see, if you had a slave circuit, we could do a quick hyperspace hop inward together and be at Nkllon in maybe an hour. Doing it this way—well, it'll take us about ten."

Han grimaced. "Great."

"We could probably set up a temporary slave circuit," Leia suggested. "Threepio knows the *Falcon*'s computer well enough to do that."

Chewbacca half turned toward her, growling a refusal that left no room for argument, even if Han had been inclined to argue. Which he wasn't. "Chewie's right," he told Leia firmly. "We don't slave this ship to anything. Ever. You copy that, shieldship?"

"Okay by me, unidentified ship," the other said. They all seemed to be taking a perverse pleasure in using that phrase. "I get paid by the hour anyway."

"Fine," Han said. "Let's get to it."

"Sure."

The transmission cut off, and Han poised his hands over the controls. The umbrella was still drifting, but nothing more. "Chewie, has he got his engines off standby yet?"

The Wookiee rumbled a negative.

"What's wrong?" Leia asked, leaning forward again.

"I don't know," Han said, looking around. With the umbrella in the way, there wasn't a lot to see. "I don't like it, though." He tapped the transmitter. "Shieldship Nine, what's the holdup?"

"Not to worry, unidentified ship," the voice came back soothingly. "We've got another craft coming in that also doesn't have a slave circuit, so we're going to take you both in together. No point in tying up two of us, right?"

The hairs on the back of Han's neck began to tingle. Another ship that just happened to be coming into Nkllon the same time they were. "You have an ID on that other ship?" he asked.

The other snorted. "Hey, friend, we don't even have an ID on *you*."

"You're a big help," Han said, muting the transmitter again. "Chewie, you got an approach yet on this guy?"

The Wookiee's reply was short and succinct. And disturbing. "Cute," Han growled. "Real cute."

"I missed that," Leia murmured, looking over his shoulder.

"He's coming in from the far side of the shieldship's central pylon," Han told her grimly, pointing to the inference brackets on the scanner scope. "Keeping it between him and us where we can't see him."

"Is he doing it on purpose?"

"Probably." Han nodded, hitting his restraint release. "Chewie, take over; I'm going to fire up the quads."

He ran back along the cockpit corridor to the central core and headed up the ladder. "Captain Solo," a nervous mechanical voice called after him from the direction of the lounge. "Is something wrong?"

"Probably, Threepio," Han shouted back. "Better strap in."

He got up the ladder, passed through the right-angle gravity discontinuity at the gun well, and dropped himself into the seat.[2] The control board went on with satisfying quickness, as he keyed for power with one hand and grabbed the headset with the other. "Anything yet, Chewie?" he called into his mike.

The other growled a negative: the approaching craft was still completely hidden by the shieldship's pylon. But the inference scope was now giving a distance reading, and from that the Wookiee had been able to compute an upper size limit for the craft. It wasn't very big. "Well, that's something," Han told him, running through his mental list of starship types and trying to figure out what the Empire might be throwing at them that would be that small. Some variety of TIE fighter, maybe? "Stay sharp—this might be a decoy."

The inference scope pinged: the unknown ship was starting to come around the pylon. Han braced himself, fingers resting lightly on the fire controls . . .

2. One of my all-time favorite movie examples of How To Do Technology Right is from *A New Hope*. During the escape from the Death Star, Han and Luke head up and down to the quad lasers. However, by the time they arrive at the gun wells, gravity has turned ninety degrees, which is what allows them to comfortably sit in the gunner seats facing up and down for firing.

This is exactly the way people do things in the real world: if you have gravity plates (or whatever), you adjust and position them to get things arranged the way you want them to be. People do that with pretty much any technology.

It's completely and properly underplayed in the movie, of course. After all, Luke and Han are used to things working this way, so they wouldn't comment on it.

But having appreciated that little touch of cleverness back when the movie came out, I wanted to remind the readers about it here.

—TZ

And with a suddenness that surprised him, the ship burst into sight, rounding the pylon in a twisting spiral. It steadied slightly—

"It's an X-wing," Leia identified it, sounding greatly relieved. "With Republic markings—"

"Hello, strangers," Luke's voice crackled into Han's ear. "Good to see you."

"Uh . . . hi," Han said, stifling the automatic urge to greet Luke by name. Theoretically, they were on a secure frequency, but it was easy enough for anyone with sufficient motivation to get around such formalities. "What are you doing here?"

"I came to see Lando," Luke told him. "Sorry if I startled you. When they told me I'd be going in with an unidentified ship I thought it might be a trap. I wasn't completely sure it was you until a minute ago."

"Ah," Han said, watching as the other ship settled into a parallel course. It was Luke's X-wing, all right.

Or at least, it *looked* like Luke's X-wing. "So," he said casually, swiveling the laser cannons around to target the other. Situated the way it was, the X-wing would have to yaw 90 degrees around before it could fire at them. Unless, of course, it had been modified. "This just a social call, or what?"

"Not really. I found an old gadget that . . . well, I thought Lando might be able to identify it." He hesitated. "I don't think we ought to discuss it out in the open like this. How about you?"

"I don't think we should talk about that, either," Han told him, mind racing. It sounded like Luke, too; but after that near-disastrous decoy attempt on Bpfassh, he wasn't about to take anything for granted. Somehow, they needed to make a positive identification, and fast.

He tapped a switch, cutting himself out of the radio circuit. "Leia, can you tell whether or not that's really Luke out there?"

"I think so," she said slowly. "I'm almost positive it is."

" 'Almost positive' won't cut it, sweetheart," he warned her.

"I know," she said. "Hang on; I've got an idea."

Han cut himself back into the radio circuit. "—said that if I had a slave circuit they could get me in a lot faster," Luke was saying. "A hyperspace jump as close to Nkllon as the gravity well will permit, and then just a few minutes of cover before I'd be in the planetary umbra and could go the rest of the way in on my own."

"Except that X-wings don't come equipped with slave circuits?" Han suggested.

"Right," Luke said, a little dryly. "Some oversight in the design phase, no doubt."

"No doubt," Han echoed, beginning to sweat a little. Whatever Leia was up to, he wished she'd get to it.

"Actually, I'm glad you don't have one," Leia spoke up. "It feels safer traveling in convoy this way. Oh, before I forget, there's someone here who wants to say hello."

"Artoo?" Threepio's prissy voice said tentatively. "Are you there?"

Han's headphone erupted with a blather of electronic beeps and twitters. "Well, I don't *know* where else you might have been," Threepio said stiffly. "From past experience, there are a considerable variety of difficulties you could have gotten yourself into. Certainly without me along to smooth things out for you."

The headphone made a noise that sounded suspiciously like an electronic snort. "Yes, well, you've *always* believed that," Threepio countered, even more stiffly. "I suppose you're entitled to your delusions."

Artoo snorted again; and, smiling tightly to himself, Han keyed off his control board and dropped the lasers back into standby status. He'd known a lot of men, back in his smuggling days, who wouldn't have wanted a wife who could sometimes think faster than they could.

Speaking for himself, Han had long ago decided he wouldn't have it any other way.[3]

3. One of the great and satisfying aspects of *Star Wars* is that no one is deadweight. All of the characters have their chance to shine, to come up with the clever way to think or fight their way out of whatever predicament they happen to be in at the moment.

Maintaining that balance was yet another of the challenges—and fun parts—of writing *Heir*.

—TZ

———◆◆◆———

The shieldship pilot hadn't been exaggerating. It was nearly ten hours later when he finally signaled that they were on their own, made one final not-quite-impolite comment, and pulled off to the side, out of the way.

There wasn't much to see; but then, Han decided, the dark side of an undeveloped planet was seldom very scenic. A homing signal winked at him from one of the scopes, and he made a leisurely turn in the indicated direction.

From behind him came the sound of a footstep. "What's happening?" Leia asked, yawning as she sat down in the copilot's seat.

"We're in Nkllon's shadow," Han told her, nodding toward the starless mass directly ahead of them. "I've got a lock on Lando's mining operation—looks like we'll be there in ten or fifteen minutes."

"Okay." Leia looked off to the side, at the running lights of the X-wing pacing them. "Have you talked with Luke lately?"

"Not for a couple of hours. He said he was going to try and get some sleep. I think Artoo's running the ship at the moment."

"Yes, he is." Leia nodded, with that slightly absent voice she always used when practicing her new Jedi skills. "Luke's not sleeping very well, though. Something's bothering him."

"Something's been bothering him for the past couple of months," Han reminded her. "He'll get over it."

"No, this is something different." Leia shook her head. "Something more—I don't know; more *urgent*, somehow." She turned back to face him. "Winter thought that maybe he'd be willing to talk to you about it."

"Well, he hasn't yet," Han said. "Look, don't worry. When he's ready to talk, he'll talk."

"I suppose so." She peered out of the cockpit at the edge

of the planetary mass they were speeding toward. "Incredible. Do you realize you can actually see part of the solar corona from here?"

"Yeah, well, don't ask me to take you out for a closer look," Han told her. "Those shieldships aren't just for show, you know—the sunlight out there is strong enough to fry every sensor we have in a few seconds and take the *Falcon's* hull off a couple of minutes later."

She shook her head wonderingly. "First Bespin, now Nkllon. Have you ever known Lando when he *wasn't* involved in some kind of crazy scheme?"

"Not very often," Han had to admit. "Though at Bespin, at least, he had a known technology to work with—Cloud City had been running for years before he got hold of it. This"—he nodded out the viewport—"they had to think up pretty much from scratch."

Leia leaned forward. "I think I see the city—that group of lights over there."

Han looked where she was pointing. "Too small," he said. "More likely it's an outrider group of mole miners. Last I heard he had just over a hundred of the things digging stuff out of the surface."

"Those are, what, those asteroid ships we helped him get from Stonehill Industries?"[4]

"No, he's using those in the outer system for tug work," Han corrected. "These are little two-man jobs that look like cones with the points chopped off. They've got a set of plasma-jet drills pointing down around the underside hatch—you just land where you want to drill, fire the jets for a minute or two to chop up the ground, then go on down through the hatch and pick up the pieces."

"Oh, right, I remember those now," Leia nodded. "They were originally asteroid miners, too, weren't they?"

"The style was. Lando found this particular batch being used in a smelting complex somewhere. Instead of just removing the plasma jets, the owners had hauled the things up whole and wedged them into place on the line."

4. Another Tuckerism: the Stonehill Science Fiction Club of Tampa, which puts on the Necronomicon convention every October.

—TZ

"I wonder how Lando got hold of them."

"We probably don't want to know."

The transmitter crackled. "Unidentified ships, this is Nomad City Control," a crisp voice said. "You've been cleared for landing on Platforms Five and Six. Follow the beacon in, and watch out for the bumps."

"Got it," Han said. The *Falcon* was skimming the ground now, the altimeter reading them as just under fifty meters up. Ahead, a low ridge rose to meet them; giving the controls a tap, Han nudged them over it—

And there, directly ahead, was Nomad City.

"Tell me again," he invited Leia, "about Lando and crazy schemes?"

She shook her head wordlessly . . . and even Han, who'd more or less known what to expect, had to admit the view was stunning. Huge, humpbacked, blazing with thousands of lights in the darkside gloom, the mining complex looked like some sort of exotic monstrous living creature as it lumbered its way across the terrain, dwarfing the low ridges over which it walked. Searchlights crisscrossed the area in front of it; a handful of tiny ships buzzed like insect parasites around its back or scuttered across the ground in front of its feet.

It took Han's brain a handful of seconds to resolve the monster into its component parts: the old Dreadnaught Cruiser on top, the forty captured Imperial AT-ATs underneath carrying it across the ground, the shuttles and pilot vehicles moving around and in front of it.

Somehow, knowing what it was didn't make it the least bit less impressive.

The transmitter crackled again. "Unidentified ship," a familiar voice said, "welcome to Nomad City. What's this about playing a hand of sabacc?"

Han grinned lopsidedly. "Hello, Lando. We were just talking about you."

"I'll bet," Lando said wryly. "Probably remarking on my business skills and creativity."

"Something like that," Han told him. "Any special trick involved in landing on that thing?"

"Not really," the other assured them. "We're only going a few kilometers an hour, after all. Is that Luke in the X-wing?"

"Yes, I'm here," Luke put in before Han could answer. "This place is amazing, Lando."

"Wait till you see it from the inside. It's about time you people came to visit, I might add. Are Leia and Chewie with you?"

"We're all here," Leia said.

"It's not exactly a social call," Han warned him. "We need a little help."

"Well, sure," Lando said, with just the slightest bit of hesitation. "Anything I can do. Look, I'm in Project Central at the moment, supervising a difficult dig. I'll have someone meet you on the landing platform and bring you down here. Don't forget there's no air here—make sure you wait for the docking tube to connect before you try popping the hatch."[5]

"Right," Han said. "Make sure your reception committee is someone you can trust."

Another slight pause. "Oh?" Lando asked, casually. "Is there something—?"

He was cut off by a sudden electronic squeal from the transmitter. "What's that?" Leia snapped.

"Someone's jamming us," Han growled, jabbing at the transmitter cutoff. The squealing vanished, leaving an unpleasant ringing in his ears as he keyed for intercom. "Chewie, we've got trouble," he called. "Get up here."

He got an acknowledgment, turned back to the transmitter. "Get us a scan of the area," he told Leia. "See if there's anything coming in."

"Right," Leia said, already working the keys. "What are you going to do?"

"I'm going to find us a clear frequency." He pulled the *Falcon* out of its approach vector, made sure they had an

5. Before he became a full-time novelist, Tim was a grad student shooting for a PhD in physics. Here is just one place where he brings his science background into play. Checking for breathable air is always a good idea before jumping out of your ship on a strange planet.

—BM

open field around them, then turned the transmitter back on, keeping the volume low. There were freq-scanning and mixing tricks that he'd used in the past against this kind of jamming. The question now was whether he was going to have the time to implement them.

Abruptly, much quicker than he'd expected, the squeal dissolved into a voice. "—peating: any ships who can read me, please check in."

"Lando, it's me," Han called. "What's going on?"

"I'm not sure," Lando said, sounding distracted. "It could be just a solar flare scrambling our communications—that happens sometimes. But the pattern here doesn't seem quite right for . . ."

His voice trailed off. "What?" Han demanded.

There was a faint hiss from the speaker, the sound of someone inhaling deeply. "Imperial Star Destroyer," Lando said quietly. "Coming in fast toward the planetary shadow."

Han looked at Leia, saw her face turn to stone as she looked back at him. "They've found us," she whispered.[6]

6. Bestselling writers often use the literary device of the cliffhanger to grip readers. How many times have you stayed up far too late at night because something enthralling happens at the end of a chapter and you simply *have* to find out what happens next? Tim brings the use of the cliffhanger to a high art in *Heir*. I defy anyone to put this book down after a closing line like Leia's.

—BM

CHAPTER 13

"I SEE IT, ARTOO, I see it," Luke soothed. "Let me worry about the Star Destroyer; you just keep trying to find a way through that jamming."

The little droid warbled a nervous-sounding acknowledgment and got back to work. Ahead, the *Millennium Falcon* had pulled out of its landing approach and was swinging back on what looked like an intercept course for the approaching ship. Hoping Han knew what he was doing, Luke keyed the X-wing for attack status and followed. *Leia?* he called silently.

Her response contained no words; but the anger and frustration and quiet fear came through all too clearly. *Hang on, I'm with you,* he told her, putting as much reassurance and confidence into the thought as he could.

A confidence which, he had to admit, he didn't particularly feel. The Star Destroyer itself didn't worry him—if Lando's descriptions of the sunlight's intensity were right, the big ship itself was probably helpless by now, its sensors and maybe even a fair amount of its armament vaporized right off its hull.

But the TIE fighters protected in its hangars weren't so handicapped . . . and as soon as the ship reached Nkllon's shadow, those fighters would be free to launch.

Abruptly, the static cleared. "Luke?"

"I'm here," Luke confirmed. "What's the plan?"

"I was hoping *you'd* have one," the other said dryly. "Looks like we're a little outnumbered here."

"Does Lando have any fighters?"

"He's scrambling what he's got, but he's going to keep them close in to protect the complex. I get the feeling the crews aren't all that experienced."

"Looks like we're the attack front, then," Luke said. A stray memory flicked through his mind: walking into Jabba's palace on Tatooine five years ago, using the Force to befuddle the Gamorrean guards. "Let's try this," he told Han. "I'll run ahead of you, try to confuse or slow down their reflexes as much as I can. You follow right behind me and take them out."

"Sounds as good as we're going to get," Han grunted. "Stay close to the ground; with luck, we'll be able to run some of them into those low ridges."

"But don't get *too* low," Leia warned. "Remember that you're not going to be able to concentrate very much on your flying."

"I can handle both," Luke assured her, giving the instruments one last scan. His first space combat as a full Jedi.[1] Distantly, he wondered if this was how the Jedi of the Old Republic had handled such battles. Or even if they'd fought like this at all.

"Here they come," Han announced. "Out of the hangar and on their way. Looks like . . . probably only one squadron. Overconfident."

"Maybe." Luke frowned at his tactical scope. "What are those other ships with them?"

---

1. This line is undoubtedly out of date now, with the other books that have been written in the gap between *Return of the Jedi* and *Heir*. But it *was* true when I wrote it.

                                    —TZ

"I don't know," Han said slowly. "They're pretty big, though. Could be troop carriers."

"Let's hope not." If this was a full-scale invasion, and not just another hit-and-fade like at Bpfassh ... "You'd better warn Lando."

"Leia's on it. You ready?"

Luke took a deep breath. The TIE fighters had formed into three four-ship groups now, sweeping directly toward them. "I'm ready," he said.

"Okay. Let's do it."

The first group was coming in fast. Half closing his eyes, flying entirely on reflex, Luke reached out with the Force.

It was a strange sensation. Strange, and more than a little unpleasant. To touch another mind with the intent of communication was one thing; to touch that same mind with the intent of deliberately distorting its perception was something else entirely.

He'd had a similar feeling at Jabba's, with those guards, but had put it down then to nervousness about his mission to rescue Han. Now, he realized that there was more to it than that. Perhaps this sort of action—even done purely in self-defense—was dangerously close to the edge of the dark areas where Jedi were forbidden to go.

He wondered why neither Yoda nor Ben had ever told him about this. Wondered what else there was about being a Jedi that he was going to have to discover on his own.

Luke?

Dimly, he felt himself being jammed into his straps as he twitched the X-wing to one side. The voice whispering into his mind ... "Ben?" he called aloud. It didn't sound like Ben Kenobi; but if it wasn't him, then who—?

You will come to me, Luke, the voice said again. *You must come to me. I will await you.*

Who are you? Luke asked, focusing as much of his strength on the contact as he could without risking a crash.

But the other mind was too elusive to track, skittering away like a bubble in a hurricane. *Where are you?*

You will find me. Even as Luke strained, he could feel the contact slipping away. *You will find me . . . and the Jedi shall rise again. Until then, farewell.*

Wait! But the call was fading into nothingness. Clenching his teeth, Luke strained . . . and gradually began to realize that another, more familiar voice was calling his name. "Leia?" he croaked back through a mouth that was inexplicably dry.

"Luke, are you all right?" Leia asked anxiously.

"Sure," he said. His voice sounded better this time. "I'm fine. What's wrong?"

"*You're* what's wrong," Han cut in. "You planning to chase them all the way home?"

Luke blinked, looking around in surprise. The buzzing TIE fighters were gone, leaving nothing but bits of wreckage strewn across the landscape. On his scope, he could see that the Star Destroyer had left Nkllon's shadow again, driving hard away from the planet toward a point far enough out of the gravity well for a lightspeed jump. Beyond it, a pair of miniature suns were approaching: two of Lando's shieldships, belatedly arriving—now that it was too late—to assist in the fight. "It's all over?" he asked stupidly.

"It's all over," Leia assured him. "We got two of the TIE fighters before the rest disengaged and retreated."

"What about the troop carriers?"

"They went back with the fighters," Han said. "We still don't know what they were doing here—we sort of lost track of them during the fight. Didn't look like they ever went very close to the city itself, though."

Luke took a deep breath, glanced at the X-wing's chrono. In and among all of that, he'd somehow lost over half an hour. Half an hour that his internal time sense had no recollection of whatsoever. Could that strange Jedi contact really have lasted that long?

It was something he would have to look into. Very carefully.

On the main bridge screen, showing as little more than a bright spot against Nkllon's dark backdrop, the *Judicator* made its jump to lightspeed. "They're clear, Admiral," Pellaeon announced, looking over at Thrawn.

"Good." The Grand Admiral gave the other displays an almost lazy examination, though there was little to worry about this far out in the Athega system. "So," he said, swiveling his chair around. "Master C'baoth?"

"They fulfilled their mission," C'baoth said, that strangely taut expression on his face again. "They obtained fifty-one of the mole miner machines you sent them for."

"Fifty-one," Thrawn repeated with obvious satisfaction. "Excellent. You had no problem guiding them in and out?"

C'baoth focused his eyes on Thrawn. "They fulfilled their mission," he repeated. "How many times do you intend to ask me the same question?"

"Until I'm sure I have the correct answer," Thrawn replied coolly. "For a while there your face looked as if you were having trouble."

"I had no trouble, Grand Admiral Thrawn," C'baoth said loftily. "What I had was conversation." He paused, a slight smile on his face. "With Luke Skywalker."

"What are you talking about?" Pellaeon snorted. "Current intelligence reports indicate that Skywalker is—"

He broke off at a gesture from Thrawn. "Explain," the Grand Admiral said.

C'baoth nodded toward the display. "He's there right now, Grand Admiral Thrawn. He arrived on Nkllon just ahead of the *Judicator*."[2]

Thrawn's glowing red eyes narrowed. "Skywalker is on Nkllon?" he asked, his voice dangerously quiet.

"In the very center of the battle," C'baoth told him, very clearly enjoying the Grand Admiral's discomfiture.

2. Coincidence is, of course, a necessary part of fiction, and *Star Wars* is no exception. What would have happened, for instance, if Han and Chewie hadn't dropped into that Mos Eisley cantina for a drink?

But unlike the case with most fiction, it can be argued that in *Star Wars* there's an underlying purpose to seemingly random events. The Force may be subtly guiding encounters such as this.

—TZ

"And you said nothing to me?" Thrawn demanded in that same deadly voice.

C'baoth's smile vanished. "I told you before, Grand Admiral Thrawn: you will leave Skywalker alone. *I* will deal with him—in my own time, in my own way. All I require of you is the fulfillment of your promise to take me to Jomark."

For a long moment Thrawn gazed at the Jedi Master, his eyes glowing red slits, his face hard and totally unreadable. Pellaeon held his breath . . . "It's too soon," the Grand Admiral said at last.

C'baoth snorted. "Why? Because you find my talents too useful to give up?"

"Not at all," Thrawn said, his voice icy. "It's a simple matter of efficiency. The rumors of your presence haven't had enough time to spread. Until we can be sure Skywalker will respond, you'll just be wasting your time there."

A strangely dreamy look seeped onto C'baoth's face. "Oh, he'll respond," he said softly. "Trust me, Grand Admiral Thrawn. He *will* respond."

"I always trust you," Thrawn said sardonically. He reached a hand up to stroke the ysalamir draped over his command chair, as if to remind the Jedi Master just how far he trusted him. "At any rate, I suppose it's your own time to waste. Captain Pellaeon, how long will it take to repair the damage to the *Judicator*?"

"Several days at the least, Admiral," Pellaeon told him. "Depending on the damage, it could take as long as three or four weeks."

"All right. We'll go to the rendezvous point, stay with them long enough to make sure repairs are properly under-way, and then take Master C'baoth to Jomark. I trust that will be satisfactory?" he added, looking back at C'baoth.

"Yes." Carefully, C'baoth unfolded himself from his chair and stood up. "I will rest now, Grand Admiral Thrawn. Alert me if you need my assistance."

"Certainly."

Thrawn watched the other wend his way back across the bridge; and as the doors slid solidly shut behind him, the Grand Admiral turned to Pellaeon. Pellaeon braced himself, trying not to wince. "I want a course projection, Captain," Thrawn said, his voice cold but steady. "The most direct line from Nkllon to Jomark, at the best speed a hyperdrive-equipped X-wing could take it."

"Yes, Admiral." Pellaeon signaled to the navigator, who nodded and got busy. "You think he's right about Skywalker going there?"

Thrawn shrugged fractionally. "The Jedi had ways of influencing people, Captain, even over considerable distances. It's possible that even out here he was close enough to Skywalker to plant a suggestion or compulsion. Whether those techniques will work on another Jedi—" He shrugged again. "We'll see."

"Yes, sir." The numbers were starting to track across Pellaeon's display now. "Well, even if Skywalker leaves Nkllon immediately, there won't be any problem getting C'baoth to Jomark ahead of him."

"I knew that much already, Captain," Thrawn said. "What I need is a bit more challenging. We're going to drop C'baoth off on Jomark, then backtrack to a point on Skywalker's projected course. A point at least twenty light-years away, I think."

Pellaeon frowned at him. The expression on Thrawn's face made the back of his neck tingle . . . "I don't understand, sir," he said carefully.

The glowing eyes regarded him thoughtfully. "It's quite simple, Captain. I mean to disabuse our great and glorious Jedi Master of his growing belief that he's indispensable to us."

Pellaeon got it then. "So we wait along Skywalker's projected approach to Jomark and ambush him?"

"Precisely." Thrawn nodded. "At which point we decide whether to capture him for C'baoth"—his eyes hardened— "or simply kill him."

Pellaeon stared at him, feeling his jaw drop. "You promised C'baoth he could have him."

"I'm reconsidering the deal," Thrawn told him coolly. "Skywalker has proved himself to be highly dangerous, and by all accounts has already withstood at least one attempt to turn him. C'baoth should have more success bending Skywalker's sister and her twins to his will."

Pellaeon glanced behind him at the closed doors, reminding himself firmly that there was no way for C'baoth to eavesdrop on their conversation with all the ysalamiri scattered around the *Chimaera*'s bridge. "Perhaps he's looking forward to the challenge, sir," he suggested cautiously.

"There will be many challenges for him to face before the Empire is reestablished. Let him save his talents and cunning for those." Thrawn turned back to his monitors. "At any rate, he'll likely forget all about Skywalker once he has the sister. I expect our Jedi Master's wants and desires will prove to be as erratic as his moods."

Pellaeon thought back. On the matter of Skywalker, at least, C'baoth's desire seemed to have remained remarkably steady. "I respectfully suggest, Admiral, that we still make every possible effort to take Skywalker alive." He had a flash of inspiration—"Particularly since his death might induce C'baoth to leave Jomark and return to Wayland."

Thrawn[3] looked back at him, glowing eyes narrowed. "Interesting point, Captain," he murmured softly. "Interesting point, indeed. You're right, of course. By all means, we must keep him off Wayland. At least until the work on the Spaarti cylinders is finished and we have all the ysalamiri there we're going to need." He smiled tightly. "His reaction to what we're doing there might not be at all pleasant."

"Agreed, sir," Pellaeon said.

Thrawn's lip twitched. "Very well, Captain: I accede to your suggestion." He straightened himself in his seat. "It's time to be going. Prepare the *Chimaera* for lightspeed."

---

3. A small thing that I never would have anticipated, and never even knew before I was invited to a *Star Wars* convention in Munich:

The *thr* combination apparently doesn't exist in German, or so I was told. German *Star Wars* fans therefore have terrific difficulty pronouncing Thrawn's name.

—TZ

Pellaeon turned back to his displays. "Yes, sir. Direct route to the rendezvous point?"

"We'll be making a short detour first. I want you to swing us around the system to the commercial outvector near the shieldship depot and drop some probes to watch for Skywalker's departure. Near-system and farther out." He looked out the viewport in Nkllon's direction. "And who knows? Where Skywalker goes, the *Millennium Falcon* often goes, as well.

"And then we'll have them all."

CHAPTER 14

"FIFTY-ONE," Lando Calrissian growled, throwing a glare at Han and Leia as he paced a convoluted path around the low chairs in the lounge. "Fifty-one of my best reconditioned mole miners. *Fifty-one.* That's almost half my workforce. You realize that?—*half* my workforce."

He dropped down into a chair, but was on his feet again almost immediately, stalking around the room, his black cloak billowing behind him like a tame storm cloud. Leia opened her mouth to offer commiseration, felt Han squeeze her hand warningly. Obviously, Han had seen Lando in this state before. Swallowing back the words, she watched as he continued his caged-animal pacing.

And without obvious warning, it was over. "I'm sorry," he said abruptly, coming to a halt in front of Leia and taking her hand. "I'm neglecting my duties as host, aren't I? Welcome to Nkllon." He raised her hand, kissed it, and waved his free hand toward the lounge window. "So. What do you think of my little enterprise?"

"Impressive," Leia said, and meant it. "How did you ever come up with the idea for this place?"

"Oh, it's been kicking around for years." He shrugged, pulling her gently to her feet and guiding her over to the window, his hand resting against the small of her back. Ever since she and Han had gotten married, Leia had noticed a resurgence of this kind of courtly behavior toward her from Lando—behavior that harkened back to their first meeting at Cloud City. She'd puzzled over that for a while, until she'd noticed that all the attention seemed to annoy Han.

Or, at least, it normally annoyed him. Right now, he didn't even seem to notice.

"I found plans for something similar once in the Cloud City files, dating back to when Lord Ecclessis Figg first built the place," Lando continued, waving a hand toward the window. The horizon rolled gently as the city walked, the motion and view reminding Leia of her handful of experiences aboard sailing ships. "Most of the metal they used came from the hot inner planet, Miser, and even with Ugnaughts doing the mining they had a devil of a time with it. Figg sketched out an idea for a rolling mining center that could stay permanently out of direct sunlight on Miser's dark side. But nothing ever came of it."

"It wasn't practical," Han said, coming up behind Leia. "Miser's terrain was too rough for something on wheels to get across easily."

Lando looked at him in surprise. "How do you know about that?"

Han shook his head distractedly, his eyes searching the landscape and the starry sky above it. "I spent an afternoon going through the Imperial files once, back when you were trying to talk Mon Mothma into helping fund this place. Wanted to make sure someone else hadn't already tried it and found out it didn't work."

"Nice of you to go to that kind of trouble." Lando cocked an eyebrow. "So, what's going on?"

"We should probably wait until Luke gets here to talk about it," Leia suggested quietly before Han could answer.

Lando glanced past Han, as if only just noticing Luke's absence. "Where is he, anyway?"

"He wanted to catch a fast shower and change," Han told him, shifting his attention to a small ore shuttle coming in for a landing. "Those X-wings don't have much in the way of comfort."

"Especially over long trips," Lando agreed, tracing Han's gaze with his eyes. "I've always thought putting a hyperdrive on something that small was a poor idea."

"I'd better see what's keeping him," Han decided suddenly. "You have a comm in this room?"

"It's over there," Lando said, pointing toward a curved wooden bar at one end of the lounge. "Key for central; they'll track him down for you."

"Thanks," Han called over his shoulder, already halfway there.

"It's bad, isn't it?" Lando murmured to Leia, his eyes following Han across the room.

"Bad enough," she admitted. "There's a chance that that Star Destroyer came here looking for me."

For a moment, Lando was silent. "You came here for help." It wasn't a question.

"Yes."

He took a deep breath. "Well . . . I'll do what I can, of course."

"Thank you," Leia said.

"Sure," he said. But his eyes drifted from Han to the window and the activity beyond it, his expression hardening as he did so. Perhaps he was thinking of the last time Han and Leia had come to him for help.

And what giving that help had cost him.

Lando listened to the whole story in silence, then shook his head. "No," he said positively. "If there was a leak, it didn't come from Nkllon."

"How can you be sure of that?" Leia asked.

"Because there's been no bounty offered for you," Lando told her. "We have our fair share of shady people here, but they're all out for profit. None of them would turn you over to the Empire just for the fun of it. Besides, why would the Imperials steal my mole miners if they were after you?"

"Harassment, maybe," Han suggested. "I mean, why steal mole miners anyway?"

"You got me," Lando conceded. "Maybe they're trying to put economic pressure on one of my clients, or maybe they just want to disrupt the New Republic's flow of raw materials generally. Anyway, that's beside the point. The point is that they took the mole miners, and they didn't take you."

"How do you know there's been no bounty offer?" Luke asked from his seat off to the right—a seat, Leia had already noted, where he and his lightsaber would be between his friends and the room's only door. Apparently, he didn't feel any safer here than she did.

"Because I'd have heard about it," Lando said, sounding a little miffed. "Just because I'm respectable doesn't mean I'm out of touch."

"I told you he'd have contacts," Han said with a grimly satisfied nod. "Great. So which of these contacts do you trust, Lando?"

"Well—" Lando broke off as a beep came from his wrist. "Excuse me," he said, sliding a compact comlink from the decorative wristband and flicking it on. "Yes?"

A voice said something, inaudible from where Leia was sitting. "What kind of transmitter?" Lando asked, frowning. The voice said something else. "All right, I'll take care of it. Continue scanning."

He closed down the comlink and replaced it in his wristband. "That was my communications section," he said, looking around the room. "They've picked up a short-range transmitter on a very unusual frequency . . . which appears to be sending from this lounge."

Beside her, Leia felt Han stiffen. "What kind of transmitter?" he demanded.

"This kind, probably," Luke said. Standing up, he pulled a flattened cylinder from his tunic and stepped over to Lando. "I thought you might be able to identify it for me."

Lando took the cylinder, hefted it. "Interesting," he commented, peering closely at the alien script on its surface. "I haven't seen one of these in years. Not this style, anyway. Where'd you get it?"

"It was buried in mud in the middle of a swamp. Artoo was able to pick it up from pretty far away, but he couldn't tell me what it was."

"That's our transmitter, all right." Lando nodded. "Amazing that it's still running."

"What exactly is it transmitting?" Han asked, eyeing the device as if it were a dangerous snake.

"Just a carrier signal," Lando assured him. "And the range is small—well under a planetary radius. Nobody used it to follow Luke here, if that's what you were wondering."

"Do you know what it is?" Luke asked.

"Sure," Lando said, handing it back. "It's an old beckon call.[1] Pre-Clone Wars vintage, from the looks of it."

"A beckon call?" Luke frowned, cupping it in his hand. "You mean like a ship's remote?"

"Right." Lando nodded. "Only a lot more sophisticated. If you had a ship with a full-rig slave system you could tap in a single command on the call and the ship would come straight to you, automatically maneuvering around any obstacles along the way. Some of them would even fight their way through opposing ships, if necessary, with a reasonable degree of skill." He shook his head in memory. "Which could be extremely useful at times."

1. Also echoes the phrase *beck and call.* Karrde isn't the only one who likes puns.

—TZ

Han snorted under his breath. "Tell that to the *Katana* fleet."[2]

"Well, of course you have to build in some safeguards," Lando countered. "But to simply decentralize important ship's functions into dozens or hundreds of droids just creates its own set of problems. The limited jump-slave circuits we use here between transports and shieldships are certainly safe enough."

"Did you use jump-slave circuits on Cloud City, too?" Luke asked. "Artoo said he saw you with one of these right after we got out of there."

"My personal ship was full-rigged," Lando said. "I wanted something I could get at a moment's warning, just in case." His lip twitched. "Vader's people must have found it and shut it down while they were waiting for you, because it sure didn't come when I called it. You say you found it in a *swamp?*"

"Yes." Luke looked at Leia. "On Dagobah."

Leia stared at him. "Dagobah?" she asked. "As in the planet that Dark Jedi from Bpfassh fled to?"

Luke nodded. "That's the place." He fingered the beckon call, an odd expression on his face. "This must have been his."[3]

"It could just as easily have been lost some other time by someone else," Lando pointed out. "Pre-Clone Wars calls could run for a century or more on standby."

"No," Luke said, shaking his head slowly. "It was his, all right. The cave where I found it absolutely tingles with the dark side. I think it must have been the place where he died."[3]

For a long moment they all sat in silence. Leia studied her brother closely, sensing the new tension lying just beneath the surface of his thoughts. Something else, besides the beckon call, must have happened to him on Dagobah. Something that tied in with the new sense of urgency she'd felt on the way in toward Nkllon . . .

Luke looked up sharply, as if sensing the flow of Leia's

2. The *Katana* fleet isn't going to become important until *Dark Force Rising.* But again, it's important to start setting things up as soon as possible.

—TZ

3. The beckon call was originally nothing more than a plot device, something to get Luke to Lando's in time for all of them to have this conversation together. The suggestion that the call had belonged to the Dark Jedi was supposed to be the complete explanation, and so I moved on to other matters and forgot about it.

But not all of the readers bought my explanation. Speculation arose that there was a plot thread lurking in there that I was planning to use somewhere down the line.

The more I thought about that, the more I liked the idea of coming up with a more interesting history for this particular piece of jetsam.

So when I was contracted for the book *The Hand of Thrawn* (which was subsequently split into *Specter of the Past* and *Vision of the Future*), that's exactly what I did.

—TZ

thoughts. "We were talking about Lando's smuggler contacts," he said. The message was clear: this was not the time to ask him about it.

"Right," Han said quickly. Apparently, he'd gotten the hint, too. "I need to know which of your marginally legal friends you can trust."

The other shrugged. "Depends on what you need to trust them with."

Han looked him straight in the eye. "Leia's life."

Seated on Han's other side, Chewbacca growled something that sounded startled. Lando's mouth fell open, just slightly. "You're not serious."

Han nodded, his eyes still locked on Lando's face. "You saw how close the Imperials are breathing down our necks. We need a place to hide her until Ackbar can find out how they're getting their information. She needs to stay in touch with what's happening on Coruscant, which means a diplomatic station we can quietly tap into."

"And a diplomatic station means encrypt codes," Lando said heavily. "And quietly tapping into encrypt codes means finding a slicer."

"A slicer you can trust."

Lando hissed softly between his teeth and slowly shook his head. "I'm sorry, Han, but I don't know any slicers I trust that far."

"Do you know any smuggler groups that have one or two on retainer?" Han persisted.

"That I trust?" Lando pondered. "Not really. The only one who might even come close is a smuggler chief named Talon Karrde—everyone I've talked to says he's extremely honest in his trade dealings."

"Have you ever met him?" Luke asked.

"Once," Lando said. "He struck me as a pretty cold fish—calculating and highly mercenary."

"I've heard of Karrde," Han said. "Been trying for months to contact him, in fact. Dravis—you remember

Dravis?—he told me Karrde's group was probably the biggest one around these days."

"Could be." Lando shrugged. "Unlike Jabba, Karrde doesn't go around flaunting his power and influence. I'm not even sure where his base is, let alone what his loyalties are."

"If he *has* any loyalties," Han grunted; and in his eyes Leia could see the echoes of all those fruitless contacts with smuggling groups who preferred to sit on the political fence. "A lot of them out there don't."

"It's an occupational hazard." Lando rubbed his chin, forehead wrinkled in thought. "I don't know, Han. I'd offer to put the two of you up here, but we just don't have the defenses to stop a really serious attack." He frowned into the distance. "Unless . . . we do something clever."

"Such as?"

"Such as taking a shuttle or living module and burying it underground," Lando said, a gleam coming into his eye. "We put it right by the dawn line, and within a few hours you'd be under direct sunlight. The Imperials wouldn't even be able to find you there, let alone get to you."

Han shook his head. "Too risky. If we ran into any problems, there also wouldn't be any way for anyone to get help to us." Chewbacca pawed at his arm, grunting softly, and Han turned to face the Wookiee.

"It wouldn't be as risky as it looks," Lando said, shifting his attention to Leia. "We should be able to make the capsule itself foolproof—we've done similar things with delicate survey instrument packs without damaging them."

"How long is Nkllon's rotation?" Leia asked. Chewbacca's grunting was getting insistent, but it still wasn't loud enough for her to make out what the discussion was all about.

"Just over ninety standard days," Lando told her.

"Which means we'd be completely out of touch with Coruscant for a minimum of forty-five. Unless you've got a transmitter that would operate on the sunside."

Lando shook his head. "The best we've got would be fried in minutes."

"In that case, I'm afraid—"

She broke off as, beside her, Han cleared his throat. "Chewie has a suggestion," he said, his face and voice a study in mixed feelings.

They all looked at him. "Well?" Leia prompted.

Han's lip twitched. "He says that if you want, he's willing to take you to Kashyyyk."[4]

Leia looked past him to Chewbacca, a strange and not entirely pleasant thrill running through her. "I was under the impression," she said carefully, "that Wookiees discouraged human visitors to their world."

Chewbacca's reply was as mixed as Han's expression. Mixed, but solidly confident. "The Wookiees were friendly enough to humans before the Empire came in and started enslaving them," Han said. "Anyway, it ought to be possible to keep the visit pretty quiet: you, Chewie, the New Republic rep, and a couple of others."

"Except that we're back to the New Republic rep knowing about me," Leia pointed out.

"Yes, but he'll be a Wookiee," Lando pointed out. "If he accepts you under his personal protection, he won't betray you. Period."

Leia studied Han's face. "Sounds good. So tell me why you don't like it."

A muscle in Han's cheek twitched. "Kashyyyk isn't exactly the safest place in the galaxy," he said bluntly. "Especially for non-Wookiees. You'll be living in trees, hundreds of meters above the ground—"

"I'll be with Chewie," she reminded him firmly, suppressing a shiver. She'd heard stories about Kashyyyk's lethal ecology, too. "You've trusted your own life to him often enough."

He shrugged uncomfortably. "This is different."

"Why don't you go with them?" Luke suggested. "Then she'll be doubly protected."

4. The name of the Wookiee home world has always bothered me—from what I've heard of Wookiee speech, I'm not convinced they can actually pronounce the word.

In fact, before I knew the world had already been named, I had planned to call it Rwookrrorro.

When I learned that Kashyyyk was already on the books, I suggested that could be the name the Republic and Empire knew it by, while Rwookrrorro was the local Wookiee name.

I was turned down, probably on the grounds that a planet with two different and completely unconnected names would be confusing.

So instead, we used Rwookrrorro as the name of the specific village Leia would be traveling to.

Interestingly, the name Rwook was later used to denote the subspecies that Chewie and some of the other Wookiees belong to.

—TZ

"Right," Han said sourly. "I was planning to; except that Chewie thinks it'll gain us more time if Leia and I split up. He takes her to Kashyyyk; I fly around in the *Falcon,* pretending she's still with me. Somehow."

Lando nodded. "Makes sense to me."

Leia looked at Luke, the obvious suggestion coming to her lips . . . and dying there unsaid. Something in his face warned her not to ask him to come with them. "Chewie and I will be fine," she said, squeezing Han's hand. "Don't worry."

"I guess that's settled, then," Lando said. "You can use my ship, of course, Chewie. In fact"—he looked thoughtful—"if you want company, Han, maybe I'll come along with you."

Han shrugged, clearly still unhappy with the arrangement. "If you want to, sure."

"Good," Lando said. "We should probably fly out of Nkllon together—I've been planning an offworld purchasing trip for a couple of weeks now, so I've got an excuse to leave. Once we're past the shieldship depot, Chewie and Leia can take my ship and no one'll be the wiser."

"And then Han sends some messages to Coruscant pretending Leia's aboard?" Luke asked.

Lando smiled slyly. "Actually, I think we can do a little bit better than that. You still have Threepio with you?"

"He's helping Artoo run a damage check on the *Falcon,*" Leia told him. "Why?"

"You'll see," Lando said, getting to his feet. "This'll take a little time, but I think it'll be worth it. Come on—let's go talk to my chief programmer."

The chief programmer was a little man with dreamy blue eyes, a thin swath of hair arcing like a gray rainbow from just over his eyebrows to the nape of his neck, and a shiny borg[5] implant wrapped around the back of his head. Luke listened as Lando outlined the procedure and watched

5. I got at least one letter from a reader who took me to task for using *borg,* which he informed me was a *Star Trek* word.

I wrote back and explained that *borg* comes from *cyborg,* which is a contraction of *cybernetic organism* and was coined by Manfred Clynes and Nathan Kline in 1960.

On top of that, the term *borg* was first used in *Star Wars* in 1978 in one of the Marvel Comics adventures, thus predating *Star Trek*'s borg concept by about eleven years.

Not that anyone's counting. Just thought you'd like to know.

—TZ

long enough to make sure it was all going smoothly. Then, quietly, he slipped out, returning to the quarters Lando's people had assigned him.

He was still there an hour later, poring uselessly over what seemed to be an endless stream of star charts, when Leia found him.

"There you are," she said, coming in and glancing at the charts on his display. "We were starting to wonder where you went."

"I had some things to check on," Luke said. "You finished already?"

"My part is," Leia said, pulling a chair over to him and sitting down. "They're working on tailoring the program now. After that it'll be Threepio's turn."

Luke shook his head. "Seems to me the whole thing ought to be simpler than all that."

"Oh, the basic technique is," Leia agreed. "Apparently, the hard part is slipping it past the relevant part of Threepio's watchdog programming without changing his personality in the process." She looked again at the screen. "I was going to ask you if you'd be interested in coming to Kashyyyk with me," she said, her voice trying hard to be casual. "But it looks like you've got somewhere else to go."

Luke winced. "I'm not running out on you, Leia," he insisted, wishing he could truly believe that. "Really I'm not. This is something that in the long run could mean more for you and the twins than anything I could do on Kashyyyk."

"All right," she said, calmly accepting the statement. "Can you at least tell me where you're going?"

"I don't know yet," he confessed. "There's someone out there I have to find, but I'm not sure yet even where to start looking." He hesitated, suddenly aware of how strange and maybe even crazy this was going to sound. But he was going to have to tell them eventually. "He's another Jedi."

She stared at him. "You're not serious."

"Why not?" Luke asked, frowning at her. Her reaction

seemed vaguely wrong, somehow. "It's a big galaxy, you know."

"A galaxy in which you were supposedly the last of the Jedi," she countered. "Isn't that what you said Yoda told you before he died?"

"Yes," he nodded. "But I'm beginning to think he might have been mistaken."

Her eyebrows lifted slightly. "Mistaken? A Jedi Master?"

A memory flashed through Luke's mind: a ghostly Obi-wan, in the middle of the Dagobah swamp, trying to explain his earlier statements about Darth Vader. "Jedi sometimes say things that are misleading," he told her. "And even Jedi Masters aren't omniscient."

He paused, gazing at his sister, wondering how much of this he should tell her. The Empire was far from defeated, and the mysterious Jedi's life might depend on his defense remaining a secret. Leia waited in silence, that concerned expression on her face . . .

"You'll have to keep this to yourself," Luke said at last. "I mean *really* to yourself. I don't even want you to tell Han or Lando, unless it becomes absolutely necessary. They don't have the resistance to interrogation that you do."

Leia shuddered, but her eyes stayed clear. "I understand," she said evenly.

"All right. Did it ever occur to you to wonder why Master Yoda was able to stay hidden from the Emperor and Vader all those years?"

She shrugged. "I suppose I assumed they didn't know he existed."

"Yes, but they should have," Luke pointed out. "They knew *I* existed by my effect on the Force. Why not Yoda?"

"Some kind of mental shielding?"

"Maybe. But I think it's more likely it was because of where he chose to live. Or maybe," he amended, "where events chose for him to live."

A faint smile brushed Leia's lips. "Is this where I finally get to find out where this secret training center of yours was?"

"I didn't want anyone else to know," Luke said, moved by some obscure impulse to try to justify that decision to her. "He was so perfectly hidden—and even after his death I was afraid the Empire might be able to do something—"

He broke off. "Anyway, I can't see that it matters now. Yoda's home was on Dagobah. Practically next door to the dark-side cave where I found that beckon call."

Her eyes widened in surprise, a surprise that faded into understanding. "Dagobah," she murmured, nodding slowly as if a private and long-standing problem had just been resolved. "I've always wondered how that renegade Dark Jedi was finally defeated. It must have been Yoda who . . ." She grimaced.

"Who stopped him," Luke finished for her, a shiver running up his back. His own skirmishes with Darth Vader had been bad enough; a full-scale Force war between Jedi Masters would be terrifying. "And he probably didn't stop him with a lot of time to spare."

"The beckon call was already on standby," Leia remembered. "He must have been getting ready to call his ship."

Luke nodded. "All of which could explain why the cave was so heavy with the dark side. What it *doesn't* explain is why Yoda decided to stay there."

He paused, watching her closely; and a moment later, the understanding came. "The cave shielded him," she breathed. "Just like a pair of positive and negative electric charges close enough together—to a distant observer they look almost like no charge at all."

"I think that's it." Luke nodded again. "And if that's really how Master Yoda stayed hidden, there's no reason why another Jedi couldn't have pulled the same trick."

"I'm sure another Jedi could have," Leia agreed, sounding reluctant. "But I don't think this C'baoth rumor is anywhere near solid enough to chase after."

Luke frowned. "What C'baoth rumor?"

It was Leia's turn to frown. "The story that a Jedi Master named Joruus C'baoth has reemerged from wherever it was he's spent the past few decades." She stared at him. "You hadn't heard it?"

He shook his head. "No."

"But then, how—?"

"Someone called to me, Leia, during the battle this afternoon. In my mind. The way another Jedi would."

For a long moment they just looked at each other. "I don't believe it," Leia said. "I just don't. Where could someone with C'baoth's power and history have hidden for so long? And why?"

"The *why* I don't know," Luke admitted. "As to the *where*—" He nodded toward the display. "That's what I've been looking for. Someplace where a Dark Jedi might once have died." He looked at Leia again. "Do the rumors say where C'baoth is supposed to be?"

"It could be an Imperial trap," Leia warned, her voice abruptly harsh. "The person who called to you could just as easily be a Dark Jedi[6] like Vader, with this C'baoth rumor dangled in front of us to lure you in. Don't forget that Yoda wasn't counting them—both Vader and the Emperor were still alive when he said you were the last Jedi."

"That's a possibility," he conceded. "It could also be just a garbled rumor. But if it's not . . ."

He let the sentence hang, unfinished, in the air between them. There were deep uncertainties in Leia's face and mind, he could see, woven through by equally deep fears for his safety. But even as he watched her he could sense her gain control over both emotions. In those aspects of her training, she was making good progress. "He's on Jomark," she said at last, her voice quiet. "At least according to the rumor Wedge quoted for us."

Luke turned to the display, called up the data on Jomark. There wasn't much there. "Not very populated," he said, glancing over the stats and the limited selection of maps. "Less than three million people, all told. Or at least back when this was compiled," he amended, searching for the publication date. "Doesn't look like anyone's taken of-

6. When Episode IV came out, Vader was described as "Dark Lord of the Sith," but at the time no one knew what that meant. The explanation of *Sith* was far in the future.

Or should that be far in the *past*? It's so hard to keep track of these things sometimes. . . .

—TZ

ficial notice of the planet in fifteen years." He looked back at Leia. "Just the sort of place a Jedi might choose to hide from the Empire."

"You'll be leaving right away?"

He looked at her, swallowing the quick and obvious answer. "No, I'll wait until you and Chewie are ready to go," he said. "That way I can fly out with your shieldship. Give you that much protection, at least."

"Thanks." Taking a deep breath, she stood up. "I hope you know what you're doing."

"So do I," he said frankly. "But whether I do or not, it's something I have to try. That much I know for sure."

Leia's lip twitched. "I suppose that's one of the things I'm going to have to get used to. Letting the Force move me around."

"Don't worry about it," Luke advised her, getting to his feet and switching off the display. "It doesn't happen all at once—you get to ease into it. Come on; let's go see how they're coming with Threepio."

"At last!" Threepio cried, waving his arms in desperate relief as Luke and Leia stepped into the room. "Master Luke! Please, *please* tell General Calrissian that what he intends is a serious violation of my primary programming."

"It'll be okay, Threepio," Luke soothed, stepping over to him. From the front the droid seemed to be just sitting there; it was only as Luke got closer that he could see the maze of wires snaking from both headpiece and dorsal junction box into the computer console behind him. "Lando and his people will be careful that nothing happens to you." He glanced at Lando, got a confirming nod in return.

"But Master Luke—"

"Actually, Threepio," Lando put in, "you could think of this as really just fulfilling your primary programming in a more complete way. I mean, isn't a translation droid supposed to speak for the person he's translating for?"

"I am primarily a protocol droid," Threepio corrected in as frosty a tone as he could probably manage. "And I say again that this is *not* the sort of thing covered by any possible stretch of protocol."

The borg looked up from the panel, nodded. "We're ready," Lando announced, touching a switch. "Give it a second . . . all right. Say something, Threepio."

"Oh, dear," the droid said—

In a perfect imitation of Leia's voice.

Artoo, standing across the room, trilled softly. "That's it," Lando said, looking decidedly pleased with himself. "The perfect decoy"—he inclined his head to Leia—"for the perfect lady."

"This feels decidedly strange," Threepio continued—Leia's voice, this time, in a thoughtful mood.

"Sounds good," Han said, looking around at the others. "We ready to go, then?"

"Give me an hour to log some last-minute instructions," Lando said, starting toward the door. "It'll take our shield-ship that long to get here, anyway."

"We'll meet you at the ship," Han called after him, stepping over to Leia and taking her arm. "Come on—we'd better get back to the *Falcon*."

She put her hand on his, smiling reassuringly up at him. "It'll be all right, Han. Chewie and the other Wookiees will take good care of me."

"They'd better," Han growled, glancing to where the borg was undoing the last of the cables connecting Threepio to the console. "Let's go, Threepio. I can hardly wait to hear what Chewie thinks of your new voice."

"Oh, dear," the droid murmured again. "Oh, *dear*."

Leia shook her head in wonder as they headed for the door. "Do I really," she asked, "sound like that?"

CHAPTER 15

HAN HAD FULLY EXPECTED that they would be attacked during the long shieldship journey out from Nkllon. For once, thankfully, his hunch was wrong. The three ships reached the shieldship depot without incident and made a short hyperspace jump together to the outer fringes of the Athega system. There, Chewbacca and Leia replaced Lando aboard his yacht-style ship, the *Lady Luck*, and started off toward Kashyyyk. Luke waited until they were safely away before securing his X-wing back from defense posture and heading off on some mysterious errand of his own.

Leaving Han alone on the *Falcon* with Lando and Threepio.

"She'll be fine," Lando assured him, punching at the nav computer from the copilot's seat. "She's as safe now as she's ever likely to be. Don't worry."

With an effort, Han turned from the viewport to face him. There was nothing to see out there, anyway—the *Lady Luck* was long gone. "You know, that's almost exactly the same thing you said back on Boordii," he reminded Lando sourly. "That botched dolfrimia run—remember? You said, 'It'll be fine; don't worry about it.' "

Lando chuckled. "Yes, but this time I mean it."

"That's nice to know. So, what do you have planned for entertainment?"

"Well, the first thing we ought to do is have Threepio send off a message to Coruscant," Lando said. "Give the impression that Leia's aboard to any Imperials who might be listening. After that, we could move a couple of systems over and send another message. And after that"—he threw Han a sideways glance—"I thought we might like to do a little sightseeing."

"Sightseeing?" Han echoed suspiciously. Lando was practically glowing with innocence, a look he almost never used except when he was trying to sucker someone into something. "You mean as in flying all over the galaxy looking for replacement mole miners?"

"Han!" Lando protested, looking hurt now. "Are you suggesting I'd stoop so low as to try and con you into helping me run my business?"

"Forgive me," Han said, trying not to sound too sarcastic. "I forgot—you're respectable now. So what sights *are* we going to see?"

"Well . . ." Casually, Lando leaned back and laced his fingers together behind his head. "You mentioned earlier that you hadn't been able to get in touch with Talon Karrde. I thought we might take another crack at it."

Han frowned at him. "You serious?"

"Why not? You want cargo ships, and you want a good slicer. Karrde can supply both."

"I don't need a slicer anymore," Han said. "Leia's as safe now as she's ever likely to be. Remember?"

"Sure—until someone leaks the news that she's there," Lando countered. "I don't think the Wookiees would, but there are non-Wookiee traders flying in and out of Kashyyyk all the time. All it takes is one person spotting her, and you'll be right back where you were when you first got here." He cocked an eyebrow. "And Karrde might also have something on this mysterious Imperial commander who's been running you in circles lately."

The commander who was almost certainly also the man behind the attacks on Leia . . . "You know how to make contact with Karrde?"

"Not directly, but I know how to get to his people. And I thought that as long as we had Threepio and his ump-teen million languages aboard anyway, we'd just go ahead and cut a new contact path."

"That'll take time."

"Not as much as you might think," Lando assured him. "Besides, a new path will cover our trail better—yours and mine both."

Han grimaced, but Lando was right. And with Leia safely hidden away, at least for now, they could afford to play it cautious. "All right," he said. "Assuming we don't wind up playing tag with a Star Destroyer or two."

"Right," Lando agreed soberly. "The last thing we want is to draw the Imperials onto Karrde's tail. We've got enough enemies out there as it is." He tapped the ship's intercom switch. "Threepio? You there?"

"Of course," Leia's voice returned.

"Come on up here," Lando told the droid. "Time for your debut performance."

1. Someone at a convention once suggested to me that, instead of art, Thrawn might do better to study an alien race's myths and legends to get insights into their cultural psyche.

In general, it's an excellent idea. The problem, from Thrawn's point of view, is that he would have to read those legends in translation, which might lose key nuances, or else spend years learning all the associated languages. Their artwork, in contrast, he can study directly, in either physical or holographic form.

—TZ

The command room was filled with sculptures instead of pictures this time: over a hundred of them, lining the walls in holographic niches as well as scattered around the floor on ornate pedestals.[1] The variety, as Pellaeon had come to expect, was astonishing, ranging from human-style chunks of simple stone and wood to others that were more like tethered living creatures than works of art. Each was illuminated by a hazy globe of light, giving sharp contrast to the darkness of the spaces between them. "Admiral?" Pellaeon called uncertainly, trying to see around the artwork and through the gloom.

. "Come in, Captain," Thrawn's coolly modulated voice beckoned. Over at the command chair, just above the hazy white of the Grand Admiral's uniform, two glowing red slits appeared. "You have something?"

"Yes, sir," Pellaeon told him, walking to the console ring and handing a data card over it. "One of our probes in the outer Athega system has picked up Skywalker. *And* his companions."

"*And* his companions," Thrawn echoed thoughtfully. He took the data card, inserted it, and for a minute watched the replay in silence. "Interesting," he murmured. "Interesting, indeed. What's that third ship—the one maneuvering to link with the *Millennium Falcon*'s dorsal hatch?"

"We've tentatively identified it as the *Lady Luck*," Pellaeon said. "Administrator Lando Calrissian's personal ship. One of the other probes copied a transmission stating that Calrissian was leaving Nkllon on a purchasing trip."

"Do we know that Calrissian did, in fact, board the ship at Nkllon?"

"Ah ... no, sir, not for certain. We can try to get that information, though."

"Unnecessary," Thrawn said. "Our enemies are clearly past the stage of such childish tricks." Thrawn pointed to the display, where the *Millennium Falcon* and the *Lady Luck* were now joined together. "Observe, Captain, their strategy. Captain Solo and his wife and probably the Wookiee Chewbacca board their ship on Nkllon, while Calrissian similarly boards his. They fly to the outer Athega system ... and there they make a switch."

Pellaeon frowned. "But we've—"

"*Shh,*" Thrawn cut him off sharply, holding up a finger for silence, his eyes on the display. Pellaeon watched, too, as absolutely nothing happened. After a few minutes the two ships separated, maneuvering carefully away from each other.

"Excellent," Thrawn said, freezing the frame. "Four minutes fifty-three seconds. They're in a hurry, of course, locked together so vulnerably. Which means . . ." His forehead furrowed in concentration, then cleared. "Three people," he said, a touch of satisfaction in his voice. "Three people transferred, in one direction or the other, between those two ships."

"Yes, sir." Pellaeon nodded, wondering how in the Empire the Grand Admiral had figured *that* one out. "At any rate, we know that Leia Organa Solo remained aboard the *Millennium Falcon.*"

"Do we?" Thrawn asked, lazily polite. "Do we indeed?"

"I believe we do, sir, yes," Pellaeon said, quietly insistent. The Grand Admiral hadn't seen the entire playback, after all. "Right after the *Lady Luck* and Skywalker's X-wing left, we intercepted a transmission from her that definitely originated from the *Millennium Falcon.*"

Thrawn shook his head. "A recording," he said, his voice leaving no room for argument. "No; they're cleverer than that. A voiceprint-doctored droid, then—probably Skywalker's Threepio protocol droid. Leia Organa Solo, you see, was one of the two people who left with the *Lady Luck.*"

Pellaeon looked at the display. "I don't understand."

2. Various readers over the years have noted certain similarities between Thrawn and Sherlock Holmes. Here's one of the spots where that kinship comes most clearly into view.

Once my current reading stack gets a little smaller, it'll probably be time for me to pull out my complete Sherlock Holmes collection and start through it again.

—TZ

"Consider the possibilities,"[2] Thrawn said, leaning back in his chair and steepling his fingertips in front of him. "Three people start out aboard the *Millennium Falcon,* one aboard the *Lady Luck.* Three people then transfer. But neither Solo nor Calrissian is the type to turn his ship over to the dubious command of a computer or droid. So each ship must end up with at least one person aboard. You follow so far?"

"Yes, sir," Pellaeon said. "That doesn't tell us who is where, though."

"Patience, Captain," Thrawn interrupted him. "Patience. As you say, the question now is that of the final makeup of the crews. Fortunately, once we know there were three transfers, there are only two possible combinations. Either Solo and Organa Solo are together aboard the *Lady Luck,* or else Organa Solo and the Wookiee are there."

"Unless one of the transfers was a droid," Pellaeon pointed out.

"Unlikely," Thrawn shook his head. "Historically, Solo has never liked droids, nor allowed them to travel aboard his ship except under highly unusual circumstances. Skywalker's droid and its astromech counterpart appear to be the sole exceptions; and thanks to your transmission data, we already know that that droid has remained on the *Millennium Falcon.*"

"Yes, sir," Pellaeon said, not entirely convinced but knowing better than to argue the point. "Shall I put out an alert on the *Lady Luck,* then?"

"That won't be necessary," Thrawn said, and this time the satisfaction came through clearly. "I know exactly where Leia Organa Solo is going."

Pellaeon stared at him. "You're not serious. Sir."[3]

"Perfectly serious, Captain," Thrawn said evenly. "Consider. Solo and Organa Solo have nothing to gain by simply transferring together to the *Lady Luck*—the *Millennium Falcon* is faster and far better defended. This exercise only makes sense if Organa Solo and the Wookiee are together." Thrawn smiled up at Pellaeon. "And given that, there is only one logical place for them to go."

Pellaeon looked at the display, feeling slightly sandbagged. But the Grand Admiral's logic tracked clean. "Kashyyyk?"

"Kashyyyk," Thrawn confirmed. "They know they can't evade our Noghri forever, and so they've decided to surround her with Wookiees. For all the good it will do them."

Pellaeon felt his lip twitch. He'd been aboard one of the ships that had been sent to Kashyyyk to capture Wookiees for the Empire's slave trade. "It may not be as easy as it sounds, Admiral," he cautioned. "Kashyyyk's ecology can best be described as a layered deathtrap. And the Wookiees themselves are extremely capable fighters."

3. Early on, I decided that I was going to use only humans as point-of-view characters. Not because I have a problem with aliens or droids, but because I was afraid that giving those POV segments a truly alien flavor might distract from the flow of the story.

That meant I would never get into Thrawn's skin and see how exactly he thought. Thus Pellaeon's role was expanded from simply Thrawn's second in command to the man through whom Thrawn was to be seen.

To be, in effect, the Dr. Watson to Thrawn's Sherlock Holmes.

—TZ

"So are the Noghri," Thrawn countered coldly. "Now. What of Skywalker?"

"His vector away from Athega was consistent with a course toward Jomark," Pellaeon told him. "Of course, he could easily have altered it once he was out of range of our probes."

"He's going there," Thrawn said, lips twisting in a tight smile. "Our Jedi Master has said so, hasn't he?" The Grand Admiral glanced at the chrono on his display board. "We'll leave for Jomark immediately. How much lead time will we have?"

"A minimum of four days, assuming that Skywalker's X-wing hasn't been overly modified. More than that, depending on how many stopovers he has to make on the way."

"He'll make no stopovers," Thrawn said. "Jedi use a hibernation state for trips of such length. For our purposes, though, four days will be quite adequate."

He straightened in his chair and touched a switch. The command room's lights came back up, the holographic sculptures fading away. "We'll need two more ships," he told Pellaeon. "An Interdictor Cruiser to bring Skywalker out of hyperspace where we want him, and some kind of freighter. An expendable one, preferably."

Pellaeon blinked. "Expendable, sir?"

"Expendable, Captain. We're going to set up the attack as a pure accident—an opportunity that will seem to have arisen while we were investigating a suspicious freighter for Rebellion munitions." He cocked an eyebrow. "That way, you see, we retain the option of turning him over to C'baoth if we choose to do so, without even Skywalker realizing he was actually ambushed."

"Understood, sir," Pellaeon said. "With your permission, I'll get the *Chimaera* underway." He turned to go—

And paused. Halfway across the room, one of the sculptures had not disappeared with the others. Sitting all alone in its globe of light, it slowly writhed on its pedestal like a wave in some bizarre alien ocean. "Yes," Thrawn said from behind him. "That one is indeed real."

"It's . . . very interesting," Pellaeon managed. The sculpture was strangely hypnotic.

"Isn't it?" Thrawn agreed, his voice sounding almost wistful. "It was my one failure, out on the Fringes. The one time when understanding a race's art gave me no insight at all into its psyche. At least not at the time. Now, I believe I'm finally beginning to understand them."

"I'm sure that will prove useful in the future," Pellaeon offered diplomatically.

"I doubt it," Thrawn said, in that same wistful voice. "I wound up destroying their world."[4]

Pellaeon swallowed. "Yes, sir," he said, starting again for the door. He winced only a little as he passed the sculpture.

4. Another mostly throwaway line, put in to remind the reader that, for all his skill and urbanity, Thrawn can be ruthless if and when necessary.

But as I read this again, I find myself intrigued by the possibilities. Somewhere in the future, I may have to tell this particular story.

—TZ

CHAPTER 16

THERE WAS NO DREAMING in the Jedi hibernation trance. No dreaming, no consciousness, virtually no awareness of the outside world. It was very much like a coma, in fact, except for one interesting anomaly: despite the absence of true consciousness, Luke's time sense still somehow managed to function. He didn't understand it, exactly, but it was something he'd learned to recognize and use.

It was that time sense, coupled with Artoo's frantic gurgling in the foggy distance, that was his first hint something was wrong.

"All right, Artoo, I'm awake," he reassured the droid as he worked his way back toward consciousness. Blinking the gummy feeling out of his eyes, he gave the instruments a quick scan. The readings confirmed what his time sense had already told him: the X-wing had come out of hyperspace nearly twenty light-years short of Jomark. The proximity indicator registered two ships practically on top of him ahead, with a third off to one side in the distance. Still blinking, he raised his head for a look.

And with a rush of adrenaline came fully awake. Directly ahead of him was what looked like a light freighter, a blazing overload in its engine section visible through crumpled and half-vaporized hull plates. Beyond it, looming like a dark cliff face, was an Imperial Star Destroyer.

Anger, fear, aggression—the dark side of the Force are they. With an effort, Luke forced down his fear. The freighter was between him and the Star Destroyer; concentrating on their larger prey, the Imperials might not even have noticed his arrival. "Let's get out of here, Artoo," he said, keying the controls back to manual and swinging the X-wing hard around. The etheric rudder whined in protest with the turn—

"Unidentified starfighter," a harsh voice boomed from the speaker. "This is the Imperial Star Destroyer *Chimaera.* Transmit your identification code and state your business."

So much for hoping he wouldn't be noticed. In the distance now, Luke could see what it was that had yanked the X-wing out of hyperspace: the third ship was an Interdictor Cruiser,[1] the Empire's favorite tool for keeping opponents from jumping to lightspeed. Obviously, they'd been lying in wait for the freighter; it was just his bad luck that he'd run across the Interdictor's projected mass shadow and been kicked out of hyperspace along with it.

The freighter. Closing his eyes briefly with concentration, Luke reached out with the Force, trying to discover whether it was a Republic ship, a neutral, or even a pirate that the *Chimaera* had caught. But there was no hint of any life aboard. Either the crew had escaped, or else they'd already been taken prisoner.

Either way, there was nothing Luke could do for them now. "Artoo, find me the nearest edge of that Interdictor's gravity-wave cone," he ordered, throwing the X-wing into

1. The Interdictor Cruiser had been invented by West End Games, keying (I assume) off Admiral Piett's line in *Return of the Jedi* that the Imperial forces at Endor weren't to attack, but merely to keep the Rebel ships from escaping.

Thrawn, typically, would come up with several interesting tactical uses for the ship and its projected gravity well during his campaign against the New Republic.

—TZ

a stomach-churning downward drop that even the acceleration compensator couldn't quite handle. If he could keep the freighter directly between him and the Star Destroyer, he might be able to get out of range before they could bring a tractor beam to bear.

"Unidentified starfighter." The harsh voice was starting to get angry. "I repeat, transmit your identification code or prepare to be detained."

"Should have brought one of Han's false ID codes with me," Luke muttered to himself. "Artoo? Where's that edge estimate?"

The droid beeped, and a diagram appeared on the computer scope. "That far, huh?" Luke murmured. "Well, nothing to do but go for it. Hang on."

"Unidentified starfighter—"

The rest of the harangue was drowned out by the roar of the drive as Luke abruptly kicked the ship to full power. Almost lost in the noise was Artoo's questioning trilling. "No, I want the deflector shields down," Luke shouted back. "We need the extra speed."

He didn't add that if the Star Destroyer was really serious about vaporizing them, the presence or absence of shields wouldn't matter much at this range, anyway. But Artoo probably already knew that.

But if the Imperials didn't seem interested in vaporizing him out of hand, neither were they willing to just let him go. On the rear scope, he could see the Star Destroyer moving up and over the damaged freighter, trying to get clear of its interference.

Luke threw a quick look at the proximity indicator. He was still within tractor beam range, and at their current relative speeds would remain so for the next couple of minutes. What he needed was some way to distract or blind them . . .

"Artoo, I need a fast reprogramming on one of the proton torpedoes," he called. "I want to drop it at zero delta-v, then have it turn around and head straight aft. No sensors or homing codes, either—I want it to go out cold. Can you do that?" There was an affirmative beep. "Good. As soon as it's ready, give me a warning and then let it go."

He turned his attention back to the rear scope, gave the X-wing's course a slight readjustment. With its guidance sensors in their normal active state, the torpedo would be subject to the Star Destroyer's impressive array of jamming equipment; going out cold like this would limit the Imperials' response to trying to shoot it down with laser fire. The flip side of that, of course, was that if it wasn't aimed *very* accurately, it would shoot right past its intended target without even a twitch.

Artoo beeped; and with a slight lurch, the torpedo was away. Luke watched it go, reaching out with the Force to give it a slight realignment tap—

And a second later, with a spectacular multiple flash of sympathetic detonations, the freighter blew up.

Luke looked at the proximity indicator, mentally crossing his fingers. Almost out of range now. If the debris from the freighter could screen off the tractor beam for a few more seconds, they should make it.

Artoo warbled a warning. Luke glanced at the translation, then at the long-range scope, and felt his stomach tighten. Artoo warbled again, more insistently this time. "I see it, Artoo," Luke growled. It was, of course, the obvious tactic for the Imperials to employ. With the freighter no longer of any interest whatsoever, the Interdictor was changing position, swinging around to try to bring its huge gravity field projectors more fully to bear on the escaping X-wing. Luke watched as the cone-shaped field area angled across the scope . . .

"Hang on, Artoo," he called; and, again too abruptly for the compensators to totally negate, he swung the X-wing into a right-angle turn, blasting laterally to their original course.

From behind him came a shocked screech. "Quiet, Artoo, I know what I'm doing," he told the droid. Off to starboard now, the Star Destroyer was belatedly trying to shift its massive bulk, pivoting to track Luke's maneuver . . . and for the first time since the beginning of the encounter, flashes of laser fire began lancing out.

Luke made a quick decision. Speed alone wasn't going to save him now, and a near miss could end the contest right here and now. "Deflectors up, Artoo," he instructed the droid, giving his full attention to his best evasive maneuvering. "Give me a balance between shield power and speed."

Artoo beeped a response, and there was a slight drop in engine noise as the shields began drawing power. They were going slower, but so far the gamble seemed to be working. Caught off balance by Luke's right-angle maneuver, the Interdictor was now rotating in the wrong direction, its gravity beam sweeping across Luke's previous course instead of tracking the current one. Its commander was obviously trying to correct that mistake, but the sheer inertia of the ship's massive gravity generators was on Luke's side. If he could stay out of the Star Destroyer's range for another few seconds, he'd be out of the beam and free to escape to hyperspace. "Stand by for lightspeed," he told Artoo. "Don't worry about direction—we can do a short hop and set things up more carefully once we're clear."

Artoo acknowledged—

And without warning, Luke was slammed hard against his harness.

The Star Destroyer's tractor beam had them.

Artoo shrilled in dismay; but Luke had no time to comfort the droid now. His straight-line course had suddenly become an arc, a sort of pseudoorbit with the Star Destroyer playing the role of planet at its center. Unlike a true orbit, though, this one wasn't stable, and as soon as the Imperials got another beam focused on him, the circle would quickly degenerate into a tight inward spiral. A spiral whose end point would be inside the Star Destroyer's hangar bay.

He dropped the shields, throwing full power once again to the drive, knowing full well it was most likely a futile gesture. And he was right—for a second the beam seemed to falter, but it quickly caught back up with him. Such a relatively minor change in speed was too small to foul up the beam's tracking equipment.

But if he could find a way to arrange a more major change in speed . . .

"Unidentified starfighter." The harsh voice was back, unmistakably gloating this time. "You have no chance of escape; further efforts will merely damage your vehicle. You are ordered to power down and prepare to dock."

Luke clenched his teeth. This was going to be dangerous, but he'd run out of choices. And he *had* heard stories of this working at least once before. Somewhere. "Artoo, we're going to try something tricky," he called to the droid. "On my signal, I want you to reverse-trigger the acceleration compensator—full power, and bypass the cutoffs if you have to." Something warbled from the control panel, and he risked a quick look at the scope. His curving arc had brought him right to the edge of the Interdictor's gravity projection. "Artoo: *now.*"

And with a scream of horribly stressed electronics, the X-wing came to a sudden dead stop.

There wasn't even enough time for Luke to wonder what aboard his ship could possibly have made a scream like that before he was again thrown, even harder this time, against his harness. His thumbs, ready on the firing buttons, jabbed down hard, sending a pair of proton torpedoes lancing forward; simultaneously, he pulled the X-wing upward. The Star Destroyer's tractor beam, tracking him along his path, had momentarily gotten lost by his sudden maneuver. If the computers guiding that lock would now be considerate enough to latch on to the proton torpedoes instead of him—

And suddenly the torpedoes were gone, leaving behind only a wisp of their exhaust trail to show that they'd been

snatched off their original course. The gamble had succeeded; the Star Destroyer was now steadily pulling in the
wrong target.

"We're free!" he snapped to Artoo, throwing full power
to the drive. "Get ready for lightspeed."

The droid trilled something, but Luke had no time to
look down at the computer scope for the translation. Realizing their error, and recognizing there was insufficient
time to reestablish a tractor lock, the Imperials had apparently decided to go for a straight kill. All the Star Destroyer's batteries seemed to open up at once, and Luke suddenly
found himself trying to dodge a virtual sandstorm of laser
fire. Forcing himself to relax, he let the Force flow through
him, allowing it to guide his hands on the controls the way
it did his lightsaber. The ship jumped once as a shot got
through; in his peripheral vision he saw the tip of his dor-
sal/starboard laser cannon flash and disappear into a
cloud of superheated plasma. A near miss burned past
overhead; another, closer, scorched a line across the
transparisteel canopy.

Another warble came from the scope: they were clear of
the Interdictor's gravity shadow. "Go!" Luke shouted to
Artoo.

And with a second, even more nerve-wrenching electronic scream from behind him, the sky ahead abruptly
turned to starlines.

They'd made it.

For what seemed like a small eternity Thrawn gazed out
the viewport, staring at the spot where Skywalker's X-wing
had been when it had vanished. Surreptitiously, Pellaeon
watched him, wondering tautly when the inevitable explosion would come. With half an ear he listened to the damage control reports coming from the Number Four tractor
beam projector, carefully not getting himself involved
with the cleanup.

The destruction of one of the *Chimaera*'s ten projectors was a relatively minor loss. Skywalker's escape was not.

Thrawn stirred and turned around. Pellaeon tensed— "Come with me, Captain," the Grand Admiral said quietly, striding away down the bridge command walkway.

"Yes, sir," Pellaeon murmured, falling into step behind him, the stories of how Darth Vader had dealt with subordinates' failures running through his mind.

The bridge was uncommonly quiet as Thrawn led the way to the aft stairway and descended into the starboard crew pit. He walked past the crewers at their consoles, past the officers standing painfully erect behind them, and came to a halt at the control station for the starboard tractor beams. "Your name," he said, his voice excruciatingly calm.

"Cris Pieterson, sir," the young man seated at the console answered, his eyes wary.

"You were in charge of the tractor beam during our engagement with the starfighter." It was a statement, not a question.

"Yes, sir—but what happened wasn't my fault."

Thrawn's eyebrows arched, just a bit. "Explain."

Pieterson started to gesture to the side, changed his mind in midmotion. "The target did something with his acceleration compensator that killed his velocity vector—"

"I'm aware of the facts," Thrawn cut in. "I'm waiting to hear why his escape wasn't your fault."

"I was never properly trained for such an occurrence, sir," Pieterson said, a flicker of defiance touching his eyes. "The computer lost the lock, but seemed to pick it up again right away. There was no way for me to know it had really picked up something else until—"

"Until the proton torpedoes detonated against the projector?"

Pieterson held his gaze evenly. "Yes, sir."

For a long moment Thrawn studied him. "Who is your officer?" he asked at last.

Pieterson's eyes shifted to the right. "Ensign Colclazure, sir."

Slowly, deliberately, Thrawn turned to the tall man standing rigidly at attention with his back to the walkway. "You are in charge of this man?"

Colclazure swallowed visibly. "Yes, sir," he said.

"Was his training also your responsibility?"

"Yes, sir," Colclazure said again.

"Did you, during that training, run through any scenarios similar to what just happened?"

"I . . . don't remember, sir," the ensign admitted. "The standard training package *does* include scenarios concerning loss of lock and subsequent reestablishment confirmation."

Thrawn threw a brief glance back down at Pieterson. "Did you recruit him as well, Ensign?"

"No, sir. He was a conscript."

"Does that make him less worthy of your training time than a normal enlistee?"

"No, sir." Colclazure's eyes flicked to Pieterson. "I've always tried to treat my subordinates equally."

"I see." Thrawn considered for a moment, then half turned to look past Pellaeon's shoulder. "Rukh."

Pellaeon started as Rukh brushed silently past him; he hadn't realized the Noghri had followed them down. Thrawn waited until Rukh was standing at his side, then turned back to Colclazure. "Do you know the difference between an error and a mistake, Ensign?"

The entire bridge had gone deathly still. Colclazure swallowed again, his face starting to go pale. "No, sir."

"Anyone can make an error, Ensign. But that error doesn't become a mistake until you refuse to correct it." He raised a finger—

And, almost lazily, pointed.

Pellaeon never even saw Rukh move. Pieterson certainly never had time to scream.

From farther down the crew pit came the sound of

someone trying valiantly not to be sick. Thrawn glanced over Pellaeon's shoulder again and gestured, and the silence was further broken by the sound of a pair of stormtroopers coming forward. "Dispose of it," the Grand Admiral ordered them, turning away from Pieterson's crumpled body and pinning Colclazure[2] with a stare. "The error, Ensign," he told the other softly, "has now been corrected. You may begin training a replacement."

He held Colclazure's eyes another heartbeat. Then, seemingly oblivious to the tension around him, he turned back to Pellaeon. "I want a full technical/tactical readout on the last few seconds of that encounter, Captain," he said, all calm business again. "I'm particularly interested in his lightspeed vector."

"I have it all here, sir," a lieutenant spoke up a bit hesitantly, stepping forward to offer the Grand Admiral a data pad.

"Thank you." Thrawn glanced at it briefly, handed it to Pellaeon. "We'll have him, Captain," he said, starting back down the crew pit toward the stairway. "Very soon now, we'll have him."

"Yes, sir," Pellaeon agreed cautiously, hurrying to catch up with the other. "I'm sure it's just a matter of time."

Thrawn raised an eyebrow. "You misunderstand me," he said mildly. "I mean that literally. He's out there right now, not very far away. And"—he smiled slyly at Pellaeon—"he's helpless."

Pellaeon frowned. "I don't understand, sir."

"That maneuver he used has an interesting side effect I suspect he didn't know about," the Grand Admiral explained. "Backfiring an acceleration compensator like that does severe damage to the adjoining hyperdrive. A light-year away, no farther, and it will fail completely. All we have to do is make a search along that vector, or persuade others to do our searching for us, and he'll be ours. You follow?"

"Yes, sir," Pellaeon said. "Shall I contact the rest of the fleet?"

2. Two more Tuckerizations, only these two were charity auction winners. Chris Peterson won the chance to be in my next book, and Brian Colclazure won the decision of whether Peterson lived or died. Since Peterson's death was his decision, I figured it might as well also be his fault.

At the time of the auction they had no idea (nor did I) that my "next book" would be *Heir*. I hope they were both surprised and pleased with their appearances.

—TZ

Thrawn shook his head. "Preparing for the Sluis Van attack is the fleet's top priority at the moment. No, I think we'll subcontract this one out. I want you to send messages to all the major smuggling chiefs whose groups operate in this area—Brasck, Karrde, Par'tah,[3] any others we have on file. Use their private frequencies and encrypt codes—a little reminder of how much we know about each of them should help ensure their cooperation. Give them Skywalker's hyperspace vector and offer a bounty of thirty thousand for his capture."

"Yes, sir." Pellaeon glanced back down the crew pit, at the activity still going on around the tractor beam station. "Sir, if you knew that Skywalker's escape was only temporary . . . ?"

"The Empire is at war, Captain," the Grand Admiral said, his voice cold. "We cannot afford the luxury of men whose minds are so limited they cannot adapt to unexpected situations."

He looked significantly at Rukh, then turned those glowing eyes back on Pellaeon. "Carry out your orders, Captain. Skywalker *will* be ours. Alive . . . or otherwise."

3. Brasck and Par'tah, mentioned here, will make important appearances in *The Last Command*.

—TZ

CHAPTER 17

IN FRONT OF LUKE, the scopes and displays glowed softly as the diagnostic messages, most of them bordered in red, scrolled past. Beyond the displays, through the canopy, he could see the X-wing's nose, lit faintly by the sheen of distant starlight. Beyond that were the stars themselves, blazing all around him with cold brilliance.

And that was all. No sun, no planets, no asteroids, no cometary bodies. No warships, transports, satellites, or probes. Nothing. He and Artoo were stranded, very literally, in the middle of nowhere.

The computer's diagnostic package came to an end. "Artoo?" he called. "What've you got?"

From behind him came a distinctly mournful electronic moan, and the droid's reply appeared on the computer scope. "That bad, huh?"

Artoo moaned again, and the computer's summary was replaced by the droid's own assessment of their situation.

It wasn't good. Luke's reverse-triggering of the acceleration compensator had caused an unanticipated feedback surge into both hyperdrive motivators—not enough to fry them on the spot, but scorching them badly enough to cause sudden failure ten minutes into their escape. At the Point Four the ship had been doing at the time, that translated into approximately half a light-year of distance. Just for good measure, the same power surge had also completely crystallized the subspace radio antenna.

"In other words," Luke said, "we can't leave, we aren't likely to be found, and we can't call for help. Does that about sum it up?"

Artoo beeped an addition. "Right." Luke sighed. "And we can't stay here. Not for long, anyway."

Luke rubbed a hand across his chin, forcing back the sense of dread gnawing at him. Giving in to fear would only rob him of the ability to think, and that was the last thing he could afford to lose at this point. "All right," he said slowly. "Try this. We take the hyperdrive motivators off both engines and see if we can salvage enough components to put together a single functional one. If we can, we remount it somewhere in the middle of the aft fuselage where it can handle both engines. Maybe where the S-Foil servo actuator[1] is now—we don't need that to get home. Possible?"

Artoo whistled thoughtfully. "I'm not asking if it'll be easy," Luke said patiently as the droid's response came up. "Just if it would be possible."

Another whistle, another pessimistic message. "Well, let's give it a try anyway," Luke told him, unstrapping his restraints and trying to wriggle around in the cramped confines of the cockpit. If he pulled off the back of the ejection seat, he would be able to get into the cargo compartment and the tools stored there.

Artoo warbled something else. "Don't worry, I'm not going to get stuck," Luke assured him, changing his mind and reaching for the in-cockpit pouches instead. The gloves and helmet seals for his flight suit were stored there; it'd be just as easy at this point to gear himself for vacuum

1. West End Games's source material included a splendid X-wing schematic, with all the cool tech stuff a writer could ever ask for.

—TZ

and then get into the cargo compartment through its underside hatch. "If you want to be helpful, you might pull up the maintenance specs and find out exactly how I go about getting one of those motivators out. And cheer up, will you? You're starting to sound like Threepio."

Artoo was still jabbering indignantly over that characterization when the last of Luke's helmet seals cut off the sound. But he *did* sound less frightened.

It took nearly two hours for Luke to get past all the other cables and tubing in the way and remove the port engine hyperdrive motivator from its socket.

It took less than a minute more to discover that Artoo's earlier pessimism had been justified.

"It's riddled with cracks," Luke told the droid grimly, turning the bulky box over in his hands. "The whole shield casing. Just hairlines, really—you can barely see some of them. But they run most of the length of the sides."

Artoo gave a soft gurgle, a comment which required no translation. Luke hadn't done a lot of X-wing maintenance, but he knew enough to recognize that without an intact superconducting shield, a hyperdrive motivator was little more than a box of interconnected spare parts. "Let's not give up yet," he reminded Artoo. "If the other motivator's casing is all right we may still be in business."

Collecting his tool kit, feeling inordinately clumsy in zero-gee freefall, he made his way under the X-wing's fuselage to the starboard engine. It took only a few minutes to remove the proper access cover and tie back some of the interfering cables. Then, trying to get both his faceplate and his glow rod together in the opening without blinding himself, he peered inside.

A careful look at the motivator casing showed that there was no need to continue the operation.

For a long moment he just hung there, one knee bumping gently against the power surge vent, wondering what in the name of the Force they were going to do now. His X-wing, so sturdy and secure in even the thick of combat, seemed now to be little more than a terribly fragile thread by which his life was hanging.

He looked around him—looked at the emptiness and the distant stars—and as he did so, the vague sense of falling that always accompanied zero-gee came flooding back in on him. A memory flashed: hanging from the underside of Cloud City, weak from fear and the shock of losing his right hand, wondering how long he would have the strength to hang on. *Leia,* he called silently, putting all the power of his new Jedi skill into the effort. *Leia, hear me. Answer me.*

There was no answer except for the echoing of the call through Luke's own mind. But then, he hadn't expected one. Leia was long gone, safe on Kashyyyk by now, under the protection of Chewbacca and a whole planet of Wookiees.

He wondered if she'd ever find out what had happened to him.

For the Jedi, there is no emotion; there is peace. Luke took a deep breath, forcing back the black thoughts. No, he would not give up. And if the hyperdrive couldn't be fixed . . . well, perhaps there was something else they could try. "I'm coming in, Artoo," he announced, replacing the access panel and again collecting his tools. "While you're waiting, I want you to pull everything we've got on the subspace radio antenna."

Artoo had the data assembled by the time Luke got the cockpit canopy sealed over him again. Like the hyperdrive data, it wasn't especially encouraging. Made of ten kilometers of ultrathin superconducting wire wound tightly around a U-shaped core, a subspace radio antenna wasn't something that was supposed to be field-repairable.

But then, Luke wasn't the average X-wing pilot, either.

"All right, here's what we're going to do," he told the droid slowly. "The antenna's outer wiring is useless, but it doesn't look like the core itself was damaged. If we can find ten kilometers of superconducting wire somewhere else on the ship, we should be able to make ourselves a new one. Right?"

Artoo thought about that, gurgled an answer. "Oh, come on now," Luke admonished him. "You mean to tell me you can't do what some nonintelligent wire-wrapping machine does all day?"

The droid's beeping response sounded decidedly indignant. The translation that scrolled across the computer scope was even more so. "Well, then, there's no problem," Luke said, suppressing a smile. "I'd guess either the repulsorlift drive or else the sensor jammer will have all the wire we need. Check on that, will you?"

There was a pause, and Artoo quietly whistled something. "Yes, I know what the life support's limitations are," Luke agreed. "That's why you'll be the one doing all the wiring. I'm going to have to spend most of the time back in hibernation trance."

Another series of whistles. "Don't worry about it," Luke assured him. "As long as I come up every few days for food and water, hibernation is perfectly safe. You've seen me do it a dozen times, remember? Now get busy and run those checks."

Neither of the two components had quite the length of wiring they needed, but after poking around a little in the more esoteric sections of his technical memory, Artoo came to the conclusion that the eight kilometers available in the sensor jammer should be adequate to create at least a low-efficiency antenna. He conceded, however, that there was no way to know for sure until they actually tried it.

It was another hour's work for Luke to get the jammer and antenna out of the ship, strip the ruined wire off the core of the latter, and move everything to the upper aft fuselage where Artoo's two graspers could reach it. Jury-rigging a framework to feed the wire and protect it from snagging took another hour, and he took a half hour more to watch the operation from inside to make sure it was going smoothly.

At which point there was nothing left for him to do.

"Now, don't forget," he warned the droid as he settled himself as comfortably into the cockpit seat as possible. "If anything goes wrong—or you even *think* something's about to go wrong—you go ahead and wake me up. Got that?"

Artoo whistled his assurances. "All right," Luke said, more to himself than to the droid. "I guess this is it, then."[2]

He took a deep breath, letting his gaze sweep one last time across the starry sky. If this didn't work . . . But there was no point in worrying about that now. He'd done all he could for the moment. It was time now for him to draw upon inner peace, and to entrust his fate to Artoo.

To Artoo . . . and to the Force.

He took another deep breath. *Leia,* he called, uselessly, one last time. Then, turning his mind and thoughts inward, he began to slow his heart.

The last thing he remembered before the darkness took him was the odd sense that someone, somewhere, had in fact heard that final call. . . .

Leia . . .

Leia jerked awake. "Luke?" she called, propping herself up on one elbow and peering into the dimness surrounding her. She could have sworn she'd heard his voice. His voice, or perhaps the touch of his mind.

But there was no one. Nothing but the cramped space of the *Lady Luck*'s main cabin and the pounding of her own heart and the familiar background sounds of a ship in flight. And, a dozen meters away in the cockpit, the unmistakable sense of Chewbacca's presence. And as she woke further, she remembered that Luke was hundreds of light-years away.

It must have been a dream.

2. It's always important that the heroes have a plan for getting out of whatever trouble the writer has thrown them into. Even if the plan is never used, or isn't used the way the character expected, heroes need to be proactive. Luke can't just sit around hoping that by some stroke of luck he'll be rescued.

Well, okay—technically, he *is* just sitting around right now. But you know what I mean.

—TZ

With a sigh, she lay back down. But even as she did so, she heard the subtle change in sound and vibration pattern as the main sublight drive shut down and the repulsorlift kicked in. Listening closer, she could hear the faint sound of air rushing past the hull.

Slightly ahead of schedule, they were coming in to Kashyyyk.

She got out of bed and found her clothes, feeling her quiet misgivings gnawing with renewed force as she got dressed. Han and Chewbacca could make all the reassuring noises they wanted, but she'd read the diplomatic reports, and she knew full well how strong the undercurrent of resentment was that the Wookiees still harbored toward humans. Whether her status as a member of the New Republic hierarchy would make up for that was, in her view, entirely problematical.

Especially given her chronic difficulty in understanding their language.

The thought made her wince, and not for the first time since leaving Nkllon, she wished she'd had Lando use some other droid for his little voice-matching trick. Having Threepio and his seven-million-language translator along would have made this whole thing so much less awkward.

The *Lady Luck* was already deep into the atmosphere by the time she arrived in the cockpit, skimming low over a surprisingly flat layer of clouds and making smooth curves around the treetops that were occasionally visible poking through them. She remembered when she'd first come across a reference to the size of Kashyyyk's trees; she'd had a full-blown argument with the Senate librarian at the time about how the government could not afford to have its records data shot through with such clearly absurd errors. Even now, with them right in front of her, she found the things hard to believe. "Is that size typical for *wroshyr* trees?" she asked Chewbacca as she slipped into the seat beside him.

Chewbacca growled a negative: the ones visible above the clouds were probably half a kilometer taller than the average. "They're the ones you put nursery rings on, then." Leia nodded.

He looked at her, and even with her limited ability to read Wookiee faces his surprise was quite evident. "Don't look so shocked," she admonished him with a smile. "Some of us humans know a little about Wookiee culture. We aren't *all* ignorant savages, you know."

For a moment he just stared at her. Then, with an urf-urf-urf of laughter, he turned back to the controls.

Ahead and to the right, a tighter group of the extra-tall *wroshyr* trees had come into view. Chewbacca turned the *Lady Luck* toward it, and within a few minutes they were close enough for Leia to see the network of cables or thin branches linking them together just above cloud height. Chewbacca circled the ship partway around, bringing it within the perimeter; and then, with just a growl of warning, dropped sharply down into the clouds.

Leia grimaced. She'd never really liked flying blind, especially in an area crowded with obstacles the size of *wroshyr* trees. But almost before the *Lady Luck* was completely enveloped by the thick white fog they were clear of it again. Immediately below them was another cloud layer. Chewbacca dropped them into that one, too, and drove through it to clear air again—

Leia inhaled sharply. Filling the entire gap between the group of massive trees, apparently hanging suspended in midair, was a city.

Not just a collection of primitive huts and fires like the Ewok tree villages on Endor. This was a real, genuine city, stretching out over a square kilometer or more of space. Even from this distance she could see that the buildings were large and complex, some of them two or three stories high, and that the avenues between them were straight and carefully laid out. The huge boles of the trees poked up around and, in some places, through the city, giving the illusion of giant brown columns supporting a rooftop of clouds. Surrounding the city on all sides, strangely colored searchlight beams lanced outward.[3]

Beside her, Chewbacca rumbled a question. "No, I've never even seen holos of a Wookiee village," she breathed. "My loss, obviously." They were getting closer now; close enough for her to see that the Cloud City–type unipod she'd expected was nowhere to be seen.

For that matter, there was no support of *any* kind visible. Was the whole city being held up by repulsorlifts?

The *Lady Luck* banked slightly to the left. Directly ahead of them now, at one edge of the city and a little above it, was a circular platform rimmed with landing lights. The platform seemed to be sticking straight out from one of the trees, and it took a few seconds for her to realize that the whole thing was nothing more or less than the remnant of a huge limb that had been horizontally cut off near the trunk.

A not insignificant engineering feat. Dimly, she wondered how they'd disposed of the rest of the limb.

The platform didn't look nearly big enough to accommodate a ship the size of the *Lady Luck,* but a quick glance back at the city itself showed that the apparent smallness was merely a trick of the tree's deceptive scale.[4] By the time Chewbacca put them down on the fire-blackened wood, in fact, it was clear that the platform could not only easily handle the *Lady Luck,* but probably full-sized passenger liners, as well.

Or, for that matter, Imperial Strike Cruisers. Perhaps, Leia decided, she shouldn't inquire too deeply into the circumstances of the platform's construction.

She had half expected the Wookiees to send a delegation out to meet her, and she turned out to have been half right. Two of the giant aliens were waiting beside the *Lady Luck* as Chewbacca lowered the entry ramp, indistinguishable to her untrained eye except for their slightly different heights and the noticeably different designs of the wide

3. This was the description of Kashyyyk that I was given: immensely tall trees with Wookiee cities perched on them, with a layered ecology that got more and more vicious as you traveled down toward the ground below. Sort of an organic version of the tall, layered cityscape of Coruscant, now that I think about it.

I was really looking forward to getting a glimpse of that world when I heard it would be featured in *Revenge of the Sith.* I was also curious as to the kind of tactics the Wookiees would use against the Separatist forces on such a battlefield. But either the planet had been redesigned when I wasn't looking, or else George simply chose to use a ground-level area of the world for that scene.

Maybe someday in a special edition . . .

—TZ

4. I got to experience this same effect on a recent cruise to Alaska. When looking over the rail at a glacier, with no trees, animals, or other objects near the ice to show scale, it was impossible for me to get a genuine feel for the size of what I was seeing. A chunk that Looks like an ice cube falls off, and a boom rolls

(cont.)
across the water, and you realize that the "ice cube" was probably the size of a refrigerator.

—TZ

5. I generally like to use brackets when I'm showing that a character is speaking in an alien language. It's always seemed to me that an odd touch like that helps add to the alienness of the speech.

—TZ

6. Just in case the brackets weren't enough alienness, I also threw in an extra letter at the end of r-ending words.
  This is the sort of thing that drives copy editors crazy . . .

—TZ

7. I needed to be able to have actual conversations with one of the Wookiees, and since I'd committed myself to never directly translating Chewie (it was never done in the movies), I came up with this idea that a "speech impediment" actually made

baldrics curving from shoulder to waist across their brown fur. The taller of the two, his baldric composed of gold-threaded tan, took a step forward as Leia headed down the ramp. She continued toward him, using all the calming Jedi techniques she knew, praying that this wouldn't be as awkward as she was very much afraid it would be. Chewbacca was hard enough for her to understand, and he'd been living out among humans for decades. A native Wookiee, speaking a native dialect, was likely to be totally incomprehensible.

The tall Wookiee bowed his head slightly and opened his mouth. Leia braced herself—

[I to you, Leiaorganasolo, bring greetings,] he roared. [I to Rwookrrorro welcome you.][5]

Leia felt her jaw drop in astonishment. "Ah . . . thank you," she managed. "I'm—ah—honored to be here."

[As we by yourr presence arre honored,] he growled politely. [I am Ralrracheen. You may find it easierr to call me Ralrra.][6]

"I'm honored to meet you," Leia nodded, still feeling a little dazed by it all. Apart from the odd extended growling of his final *r* sounds, Ralrra's Wookiee speech was perfectly understandable. Listening to him, in fact, it was as if all the static she'd always had to plow through had suddenly cleared away. She could feel her face warming, and hoped her surprise didn't show.

Apparently, it did. Beside her, Chewbacca was urf-urf-urfing quietly again. "Let me guess," she suggested dryly, looking up at him. "You've had a speech impediment all these years and never thought to mention it to me?"

Chewbacca laughed even louder. [Chewbacca speaks most excellently,] Ralrra told her. [It is I who has a speech impediment. Strangely, it is the kind of trouble that humans find easierr to understand.][7]

"I see," Leia said, though she didn't entirely. "Were you an ambassador, then?"

Abruptly, the air around her seemed to grow chilly. [I

STAR WARS: HEIR TO THE EMPIRE   203

was a slave to the Empirre,] Ralrra growled softly. [As was
Chewbacca also, beforre Hansolo freed him. My captorrs
found me useful, to speak with the otherr Wookiee slaves.]

Leia shivered. "I'm sorry," was all she could think of to
say.

[You must not be,] he insisted. [My role gave me much
information about the Empirre's forces. Information that
proved useful when yourr Alliance freed us.]

Abruptly, Leia realized that Chewbacca was no longer
standing at her side. To her shock, she saw that he was
locked in a death grip with the other Wookiee, his bowcaster trapped uselessly against his shoulder by the other's
massive arm. "Chewie!" she snapped, hand dropping to
the blaster belted at her side.

She'd barely gotten hold of it, though, before Ralrra's
shaggy hand landed in an iron grip on top of hers. [Do not
disturb them,] the Wookiee told her firmly. [Chewbacca
and Salporin have been friends since childhood, and have
not seen each otherr in many yearrs. Theirr greeting must
not be interrupted.]

"Sorry," Leia murmured, dropping her hand to her side
and feeling like an idiot.[8]

[Chewbacca said in his message that you requirre sanc-
tuary,] Ralrra continued, perhaps recognizing her embarrassment. [Come. I will show you the preparations we
have made.]

Leia's eyes flicked to Chewbacca and Salporin, still
clinging to each other. "Perhaps we should wait for the
others," she suggested, a little uncertainly.

[Therre will be no dangerr.] Ralrra drew himself up to
his full height. [Leiaorganasolo, you must understand.
Without you and yourr people many of us would still be
slaves to the Empirre. Slaves, orr dead at theirr hand. To
you and yourr Republic we owe a life debt.]

"Thank you," Leia said, feeling the last bit of residual
tension draining away. There was a great deal about Wookiee culture and psychology that was still opaque to her; but

(cont.)
Ralrra easier for humans
to understand.
                    —TZ

8. A close hug *does* look
a lot like vertical wrestling,
after all. Probably even
more so with Wookiees.
                    —TZ

the life debt, at least, she understood very well. Ralrra had formally committed himself to her safety now, that commitment backed up by Wookiee honor, tenacity, and raw strength.

[Come,] Ralrra growled, gesturing toward what looked like an open-cage liftcar at the edge of the platform. [We will go to the village.]

"Certainly," Leia said. "That reminds me—I was going to ask how you keep the village in place. Do you use repulsorlifts?"

[Come,] Ralrra said. [I will show you.]

The village was not, in fact, being held up by repulsorlifts. Nor with unipods, tractor anchorlines, or any other clever scheme of modern technology. Which made it all the more sobering for Leia to realize that the Wookiees' method was, in its own way, more sophisticated than any of them.

The village was held up by branches.

[It was a great task, a village of this size to build,] Ralrra told her, waving a massive hand upward at the latticework above them. [Many of the branches at the level desired werre removed. Those which remained then grew stronggerr and fasterr.]

"It looks almost like a giant spiderweb," Leia commented, peering from the liftcar at the underside of the village and trying not to think about the kilometers of empty space directly beneath them. "How did you mesh them together like that?"

[We did not. Through theirr own growth they arre a unity.]

Leia blinked. "Excuse me?"

[They have grown togetherr,] Ralrra explained. [When two *wroshyr* branches meet, they grow into one. Togetherr then they sprout new branches in all directions.]

He growled something under his breath, a word or

phrase for which Leia had no translation. [It is a living reminderr of the unity and strength of the Wookiee people,] he added, almost to himself.

Leia nodded silently. It was also, she realized, a strong indication that all the *wroshyr* trees in this bunch were a single giant plant, with a unified or at least an intermixed root system. Did the Wookiees realize that? Or had their obvious reverence for the trees forbidden such thinking and research?

Not that curiosity would help them all that much in this case. Dropping her gaze, she peered down into the hazy dimness beneath the liftcar. Somewhere down there were the shorter *wroshyrs* and hundreds of other types of trees that made up the vast jungles of Kashyyyk. Several different arboreal ecosystems were reputed to exist in the jungle, arranged in roughly horizontal layers descending toward the ground, each layer more deadly than the one above. She didn't know whether the Wookiees had ever even made it all the way down to the surface; it was for sure that no one who had would have taken the time for leisurely botanical studies.

[They arre called *kroyies*,][9] Ralrra said.

Leia blinked at the odd non sequitur. But even as she opened her mouth to ask what he was talking about, she spotted the double wedge of birds flying swiftly through the sky beneath them. "Those birds?" she asked.

[Yes. Once they werre a prize food to the Wookiee people. Now even the poorr may eat them.] He pointed toward the edge of the village above them, to the haze of light coming from the searchlights she'd seen during their approach. [*Kroyies* will come to those lights,] he explained. [Hunterrs therre await them.]

Leia nodded understanding; she'd seen visual lures of varying degrees of sophistication used to attract food animals on other worlds. "Don't all those clouds interfere with their effectiveness, though?"

9. One of the neat things about the *Star Wars* universe is that there's always room for something new. Jumping off of the Kashyyyk background that I'd been given, I was able to add a few new things, such as the *kroyies*, into the ecological system.

—TZ

[Through the clouds they work best,] Ralrra said. [The clouds spread the light. A *kroyie* will see it from great distances and come.]

As he spoke, the double wedge of birds banked sharply, climbing toward the clouds overhead and the lights playing against them. [Even so, you see. Tonight we shall perhaps dine on one of them.]

"I'd like that," she said. "I remember Chewie saying once that they were delicious."

[Then we must return to the village,] Ralrra said, touching the liftcar's control. With a creak of the cable, it started upward. [We had hoped to shelterr you in one of the morre luxurious homes,] he commented as they started upward. [But Chewbacca would not allow it.]

He gestured, and for the first time Leia noticed the homes built directly into the tree beside them. Some of them were multistoried and quite elaborate; all of them seemed to open up directly onto empty space. "Chewbacca understands my preferences," she told Ralrra, suppressing a shiver. "I was wondering why the liftcar went this far down past the village proper."

[The liftcarr is used mainly forr cargo transportation orr the ill,] Ralrra said. [Most Wookiees preferr to climb the trees naturally.]

He held out a hand to her, palm up; and as the muscles under the skin and fur flexed, a set of wickedly curved claws slid into sight from hidden fingertip sheaths.[10]

Leia swallowed hard. "I didn't realize Wookiees had claws like those," she said. "Though I suppose I should have. You *are* arboreal, after all."

[To live among trees without them would be impossible,] Ralrra agreed. The claws retracted again, and the Wookiee waved the hand upward. [Even vine travel would be difficult without them.]

"Vines?" Leia echoed, frowning up through the liftcar's transparent roof. She hadn't noticed any vines on the trees earlier, and didn't really see any now. Her eyes fell on the

10. I liked the idea of Wookiees being arboreal and living on huge trees kilometers above the ground. The problem was that they didn't seem to be built for that sort of life. So I added the protractible claws to make tree climbing practical.

   Unfortunately, in the process I forgot my own admonition that I needed to pay attention to what *wasn't* seen in the movies. Specifically, why weren't these claws ever seen, particularly when Chewie was fighting for his life?

   Fortunately, the West End Games folks also spotted the lapse and came to my rescue. In one of the later sourcebooks they explained that it was a matter of honor that Wookiees never used these claws in combat, but kept them strictly for climbing.

   —TZ

cable running from the liftcar up into the leaves and branches above . . .

The dark *green* cable.

"That cable?" she asked carefully, nodding toward it. "That's a vine?"

[It a *kshyy* vine is,] he assured her. [Do not worry about its strength. It is strongerr than composite cable material, and cannot even by blasterrs be cut. Too, it is self-repairing.]

"I see," Leia said, staring at the vine and fighting hard against the sudden sense of panic. She'd flown all around the galaxy in hundreds of different types of airspeeders and spaceships without the slightest twinge of acrophobia, but this hanging out on the edge of nowhere without a solid powered cockpit around her was something else entirely.[11] The warm sense of security she'd been feeling at being on Kashyyyk was starting to evaporate. "Have the vines ever broken?" she asked, trying to sound casual.

[In the past, it sometimes happened,] Ralrra said. [Various parasites and fungi, if unchecked, can erode them. Now, we employ safeguards which ourr ancestorrs did not have. Liftcarrs such as this one contain emergency repulsorlift systems.]

"Ah," Leia said, the momentary discomfort easing as she once again found herself feeling like a raw and not very bright diplomatic beginner. It was easy to forget that, despite their somewhat quaint-looking arboreal villages and their own animalistic appearance, Wookiees generally were quite at home with high technology.

The liftcar rose above the level of the village floor. Chewbacca and Salporin were standing there waiting for them, the former fingering his bowcaster and giving the little twitches that Leia had learned to associate with impatience. Ralrra brought them to a stop at the level of the wide exit ramp and opened the door, Salporin stepping forward as he did so to offer Leia his hand in assistance.

[We have made arrangements forr you and Chewbacca

11. Art imitating life. I have the same problem that I'm attributing here to Leia. Airplanes don't bother me; the Seattle Space Needle observation deck does.

—TZ

to stay at Salporin's home,] Ralrra said as they stepped out onto relatively solid ground again. [It is not farr. Therre arre transports available, if you wish.]

Leia looked out across the nearest parts of the village. She wanted very much to walk, to get out among the people and start getting the feel of the place. But after all the effort they'd put into sneaking her onto Kashyyyk in the first place, parading herself in front of the whole population would probably not be the smartest thing to do. "A transport would probably be best," she told Ralrra.

Chewbacca growled something as they came up to him. [She wished to see the village's structurre,] Ralrra told him. [We arre now ready to go.]

Chewbacca gave another growl of displeasure, but returned his bowcaster to his shoulder and strode off without further comment toward a repulsor sled parked at the side of the road perhaps twenty meters away. Ralrra and Leia followed, with Salporin bringing up the rear. The houses and other buildings began right at the edge of the matted branches, Leia had already noted, without anything more substantial than a few twisted *kshyy* vines between them and empty space. Ralrra had implied that the homes clinging to the trees themselves were the more prestigious ones; perhaps those here at the edge belonged to the upper middle class. Idly, she looked at the nearest of them, glancing into the windows as they passed. A face moved into view in the shadows behind one of them, catching her eye—

"Chewie!" she gasped. Even as her hand darted for her blaster the face vanished. But there was no mistaking those bulging eyes and protruding jaw and steel-gray skin.

Chewbacca was at her side in an instant, bowcaster in hand. "One of those creatures who attacked us on Bimmisaari is in there," she told him, reaching out with all the Jedi sense she could muster. Nothing. "At that window," she added, pointing with her blaster. "He was right there."

Chewbacca barked an order, sliding his massive bulk

between Leia and the house and easing her slowly backward, his bowcaster weaving back and forth across the
structure in a covering pattern. Ralrra and Salporin were
already at the house, each carrying a pair of wicked-
looking knives they'd pulled from somewhere. They took
up flanking positions beside the front door; and with a
brilliant flash from his bowcaster, Chewbacca shot the
door in.

From somewhere in toward the center of the village
someone roared—a long, ululating Wookiee howl of anger
or alarm that seemed to echo from the buildings and massive trees. Even before Ralrra and Salporin had disappeared into the house the howl was being taken up by
other voices, rising in number and volume until it seemed
as if half the village had joined in. Leia found herself pressing against Chewbacca's hairy back, wincing at the sheer
ferocity in that call and flashing back to the Bimmisaari
marketplace reacting to her jewelry theft.

Except that these weren't funny little yellow-clad
Bimms. They were giant, violently strong Wookiees.

A large crowd had begun to form by the time Ralrra
and Salporin emerged from the house—a crowd that
Chewbacca paid no more attention to than he had the
howling as he kept his eyes and bowcaster trained on the
house. The other two Wookiees also ignored the crowd,
disappearing around opposite sides of the house. They reappeared seconds later, their manner that of hunters
who'd come up dry.

"He was there," Leia insisted as they returned to where
she and Chewbacca stood. "I saw him."

[That may be true,] Ralrra said, slipping his knives back
into hidden sheaths behind his baldric. Salporin, his attention still back on the house, kept his own knives ready.
[But we found no trace of anyone.]

Leia bit at her lip, eyes flicking across the area. There
were no other houses near enough for the alien to have
crossed to without her and Chewbacca seeing him. No

cover of any sort, for that matter, on this side of the house. On the other side, there was nothing but the edge of the village.

"He went over the edge," she realized suddenly. "He must have. Either worked his way under the village with climbing gear or else met a craft hovering down below."

[That is unlikely,] Ralrra said, starting past her. [But possible. I will go down the liftcarr, to try and discoverr him.]

Chewbacca reached a hand out to stop him, growling a negative. [You arre right,] Ralrra conceded, though clearly reluctantly. [Yourr safety, Leiaorganasolo, is the most important thing at this point. We will take you to safety first, and then make inquiries about this alien.]

To safety. Leia gazed at the house, a shiver running up her back. And wondered if there would ever again be such a thing for her as safety.

CHAPTER 18

THE TRILLING CODE, coming from somewhere far
behind him, startled Luke up out of his dreamless sleep.
"Okay, Artoo, I'm awake," he said groggily, reaching up to
rub at his eyes. His knuckles bumped into the visor of his
flight helmet, and the impact did a bit to dissipate the fog
still swirling through his mind. He couldn't remember exactly the circumstances under which he'd gone into hibernation, but he had the distinct feeling that Artoo had
brought him out too soon. "Is anything wrong?" he asked,
trying to track down exactly what it was the droid was
supposed to be doing.

The trilling changed to an anxious-sounding warble.
Still fighting to get his eyes properly focused, Luke searched
out the computer scope for the translation. To his mild surprise, it was dark. As were all the rest of his instruments;
and then it came back to him. He was trapped in deep
space, with all the X-wing's systems shut down except
power for Artoo and minimal life support for himself.

And Artoo was supposed to be winding a new subspace

radio antenna. Twisting a slightly stiff neck, he turned halfway around to look back at the droid, wondering what the problem was—

And felt his muscles twitch with surprise. There, bearing rapidly down on them, was another ship.

He spun back around, fully awake now, hands jabbing for the bank of power switches and slapping them all on. But it was so much useless reflex. Even with shortcuts, it would still take nearly fifteen minutes to bring the X-wing's engines from a cold start to any serious possibility of flight, let alone combat. If the intruder was unfriendly . . .

Using the emergency maneuvering jets, he got the X-wing turning slowly around to face the approaching ship. The scopes and sensors were starting to come back online again, confirming what his eyes had already told him: his visitor was a midsized, slightly dilapidated-looking Corellian bulk freighter. Not the sort of ship the Imperials usually used, and there were certainly no Imperial markings on its hull.

But under the circumstances, it was just as unlikely that it was an innocent freight handler, either. A pirate, perhaps? Luke reached out with the Force, trying to get a sense of the crew . . .

Artoo warbled, and Luke glanced down at the computer scope. "Yes, I noticed that, too," Luke told him. "But a normal bulk freighter might be able to pull that kind of deceleration if it was empty. Why don't you do a quick analysis of the sensor readings, see if you can spot any weapons emplacements."

The droid beeped an acknowledgment, and Luke gave the other instruments a quick scan. The primary laser cannon capacitors were at half charge now, with the main sublight drive about halfway through its preflight sequence.

And the flashing radio signal indicated that he was being hailed.

Bracing himself, Luke flipped on the receiver. "—need assistance?" a cool female voice said. "Repeating: unidentified starfighter, this is the freighter *Wild Karrde.* Do you need assistance?"

"*Wild Karrde,* this is New Republic X-wing AA-589," Luke identified himself. "As a matter of fact, yes, I could use some help."

"Acknowledged, X-wing," the other said. "What seems to be the problem?"

"Hyperdrive," Luke told her, watching the ship closely as it continued its approach. A minute earlier he'd rotated to face the freighter's approach; the other pilot had responded with a slight sidling drift of her own, with the result that the *Wild Karrde* was no longer in line with the X-wing's lasers. Probably just being cautious . . . but there were other possibilities. "I've lost both motivators," he continued. "Cracked shield cases, probably some other problems, too. I don't suppose you'd be carrying any spares?"

"Not for a ship that size." There was a short pause. "I'm instructed to tell you that if you'd care to come aboard, we can offer you passage to our destination system."

Luke reached out with the Force, trying to measure the sense behind the words. But if there was deceit there, he couldn't detect it. And even if there was, he had precious little choice. "Sounds good," he said. "Any chance you could take my ship, too?"

"I doubt you could afford our shipping rates," the other told him dryly. "I'll check with the captain, but don't get your hopes up. We'd have to take it in tow, anyway—our holds are pretty full at the moment."

Luke felt his lip twitch. A fully loaded bulk freighter couldn't possibly have managed the deceleration profile Artoo had noted earlier. Either they were lying about that, or else that normal-looking drive system had undergone a complete and massive upgrading.[1]

Which made the *Wild Karrde* either a smuggler, a pirate, or a disguised warship. And the New Republic had no disguised warships.

The other pilot was talking again. "If you'll hold your

1. Someone asked me once what kind of modern-day car Karrde would drive. I told him that it would probably be a nice, simple, family-style sedan or minivan. A Toyota or Ford maybe . . . with a Lamborghini V-12 engine tucked away under the hood.

—TZ

present position, X-wing, we'll move up close enough to throw a force cylinder out to you," she said. "Unless you'd rather suit up and spacewalk across."

"The cylinder sounds fastest," Luke said, deciding to try a light verbal probe. "I don't suppose either of us has any reason to hang around this place. How did you happen to wind up out here, anyway?"

"We can handle a limited amount of baggage," the other went on, ignoring the question. "I imagine you'll want to bring your astromech droid along, too."

So much for the light verbal probe. "Yes, I will," he told her.

"All right, then, stand by. Incidentally, the captain says the transport fee will be five thousand."

"Understood," Luke said, unstrapping his restraints. Opening the side pouches, he pulled out his gloves and helmet seal and folded them into his flight suit's chest pockets where he'd have quick access to them. A force cylinder was relatively foolproof, but accidents could always happen. Besides which, if the *Wild Karrde*'s crew was hoping to pick themselves up a free X-wing, shutting the cylinder down halfway through the operation would be the simplest and least messy way to dispose of him.

The crew. Luke paused, straining his senses toward the ship moving steadily toward him. There was something wrong there; something he could feel but couldn't quite track down.

Artoo warbled anxiously. "No, she didn't answer the question," Luke agreed. "But I can't think of any legitimate reason for them to be out this far. Can you?"

The droid gave a soft, electronic moan. "Agreed." Luke nodded. "But refusing the offer doesn't buy us anything at all. We'll just have to stay alert."

Reaching into the other side pouch, he pulled out his blaster, checked its power level, and slid it into the holster pocket built into his flight suit. His comlink went into another pocket, though what use it would be aboard the

Wild Karrde he couldn't imagine. The emergency survival pack went around his waist, awkward to fasten in the cramped quarters. And last, he pulled out his lightsaber and fastened it to his belt.

"Okay, X-wing, we've got the cylinder[2] established," the voice came. "Whenever you're ready."

The *Wild Karrde*'s small docking bay was directly above him, its outer door gaping invitingly. Luke checked his instruments, confirmed there was indeed a corridor of air between the two ships, and took a deep breath. "Here we go, Artoo," he said, and popped the canopy.

A puff of breeze brushed across his face as the air pressures equalized. Giving himself a careful push, he eased up and out, gripping the edge of the canopy to turn himself around. Artoo, he saw, had ejected from his socket and was drifting freely just above the X-wing, making distinctly unhappy noises about his situation. "I've got you, Artoo," Luke soothed, reaching out with the Force to pull the droid toward him. Getting his bearings one last time, he bent his knees and pushed off.

He reached the airlock at the back of the bay a half second ahead of Artoo, grabbed hold of the straps fastened to the walls, and brought both of them to a smooth halt. Someone was obviously watching; they were still moving when the outer lock door slid shut. Gravity came back, slowly enough for him to adjust his stance to it, and a moment later the inner door slid open.

There was a young man waiting for them, wearing a casual coverall of an unfamiliar cut. "Welcome aboard the *Wild Karrde*," he said, nodding gravely. "If you'll follow me, the captain would like to see you."

Without waiting for a reply, he turned and headed down the curving corridor. "Come on, Artoo," Luke murmured, starting after him and reaching out with the Force for a quick survey of the ship. Aside from their guide, he could sense only four others aboard, all of them in the forward sections. Behind him, in the aft sections . . .

2. I envisioned a force cylinder as being a cylindrical version of the atmosphere screen we saw in the movies in big hatchways like those of the Death Star. An emergency docking tube, probably meant for temporary use only.

But given the prominent use of the term *the Force*, I really should have come up with a different name for this. Vac-walk cylinder, maybe. Way too late now.

—TZ

3. Somewhere along the line, one of the artists tackling Karrde either missed this description or else ignored it, and drew the man with long, flowing hair and a goatee. That's the image that has now stuck for him.

Which is fine with me. Karrde is the type who would probably find it useful to change appearance every so often anyway, and by the end of the Thrawn Trilogy he could very well have looked like that.

It was also that image that Decipher used when they brought Mike Stackpole and me out to Virginia for a photo session to create their special Talon Karrde and Corran Horn cards.

I would never have guessed, as I was writing *Heir,* that I might someday end up on a collectible card. Life can be very strange sometimes.

                  –TZ

4. This became the basis of a line in the Essential Guides, which then became an entire book: *Luke Skywalker and the Shadows of Mindor* by Matthew Stover.

                  –TZ

He shook his head, trying to clear it. It didn't help: the aft sections of the ship still remained oddly dark to him. An aftereffect of the long hibernation, probably. It was for certain, though, that there were no crew members or droids back there, and that was all he needed to know for the moment.

The guide led them to a door, which slid open as he stepped to one side. "Captain Karrde will see you now," he said, waving toward the open door.

"Thank you." Luke nodded to him. With Artoo bumping against his heels, he stepped into the room.

It was an office of sorts; small, with much of its wall space taken up with what looked like highly sophisticated communications and encrypt equipment. In the center was a large desk/console combination . . . and seated behind it, watching Luke's approach, was a slender man, thin-faced, with short dark hair and pale blue eyes.[3]

"Good evening," he said in a cool, carefully modulated voice. "I'm Talon Karrde." His eyes flicked up and down Luke, as if measuring him. "And you, I presume, are Commander Luke Skywalker."

Luke stared at him. How in the worlds . . . ? "Private citizen Skywalker," he said, striving to keep his own voice calm. "I resigned my Alliance commission nearly four years ago."[4]

An almost-smile twitched the corners of Karrde's mouth. "I stand corrected. I must say, you've certainly found a good place to get away from it all."

The question was unstated, but no less obvious for that. "I had some help choosing it," Luke told him. "A small run-in with an Imperial Star Destroyer about half a light-year away."

"Ah," Karrde said, without any surprise that Luke could see or sense. "Yes, the Empire is still quite active in this part of the galaxy. Growing more so, too, particularly of late." He cocked his head slightly to the side, his eyes never leaving Luke's face. "Though I presume you've already noticed that. Incidentally, it looks like we'll be able to take your ship in tow, after all. I'm having the cables rigged now."

"Thank you," Luke said, feeling the skin on the back of his neck start to tingle. Whether a pirate or a smuggler, Karrde should certainly have reacted more strongly to the news that there was a Star Destroyer in the area. Unless, of course, he already had an understanding with the Imperials . . . "Allow me to thank you for the rescue, as well," he continued. "Artoo and I are lucky you happened along."

"And Artoo is—? Oh, of course—your astromech droid." The blue eyes flicked down briefly. "You must be a formidable warrior indeed, Skywalker—escaping from an Imperial Star Destroyer is no mean trick. Though I imagine a man like yourself is accustomed to giving the Imperials trouble."

"I don't see much front-line action anymore," Luke told him. "You haven't told me how you came to be out here, Captain. Or, for that matter, how you knew who I was."

Another almost-smile. "With a lightsaber attached to your belt?" he asked wryly. "Come now. You were either Luke Skywalker, Jedi, or else someone with a taste for antiques and an insufferably high opinion of his swordsmanship." Again, the blue eyes flicked up and down Luke. "You're not really what I expected, somehow. Though I suppose that's not all that surprising—the vast majority of Jedi lore has been so twisted by myth and ignorance that to get a clear picture is almost impossible."

The warning bell in the back of Luke's mind began to ring louder. "You almost sound as if you were expecting to find me here," he said, easing his body into a combat stance and letting his senses reach out. All five of the crewers were still more or less where they'd been a few minutes earlier, farther up toward the forward part of the ship. None except Karrde himself was close enough to pose any kind of immediate threat.

"As a matter of fact, we were," Karrde agreed calmly. "Though I can't actually take any of the credit for that. It was one of my associates, Mara Jade, who led us here." His head inclined slightly to his right. "She's on the bridge at the moment."

He paused, obviously waiting. It could be a setup, Luke knew; but the suggestion that someone might actually have been able to sense his presence from light-years away was too intriguing to pass up. Keeping his overall awareness clear, Luke narrowed a portion of his mind to the *Wild Karrde*'s bridge. At the helm was the young woman he'd spoken to earlier from the X-wing. Beside her, an older man was busy running a calculation through the nav computer. And sitting behind them—

The jolt of that mind shot through him like an electric current. "Yes, that's her," Karrde confirmed, almost offhandedly. "She hides it quite well, actually—though not, I suppose, from a Jedi. It took me several months of careful observation to establish that it was you, and you personally, for whom she had these feelings."

It took Luke another second to find his voice. Never before, not even from the Emperor, had he ever felt such a black and bitter hatred. "I've never met her before," he managed.

"No?" Karrde shrugged. "A pity. I was rather hoping you'd be able to tell me why she feels this way. Ah, well." He got to his feet. "I suppose, then, there's nothing more for us to talk about for the moment . . . and let me say in advance that I'm very sorry it has to be this way."

Reflexively, Luke's hand darted for his lightsaber. He'd barely begun the movement when the shock of a stun weapon coursed through him from behind.

There were Jedi methods for fighting off unconsciousness. But they all took at least a split second of preparation—a split second that Luke did not have. Dimly, he felt himself falling; heard Artoo's frantic trilling in the distance; and wondered with his last conscious thought how in the worlds Karrde had done this to him.

CHAPTER 19

HE AWOKE SLOWLY, in stages, aware of nothing but the twin facts that, one, he was lying flat on his back and, two, he felt terrible.

Slowly, gradually, the haze began to coalesce into more localized sensations. The air around him was warm but damp, a light and shifting breeze carrying several unfamiliar odors along with it. The surface beneath him had the soft/firm feel of a bed; the general sense of his skin and mouth implied he'd been asleep for probably several days.

It took another minute for the implications of that to percolate through the mental fog filling his brain. More than an hour or two was well beyond the safe capabilities of any stun weapon he'd ever heard of. Clearly, after being shot, he'd been drugged.

Inwardly, he smiled. Karrde was probably expecting him to be incapacitated for a while longer; and Karrde was in for a surprise. Forcing his mind into focus, he ran through the Jedi technique for detoxifying poisons and then waited for the haze to clear.

It took him some time to realize that nothing was, in fact, happening.

Somewhere in there he fell asleep again; and when he next awoke, his mind had cleared completely. Blinking against the sunlight streaming across his face, he opened his eyes and lifted his head.

He was lying on a bed, still in his flight suit, in a small but comfortably furnished room. Directly across from him was an open window, the source of the aroma-laden breezes he'd already noted. Through the window, too, he could see the edge of a forest fifty meters or so away, above which a yellowish-orange sun hovered—rising or setting, he didn't know which. The furnishings of the room itself didn't look much like those of a prison cell—

"Finally awake, are you?" a woman's voice said from the side.

Startled, Luke twisted his head toward the voice. His first, instantaneous thought was that he had somehow missed sensing whoever was over there; his second, following on the heels of the first, was that that was clearly ridiculous and that the voice must be coming instead from an intercom or comlink.

He finished his turn, to discover that the first thought had indeed been correct.

She was sitting in a high-backed chair, her arms draped loosely over the arms in a posture that seemed strangely familiar: a slender woman about Luke's own age, with brilliant red-gold hair and equally brilliant green eyes. Her legs were casually crossed; a compact but wicked-looking blaster lay on her lap.

A genuine, living human being . . . and yet, impossibly, he couldn't sense her.

The confusion must have shown in his face. "That's right," she said, favoring him with a smile. Not a friendly or even a polite smile, but one that seemed to be made up of equal parts bitterness and malicious amusement. "Welcome back to the world of mere mortals."

—and with a surge of adrenaline, Luke realized that the strange mental veiling wasn't limited to just her. He couldn't sense *anything.* Not people, not droids, not even the forest beyond his window.

It was like suddenly going blind.

"Don't like it, do you?" the woman mocked. "It's not easy to suddenly lose everything that once made you special, is it?"

Slowly, carefully, Luke eased his legs over the side of the bed and sat up, giving his body plenty of time to get used to moving again. The woman watched him, her right hand dropping to her lap to rest on top of the blaster. "If the purpose of all this activity is to impress me with your remarkable powers of recuperation," she offered, "you don't need to bother."

"Nothing so devious," Luke advised, breathing hard and trying not to wheeze. "The purpose of all this activity is to get me back on my feet." He looked her hard in the eye, wondering if she would flinch away from his gaze. She didn't even twitch. "Don't tell me; let me guess. You're Mara Jade."

"That doesn't impress me, either," she said coldly. "Karrde already told me he'd mentioned my name to you."

Luke nodded. "He also told me that you were the one who found my X-wing. Thank you."

Her eyes flashed. "Save your gratitude," she bit out. "As far as I'm concerned, the only question left is whether we turn you over to the Imperials or kill you ourselves."

Abruptly she stood up, the blaster ready in her hand. "On your feet. Karrde wants to see you."

Carefully, Luke stood up, and as he did so, he noticed for the first time that Mara had attached his lightsaber to her own belt. Was she, then, a Jedi herself? Powerful enough, perhaps, to smother Luke's abilities? "I can't say that either of those options sounds appealing," he commented.

"There's one other one." She took half a step forward,

moving close enough that he could have reached out and touched her. Lifting the blaster, she pointed it directly at his face. "You try to escape . . . and I kill you right here and now."

For a long moment they stood there, frozen. The bitter hatred was blazing again in those eyes . . . but even as Luke gazed back at her, he saw something else along with the anger. Something that looked like a deep and lingering pain.

He stood quietly, not moving; and almost reluctantly, she lowered the weapon. "Move. Karrde's waiting."

Luke's room was at the end of a long hallway with identical doors spaced at regular intervals along its length. A barracks of sorts, he decided, as they left it and started across a grassy clearing toward a large, high-roofed building. Several other structures clustered around the latter, including another barracks building, a handful that looked like storehouses, and one that was clearly a servicing hangar. Grouped around the hangar on both sides were over a dozen starships, including at least two bulk cruisers like the *Wild Karrde* and several smaller craft, some of them hidden a ways back into the forest that pressed closely in on the compound from all sides. Tucked away behind one of the bulk cruisers, he could just see the nose of his X-wing. For a moment he considered asking Mara what had happened to Artoo, decided he'd do better to save the question for Karrde.

They reached the large central building and Mara reached past Luke to slap the sensor plate beside the door. "He's in the greatroom," Mara said as the panel slid open in response. "Straight ahead."

They walked down a long hallway, passing a pair of what seemed to be medium-sized dining and recreation rooms. Ahead, a large door at the end of the hallway slid open at their approach. Mara ushered him inside—

And into a scene straight out of ancient legend.

For a moment Luke just stood in the doorway, staring. The room was large and spacious, its high ceiling translucent and crisscrossed by a webwork of carved rafters. The walls were composed of a dark brown wood, much of it elaborately open-mesh carved, with a deep blue light glowing through the interstices.[1] Other luxuries were scattered sparingly about: a small sculpture here, an unrecognizable alien artifact there. Chairs, couches, and large cushions were arranged in well-separated conversation circles, giving a distinctly relaxed, almost informal air to the place.

But all that was secondary, taken in peripherally or at a later time entirely. For that first astonishing moment Luke's full attention was fixed solidly on the tree growing through the center of the room.

Not a small tree, either, like the delicate saplings that lined one of the hallways in the Imperial Palace. This one was huge, a meter in diameter at the base, extending from a section of plain dirt floor through the translucent ceiling and far beyond. Thick limbs starting perhaps two meters from the ground stretched their way across the room, some of them nearly touching the walls, almost like arms reaching out to encompass everything in sight.[2]

"Ah; Skywalker," a voice called from in front of him. With an effort, Luke shifted his gaze downward, to find Karrde sitting comfortably in a chair at the base of the tree. On either side two long-legged quadrupeds crouched, their vaguely doglike muzzles pointing stiffly in Luke's direction. "Come and join me."

Swallowing, Luke started toward him. There were stories he remembered from his childhood about fortresses with trees growing up through them. Frightening stories, some of them, full of danger and helplessness and fear.

And in every one of those stories, such fortresses were the home of evil.

"Welcome back to the land of the living," Karrde said as

1. This image of carved wood with blue light shining through the gaps comes from a couple of visits we made to a place called the House on the Rock in Wisconsin. It's an absolutely stunning architectural masterpiece, and several of the rooms have this sort of background lighting.

—TZ

2. I read mythology voraciously when I was a child, and my favorites were the Norse myths. This one is straight out of the Siegfried legend—all we're missing is a sword stuck in the tree.

—TZ

Luke approached. He picked up a silvery pitcher from the low table at his side, poured a reddish liquid into a pair of cups. "I must apologize for having kept you asleep all this time. But I'm sure you appreciate the special problems involved in making sure a Jedi stays where you've put him."

"Of course," Luke said, his attention on the two animals beside Karrde's chair. They were still staring at him with an uncomfortable intensity. "Though if you'd just asked nicely," he added, "you might have found me quite willing to cooperate."

A flicker of a smile touched Karrde's lips. "Perhaps. Perhaps not." He gestured to the chair across from him. "Please sit down."

Luke started forward; but as he did so, one of the animals rose up slightly on his haunches, making a strange sort of choked purr. "Easy, Sturm," Karrde admonished, looking down at the animal. "This man is our guest."

The creature ignored him, its full attention clearly on Luke. "I don't think it believes you," Luke suggested carefully. Even as he spoke, the second animal made the same sort of sound as the first had.

"Perhaps not." Karrde had a light grip on each of the animals' collars now and was glancing around the room. "Chin!" he called toward the three men lounging in one of the conversation circles. "Come and take them out, will you?"

"Sure." A middle-aged man with a Froffli-style haircut[3] got up and trotted over. "Come on, fellows," he grunted, taking over Karrde's grip on the collars and leading the animals away. "What hai we go for a walk, hee?"

"My apologies, Skywalker," Karrde said, frowning slightly as he watched the others go. "They're usually better behaved than that with guests. Now; please sit down."

Luke did so, accepting the cup Karrde offered him. Mara stepped past him and took up position next to her chief. Her blaster, Luke noted, was now in a wrist holster

---

3. "What is a Froffli-style haircut?"

I got asked this kind of question a lot with *Heir* and the other two books. The questions came from my editor, Lucasfilm, the copy editor, or sometimes all three.

The answer: I don't know. The idea was to sprinkle these alien non-Earth references throughout the books, with the intent being to add a little more *Star Wars* feeling to it.

Of course, the throwaway lines also served another, more devious purpose. The reader never knew whether one of these things was merely some local color, or whether it was a subtle setup to an important plot point somewhere down the line.

An aside: the comics depict Chin's hair as spiky.

—TZ

on her left forearm, nearly as accessible as it would have been in her hand.

"It's just a mild stimulant," Karrde said, nodding to the cup in Luke's hand. "Something to help you wake up." He took a drink from his own cup and set it back down on the low table.

Luke took a sip. It tasted all right; and anyway, if Karrde had wanted to drug him, there was hardly any need to stoop to such a childish subterfuge. "Would you mind telling me where my droid is?"

"Oh, he's perfectly all right," Karrde assured him. "I have him in one of my equipment sheds for safekeeping."

"I'd like to see him, if I may."

"I'm sure that can be arranged. But later." Karrde leaned back in his seat, his forehead furrowing slightly. "Perhaps after we've figured out just exactly what we're going to do with you."

Luke glanced up at Mara. "Your associate mentioned the possibilities. I'd hoped I could add another to the list."

"That we send you back home?" Karrde suggested.

"With due compensation, of course," Luke assured him. "Say, double whatever the Empire would offer?"

"You're very generous with other people's money," Karrde said dryly. "The problem, unfortunately, doesn't arise from money, but from politics. Our operations, you see, extend rather deeply into both Imperial and Republic space. If the Empire discovered we'd released you back to the Republic, they would be highly displeased with us."

"And vice versa if you turned me over to the Empire," Luke pointed out.

"True," Karrde said. "Except that given the damage to your X-wing's subspace radio, the Republic presumably has no idea what happened to you. The Empire, unfortunately, does."

"And it's not what they *would* offer," Mara put in. "It's what they *have* offered. Thirty thousand."[4]

4. The official currency of the *Star Wars* galaxy is the credit, but I never really liked that term—I guess it always seemed too fifties SF to me. (So do blasters, actually, but for some reason that one doesn't bother me nearly as much.)

So I took a page from Han's bargaining with Obi-Wan for the Alderaan trip and tried wherever possible to simply avoid mentioning the type of currency, figuring that it would be understood by both parties.

—TZ

Luke pursed his lips. "I had no idea I was so valuable," he said.

"You could be the difference between solvency and failure for any number of marginal operators," Karrde said bluntly. "There are probably dozens of ships out there right now, ignoring schedules and prior commitments to hunt for you." He smiled tightly. "Operators who haven't given even a moment of consideration to how they would hold on to a Jedi even if they caught one."

"Your method seems to work pretty well," Luke told him. "I don't suppose you'd be willing to tell me how you've managed it."

Karrde smiled again. "Secrets of that magnitude are worth a great deal of money. Have you any secrets of equal value to trade?"

"Probably not," Luke said evenly. "But, again, I'm sure the New Republic would be willing to pay market value."

Karrde sipped from his drink, eyeing Luke thoughtfully over the rim of the cup. "I'll make you a deal," he said, putting the cup back on the table beside him. "You tell me why the Empire is suddenly so interested in you, and I'll tell you why your Jedi powers aren't working."

"Why don't you ask the Imperials directly?"

Karrde smiled. "Thank you, but no. I'd just as soon not have them start wondering at my sudden interest. Particularly after we pleaded prior commitments when the request came in for us to help hunt you down."

Luke frowned at him. "You weren't hunting for me?"

"No, we weren't." Karrde's lip twisted. "One of those little ironies that make life so interesting. We were simply returning from a cargo pickup when Mara dropped us out of hyperspace on the spur of the moment to do a nav reading."

Luke studied Mara's stony expression. "How fortunate for you," he said.

"Perhaps," Karrde said. "The net result, though, was to

put us in the middle of the exact situation that I'd hoped to avoid."

Luke held his hands out, palms upward. "Then let me go and pretend none of this happened. I give you my word I'll keep your part in it quiet."

"The Empire would find out anyway." Karrde shook his head. "Their new commander is extremely good at piecing bits of information together. No, I think your best hope right now is for us to find a compromise. Some way we can let you go while still giving the Imperials what they want." He cocked his head slightly. "Which leads us back to my original question."

"And from there back to my original answer," Luke said. "I really *don't* know what the Empire wants with me." He hesitated, but Leia should be well beyond Imperial reach by now. "I can tell you, though, that it's not just me. There have been two attempts on my sister Leia, too."

"Killing attempts?"

Luke thought about it. "I don't think so. The one I was present for felt more like a kidnapping."

"Interesting," Karrde murmured, his eyes defocusing slightly. "Leia Organa Solo. Who is in training to be a Jedi like her brother. That could explain . . . certain recent Imperial actions."

Luke waited, but after a moment it became clear that Karrde wasn't going to elaborate. "You spoke of a compromise," he reminded the other.

Karrde seemed to pull his thoughts back to the room. "Yes, I did," he said. "It's occurred to me that your privileged position in the New Republic might be what the Empire was interested in—that they wanted information on the inner workings of the Provisional Council. In such a case, we might have been able to work out a deal whereby you went free while your Artoo droid went to the Imperials for debriefing."

Luke felt his stomach tighten. "It wouldn't do them any

good," he said as casually as he could manage. The thought of Artoo being sold into Imperial slavery . . . "Artoo has never been to any of the Council meetings."

"But he does have a great deal of knowledge of you personally," Karrde pointed out. "As well as of your sister, her husband, and various other highly placed members of the New Republic." He shrugged. "It's a moot question now, of course. The fact that the focus is exclusively on the New Republic's Jedi and potential Jedi means they're not simply after information. Where did these two attacks take place?"

"The first was on Bimmisaari, the second on Bpfassh."

Karrde nodded. "We've got a contact on Bpfassh; perhaps we can get him to do some backtracking on the Imperials. Until then, I'm afraid you'll have to remain here as our guest."

It sounded like a dismissal. "Let me just point out one other thing before I go," Luke said. "No matter what happens to me—or what happens to Leia, for that matter—the Empire is still doomed. There are more planets in the New Republic now than there are under Imperial rule, and that number increases daily. We'll win eventually, if only by sheer weight of numbers."

"I understand that was the Emperor's own argument when discussing your Rebellion," Karrde countered dryly. "Still, that *is* the crux of the dilemma, isn't it? While the Empire will wreak swift retribution on me if I don't give you over to them, the New Republic looks more likely to win out in the long run."

"Only if he and his sister are there to hold Mon Mothma's hand," Mara put in contemptuously. "If they aren't—"

"If they aren't, the final time frame is somewhat less clear," Karrde agreed. "At any rate, I thank you for your time, Skywalker. I hope we can come to a decision without too much of a delay."

"Don't hurry on my account," Luke told him. "This seems a pleasant enough world to spend a few days on."

"Don't believe it for a moment," Karrde warned. "My two pet vornskrs have a large number of relatives out in the forest. Relatives who haven't had the benefits of modern domestication."

"I understand," Luke said. On the other hand, if he could get out of Karrde's encampment and clear of whatever this strange interference was they were using on him . . .

"And don't count on your Jedi skills to protect you, either," Karrde added, almost lazily. "You'll be just as helpless in the forest. Probably more so." He looked up at the tree towering above him. "There are, after all, considerably more ysalamiri out there than there are here."

"Ysalamiri?" Luke followed his gesture . . . and for the first time noticed the slender, gray-brown creature hanging on to the tree limb directly over Karrde's head. "What is it?"

"The reason you're staying where we put you," Karrde said. "They seem to have the unusual ability to push back the Force—to create bubbles, so to speak, where the Force simply doesn't exist."

"I've never heard of them," Luke said, wondering if there was any truth at all to the story. Certainly neither Yoda nor Ben had ever mentioned the possibility of such a thing.

"Not very many have," Karrde agreed. "And in the past, most of those who did had a vested interest in keeping it that way. The Jedi of the Old Republic avoided the planet, for obvious reasons, which was why a fair number of smuggling groups back then had their bases here. After the Emperor destroyed the Jedi, most of the groups pulled up roots and left, preferring to be closer to their potential markets. Now that the Jedi are rising again"—he nodded gravely to Luke—"perhaps some of them will return. Though I daresay the general populace would probably not appreciate that."

Luke glanced around the tree. Now that he knew what

to look for, he could see several other ysalamiri wrapped around and across various of the limbs and branches. "What makes you think it's the ysalamiri and not something else that's responsible for this bubbling in the Force?"

"Partly local legend," Karrde said. "Mainly, the fact that you're standing here talking with me. How else could a man with a stun weapon and an extremely nervous mind have walked right up behind a Jedi without being noticed?"

Luke looked at him sharply, the last piece falling into place. "You had ysalamiri aboard the *Wild Karrde*."

"Correct," Karrde said. "Purely by chance, actually. Well—" He looked up at Mara. "Perhaps not *entirely* by chance."

Luke glanced again at the ysalamiri above Karrde's head. "How far does this bubbling extend?"

"Actually, I'm not sure anyone knows," Karrde conceded. "Legend says that individual ysalamiri have bubbles from one to ten meters in radius, but that groups of them together have considerably larger ones. Some sort of reinforcement, I gather. Perhaps you'll do us the courtesy of participating in a few experiments regarding them before you leave."[5]

"Perhaps," Luke said. "Though that probably depends on which direction I'm headed at the time."

"It probably will," Karrde agreed. "Well. I imagine you'd like to get cleaned up—you've been living in that flight suit for several days now. Did you bring any changes of clothing with you?"

"There's a small case in the cargo compartment of my X-wing," Luke told him. "Thank you for bringing it along, incidentally."

"I try never to waste anything that may someday prove useful," Karrde said. "I'll have your things sent over as soon as my associates have determined that there are no hidden weapons or other equipment among them." He smiled slightly. "I doubt that a Jedi would bother with such things, but I believe in being thorough. Good evening, Skywalker."

5. When I was offered this first *Star Wars* contract, and I was wandering the house trying to think up a story, the ysalamiri and their effect on the Force was the first thing that came to my mind. The initial idea was to use them to build a sort of cage around a captured Jedi.

Interestingly enough, even though that was the first idea I had, the story ended up growing in another direction and it never actually made it into any of the three books. That specific aspect of the idea had to wait several more years, until *Vision of the Future*.

—TZ

Mara had her tiny blaster in hand again. "Let's go," she said, gesturing with the weapon.

Luke stood up. "Let me offer you one other option," he said to Karrde. "If you decide you'd rather pretend none of this ever happened, you could just return Artoo and me to where you found us. I'd be willing to take my chances with the other searchers."

"Including the Imperials?" Karrde asked.

"Including the Imperials." Luke nodded.

A small smile touched Karrde's lips. "You might be surprised. But I'll keep the option in mind."

The sun had disappeared behind the trees and the sky was noticeably darker as Mara escorted him back across the compound. "Did I miss dinner?" he asked as they walked down the corridor toward his room.

"Something can be brought to you," Mara said, her voice little more than a thinly veiled snarl.

"Thank you." Luke took a careful breath. "I don't know why you dislike me so much—"

"Shut up," she cut him off. "Just shut up."

Grimacing, Luke did so. They reached his room and she nudged him inside. "We don't have any lock for the window," she said, "but there's an alarm on it. You try going out, and it'll be a toss-up as to whether the vornskrs get to you before I do." She smiled, mock-sweetly. "But don't take my word for it. Try it and find out."

Luke looked at the window, then back at Mara. "I'll pass, thanks."

Without another word she left the room, closing the door behind her. There was the click of an electronic lock being engaged, and then silence.

He went to the window, peered out. There were lights showing in some of the other barracks windows, though he hadn't noticed any other lights in his own building. Which made sense, he supposed. Whether Karrde decided to turn him over to the Empire or release him back to the New Republic, there was no point in more of his associates knowing about it than absolutely necessary.

All the more so if Karrde decided to take Mara's advice and just kill him.

He turned away from the window and went back to his bed, fighting back the fear trying to rise inside him. Never since facing the Emperor had he felt so helpless.

Or, for that matter, actually *been* so helpless.

He took a deep breath. *For the Jedi, there is no emotion; there is peace.* Somehow, he knew, there had to be a way out of this prison.

All he had to do was to stay alive long enough to find it.

CHAPTER 20

"NO, I ASSURE YOU, everything is fine," Threepio said in Leia's voice, looking just about as unhappy beneath his headset as a droid could possibly look. "Han and I decided that as long as we were out this way we might as well take a look around the Abregado system."

"I understand, Your Highness," Winter's voice came back over the *Falcon*'s speaker. To Han, she sounded tired. Tired, and more than a little tense. "May I recommend, though, that you don't stay away too much longer."

Threepio looked helplessly at Han. "We'll be back soon," Han muttered into his comlink.

"We'll be back soon," Threepio echoed into the *Falcon*'s mike.

"I just want to check out—"
"I just want to check out—"
"—the Gados's—"
"—the Gados's—"
"—manufacturing infrastructure."
"—manufacturing infrastructure."

"Yes, Your Highness," Winter said. "I'll pass that information on to the Council. I'm sure they'll be pleased to hear it." She paused, just noticeably. "I wonder if I might be permitted to speak with Captain Solo for a moment."

Across the cockpit, Lando grimaced. *She knows,* he mouthed silently.

No kidding, Han mouthed back. He caught Threepio's eye and nodded. "Of course," the droid said, sagging with obvious relief. "Han—?"

Han switched his comlink over. "I'm here, Winter. What's up?"

"I wanted to know if you had any idea yet when you and Princess Leia would be returning," she said. "Admiral Ackbar, particularly, has been asking about you."

Han frowned at the comlink. Ackbar probably hadn't spoken two words to him outside of official business since he'd resigned his general's commission a few months back. "You'll have to thank the Admiral for his interest," he told Winter, picking his words carefully. "I trust he's doing all right himself?"

"About as usual," Winter said. "He's having some problems with his family, though, now that school is in full swing."

"A little squabbling among the children?" Han suggested.

"Bedtime arguments, mainly," she said. "Problems with the little one over who's going to get to stay up and read— that sort of thing. You understand."

"Yeah," Han said. "I know the kids pretty well. How about the neighbors? He still having trouble with them?"

There was a brief pause. "I'm . . . not exactly sure," she said. "He hasn't mentioned anything about them to me. I can ask, if you'd like."

"It's no big deal," Han said. "As long as the family's doing okay—that's the important thing."

"I agree. At any rate, I think he mainly just wanted to be remembered to you."

"Thanks for passing on the message." He threw Lando a look. "Go ahead and tell him that we won't be out here too much longer. We'll go to Abregado and maybe look in on a couple of others and then head back."

"All right," Winter said. "Anything else?"

"No—yes," Han corrected himself. "What's the latest on the Bpfasshi recovery program?"

"Those three systems the Imperials hit?"

"Right." And where he and Leia had had their second brush with those gray-skinned alien kidnappers; but there was no point in dwelling on that.

"Let me call up the proper file," Winter said. ". . . It's coming along reasonably well. There were some problems with supply shipments, but the material seems to be moving well enough now."

Han frowned at the speaker. "What did Ackbar do, dig up some mothballed container ships from somewhere?"

"Actually, he made his own," Winter came back dryly. "He's taken some capital ships—Star Cruisers and Attack Frigates, mostly—cut the crews back to skeleton size and put in extra droids, and turned them into cargo ships."

Han grimaced. "I hope he's got some good escorts along with them. Empty Star Cruisers would make great target practice for the Imperials."

"I'm sure he's thought of that," Winter assured him. "And the orbit dock and shipyards at Sluis Van are very well defended."

"I'm not sure anything's really well defended these days," Han returned sourly. "Not with the Imperials running loose like they are. Anyway. Got to go; talk to you later."

"Enjoy your trip. Your Highness? Good-bye."

Lando snapped his fingers at Threepio. "Good-bye, Winter," the droid said.

Han made a slashing motion across his throat, and Lando shut off the transmitter. "If those Star Cruisers had been built with proper slave circuits, they wouldn't have to load them with droids to make container ships out of them," he pointed out innocently.

"Yeah." Han nodded, his mind just barely registering Lando's words. "Come on—we've got to cut this short and get back." He climbed out of the cockpit seat and checked his blaster. "Something's about to burn through on Coruscant."

"You mean all that stuff about Ackbar's family?" Lando asked, standing up.

"Right," Han said, heading back toward the *Falcon*'s hatchway. "If I'm reading Winter right, it sounds like Fey'lya has started a major push toward Ackbar's territory. Come on, Threepio—you need to lock up behind us."

"Captain Solo, I must once again protest this whole arrangement," the droid said plaintively, scuttling up behind Han. "I really feel that to impersonate Princess Leia—"

"All right, all right," Han cut him off. "As soon as we get back, I'll have Lando undo the programming."

"It's over already?" Lando asked, pushing past Threepio to join Han at the lock. "I thought you told Winter—"

"That was for the benefit of anyone tapping in," Han said. "As soon as we've worked through this contact, we're going to head back. Maybe even stop by Kashyyyk on the way and pick up Leia."

Lando whistled softly. "That bad, huh?"

"It's hard to say, exactly," Han had to admit as he slapped the release. The ramp dropped smoothly down to the dusty permcrete beneath them. "That 'staying up late to read' is the part I don't understand. I suppose it could mean some of the intelligence work that Ackbar's been doing along with the Supreme Commander position. Or worse—maybe Fey'lya's going for the whole sabacc pot."

"You and Winter should have worked out a better verbal code," Lando said as they started down the ramp.

"We should have worked out a verbal code, period," Han growled back. "I've been meaning for three years to sit down with her and Leia and set one up. Never got around to it."[1]

"Well, if it helps, the analysis makes sense," Lando offered, glancing around the docking pit. "It fits the rumors I've heard, anyway. I take it the neighbors you referred to are the Empire?"

"Right. Winter should have heard something about it if Ackbar had had any luck plugging the security leaks."

"Won't that make it dangerous to go back, then?" Lando asked as they started toward the exit.

"Yeah," Han agreed, feeling his lip twist. "But we're going to have to risk it. Without Leia there to play peacemaker, Fey'lya might just be able to beg or bully the rest of the Council into giving him whatever it is he wants."

"Mmm." Lando paused at the bottom of the ramp leading to the docking pit exit and looked up. "Let's hope this is the last contact in the line."

"Let's hope first that the guy shows," Han countered, heading up the ramp.

The Abregado-rae Spaceport had had a terrible reputation among the pilots Han had flown with in his smuggling days, ranking right down at the bottom with places like the Mos Eisley port on Tatooine. It was therefore something of a shock, though a pleasant one, to find a bright, clean cityscape waiting for them when they stepped through the landing pit door. "Well, well," Lando murmured from beside him. "Has civilization finally come to Abregado?"

"Stranger things have happened," Han agreed, looking around. Clean and almost painfully neat, yet with that same unmistakable air that every general freight port seemed to have. That air of the not-entirely tame . . .

"Uh-oh," Lando said quietly, his eyes on something past Han's shoulder. "Looks like someone's just bought the heavy end of the hammer."

Han turned. Fifty meters down the port perimeter street, a small group of uniformed men with light-armor

1. Thanksgiving weekend 1989, a couple of weeks after I'd been given the Thrawn Trilogy, was the local Chambanacon SF convention, which as usual we were attending. On Saturday evening we went out to dinner at a nearby Sizzler with four close friends, friends to whom I'd entrusted the still-secret project I'd just been handed. And not just entrusted with the knowledge: I'd let them read the first-draft outline I'd written up for the trilogy.

Naturally, I wanted to discuss the story with them and get whatever feedback they'd come up with. But as we sat there, we realized we had a problem. All around us were other SF fans from the convention, and at the first utterance of the names "Han," "Luke," or "Leia" ears would rotate like radar dishes, and I would be in big trouble with Lucasfilm.

So we did exactly what I had Han and Winter do here: we came up with a code on the fly. Luke and Leia became Brother and Sister; Han became Friend, Chewie became Copilot, and so on. Names like *Mara* and *Thrawn* weren't a problem, of course, since they would be meaningless to anyone else.

238

TIMOTHY ZAHNZAHN

(cont.))

I was actually surprised at how well we all pulled it off, especially without any prior consultation.

They say "write what you know." In this case, I definitely did.

—TZ

2. Another Tuckerism: more friends from Tampa.

—TZ

3. Mike LoBue plays bagpipes, and plays them very well. So I'm *sure* this "annoying music" wasn't bagpipes. Certainly not his.

—TZ

vests and blaster rifles had gathered at one of the other landing pit entrances. Even as Han watched, half of them slipped inside, leaving the rest on guard in the street. "That's the hammer, all right," Han agreed, craning his neck to try to read the number above the door. Sixty-three. "Let's hope that's not our contact in there. Where are we meeting him, anyway?"

"Right over there," Lando said, pointing to a small windowless building built in the gap between two much older ones. A carved wooden plank with the single word "LoBue"[2] hung over the door. "We're supposed to take one of the tables near the bar and the casino area and wait. He'll contact us there."

The LoBue was surprisingly large, given its modest street front, extending both back from the street and also into the older building to its left. Just inside the entrance were a group of conversation-oriented tables overlooking a small but elaborate dance floor, the latter deserted but with some annoying variety of taped music playing in the background.[3] On the far side of the dance floor were a group of private booths, too dark for Han to see into. Off to the left, up a few steps and separated from the dance floor by a transparent etched plastic wall, was the casino area. "I think I see the bar up there," Lando murmured. "Just back of the sabacc tables to the left. That's probably where he wants us."

"You ever been here before?" Han asked over his shoulder as they skirted the conversation tables and headed up the steps.

"Not this place, no. Last time I was at Abregado-rae was years ago. It was worse than Mos Eisley, and I didn't stay long." Lando shook his head. "Whatever problems you might have with the new government here, you have to admit they've done a good job of cleaning the planet up."

"Yeah, well, whatever problems you have with the new government, let's keep them quiet, okay?" Han warned. "Just for once, I'd like to keep a low profile."

Lando chuckled. "Whatever you say."

The lighting in the bar area was lower than that in the casino proper, but not so low that seeing was difficult. Choosing a table near the gaming tables, they sat down. A holo of an attractive girl rose from the center of the table as they did so. "Good day, gentles," she said in pleasantly accented Basic. "How may I serve?"

"Do you have any Necr'ygor Omic[4] wine?" Lando asked.

"We do, indeed: '47, '49, '50, and '52."

"We'll have a half carafe of the '49,"[5] Lando told her.

"Thank you, gentles," she said, and the holo vanished.

"Was that part of the countersign?" Han asked, letting his gaze drift around the casino. It was only the middle of the afternoon, local time, but even so over half the tables were occupied. The bar area, in contrast, was nearly empty, with only a handful of humans and aliens scattered around. Drinking, apparently, ranked much lower than gambling on the list of popular Gado vices.

"Actually, he didn't say anything about what we should order," Lando said. "But since I happen to like a good Necr'ygor Omic wine—"

"And since Coruscant will be picking up the tab for it?"

"Something like that."

The wine arrived on a tray delivered through a slide-hatch in the center of the table. "Will there be anything else, gentles?" the holo girl asked.

Lando shook his head, picking up the carafe and the two glasses that had come with it. "Not right now, thank you."

"Thank you." She and the tray disappeared.

"So," Lando said, pouring the wine. "I guess we wait."

"Well, while you're busy waiting, do a casual one-eighty," Han said. "Third sabacc table back—five men and a woman. Tell me if the guy second from the right is who I think it is."

Lifting his wineglass, Lando held it up to the light, as if

4. Tuckerism: Necronomicon, mushed together with their traditional Ygor/Igor party.

—TZ

5. The numbers here don't fit with any of the various *Star Wars* dating schemes, but are references to the local planetary dating system. Another subtle indication that the New Republic's hold on these systems isn't as strong as they might like.

—TZ

studying its color. In the process he turned halfway around— "Not Fynn Torve?"

"Sure looks like him to me," Han agreed. "I figured you'd probably seen him more recently than I have."

"Not since the last Kessel run you and I did together." Lando cocked an eyebrow at Han. "Just before that *other* big sabacc table," he added dryly.

Han gave him an injured look. "You're not still sore about the *Falcon,* are you?"

"Now . . ." Lando considered. "No, probably not. No sorer than I was at losing the game to an amateur like you in the first place."

"Amateur?"

"—but I'll admit there were times right afterward when I lay awake at night plotting elaborate revenge. Good thing I never got around to doing any of it."

Han looked back at the sabacc table. "If it makes you feel any better . . . if you hadn't lost the *Falcon* to me, we probably wouldn't be sitting here right now. The Empire's first Death Star would have taken out Yavin and then picked the Alliance apart planet by planet. And that would have been the end of it."

Lando shrugged. "Maybe; maybe not. With people like Ackbar and Leia running things—"

"Leia would have been dead," Han cut him off. "She was already slated for execution when Luke, Chewie, and I pulled her out of the Death Star." A shiver ran through him at the memory. He'd been *that* close to losing her forever. And would never even have known what he'd missed.

And now that he knew . . . he might still lose her.

"She'll be okay, Han," Lando said quietly. "Don't worry." He shook his head. "I just wish we knew what the Imperials wanted with her."

"I know what they want," Han growled. "They want the twins."

Lando stared at him, a startled look on his face. "Are you sure?"

"As sure as I am of any of this," Han said. "Why else didn't they just use stun weapons on us in that Bpfassh ambush? Because the things have a better than fifty-fifty chance of sparking a miscarriage, that's why."

"Sounds reasonable," Lando agreed grimly. "Does Leia know?"

"I don't know. Probably."

He looked at the sabacc tables, the cheerful decadence of the whole scene suddenly grating against his mood. If Torve really was Karrde's contact man, he wished the other would quit this nonsense and get on with it. It wasn't like there were a lot of possibilities hanging around here to choose from.

His eyes drifted away from the casino, into the bar area . . . and stopped. There, sitting at a shadowy table at the far end, were three men.

There was an unmistakable air about a general freight port, a combination of sounds and smells and vibrations that every pilot who'd been in the business long enough knew instantly. There was an equally unmistakable air about planetary security officers. "Uh-oh," he muttered.

"What?" Lando asked, throwing a casual glance of his own around the room. The glance reached the far table— "Uh-oh, indeed," he agreed soberly. "Offhand, I'd say that explains why Torve's hiding at a sabacc table."

"And doing his best to ignore us," Han said, watching the security agents out of the corner of his eye and trying to gauge the focus of their attention. If they'd tumbled to this whole contact meeting there probably wasn't much he could do about it, short of hauling out his New Republic ID and trying to pull rank on them. Which might or might not work; and he could just hear the polite screaming fit Fey'lya would have over it either way.

But if they were just after Torve, maybe as part of that landing pit raid he and Lando had seen on the way in . . .

It was worth the gamble. Reaching over, he tapped the center of the table. "Attendant?"

The holo reappeared. "Yes, gentles?"

"Give me twenty sabacc chips, will you?"

"Certainly," she said, and vanished.

"Wait a minute," Lando said cautiously as Han drained his glass. "You're not going to go over there, are you?"

"You got a better idea?" Han countered, reaching down to resettle his blaster in its holster. "If he's our contact, I sure don't want to lose him now."

Lando gave a sigh of resignation. "So much for keeping a low profile. What do you want me to do?"

"Be ready to run some interference." The center of the table opened up and a neat stack of sabacc chips arrived. "So far it looks like they're just watching him—maybe we can get him out of here before their pals arrive in force."

"If not?"

Han collected the chips and got to his feet. "Then I'll try to create a diversion, and meet you back at the *Falcon.*"

"Right. Good luck."

There were two seats not quite halfway across the sabacc table from Torve. Han chose one and sat down, dropping his stack of chips onto the table with a metallic *thud.* "Deal me in," he said.

The others looked up at him, their expressions varying from surprised to annoyed. Torve himself glanced up, came back for another look. Han cocked an eyebrow at him. "You the dealer, sonny? Come on, deal me in."[6]

"Ah—no, it's not my deal," Torve said, his eyes flicking to the pudgy man on his right.

"And we've already started," the pudgy man said, his voice surly. "Wait until the next game."

"What, you haven't all even bet yet," Han countered, gesturing toward the handful of chips in the hand pot. The sabacc pot, in contrast, was pretty rich—the session must have been going for a couple of hours at least. Probably one reason the dealer didn't want fresh blood in the game who might conceivably win it all. "Come on, give me my cards," he told the other, tossing a chip into the hand pot.

6. Once again, I'm indebted to West End Games for the rules and subtleties of sabacc.

—TZ

Slowly, glaring the whole time, the dealer peeled the top two cards off the deck and slid them over. "That's more like it," Han said approvingly. "Brings back memories, this does. I used to drop the heavy end of the hammer on the guys back home all the time."

Torve looked at him sharply, his expression freezing to stone. "Did you, now," he said, his voice deliberately casual. "Well, you're playing with the big boys here, not the little people. You may not find the sort of rewards you're used to."

"I'm not exactly an amateur myself," Han said airily. The locals at the spaceport had been raiding landing pit sixty-three . . . "I've won—oh, probably sixty-three[7] games in the last month alone."

7. Another code created on the fly. One of Han's many hidden talents. —TZ

Another flicker of recognition crossed Torve's face. So it *was* his landing pit. "Lot of rewards in numbers like that," he murmured, letting one hand drop beneath the level of the table. Han tensed, but the hand came back up empty. Torve's eyes flicked around the room once, lingering for a second on the table where Lando was sitting before turning back to Han. "You willing to put your money where your mouth is?"

Han met his gaze evenly. "I'll meet anything you've got."

Torve nodded slowly. "I may just take you up on it."

"This is all very interesting, I'm sure," one of the other players spoke up. "Some of us would like to play cards, though."

Torve raised his eyebrows at Han. "The bet's at four," he invited.

Han glanced at his cards: the Mistress of Staves and the four of Coins. "Sure," he said, lifting six chips from his stack and dropping them into the hand pot. "I'll see the four, and raise you two." There was a rustle of air behind him—

"Cheater!" a deep voice bellowed in his ear.

Hans jumped and spun around, reaching reflexively toward his blaster, but even as he did so a large hand shot over his shoulder to snatch the two cards from his other hand. "You are a *cheater, sir,*" the voice bellowed again.

"I don't know what you're talking about," Han said, craning his neck up to get a look at his assailant.

He was almost sorry he had. Towering over him like a bushy-bearded thundercloud twice his own size, the man was glaring down at him with an expression that could only be described as enflamed with religious fervor. "You know full well what I'm talking about," the man said, biting out each word. "This card"—he waved one of Han's cards—"is a *skifter.*"[8]

Han blinked. "It is not," he protested. A crowd was rapidly gathering around the table: casino security and other employees, curious onlookers, and probably a few who were hoping to see a little blood. "It's the same card I was dealt."

"Oh, is it?" The man cupped the card in one massive hand, held it in front of Han's face, and touched the corner with a fingertip.

The Mistress of Staves abruptly became the six of Sabres. The man tapped the corner again and it became the Moderation face card. And then the eight of Flasks . . . and then the Idiot face card . . . and then the Commander of Coins . . .

"That's the card I was dealt," Han repeated, feeling sweat starting to collect under his collar. So much, indeed, for keeping a low profile. "If it's a skifter, it's not my fault."

A short man with a hard-bitten face elbowed past the bearded man. "Keep your hands on the table," he ordered Han in a voice that matched his face. "Move aside, Reverend—we'll handle this."

Reverend? Han looked up at the glowering thundercloud again, and this time he saw the black, crystal-embedded band nestled against the tufts of hair at the other's throat. "Reverend, huh?" he said with a sinking feeling. There were extreme religious groups all over the galaxy, he'd found, whose main passion in life seemed to

8. The established rules of sabacc included the random shifting of the cards' values. The skifter itself, though, was my creation.

—TZ

be the elimination of all forms of gambling. And all forms of gamblers.

"Hands on the table, I said," the security man snapped, reaching over to pluck the suspect card from the Reverend's hand. He glanced at it, tried it himself, and nodded. "Cute skifter, con," he said, giving Han what was probably his best scowl.

"He must have palmed the card he was dealt," the Reverend put in. He hadn't budged from his place at Han's side. "Where is it, cheater?"

"The card I was dealt is right there in your friend's hand," Han snapped back. "I don't need a skifter to win at sabacc. If I had one, it's because it was dealt to me."

"Oh, really?" Without warning, the Reverend abruptly turned to face the pudgy sabacc dealer, still sitting at the table but almost lost in the hovering crowd. "Your cards, sir, if you don't mind," he said, holding out his hand.

The other's jaw dropped. "What are you talking about? Why would I give someone else a skifter? Anyway, it's a house deck—see?"

"Well, there's one way to be sure, isn't there?" the Reverend said, reaching over to scoop up the deck. "And then you—*and* you"—he leveled fingers at the dealer and Han—"can be scanned to see who's hiding an extra card. I dare say that would settle the issue, wouldn't you, Kampl?" he added, looking down at the scowling security man.

"Don't tell us our job, Reverend," Kampl growled. "Cyru—get that scanner over here, will you?"

The scanner was a small palm-fitting job, obviously designed for surreptitious operation. "That one first," Kampl ordered, pointing at Han.

"Right." Expertly, the other circled Han with the instrument. "Nothing."

The first touch of uncertainty cracked through Kampl's scowl. "Try it again."

The other did so. "Still nothing. He's got a blaster, comlink, and ID, and that's it."

For a long moment Kampl continued staring at Han. Then, reluctantly, he turned to the sabacc dealer. "I protest!" the dealer sputtered, pushing himself to his feet. "I'm a Class Double-A citizen—you have no right to put me through this sort of *totally* unfounded accusation."

"You do it here or down at the station," Kampl snarled. "Your choice."

The dealer threw a look at Han that was pure venom, but he stood in stiff silence while the security tech scanned him down. "He's clean, too," the other reported, a slight frown on his face.

"Scan around the floor," Kampl ordered. "See if someone ditched it."

"And count the cards still in the deck," the Reverend spoke up.

Kampl spun to face him. "For the last time—"

"Because if all we have here are the requisite seventy-six cards," the Reverend cut him off, his voice heavy with suspicion, "perhaps what we're really looking at is a fixed deck."

Kampl jerked as if he'd been stung. "We don't fix decks in here," he insisted.

"No?" the Reverend glared. "Not even when special people are sitting in on the game? People who might know to look for a special card when it comes up?"

"That's ridiculous," Kampl snarled, taking a step toward him. "The LoBue is a respectable and perfectly legal establishment. None of these players has any connection with—"

"Hey!" the pudgy dealer said suddenly. "The guy who was sitting next to me—where'd he go?"

The Reverend snorted. "So. None of them has any connection with you, do they?"

Someone swore violently and started pushing his way through the crowd—one of the three planetary security types who'd been watching the table. Kampl watched him go, took a deep breath, and turned to glare at Han. "You want to tell me your partner's name?"

"He wasn't my partner," Han said. "And I was not cheating. You want to make a formal accusation, take me down to the station and do it there. If you don't"—he got to his feet, scooping up his remaining chips in the process— "then I'm leaving."

For a long moment he thought Kampl was going to call his bluff. But the other had no real evidence, and he knew it; and apparently he had better things to do than indulge in what would be really nothing more than petty harassment. "Sure—get out of here," the other snarled. "Don't ever come back."

"Don't worry," Han told him.

The crowd was starting to dissolve, and he had no trouble making his way back to his table. Lando, not surprisingly, was long gone. What *was* surprising was that he'd settled the bill before he had left.

"That was quick," Lando greeted him from the top of the *Falcon*'s entry ramp. "I wasn't expecting them to turn you loose for at least an hour."

"They didn't have much of a case," Han said, climbing up the ramp and slapping the hatch button. "I hope Torve didn't give you the slip."

Lando shook his head. "He's waiting in the lounge." He raised his eyebrows. "And considers himself in our debt."

"That could be useful," Han agreed, heading down the curved corridor.

Torve was seated at the lounge holo board, three small datapads spread out in front of him. "Good to see you again, Torve," Han said as he stepped in.

"You, too, Solo," the other said gravely, getting to his feet and offering Han his hand. "I've thanked Calrissian already, but I wanted to thank you, too. Both for the warning and for helping me get out of there. I'm in your debt."

"No problem," Han waved the thanks away. "I take it that *is* your ship in pit sixty-three?"

"My employer's ship, yes," Torve said, grimacing. "Fortunately, there's nothing contraband in it at the moment—I've already off-loaded. They obviously suspect me, though."

"What kind of contraband were you running?" Lando asked, coming up behind Han. "If it's not a secret, that is?"

Torve cocked an eyebrow. "No secret, but you're not going to believe it. I was running food."

"You're right," Lando said. "I don't believe it."

Torve nodded vaguely off to one side. "I didn't either, at first. Seems there's a clan of people living off in the southern hills who don't find much about the new government to appreciate."

"Rebels?"

"No, and that's what's strange about it," Torve said. "They're not rebelling or making trouble or even sitting on vital resources. They're simple people, and all they want is to be left alone to continue living that way. The government's apparently decided to make an example of them, and among other things has cut off all food and medical supplies going that way until they agree to fall into step like everyone else."

"That sounds like this government," Lando agreed heavily. "Not much into regional autonomy of any kind."

"Hence, we smuggle in food,"[9] Torve concluded. "Crazy business. Anyway, it's nice to see you two again. Nice to see you're still working together, too. So many teams have broken up over the past few years, especially since Jabba bought the *really* heavy end of the hammer."

Han exchanged glances with Lando. "Well, it's actually more like we're *back* together," he corrected Torve. "We sort of wound up on the same side during the war. Up till then . . ."

"Up till then I wanted to kill him," Lando explained helpfully. "No big deal, really."

"Sure," Torve said guardedly, looking back and forth between them. "Let me guess: the *Falcon,* right? I remember hearing rumors that you stole it."

9. Just one more indication that Karrde has an ethical core lurking under the surface.

  Also another indication of how many of Lando's contacts are of the somewhat dubious sort.

—TZ

Han looked at Lando, eyebrows raised. "*Stole* it?"

"Like I said, I was mad." Lando shrugged. "It wasn't an out-and-out theft, actually, though it came pretty close. I had a little semilegit clearinghouse for used ships at the time, and I ran short of money in a sabacc game Han and I were playing. I offered him his pick of any of my ships if he won." He threw Han a mock glare. "He was *supposed* to go for one of the flashy chrome-plate yachts that had been collecting dust on the front row, not the freighter I'd been quietly upgrading on the side for myself."

"You did a good job, too," Han said. "Though Chewie and I wound up pulling a lot of the stuff out and redoing it ourselves."

"Nice," Lando growled. "Another crack like that and I may just take it back."

"Chewie would probably take great exception to that," Han said. He fixed Torve with a hard look. "Of course, you knew all this already, didn't you."

Torve grinned. "No offense, Solo. I like to feel out my customers before we do business—get an idea of whether I can expect 'em to play straight with me. People who lie about their history usually lie about the job, too."

"I trust we passed?"

"Like babes in the tall grass." Torve nodded, still grinning. "So. What can Talon Karrde do for you?"

Han took a careful breath. Finally. Now all he had to worry about was fouling this up. "I want to offer Karrde a deal: the chance to work directly with the New Republic."

Torve nodded. "I'd heard that you were going around trying to push that scheme with other smuggling groups. The general feeling is that you're trying to set them up for Ackbar to take down."

"I'm not," Han assured him. "Ackbar's not exactly thrilled at the idea, but he's accepted it. We need to get more shipping capacity from somewhere, and smugglers are the logical supply to tap."

Torve pursed his lips. "From what I've heard it sounds

like an interesting offer. 'Course, I'm not the one who makes decisions like that."

"So take us to Karrde," Lando suggested. "Let Han talk to him directly."

"Sorry, but he's at the main base at the moment," Torve said, shaking his head. "I can't take you there."

"Why not?"

"Because we don't let strangers just flit in and out," Torve said patiently. "We don't have anything like the kind of massive, overbearing security Jabba had on Tatooine, for starters."

"We're not exactly—" Lando began.

Han cut him off with a gesture. "All right, then," he said to Torve. "How are you going to get back there?"

Torve opened his mouth, then closed it again. "I guess I'll have to figure out a way to get my ship out of impoundment, won't I?"

"That'll take time," Han pointed out. "Besides which, you're known here. On the other hand, someone who showed up with the proper credentials could probably pry it loose before anyone knew what had happened."

Torve cocked an eyebrow. "You, for instance?"

Han shrugged. "I might be able to. After that thing at the LoBue I probably should lie low, too. But I'm sure I could set it up."

"I'm sure," Torve said, heavily sardonic. "And the catch . . . ?"

"No catch," Han told him. "All I want in return is for you to let us give you a lift back to your base, and then have fifteen minutes to talk with Karrde."

Torve gazed at him, his mouth tight. "I'll get in trouble if I do this. You know that."

"We're not exactly random strangers," Lando reminded him. "Karrde met me once, and both Han and I kept major military secrets for the Alliance for years. We've got a good record of people being able to trust us."

Torve looked at Lando. Looked again at Han. "I'll get in

trouble," he repeated with a sigh. "But I guess I really *do* owe you. One condition, though: I do all the navigation on the way in, and set it up in a coded, erasable module. Whether you have to do the same thing on the way out will be up to Karrde."

"Good enough," Han agreed. Paranoia was a common enough ailment among smugglers. Anyway, he had no particular interest in knowing where Karrde had set up shop. "When can we leave?"

"As soon as you're ready." Torve nodded at the sabacc chips cupped in Han's hand. "Unless you want to go back to the LoBue and play those," he added.

Han had forgotten he was still holding the chips. "Forget it," he growled, dropping the stack onto the holo board. "I try not to play sabacc when there are fanatics breathing down my neck."

"Yes, the Reverend put on a good show, didn't he?" Torve agreed. "Don't know what we would have done without him."

"Wait a minute," Lando put in. "You *know* him?"

"Sure." Torve grinned. "He's my contact with the hill clan. He couldn't have made nearly so much fuss without a stranger like you there for him to pick on, though."

"Why, that rotten—" Han clamped his teeth together. "I suppose that was *his* skifter, huh?"

"Sure was." Torve looked innocently at Han. "What are you complaining about? You got what you wanted—I'm taking you to see Karrde. Right?"

Han thought about it. Torve was right, of course. But still . . . "Right," he conceded. "So much for heroics, I guess."

Torve snorted gently. "Tell me about it. Come on, let's get into your computer and start coding up a nav module."

CHAPTER 21

MARA STEPPED UP to the comm room door, wondering uneasily what this sudden summons was all about. Karrde hadn't said, but there had been something in his voice that had set her old survival instincts tingling. Checking the tiny blaster hanging upside down in its sleeve sheath, she slapped at the door release.

She'd expected to find at least two people already in the room: Karrde plus the comm room duty man plus whoever else had been called in on this. To her mild surprise, Karrde was alone. "Come in, Mara," he invited, looking up from his datapad. "Close the door behind you."

She did so. "Trouble?" she asked.

"A minor problem only," he assured her. "A bit of an awkward one, though. Fynn Torve just called to say he was on his way in . . . and he has guests. Former New Republic generals Lando Calrissian and Han Solo."

Mara felt her stomach tighten. "What do they want?"

Karrde shrugged fractionally. "Apparently, just to talk to me."

For a second, Mara's thoughts flicked to Skywalker, still locked away in his barracks room across the compound. But, no—there was no way anyone in the New Republic could possibly know he was here. Most of Karrde's own people didn't know it, including the majority of those right here on Myrkr. "Did they bring their own ship?" she asked.

"Theirs is the only one coming in, actually," Karrde nodded. "Torve's riding with them."

Mara's eyes flicked to the comm equipment behind him. "A hostage?"

Karrde shook his head. "I don't think so. He gave all the proper all-clear passwords. The *Etherway*'s still on Abregado—been impounded by the local authorities or some such. Apparently, Calrissian and Solo helped Torve avoid a similar fate."

"Then thank them, have them put Torve down, and tell them to get off the planet," she said. "You didn't invite them here."

"True," Karrde agreed, watching her closely. "On the other hand, Torve seems to think he's under a certain obligation to them."

"Then let him pay it back on his own time."

The skin around Karrde's eyes seemed to harden. "Torve is one of my associates," he said, his voice cold. "His debts are the organization's. You should know that by now."

Mara's throat tightened as a sudden, horrible thought occurred to her. "You're not going to give Skywalker to them, are you?" she demanded.

"Alive, you mean?" Karrde countered.

For a long moment Mara just stared at him; at that small smile and those slightly heavy eyelids and the rest of that carefully constructed expression of complete disinterest in the matter. But it was all an act, and she knew it. He wanted to know why she hated Skywalker, all right—wanted it with as close to genuine passion as the man ever got.

And as far as she was concerned, he could go right on wanting it. "I don't suppose it's occurred to you," she bit out, "that Solo and Calrissian might have engineered this whole thing, including the *Etherway*'s impoundment, as a way of finding this base."

"It's occurred to me, yes," Karrde said. "I dismissed it as somewhat far fetched."

"Of course," Mara said sardonically. "The great and noble Han Solo would never do something so devious, would he? You never answered my question."

"About Skywalker? I thought I'd made it clear, Mara, that he stays here until I know why Grand Admiral Thrawn is so interested in acquiring him. At the very least, we need to know what he's worth, and to whom, before we can set a fair market price for him. I have some feelers out; with luck, we should know in a few more days."

"And meanwhile, his allies will be here in a few more minutes."

"Yes," Karrde agreed, his lips puckering slightly. "Skywalker will have to be moved somewhere a bit more out of the way—we obviously can't risk Solo and Calrissian stumbling over him. I want you to move him to the number four storage shed."

"That's where we're keeping that droid of his," Mara reminded him.

"The shed's got two rooms; put him in the other one." Karrde waved toward her waist. "And do remember to lose that before our guests arrive. I doubt they'd fail to recognize it."

Mara glanced down at Skywalker's lightsaber hanging from her belt. "Don't worry. If it's all the same to you, I'd just as soon not have much to do with them."

"I wasn't planning for you to," Karrde assured her. "I'd like you here when I greet them, and possibly to join us for dinner, as well. Other than that, you're excused from all social activities."

"So they're staying the day?"

"And possibly the night, as well." He eyed her. "Requirements of a proper host aside, can you think of a better way for us to prove to the Republic, should the need arise, that Skywalker was never here?"

It made sense. But that didn't mean she had to like it. "Are you warning the rest of the *Wild Karrde*'s crew to keep quiet?"

"I'm doing better than that," Karrde said, nodding back toward the comm equipment. "I've sent everyone who knows about Skywalker off to get the *Starry Ice* prepped. Which reminds me—after you move Skywalker, I want you to run his X-wing farther back under the trees. No more than half a kilometer—I don't want you to go through any more of the forest alone than you have to. Can you fly an X-wing?"

"I can fly anything."

"Good," he said, smiling slightly. "You'd better be off, then. The *Millennium Falcon* will be landing in less than twenty minutes."

Mara took a deep breath. "All right," she said. Turning, she left the room.

The compound was empty as she walked across it to the barracks building. By Karrde's design, undoubtedly; he must have shifted people around to inside duties to give her a clear path for taking Skywalker to the storage shed. Reaching his room, she keyed off the lock and slid open the door.

He was standing by the window, dressed in that same black tunic, pants, and high boots that he'd worn that day at Jabba's palace.

That day she'd stood silently by and watched . . . and let him destroy her life.

"Get your case and let's go," she growled, gesturing with the blaster. "It's moving day."

His eyes stayed on her as he stepped over to the bed. Not on the blaster in her hand, but on her face. "Karrde's made a decision?" he asked calmly as he picked up the case.

For a long moment she was tempted to tell him that, no, this was on her own initiative, just to see if the implications would crack that maddening Jedi serenity. But even a Jedi would probably fight if he thought he was going to his death, and they were on a tight enough schedule as it was. "You're moving to one of the storage sheds," she told him. "We've got company coming, and we don't have any formal wear your size. Come on, move."

She walked him past the central building to the number four shed, a two-room structure tucked conveniently back out of the compound's major traffic patterns. The room on the left, normally used for sensitive or dangerous equipment, was also the only one of the storage areas with a lock, undoubtedly the reason Karrde had chosen it to serve the role of impromptu prison. Keeping one eye on Skywalker, she keyed open the lock, wondering as she did so whether Karrde had had time to disable the inside mechanism. A quick look as the door slid open showed that he hadn't.

Well, that could easily be corrected. "In here," she ordered, flicking on the inside light and gesturing for him to enter.

He complied. "Looks cozy," he said, glancing around the windowless room and the piled shipping boxes that took up perhaps half the floor space to the right. "Probably quiet, too."

"Ideal for Jedi meditation," she countered, stepping over to an open box marked *Blasting Disks* and taking a look inside. No problem; it was being used for spare coveralls at the moment. She gave the rest of the box markings a quick check, confirmed that there was nothing here he could possibly use to escape. "We'll get a cot or something in for you later," she said, moving back to the door. "Food, too."

"I'm all right for now."

"Ask me if I care." The inner lock mechanism was behind a thin metal plate. Two shots from her blaster unsealed one end of the plate and curled it back; a third vaporized a selected group of wires. "Enjoy the quiet," she said, and left.

The door closed behind her, and locked . . . and Luke was once again alone.

He looked around him. Piled boxes, no windows, a single locked door. "I've been in worse places," he muttered under his breath. "At least there's no Rancor here."

For a moment he frowned at the odd thought, wondering why the Rancor pit at Jabba's palace should suddenly have flashed to mind. But he gave it only a moment. The lack of proper preparation and facilities in his new prison strongly suggested that moving him here had been a spur-of-the-moment decision, possibly precipitated by the imminent arrival of whoever the visitors were Mara had mentioned.

And if so, there was a good possibility that somewhere in the mad scramble they might finally have made a mistake.

He went over to the door, easing the still-warm metal plate a little farther back and kneeling down to peer inside at the lock mechanism. Han had spent a few idle hours once trying to teach him the finer points of hot-wiring locks, and if Mara's shot hadn't damaged it too badly, there was a chance he might be able to persuade it to disengage.

It didn't look promising. Whether by design or accident, Mara's shot had taken out the wires to the inside control's power supply, vaporizing them all the way back into the wall conduit, where there was no chance at all of getting hold of them.

But if he could find another power supply . . .

He got to his feet again, brushed off his knees, and headed over to the neatly piled boxes. Mara had glanced at their labels, but she'd actually looked inside only one of them. Perhaps a more complete search would turn up something useful.

The search, unfortunately, took even less time than his examination of the ruined lock. Most of the boxes were sealed beyond his capability to open without tools, and the handful that weren't held such innocuous items as clothing or replacement equipment modules.

All right, then, he told himself, sitting down on the edge of one of the boxes and looking around for inspiration. *I can't use the door. There aren't any windows.* But there *was* another room in this shed—he'd seen the other door while Mara was opening this one. Perhaps there was some kind of half-height doorway or crawl space between them, hidden out of sight behind the stacked boxes.

It wasn't likely, of course, that Mara would have missed anything that obvious. But he had time, and nothing else to occupy it. Getting up from his seat, he began unstacking the boxes and moving them away from the wall.

He'd barely begun when he found it. Not a doorway, but something almost as good: a multisocket power outlet, set into the wall just above the baseboard.

Karrde and Mara had made their mistake.[1]

The metal doorplate, already stressed by the blaster fire Mara had used to peel it back, was relatively easy to bend. Luke kept at it, bending it back and forth, until a roughly triangular piece broke off in his hand. It was too soft to be of any use against the sealed equipment boxes, but it would probably be adequate for unscrewing the cover of a common power outlet.

He returned to the outlet and lay down in the narrow gap between wall and boxes. He was just trying to wedge his makeshift screwdriver against the first screw when he heard a quiet beep.

He froze, listening. The beep came again, followed by a series of equally soft warbles. Warbles that sounded very familiar . . . "Artoo?" he called softly. "Is that you?"

For a pair of heartbeats there was silence from the other room. Then, abruptly, the wall erupted with a minor explosion of electronic jabbering. Artoo, without a doubt.

---

1. Ideally, any confrontation between characters should play out as a sort of stylized chess game, with the writer playing both sides. One side makes a move—Mara sealing the door—and then the other side makes a countermove—Luke searching for and finding the power outlet.

Also ideally, the side that wins a particular round does so out of cleverness, and the side that loses does so not so much out of stupidity but because they missed something. Here, there's a little fact about Luke that Mara and Karrde either didn't know or, in the rush of the moment, didn't think all the way through.

Just as the heroism of your hero is measured against the villainy of your villain, so too is the hero's cleverness measured against that of his opponents.

—TZ

"Steady, Artoo," Luke called back. "I'm going to try and get this power outlet open. There's probably one on your side, too—can you get it open?"

There was a distinctly disgusted-sounding gurgle. "No, huh? Well, just hang on, then."

The broken metal triangle wasn't the easiest thing to work with, particularly in the cramped space available. Still, it took Luke only a couple of minutes to get the cover plate off and pull the wires out of his way. Hunching forward, he could see through the hole to the back of the outlet in Artoo's room. "I don't think I can get your outlet open from here," he called to the droid. "Is your room locked?"

There was a negative beep, followed by an odd sort of whining, as if Artoo was spinning his wheels. "Restraining bolt?" Luke asked. The spinning/whine came again—"Or a restraint collar?"

An affirmative beep, with frustrated overtones. It figured, in retrospect: a restraining bolt would leave a mark, whereas a collar snugged around Artoo's lower half would do nothing but let him wear out his wheels a little. "Never mind," Luke reassured him. "If there's enough wire in here to reach to the door, I should be able to unlock it. Then we can both get out of here."

Carefully, mindful of the possibility of shock from the higher-current lines nearby, he found the low-voltage wire and started easing it gently toward him out of the conduit. There was more than he'd expected; he got nearly one and a half meters coiled on the floor by his head before it stopped coming.

More than he'd expected, but far less than he needed. The door was a good four meters away in a straight line, and he would need some slack to get it spliced into the lock mechanism. "It's going to be a few more minutes," he called to Artoo, trying to think. The low-power line had a meter and a half of slack to it, which implied the other lines probably did, as well. If he could cut that much length off two of them, he should have more than enough to reach the lock.

Which left only the problem of finding something to cut them with. And, of course, managing to not electrocute himself along the way.

"What I wouldn't give to have my lightsaber back for a minute," he muttered, examining the edge of his makeshift screwdriver. It wasn't very sharp; but then, the superconducting wires weren't very thick, either.

It was the work of a couple of minutes to pull the other wires as far out of the conduit as they would go. Standing up, he took off his tunic, wrapped one of the sleeves twice around the metal, and started sawing.

He was halfway through the first of the wires when his hand slipped off the insulating sleeve and for a second touched the bare metal. Reflexively he jerked back, banging his hand against the wall.

And then his brain caught up with him. "Uh-oh," he murmured, staring at the half-cut wire.

There was an interrogative whistle from the other room. "I just touched one of the wires," he told the droid, "and I didn't get a shock."

Artoo whistled. "Yeah," Luke agreed. He tapped at the wire . . . touched it again . . . held his finger against it.

So Karrde and Mara hadn't made a mistake, after all. They'd already cut the power to the outlet.

For a moment he knelt there, holding the wire, wondering what he was going to do now. He still had all this wire, but no power supply for it to connect with. Conversely, there were probably any number of small power sources in the room, attached to the stored replacement modules, but they were all packed away in boxes he couldn't get into. Could he somehow use the wire to get into the boxes? Use it to slice through the outer sealant layer, perhaps?

He got a firm grip on the wire and pulled on it, trying to judge its tensile strength. His fingers slipped along the insulation; shifting his grip, he wrapped it firmly around his right hand—

And stopped, a sudden prickly feeling on the back of his neck. His right hand. His artificial right hand. His artificial, dual-power-supply right hand . . . "Artoo, you know anything about cybernetic limb replacements?" he called, levering the wrist access port open with his metal triangle.

There was a short pause, then a cautious and ambiguous-sounding warble. "It shouldn't take too much," he reassured the droid, peering at the maze of wiring and servos inside his hand. He'd forgotten how incredibly complex the whole thing was. "All I need to do is get one of the power supplies out. Think you can walk me through the procedure?"

The pause this time was shorter, and the reply more confident. "Good," Luke said. "Let's get to it."

CHAPTER 22

HAN FINISHED HIS PRESENTATION, sat back in his chair, and waited.

"Interesting," Karrde said, that faintly amused, totally noncommittal expression of his hiding whatever it was he was really thinking. "Interesting, indeed. I presume the Provisional Council would be willing to record legal guarantees of all this."

"We'll guarantee what we can," Han told him. "Your protection, legality of operation, and so forth. Naturally, we can't guarantee particular profit margins or anything like that."

"Naturally," Karrde agreed, his gaze shifting to Lando. "You've been rather quiet, General Calrissian. How exactly do you fit into all of this?"

"Just as a friend," Lando said. "Someone who knew how to get in touch with you. And someone who can vouch for Han's integrity and honesty."

A slight smile touched Karrde's lips. "Integrity and honesty," he repeated. "Interesting words to use in regard to a man with Captain Solo's somewhat checkered reputation."

Han grimaced, wondering which particular incident Karrde might be referring to. There were, he had to admit, a fair number to choose from.[1] Any checkering that existed is all in the past," he said.

"Of course," Karrde agreed. "Your proposal is, as I said, very interesting. But not, I think, for my organization."

"May I ask why not?" Han asked.

"Very simply, because it would look to certain parties as if we were taking sides," Karrde explained, sipping from the cup at his side. "Given the extent of our operations, and the regions in which those operations take place, that might not be an especially politic thing to do."

"I understand." Han nodded. "I'd like the chance to convince you that there are ways to keep your other clients from knowing about it."

Karrde smiled again. "I think you underestimate the Empire's intelligence capabilities, Captain Solo," he said. "They know far more about Republic movements than you might think."

"Tell me about it," Han grimaced, glancing at Lando. "That reminds me of something else I wanted to ask you. Lando said you might know a slicer who was good enough to crack diplomatic codes."

Karrde cocked his head slightly to the side. "Interesting request," he commented. "Particularly coming from someone who should already have access to such codes. Is intrigue beginning to form among the New Republic hierarchy, perhaps?"

That last conversation with Winter, and her veiled warnings, flashed through Han's mind. "This is purely personal," he assured Karrde. "Mostly personal, anyway."

"Ah," the other said. "As it happens, one of the best slicers in the trade will be at dinner this afternoon. You'll join us, of course?"

Han glanced at his watch[2] in surprise. Between business and small talk, the fifteen-minute interview that

1. And now, with all the other books being written in the Expanded Universe, there are even *more* such incidents for Karrde to be thinking of.

—TZ

2. I used both *watch* and *chrono* to designate time-keepers in *Heir*. The former I envisioned as small, personal timepieces, while the latter would be located aboard ships or the equivalent of wall or desk clocks.

I don't think anything like watches ever showed up in the movies. But surely people there still needed easily portable ways to tell time.

—TZ

Torve had promised him with Karrde had now stretched out into two hours. "We don't want to impose on your time—"

"It's no imposition at all," Karrde assured him, setting his cup down and standing. "With the press of business and all, we tend to miss the midday meal entirely and compensate by pushing the evening dinner up to late afternoon."[3]

"I remember those wonderful smuggler schedules," Han nodded wryly, memories flashing through his mind. "You're lucky to get even two meals."

"Indeed," Karrde agreed. "If you'll follow me . . . ?"

The main building, Han had noted on the way in, seemed to be composed of three or four circular zones centering on the greatroom with the strange tree growing through it. The room Karrde took them to now was in the layer just outside the greatroom, taking perhaps a quarter of that circle. A number of round tables were set up, with several of them already occupied. "We don't stand on protocol regarding meals here," Karrde said, leading the way to a table in the center of the room. Four people were already sitting there: three men and a woman.

Karrde steered them to three vacant seats. "Good evening, all." He nodded to the others at the table. "May I present Calrissian and Solo, who'll be dining with us tonight." He gestured to each of the men in turn. "Three of my associates: Wadewarn,[4] Chin, and Ghent. Ghent is the slicer I mentioned; possibly the best in the business." He waved to the woman. "And of course you've already met Mara Jade."

"Yes," Han agreed, nodding to her and sitting down, a small shiver running up his back. Mara had been with Karrde when he'd first welcomed them into that makeshift throne room of his. She hadn't stayed long; but for the whole of that brief time she'd glowered darkly at Lando and him with those incredible green eyes of hers.

3. More art imitating life. In those days, whenever I found myself on my own (usually when I was off on one of my three-day, writing-intensive retreats), I would follow this same schedule: early breakfast, early dinner, no lunch.
—TZ

4. Tuckerism: Wade Warren, another Tampa fan.
—TZ

Almost exactly the same way she was glowering at them right now.

"So you're Han Solo," the slicer, Ghent, said brightly. "I've heard a lot about you. Always wanted to meet you."

Han shifted his attention away from Mara to Ghent. He wasn't much more than a kid, really, barely out of his teens. "It's nice to be famous," Han told him. "Just remember that whatever you've heard has been hearsay. And that hearsay stories grow an extra leg every time they're told."

"You're too modest," Karrde said, signaling to the side. In response, a squat droid rolled toward them from around the room's curve, a tray of what looked like rolled leaves perched on top of it. "It would be difficult to embellish that Zygerrian slaver incident, for example."

Lando looked up from the droid's tray. "Zygerrian slavers?" he echoed. "You never told me that one."

"It wasn't anything important," Han said, warning Lando with a look to drop the subject.

Unfortunately, Ghent[5] either missed the look or was too young to know what it meant. "He and Chewbacca attacked a Zygerrian slaver ship," the kid explained eagerly. "Just the two of them. The Zygerrians were so scared they abandoned ship."

"They were more pirates than slavers," Han said, giving up. "And they weren't afraid of me—they abandoned ship because I told them I had twenty stormtroopers with me and was coming aboard to check their shipping licenses."

Lando raised his eyebrows. "And they *bought* that?"

Han shrugged. "I was broadcasting a borrowed Imperial ID at the time."

"But then you know what he did?" Ghent put in. "He gave the ship over to the slaves they found locked up in the hold. *Gave* it to them—just like that! Including all the cargo, too."

"Why, you old softie." Lando grinned, taking a bite from one of the rolled leaves. "No wonder you never told me that one."

5. For someone who was never intended to be anything but a minor character, Ghent has picked up a surprising following among the readers over the years.

No doubt it's a combination of his computer skills, his open-faced honesty, and his complete oblivioun to all the political machinations swirling around him.

If he's not the king of the *Star Wars* nerds, he's certainly one of the royal family.

—TZ

6. An odd echo (pre-
echo?) of the
"Jaynestown" episode of
the TV series *Firefly*, where
an action that was seen
by some as heroic was re-
ally nothing more than
pure pragmatism on the
part of the person in-
volved.

In this case, Ghent saw
Han's donation of the slaver ship and cargo to the
victims as an act of charity, whereas Han's motivations had been less
altruistic than practical.

I adopted this particular
incident from the *Star
Wars Sourcebook,* where
it was described briefly by
one of the slavers' victims.
I thought it would be in-
teresting to show Han's
side of it, especially since
back then he wasn't the
noble yet lovable rogue we
all know from the movies.
—TZ

With an effort, Han held on to his patience. "The cargo was pirate plunder," he growled. "Some of it extremely traceable. We were off Janodral Mizar—they had a strange local law at the time that pirate or slaver victims got to split up the proceeds if the pirates were taken or killed."[6]

"That law's still in force, as far as I know," Karrde murmured.

"Probably. Anyway, Chewie was with me . . . and you know Chewie's opinion of slavers."

"Yeah," Lando said dryly. "They'd have had a better chance with the twenty stormtroopers."

"And if I hadn't just given away the ship—" Han broke off as a quiet beep sounded.

"Excuse me," Karrde said, pulling a comlink from his belt. "—Karrde here."

Han couldn't hear what was being said . . . but abruptly Karrde's face seemed to tighten. "I'll be right there."

He got to his feet and slipped the comlink back onto his belt. "Excuse me again," he said. "A small matter needs my attention."

"Trouble?" Han asked.

"I hope not." Karrde glanced across the table, and Han turned in time to see Mara stand up. "Hopefully, this will only take a few minutes. Please enjoy your meal."

They left the table, and Han looked back at Lando. "I've got a bad feeling about this," he muttered.

Lando nodded, his eyes still following Mara and Karrde, a strange expression on his face. "I've seen her before, Han," he murmured back. "I don't know where, but I know I've seen her . . . and I don't think she was a smuggler at the time."

Han looked around the table at the others, at the wariness in their eyes and the guarded murmuring back and forth between them. Even Ghent had noticed the sudden tension and was studiously eating away at his appetizers. "Well, figure it out fast, buddy," he told Lando quietly. "We might be about to wear out our welcome."

"I'm working on it. What do we do until then?"

Another droid was trundling up, his tray laden with filled soup bowls. "Until then," Han said, "I guess we enjoy our meal."

"He came in from lightspeed about ten minutes ago," Aves said tightly, tapping the mark on the sensor display. "Captain Pellaeon signaled two minutes later. Asking for you personally."

Karrde rubbed a finger gently across his lower lip. "Any signs of landing craft or fighters?" he asked.

"Not yet." Aves shook his head. "But from his insertion angle, I'd guess he'll be dropping some soon—downpoint probably somewhere in this part of the forest."

Karrde nodded thoughtfully. Such propitious timing . . . for someone. "Where did we wind up putting the *Millennium Falcon*?"

"It's over on pad eight," Aves said.

Back in under the edge of the forest, then. That was good—the high metal content of Myrkr's trees would help shield it from the *Chimaera*'s sensors. "Take two men and go throw a camo net over it," he told the other. "There's no point in taking chances. And do it quietly—we don't want to alarm our guests."

"Right." Aves pulled off his headset and headed out of the room at a brisk trot.

Karrde looked at Mara. "Interesting timing, this visit."

She met his gaze without flinching. "If that's a subtle way of asking whether or not I called them, don't bother. I didn't."

He cocked his head. "Really. I'm a little surprised."

"So am I," she countered. "I should have thought of it days ago." She nodded toward the headset. "You going to talk to him or not?"

"I don't suppose I have much choice." Mentally bracing himself, Karrde sat down in the seat Aves had just vacated and touched a switch. "Captain Pellaeon, this is Talon Karrde," he said. "My apologies for the delay. What can I do for you?"

The distant image of the *Chimaera* disappeared, but it wasn't Pellaeon's face that replaced it. This face was a nightmare image: long and lean, with pale blue skin and eyes that glittered like two bits of red-hot metal. "Good afternoon, Captain Karrde," the other said, his voice clear and smooth and very civilized. "I'm Grand Admiral Thrawn."

"Good afternoon, Admiral." Karrde nodded in greeting, taking it in stride. "This is an unexpected honor. May I ask the purpose of your call?"

"Part of it I'm sure you've already guessed," Thrawn told him. "We find ourselves in need of more ysalamiri, and would like your permission to harvest some more of them."

"Certainly," Karrde said, a funny feeling starting to tug at the back of his mind. There was something strange about Thrawn's posture . . . and the Imperials hardly needed his permission to come pull ysalamiri off their trees. "If I may say so, you seem to be running through them rather quickly. Are you having trouble keeping them alive?"

Thrawn raised an eyebrow in polite surprise. "None of them has died, Captain. We simply need more of them."

"Ah," Karrde said. "I see."

"I doubt that. But no matter. It occurred to me, Captain, that as long as we were coming here, it might be a good time for us to have a little talk."

"What sort of talk?"

"I'm sure we can find some topics of mutual interest," Thrawn said. "For example, I'm in the market for new warships."

Long practice kept any guilty reaction from leaking out through Karrde's face or voice. But it was a near thing. "Warships?" he asked carefully.

"Yes." Thrawn favored him with a thin smile. "Don't worry—I'm not expecting you to actually have any capital starships in stock. But a man with your contacts may possibly be able to acquire them."

"I doubt that my contacts are quite that extensive, Admiral," Karrde told him, trying hard to read that not-quite-human face. Did he know? Or was the question merely an exquisitely dangerous coincidence? "I don't think we'll be able to help you."[7]

Thrawn's expression didn't change ... but abruptly there was an edge of menace to his smile. "You'll try anyway. And then there's the matter of your refusal to help in our search for Luke Skywalker."

Some of the tightness in Karrde's chest eased. This was safer territory. "I'm sorry we were also unable to help there, Admiral. As I explained before to your representative, we were under several tight scheduling deadlines at the time. We simply couldn't spare the ships."

Thrawn's eyebrows lifted slightly. "At the time, you say? But the search is still going on, Captain."

Silently, Karrde cursed himself for the slip. "Still going on?" he echoed, frowning. "But your representative said Skywalker was flying an Incom X-wing starfighter. If you haven't found him by now, his life support will surely have given out."

"Ah," Thrawn said, nodding. "I see the misunderstanding. Normally, yes, you'd be correct. But Skywalker is a Jedi; and among a Jedi's bag of tricks is the ability to go into a sort of comatose state." He paused, and the image on the screen flickered momentarily. "So there's still plenty of time for you to join in the hunt."

"I see," Karrde said. "Interesting. I suppose that's just one of the many things the average person never knew about Jedi."

"Perhaps we'll have time to discuss such things when I arrive on Myrkr," Thrawn said.

Karrde froze, a horrible realization shooting through him like an electric shock. That brief flickering of Thrawn's image—

7. Again, a bit of foreshadowing for something that won't become important until the next book.

—TZ

A glance at the auxiliary sensor display confirmed it: three *Lambda*-class shuttles and a full TIE fighter escort had left the *Chimaera,* heading toward the surface. "I'm afraid we don't have much to entertain you with," he said between suddenly stiff lips. "Certainly not on such short notice."

"No need for entertainment," Thrawn assured him. "As I said, I'm simply coming for a talk. A *brief* talk, of course; I know how busy you are."

"I appreciate your consideration," Karrde said. "If you'll excuse me, Admiral, I need to begin the preparations to receive you."

"I look forward to our meeting," Thrawn said. His face vanished, and the display returned to its distant view of the *Chimaera.*

For a long moment Karrde just sat there, the possibilities and potential disasters flipping through his mind at top speed. "Get on the comlink to Chin," he told Mara. "Tell him we have Imperial guests coming, and he's to begin preparations to receive them properly. Then go to pad eight and have Aves move the *Millennium Falcon* farther back under cover. Go there in person—the *Chimaera* and its shuttles might be able to tap into our comlink transmissions."

"What about Solo and Calrissian?"

Karrde pursed his lips. "We'll have to get them out, of course. Move them into the forest, perhaps at or near their ship. I'd better deal with that myself."

"Why not turn them over to Thrawn?"

He looked up at her. At those burning eyes and that rigid, tightly controlled face . . . "With no offer of a bounty?" he asked. "Relying on the Grand Admiral's generosity after the fact?"

"I don't find that a compelling reason," Mara said bluntly.

"Neither do I," he countered coldly. "What I *do* find compelling is that they're our guests. They've sat at our table and eaten our food . . . and like it or not, that means they're under our protection."

Mara's lip twitched. "And do these rules of hospitality apply to Skywalker, too?" she asked sardonically.

"You know they don't," he said. "But now is not the time or the place to turn him over to the Empire, even if that's the way the decision ultimately goes. Do you understand?"

"No," she growled. "I don't."

Karrde eyed her, strongly tempted to tell her that she didn't need to understand, only to obey. "It's a matter of relative strength," he told her instead. "Here on the ground, with an Imperial Star Destroyer orbiting overhead, we have no bargaining position at all. I wouldn't do business under such circumstances even if Thrawn was the most trustworthy client in the galaxy. Which he's not. *Now* do you understand?"

She took a deep breath, let it out. "I don't agree," she gritted. "But I'll accept your decision."

"Thank you. Perhaps after the Imperials leave, you can ask General Calrissian about the perils of making bargains while stormtroopers are strolling around your territory." Karrde looked back at the display. "So. *Falcon* moved; Solo and Calrissian moved. Skywalker and the droid should be all right where they are—the four shed has enough shielding to keep out anything but a fairly determined probe."

"And if Thrawn *is* determined?"

"Then we may have trouble," Karrde agreed calmly. "On the other hand, I doubt that Thrawn would be coming down himself if he thought there was the possibility of a firefight. The upper military ranks don't achieve that status by risking their own lives unnecessarily." He nodded at the door. "Enough talk. You have your job; I have mine. Let's get to them."

She nodded and turned to the door; and as she did so, a sudden thought struck him. "Where did you put Skywalker's lightsaber?" he asked.

"It's in my room," she said, turning back. "Why?"

"Better get it and put it somewhere else. Lightsabers aren't supposed to be highly detectable, but there's no point in taking chances. Put it in with the resonator cavities in three shed; they ought to provide adequate shielding from stray sensor probes."

"Right." She regarded him thoughtfully. "What was all that business about capital starships?"

"You heard everything that was said."

"I know. I was talking about your reaction to it."

He grimaced to himself. "I'd hoped it wasn't that obvious."

"It wasn't." She waited expectantly.

He pursed his lips. "Ask me again later. Right now, we have work to do."

For another second she studied him. Then, without a word, she nodded and left.

Taking a deep breath, Karrde got to his feet. First thing to do would be to get back to the dining room and inform his guests of the sudden change in plans. And after that, to prepare himself for a face-to-face confrontation with the most dangerous man in the Empire. With Skywalker and spare warships as two of the topics of conversation.

It was going to be a most interesting afternoon.

"Okay, Artoo," Luke called as he made the last of the connections. "I think we're ready to try it. Cross your fingers."

From the next room came a complicated series of electronic jabbers. Probably, Luke decided, the droid reminding him that he didn't have any fingers to cross.

Fingers. For a moment Luke looked down at his right hand, flexing his fingers and feeling the unpleasant pins-and-needles tingling/numbness there. It had been five years since he'd really thought of the hand as being a machine attached to his arm. Now, suddenly, it was impossible to think of it as anything but that.

Artoo beeped impatiently. "Right," Luke agreed, forcing

his attention away from his hand as best he could and moving the end of the wire toward what he hoped was the proper contact point. It could have been worse, he realized: the hand could have been designed with only a single power supply, in which case he wouldn't have even this much use of it. "Here goes," he said, and touched the wire.

And with no fuss or dramatics whatsoever, the door slid quietly open.

"Got it," Luke hissed. Carefully, trying not to lose the contact point, he leaned over and peered outside.

The sun was starting to sink behind the trees, throwing long shadows across the compound. From his position Luke could see only a little of the grounds, but what he could see seemed to be deserted. Setting his feet, he let go of the wire and dived for the doorway.

With the contact broken, the door slid shut again, nearly catching his left ankle as he hit the ground and rolled awkwardly into a crouch. He froze, waiting to see if the noise would spark any reaction. But the silence continued; and after a few seconds, he got to his feet and ran to the shed's other door.

Artoo had been right: there was indeed no lock on this half of the shed. Luke hit the release, threw one last glance around, and slipped inside.

The droid beeped an enthusiastic greeting, bobbing back and forth awkwardly in the restraint collar, a torus-shaped device that fit snugly around his legs and wheels.[8] "Quiet, Artoo," Luke warned the other, kneeling down to examine the collar. "And hold still."

8. Droid rhino boot! This concept made me laugh. But it's so believable!
—BM

He'd been worried that the collar would be locked or intertwined into Artoo's wheel system in some way, requiring special tools to disengage. But the device was much simpler than that—it merely held enough of the droid's weight off the floor so that he couldn't get any real traction. Luke released a pair of clasps and pushed the hinged halves apart, and Artoo was free. "Come on," he told the droid, and headed back to the door.

As far as he could see, the compound was still deserted. "The ship's around that way," he whispered, pointing toward the central building. "Looks like the best approach would be to circle to the left, keeping inside the trees as much as we can. Can you handle the terrain?"

Artoo raised his scanner, beeped a cautious affirmative. "Okay. Keep an eye out for anyone coming out of the buildings."

They'd made it into the woods, and were perhaps a quarter of the way around the circle, when Artoo gave a warning chirp. "Freeze," Luke whispered, stopping dead beside a large tree trunk and hoping they were enough in the shadows. His own black outfit should blend adequately into the darkening forest background, but Artoo's white and blue were another matter entirely.

Fortunately, the three men who came out of the central building never looked in their direction, but headed straight toward the edge of the forest.

Headed there at a fast, determined trot . . . and just before they disappeared into the trees, all three drew their blasters.

Artoo moaned softly. "I don't like it, either," Luke told him. "Let's hope it doesn't have anything to do with us. All clear?"

The droid beeped affirmation, and they started off again. Luke kept half an eye on the forest behind them, remembering Mara's veiled hints about large predators. It could have been a lie, of course, designed to discourage him from trying to escape. For that matter, he'd never spotted any real evidence that the window of his previous room had had an alarm on it.

Artoo beeped again. Luke twisted his attention back to the compound . . . and froze.

Mara had stepped out of the central building.

For what seemed like a long time she just stood there on the doorstep, looking distractedly up into the sky. Luke watched her, not daring even to look down to see how well concealed Artoo might be. If she turned in their direction—or if she went to the shed to see how he was doing . . .

Abruptly, she looked down again, a determined expression on her face. She turned toward the second barracks building and headed off at a brisk walk.

Luke let out a breath he hadn't realized he'd been holding. They were far from being out of danger—all Mara had to do was turn her head 90 degrees to her left and she'd be looking directly at them. But something about her posture seemed to indicate that her attention and thoughts were turned inward.

As if she'd suddenly made a hard decision . . .

She went into the barracks, and Luke made a quick decision of his own. "Come on, Artoo," he murmured. "It's getting too crowded out here. We're going to cut farther into the forest, come up on the ships from behind."

It was, fortunately, a short distance to the maintenance hangar and the group of ships parked alongside it. They arrived after only a few minutes—to discover their X-wing gone.

"No, I don't know where they've moved it to," Luke gritted, looking around as best he could while still staying undercover. "Can your sensors pick it up?"

Artoo beeped a negative, adding a chirping explanation Luke couldn't even begin to follow. "Well, it doesn't matter," he reassured the droid. "We'd have had to put down somewhere else on the planet and find something with a working hyperdrive, anyway. We'll just skip that step and take one of these."

He glanced around, hoping to find a Z-95 or Y-wing or something else he was at least marginally familiar with. But the only ships he recognized were a Corellian Corvette[9] and what looked like a downsized bulk freighter. "Got any suggestions?" he asked Artoo.

The droid beeped a prompt affirmative, his little sensor dish settling on a pair of long, lean ships about twice the length of Luke's X-wing. Fighters, obviously, but not like

9. Like the use of *borg* earlier, the term *corvette* got me another letter chastising me for using such a non-*Star Wars* term—and this one the name of a modern car, to boot.

I had to write back and explain that a Corvette was originally a seventeenth-century warship, that its use was already well established in the *Star Wars* universe, and that there was nothing we could do about General Motors having borrowed the name before we got to it.

—TZ

anything the Alliance had ever used. "One of those?" he asked doubtfully.

Artoo beeped again, a distinct note of impatience to the sound. "Right; we're a little pressed for time," Luke agreed.

They made it across to one of the fighters without incident. Unlike the X-wing design, the entrance was a hinged hatchway door in the side—possibly one reason Artoo had chosen it, Luke decided as he manhandled the droid inside. The pilot's cockpit wasn't much roomier than an X-wing's, but directly behind it was a three-seat tech/weapons area. The seats weren't designed for astromech droids, of course, but with a little ingenuity on Luke's part and some stretch on the restraints, he managed to get Artoo wedged between two of the seats and firmly strapped in place. "Looks like everything's already on standby," he commented, glancing at the flickering lights on the control boards. "There's an outlet right there—give everything a quick check while I strap in. With a little luck, maybe we can be out of here before anyone even knows we're gone."

She had delivered the open comlink message to Chin, and the quieter ones to Aves and the others at the *Millennium Falcon;* and as she stalked her way glowering across the compound toward the number three shed, Mara decided once more that she hated the universe.

She'd been the one who'd found Skywalker. She, by herself, alone. There was no question about that; no argument even possible. It should be she, not Karrde, who had the final say on his fate.

I should have left him out there, she told herself bitterly as she stomped across the beaten ground. *Should have just let him die in the cold of space.* She'd considered that, too, at the time. But if he'd died out there, all alone, she might never have known for sure that he was, in fact, dead.

And she certainly wouldn't have had the satisfaction of killing him herself.

She looked down at the lightsaber clenched in her hand, watching the afternoon sunlight glint from the silvery metal as she hefted its weight. She could do it now, she knew. Could go in there to check on him and claim he had tried to jump her. Without the Force to call on, he would be an easy target, even for someone like her who hadn't picked up a lightsaber more than a handful of times in her life.[10] It would be easy, clean, and very fast.

And she didn't owe Karrde anything, no matter how well his organization might have treated her. Not about something like this.

And yet . . .

She was coming up on four shed, still undecided, when she heard the faint whine of a repulsorlift.

She peered up into the sky, shading her eyes with her free hand as she tried to spot the incoming ship. But nothing was visible . . . and as the whine grew louder, she realized abruptly that it was the sound of one of their own vehicles. She spun around and looked over toward the maintenance hangar—

Just in time to see one of their two Skipray blastboats rise above the treetops.

For a pair of heartbeats she stared at the ship, wondering what in the Empire Karrde thought he was doing. Sending an escort or pilot ship for the Imperials, perhaps?

And then, abruptly, it clicked.

She twisted back and sprinted for the four shed, pulling her blaster from its forearm sheath as she ran. The lock on the room inexplicably refused to open; she tried it twice and then blasted it.

Skywalker was gone.

She swore, viciously, and ran out into the compound. The Skipray had shifted to forward motion now, disappearing behind the trees to the west. Jamming her blaster back into its sheath, she grabbed the comlink off her belt—

And swore again. The Imperials could be here at any

10. On the surface, this looks like another comment that's since been overthrown by other stories, including a bunch of my own.

But it's clear from the rest of *Heir* and the other books of the trilogy that she's actually quite skilled with a lightsaber. I don't remember what exactly I was thinking at the time I wrote this line, but my guess is that she's merely being sarcastic.

Either that or it's a flat-out typo, and I meant to say that she hadn't picked up a lightsaber very often in the past few years.

One of those questions where the answer is now unfortunately lost in the mists of time.

—TZ

minute, and any mention of Skywalker's presence would land them all in very deep trouble indeed.

Which left her with exactly one option.

She reached the second Skipray at a dead run and had it in the air within two minutes. Skywalker would not— would *not*—get away now.

Kicking the drive to full power, she screamed off in pursuit.

CHAPTER 23

THEY SHOWED UP almost simultaneously on the scopes: the other of Karrde's fighter ships pursuing him from behind, and the Imperial Star Destroyer in orbit far overhead. "I think," Luke called back to Artoo, "that we're in trouble."

The droid's reply was almost swallowed up in the roar as Luke gingerly eased the drive up as high as he dared. The strange fighter's handling wasn't even remotely like anything he'd ever flown before; slightly reminiscent of the snowspeeders the Alliance had used on Hoth, but with the kind of sluggish response time that implied a great deal of armor and engine mass. With time, he was pretty sure he'd be able to master it.

But time was something he was rapidly running out of.

He risked a glance at the aft-vision display. The other fighter was coming up fast, with no more than a minute or two now separating the two ships. Obviously, the pilot had far more experience with the craft than Luke had. That, or else such a fierce determination to recapture Luke that it completely overrode normal commonsense caution.

Either way, it meant Mara Jade.

The fighter dipped a little too deep, scraping its ventral tail fin against the tops of the trees and drawing a sharp squeal of protest from Artoo. "Sorry," Luke called back, feeling a fresh surge of perspiration break out on his forehead as he again carefully eased the drive up a notch. Speaking of overriding common sense . . . But at the moment, sticking to the treetops was about the only option he had. The forest below, for some unknown reason, seemed to have a scattering or scrambling effect on sensor scans, both detection and navigational. Staying low forced his pursuer to stay low, too, lest she lose visual contact with him against the mottled forest backdrop, and also at least partially hid him from the orbiting Star Destroyer.

The Star Destroyer. Luke glanced at the image on his overhead scope, feeling his stomach tighten. At least he knew now who the company was Mara had mentioned. It looked like he'd gotten out just in the nick of time.

On the other hand, perhaps the move to that storage shed implied that Karrde had decided not to sell him to the Imperials after all. It might be worth asking Karrde about someday. Preferably from a great distance.

Behind him, Artoo suddenly trilled a warning. Luke jerked in his seat, eyes flickering across the scopes as he searched for the source of the trouble—

And jerked again. There, directly above his dorsal tail fin and less than a ship's length away, was the other fighter.

"Hang on!" Luke shouted at Artoo, clenching his teeth tightly together. His one chance now was to pull a dropkick Koiogran turn,[1] killing his forward momentum and loop-rolling into another direction. Twisting the control stick with one hand, he jammed the throttle forward with the other—

And abruptly, the cockpit canopy exploded into a slapping tangle of tree branches, and he was thrown hard

1. In the real world, this maneuver (minus the throttle cutback) is called an Immelmann turn. It's not much used by modern-day fighters, but shows up frequently in air shows.

　　　　　　　–TZ

against his restraints as the fighter spun and twisted and rolled out of control.

The last thing he heard before the darkness took him was Artoo's shrill electronic scream.

The three shuttles came to a perfectly synchronized landing as, overhead, the TIE fighter escort shot by in equally perfect formation. "The Empire's parade-ground expertise hasn't eroded, anyway," Aves murmured.

"Quiet," Karrde murmured back, watching the shuttle ramps lower to the ground. The center one, almost certainly, would be Thrawn's.

Marching with blaster rifles held ceremonially across their chests, a line of stormtroopers filed down each of the three ramps. Behind them, emerging not from the center but from the rightmost of the shuttles, came a handful of midranking officers. Following them came a short, wiry being of unknown race with dark gray skin, bulging eyes, a protruding jaw, and the look of a bodyguard. Following him came Grand Admiral Thrawn.

So much, Karrde thought, *for him doing things the obvious way.* It would be something to make a note of for future reference.

With his small reception committee beside him, he walked toward the approaching group of Imperials, trying to ignore the stares of the stormtroopers. "Grand Admiral Thrawn." He nodded in greeting. "Welcome to our little corner of Myrkr. I'm Talon Karrde."

"Pleased to meet you, Captain," Thrawn said, inclining his head slightly. Those glowing eyes, Karrde decided, were even more impressive in person than they were on a comm display. And considerably more intimidating.

"I apologize for our somewhat less than formal greeting," Karrde continued, waving a hand at his group. "We don't often entertain people of your status here."

Thrawn cocked a blue-black eyebrow. "Really. I'd have

thought a man in your position would be used to dealing with the elite. Particularly high planetary officials whose cooperation, shall we say, you find you require?"

Karrde smiled easily. "We deal with the elite from time to time. But not here. This is—was, I should say," he added, glancing significantly at the stormtroopers, "—our private operations base."

"Of course," Thrawn said. "Interesting drama a few minutes ago out there to the west. Tell me about it."

With an effort, Karrde hid a grimace. He'd hoped the sensor-scrambling effect of Myrkr's trees would have hidden the Skipray chase from Thrawn's view. Obviously, it hadn't. "Merely a small internal problem," he assured the Grand Admiral. "A former and somewhat disgruntled employee broke into one of our storage sheds, stole some merchandise, and made off with one of our ships. Another of our people is in pursuit."

"*Was* in pursuit, Captain," Thrawn corrected lazily, those eyes seeming to burn into Karrde's face. "Or didn't you know they both went down?"

Karrde stared at him, a thin needle of ice running through him. "I didn't know that, no," he said. "Our sensors—the metallic content of the trees fouls them up badly."

"We had a higher observation angle," Thrawn said. "It looked as if the first ship hit the trees, with the pursuer getting caught in the slipstream." He regarded Karrde thoughtfully. "I take it the pursuer was someone special?"

Karrde let his face harden a bit. "All my associates are special," he said, pulling out his comlink. "Please excuse me a moment; I have to get a rescue team organized."

Thrawn took a long step forward, reaching two pale blue fingers to cover the top of the comlink. "Permit me," he said smoothly. "Troop commander?"

One of the stormtroopers stepped forward. "Sir?"

"Take a detail out to the crash site," Thrawn ordered, his

eyes still on Karrde. "Examine the wreckage, and bring back any survivors. And anything that looks like it wouldn't normally belong in a Skipray blastboat."

"Yes, sir." The other gestured, and one of the columns of stormtroopers turned and retraced their steps up the ramp of the leftmost shuttle.

"I appreciate your assistance, Admiral," Karrde said, his mouth suddenly a little dry. "But it really isn't necessary."

"On the contrary, Captain," Thrawn said softly. "Your assistance with the ysalamiri has left us in your debt. How better for us to repay you?"

"How better, indeed?" Karrde murmured. The ramp lifted into place, and with the hum of repulsorlifts, the shuttle rose into the air. The cards were dealt, and there was nothing he could do now to alter them. He could only hope that Mara somehow had things under control.

With anyone else, he wouldn't have bet on it. With Mara . . . there was a chance.

"And now," Thrawn said, "I believe you were going to show me around?"

"Yes." Karrde nodded. "If you'll come this way, please?"

"Looks like the stormtroopers are leaving," Han said quietly, pressing the macrobinoculars[2] a little harder against his forehead. "Some of them, anyway. Filing back into one of the shuttles."

"Let me see," Lando muttered from the other side of the tree.

Keeping his movements slow and careful, Han handed the macrobinoculars over. There was no telling what kind of equipment they had on those shuttles and TIE fighters, and he didn't especially trust all this talk about how good the trees were at sensor shielding.

"Yes, it seems to be just the one shuttle that's going," Lando agreed.

2. The preferred generic term for these things is now *electrobinoculars*, with the older *macrobinoculars* referring to a somewhat lower-quality version of the devices.

—TZ

Han half turned, the serrated, grasslike plants they were lying on top of digging into his shirt with the movement. "You get Imperial visitors here often?" he demanded.

"Not here," Ghent shook his head nervously, his teeth almost chattering with tension. "They've been to the forest once or twice to pick up some ysalamiri, but they've never come to the base. At least, not while I was here."

"Ysalamiri?" Lando frowned. "What are those?"

"Little furry snakes with legs," Ghent said. "I don't know what they're good for. Look, couldn't we get back to the ship now? Karrde told me I was supposed to keep you there, where you'd be safe."

Han ignored him. "What do you think?" he asked Lando.

The other shrugged. "Got to have something to do with that Skipray that went burning out of here just as Karrde was herding us out."

"There was some kind of prisoner," Ghent offered. "Karrde and Jade had him stashed away—maybe he got out. Now, can we *please* get back to—"

"A prisoner?" Lando repeated, frowning back at the kid. "When did Karrde start dealing with prisoners?"

"Maybe when he started dealing with kidnappers," Han growled before Ghent could answer.

"We don't deal with kidnappers," Ghent protested.

"Well, you're dealing with one now," Han told him, nodding toward the group of Imperials. "That little gray guy in there?—that's one of the aliens who tried to kidnap Leia and me."

"What?" Lando peered through the macrobinoculars again. "Are you sure?"

"It's one of the species, anyway. We didn't stop at the time to get names." Han looked back at Ghent. "This prisoner—who was he?"

"I don't know," Ghent shook his head. "They brought him back on the *Wild Karrde* a few days ago and put him in the short-term barracks. I think they'd just moved him over to one of the storage sheds when we got the word that the Imperials were coming down for a visit."

"What did he look like?"

"I don't *know*!" Ghent hissed, what little was left of his composure going fast. Skulking around forests and spying on armed stormtroopers was clearly not the sort of thing an expert slicer was supposed to have to put up with. "None of us was supposed to go near him or ask any questions about him."

Lando caught Han's eye. "Could be someone they don't want the Imperials to get hold of. A defector, maybe, trying to get to the New Republic?"

Han felt his lip twist. "I'm more worried right now about them having moved him out of the barracks. That could mean the stormtroopers are planning to move in for a while."

"Karrde didn't say anything about that," Ghent objected.

"Karrde may not know it yet," Lando said dryly. "Trust me—I was on the short end of a stormtrooper bargain once." He handed the macrobinoculars back to Han. "Looks like they're going inside."

They were, indeed. Han watched as the procession set off: Karrde and the blue-skinned Imperial officer in front, their respective entourages following, the twin columns of stormtroopers flanking the whole parade. "Any idea who that guy with the red eyes is?" he asked Ghent.

"I think he's a Grand Admiral or something," the other said. "Took over Imperial operations a while back. I don't know his name."

Han looked at Lando, found the other sending the same look right back at him. "A Grand Admiral?" Lando repeated carefully.

"Yeah. Look, they're going—there's nothing else to see. Can we *please*—?"

"Let's get back to the *Falcon*," Han muttered, stowing the macrobinoculars in their belt pouch and starting a backward elbows-and-knees crawl from their covering tree. A Grand Admiral. No wonder the New Republic had been getting the sky cut out from under them lately.

"I don't suppose you have any records on Imperial Grand Admirals back on the *Falcon*," Lando murmured, backing up alongside him.

"No," Han told him. "But they've got 'em on Coruscant."

"Great," Lando said, the words almost lost in the hissing of the sharp-bladed grass as they elbowed their way through it. "Let's hope we live long enough to get this tidbit back there."

"We will," Han assured him grimly. "We'll stick around long enough to find out what kind of game Karrde's playing, but then we're gone. Even if we have to blow out of here with that camo net still hanging off the ship."

The strangest thing about waking up this time, Luke decided dimly, was that he didn't actually hurt anywhere.

And he should have. From what he remembered of those last few seconds—and from the view of splintered trees outside the fighter's twisted canopy—he would have counted himself lucky even to be alive, let alone undamaged. Clearly, the restraints and crash balloons had been augmented by something more sophisticated—an emergency acceleration compensator, perhaps.

A shaky sort of gurgle came from behind him. "You okay, Artoo?" he called, levering himself out of his seat and climbing awkwardly across the canted floor. "Hang on, I'm coming."

The droid's information retrieval jack had been snapped off in the crash, but apart from that and a couple of minor dents, he didn't seem to have been damaged. "We'd better get moving," Luke told him, untangling him from his restraints. "That other ship could be back with a ground party anytime."

With an effort, he got Artoo aft. The hatchway door popped open without serious complaint; hopping down, he looked around.

The second fighter would not be returning with any ground parties. It was right here. In worse shape, if possible, than Luke's.

From the hatchway, Artoo whistled in squeamish-sounding awe.[3] Luke glanced up at him, looked back at the ruined craft. Given the fighters' safety equipment, it was unlikely that Mara was seriously injured. A backup flight was inevitable—she would probably be able to hold out until then.

But then again, she might not.

"Wait here, Artoo," he told the droid. "I'm going to take a quick look."

Even though the exterior of the fighter was in worse shape than Luke's, the interior actually seemed to be a little better off. Crunching his way across the bits of debris in the weapons/tech area, he stepped into the cockpit doorway.

Only the top of the pilot's head showed over the seat back, but that shimmering red-gold hair was all he needed to see to know that his earlier guess had been correct. It was indeed Mara Jade who'd been chasing him.

For a pair of heartbeats he stayed where he was, torn between the need for haste and the need to satisfy his internal sense of ethics. He and Artoo had to get out of here with all possible speed; that much was obvious. But if he turned his back on Mara now, without even pausing to check her condition . . .

His mind flashed back to Coruscant, to the night Ben Kenobi had said his final farewells. *In other words,* he'd told Threepio later up on the roof, *a Jedi can't get so caught up in matters of galactic importance that it interferes with his concern for individual people.* And it would, after all, only take a minute. Stepping into the room, he looked around the seat back.

3. Writing dialogue that mirrors the human characters' voices is one thing, but Tim also manages to reproduce a distinctive range of machine-made noises. I had no trouble throughout this book hearing the correct R2-D2 utterance, whether it was a warbling question, a surprised squeal, a shriek of warning, or here, the "squeamish-sounding awe."

—BM

Directly into a pair of wide-open, perfectly conscious green eyes. Green eyes that stared at him over the barrel of a tiny blaster.

"I figured you'd come," she said, her voice grimly satisfied. "Back up. Now."

He did as ordered. "Are you hurt at all?" he asked.

"None of your business," she retorted. She climbed out of the seat, pulling a small flat case from under the chair with her free hand as she stood up. Another glitter caught his eye: she was again wearing his lightsaber on her belt. "There's a case in that compartment just over the exit hatch," she told him. "Get it."

He found the release and got the compartment open. Inside was an unfamiliarly labeled metal case with the very familiar look of a survival kit to it. "I hope we're not going to have to walk the whole way back," he commented, pulling the bag out and dropping out the hatchway.

"*I* won't," she countered. She seemed to hesitate, just a little, before following him down to the ground. "Whether you make the trip back at all is another question."

He locked gazes with her. "Finishing what you started with this?" he asked, nodding at his wrecked ship.

She snorted. "Listen, buddy boy, it was *you* who took us down, not me. My only mistake was being stupid enough to be sitting too close to your tail when you hit the trees. Put the bag down and get that droid out of there."

Luke did as he was told. By the time Artoo was down beside him she had the survival kit's lid open and was fiddling one-handed with something inside. "Just stay right there," she told him. "And keep your hands where I can see them."

She paused, cocking her head slightly to the side as if listening. A moment later, in the distance, Luke could hear the faint sound of an approaching ship. "Sounds like our ride back is already on the way," Mara said. "I want you and the droid—"

She stopped in midsentence, her eyes going strangely

unfocused, her throat tight with concentration. Luke frowned, eyes and ears searching for the problem . . .

Abruptly, she slammed the survival kit lid shut and scooped it up. "Move!" she snapped, gesturing away from the wrecked fighters. With her blaster hand she picked up the flat box she'd been carrying and wedged it under her left arm. "Into the trees—both of you. I said *move!*"

There was something in her voice—command, or urgency, or both—that stifled argument or even question. Within a handful of seconds Luke and Artoo were under cover of the nearest trees. "Farther in," she ordered. "Come on, move it."

Belatedly, it occurred to Luke that this might all be some macabre joke—that all Mara really wanted was to shoot him in the back and be able to claim afterward that he'd been running away. But she was right behind him, close enough that he could hear her breathing and occasionally feel the tip of her blaster as it brushed his back. They made it perhaps ten meters farther in—Luke leaned down to help Artoo across a particularly wide root—

"Far enough," Mara hissed in his ear. "Hide the droid and then hit dirt."

Luke got Artoo over the root and behind a tree . . . and as he dropped down beside Mara, he suddenly understood.

Hanging in midair over the wrecked fighters, rotating slowly like a hovering raptor searching for prey, was an Imperial shuttle.

A small motion caught the corner of his eye, and he turned his head to look directly into the muzzle of Mara's blaster. "Not a move," she whispered, her breath warm on his cheek. "Not a sound."

He nodded understanding and turned back to watch the shuttle. Mara slid her arm over his shoulders, pressed her blaster into the hinge of his jaw, and did the same.

The shuttle finished its circle and settled gingerly to the torn-up ground between the ruined fighters. Even before

it was completely down, the ramp dropped and began dis-
gorging stormtroopers.

Luke watched as they split up and headed off to search
the two ships, the strangeness of the whole situation adding an unreal tinge to the scene. There, less than twenty
meters away, was Mara's golden opportunity to turn him
over to the Imperials . . . and yet, here they both lay, hiding
behind a tree root and trying not to breathe too loudly.
Had she suddenly changed her mind?

Or was it simply that she didn't want any witnesses
nearby when she killed him?

In which case, Luke realized abruptly, his best chance
might actually be to find some way of surrendering to the
stormtroopers. Once away from this planet, with the Force
as his ally again, he would at least have a fighting chance.
If he could just find a way to distract Mara long enough to
get rid of her blaster . . .

Lying pressed against his side, her arm slung across his
shoulders, she must have sensed the sudden tensing of
muscles. "Whatever you're thinking about trying, don't,"
she breathed in his ear, digging her blaster a little harder
into his skin. "I can easily claim you were holding me prisoner out here and that I managed to snatch the blaster
away from you."

Luke swallowed, and settled in to wait.

The wait wasn't very long. Two groups of stormtroopers
disappeared into the fighters, while the rest walked around
the edge of the newly created clearing, probing with eyes
and portable sensors into the forest. After a few minutes
those inside the fighters emerged, and what seemed to be a
short meeting was held between them at the base of the
shuttle ramp. At an inaudible command the outer ring of
searchers came back in to join them, and the whole crowd
trooped into their ship. The ramp sealed, and the shuttle
disappeared once more into the sky, leaving nothing but
the hum of its repulsorlifts behind. A minute later, even
that was gone.

Luke got his hands under him, started to get up. "Well—"

He broke off at another jab of the blaster. "Quiet," Mara muttered. "They'll have left a sensor behind, just in case someone comes back."

Luke frowned. "How do you know?"

"Because that's standard stormtrooper procedure in a case like this," she growled. "Real quiet, now; we get up and grab some more distance. And keep the droid quiet, too."

They were completely out of sight of the wrecked fighters, and probably another fifty meters past that, before she called a halt. "What now?" Luke asked.

"We sit down," she told him.

Luke nodded and eased to the ground. "Thank you for not turning me in to the stormtroopers."

"Save it," she said shortly, sitting down carefully herself and laying her blaster on the ground beside her. "Don't worry, there wasn't anything altruistic about it. The incoming shuttles must have seen us and sent a group over to investigate. Karrde's going to have to spin them some sort of sugar story about what happened, and I can't just walk into their arms until I know what that story is." She set the small flat box on her lap and opened it.

"You could call him," Luke reminded her.

"I could also call the Imperials directly and save myself some time," she retorted. "Unless you don't think they've got the equipment to monitor anything I send. Now shut up; I've got work to do."

For a few minutes she worked at the flat box in silence, fiddling with a tiny keyboard and frowning at something Luke couldn't see from his angle. At irregular intervals she looked up, apparently to make sure he wasn't trying anything. Luke waited; and abruptly she grunted in satisfaction. "Three days," she said aloud, closing the box.

"Three days to what?" Luke asked.

"The edge of the forest," she told him, gazing at him

4. Tuckerism: Ken and
Denise Hillyard of Tampa.
—TZ

with unblinking eyes. "Civilization. Well, Hyllyard City,[4] anyway, which is about as close as this part of the planet gets to it."

"And how many of us will be going there?" Luke asked quietly.

"That's the question, isn't it?" she agreed, her tone icy. "Can you give me any reason why I should bother taking you along?"

"Sure." Luke inclined his head to the side. "Artoo."

"Don't be absurd." Her eyes flicked to the droid, back at Luke. "Whatever happens, the droid stays here. In pieces."

Luke stared at her. "In *pieces?*"

"What, you need it spelled out?" she retorted. "The droid knows too much. We can't leave it here for the stormtroopers to find."

"Knows too much about what?"

"You, of course. You, Karrde, me—this whole stupid mess."

Artoo moaned softly. "He won't tell them anything," Luke insisted.

"Not after it's in pieces, no," Mara agreed.

With an effort, Luke forced himself to calm down. Logic, not fervor, was the only way to change her mind. "We need him," he told her. "You told me yourself the forest was dangerous. Artoo has sensors that can spot predators before they get close enough to strike."

"Maybe; maybe not," she countered. "The vegetation here limits sensor ranges down to practically zero."

"It'll still be better than you or I could do," Luke said. "And he'll also be able to watch while we're sleeping."

She raised her eyebrows slightly. "*We?*"

"We," Luke said. "I don't think he'll be willing to protect you unless I'm along."

Mara shook her head. "No good," she said, picking up her blaster. "I can get along without him. And I certainly don't need you."

Luke felt his throat tighten. "Are you sure you're not letting your emotions get in the way of your judgment?" he asked.

He hadn't thought her eyes could get any harder than they already were. He was wrong. "Let me tell you something, Skywalker," she said in a voice almost too soft for him to hear. "I've wanted to kill you for a long time. I dreamed about your death every night for most of that first year. Dreamed it, plotted it—I must have run through a thousand scenarios, trying to find exactly the right way to do it. You can call it a cloud on my judgment if you want to; I'm used to it by now. It's the closest thing I've got to a permanent companion."

Luke looked back into those eyes, shaken right down to the core of his soul. "What did I do to you?" he whispered.

"You destroyed my life," she said bitterly. "It's only fair that I destroy yours."

"Will killing me bring your old life back?"

"You know better than that," she said, her voice trembling slightly. "But it's still something I have to do. For myself, and for—" She broke off.

"What about Karrde?" Luke asked.

"What about him?"

"I thought he still wanted me kept alive."

She snorted. "We all want things we can't have."

But for just a second, there was something in her eyes. Something else that had flickered through the hatred . . .

But whatever it was, it wasn't enough. "I almost wish I could drag it out a little more," she said, glacially calm again as she lifted the blaster. "But I don't have the time to spare."

Luke stared at the muzzle of her blaster, his mind frantically searching for inspiration . . . "Wait a minute," he said suddenly. "You said you needed to find out what Karrde had told the Imperials. What if I could get you a secure comm channel to him?"

The muzzle of the blaster wavered. "How?" she asked suspiciously.

Luke nodded toward her survival kit. "Does the communicator in there have enough range to reach back to the base? I mean, without satellite boosting or anything."

She was still looking suspicious. "There's a sonde balloon included that can take the antenna high enough to get past most of the forest damping. But it's nondirectional, which means the Imperials and anyone else in this hemisphere will be able to listen in."

"That's okay," Luke said. "I can encrypt it so that no one else will be able to get anything out of it. Or rather, Artoo can."

Mara smiled thinly. "Wonderful. Except for one minor detail: if the encrypt is that good, how is Karrde supposed to decrypt it?"

"He won't have to," Luke told her. "The computer in my X-wing will do it for him."

The thin smile vanished from Mara's face. "You're stalling," she snarled. "You can't do a counterpart encrypt between an astromech droid and a ship computer."

"Why not? Artoo's the only droid who's worked with that computer in more than five years, with close to three thousand hours of flight time. He's bound to have molded it to his own personality by now. In fact, I know he has— the ground maintenance people have to run diagnostics through him to make any sense out of them."

"I thought standard procedure was to wipe and reload droid memories every six months to keep that from happening."

"I like Artoo the way he is," Luke said. "And he and the X-wing work better together this way."

"How much better?"

Luke searched his memory. Maintenance had run that test just a few months ago. "I don't remember the exact number. It was something like thirty percent faster than a baseline astromech/X-wing interface. Maybe thirty-five."

Mara was staring hard at Artoo. "That's counterpart-level speed, all right," she agreed reluctantly. "The Imperials could still crack it, though."

"Eventually. But it would take some specialized equipment to do it. And you said yourself we'd be out of here in three days."

For a long minute she stared at him, her jaw tight with clenched teeth, her face a mirror of fiercely battling emotions. Bitterness, hatred, desire for survival . . . and something else. Something that Luke could almost believe might be a touch of loyalty. "Your ship's sitting all alone out in the forest," she growled at last. "How are you going to get the message back to Karrde?"

"Someone's bound to check on the ship eventually," he pointed out. "All we have to do is dump the message into storage and leave some kind of signal flashing that it's there. You have people who know how to pull a dump, don't you?"

"Any idiot knows how to pull a dump." Mara glared at him. "Funny, isn't it, how this scheme just *happens* to require that I keep both of you alive a while longer."[5]

Luke remained silent, meeting that bitter gaze without flinching . . . and then, abruptly, Mara's internal battle seemed to end. "What about the droid?" she demanded. "It'll take forever to get it across this terrain."

"Artoo's made it through forests before. However . . ." Luke looked around, spotted a tree with two low branches just the right size. "I should be able to rig up a dragging frame to carry him on—a travois, or something like that." He started to get up. "If you'll give me my lightsaber for a minute I can cut a couple of those branches off."

"Sit down," she ordered, standing up. "I'll do it."

Well, it had been worth a try. "Those two," he told her, pointing. "Be careful—lightsabers are tricky to handle."

"Your concern for my welfare is touching," she said, her voice dripping sarcasm. She drew the lightsaber and stepped over to the indicated tree, keeping an eye on Luke the whole time. She raised the weapon, ignited it—

And in a handful of quick, sure swipes trimmed, shortened, and cut the branches from the tree.

5. In my original outline, this scene had the same ultimate result—Mara grudgingly agreeing to work with Luke to get out of the forest alive—but I didn't yet have any of the details worked out. Betsy spotted that, and pointed out that I needed a good reason for Mara putting aside her desire to just kill Luke then and there.

I agreed, and just to be on the safe side I gave her *two* reasons: R2's sensors, and the counterpart encryption system that would let her find out what Karrde had told the Imperials and, therefore, what she would need to say to make their stories match up.

And of course, both reasons also require her to keep R2 intact, which she also didn't want to do. Given subsequent events, it's just as well she gave in on that point, too.

—TZ

She closed down the weapon and returned it to her belt in a single smooth motion. "Help yourself," she said, moving away.

"Right," Luke said mechanically, his mind tingling with astonishment as he stumbled over to collect the branches. The way she'd done that . . . "You've used a lightsaber before."

She gazed at him coldly. "Just so you know I can handle it. In case you should feel tempted to try and make a grab for my blaster." She glanced upward at the darkening sky. "Come on—get busy with that travois. We'll need to find some kind of clearing to put the sonde balloon up, and I want to get that done before nightfall."

CHAPTER 24

"I MUST APOLOGIZE for chasing you out like that," Karrde said as he walked Han toward the central building. "Particularly in the middle of a meal. Not exactly the sort of hospitality we strive for here."

"No problem," Han told him, eyeing him as best he could in the gathering dusk. The light from the building ahead was casting a faint glow on Karrde's face; with luck, it would be enough to read the other's expression by. "What was that all about, anyway?"

"Nothing serious," Karrde assured him easily. "Some people with whom I've had business dealings wanted to come and look the place over."

"Ah," Han said. "So you're working directly for the Empire now?"

Karrde's expression cracked, just a little. Han expected him to make some sort of reflexive denial; instead, he stopped and turned to look at Lando and Ghent, walking behind them. "Ghent?" he asked mildly.

"I'm sorry, sir," the kid said, sounding miserable. "They insisted on coming out to see what was happening."

"I see." Karrde looked back at Han, his face calm again. "No harm done, probably. Not the wisest of risks to take, though."

"I'm used to taking risks," Han told him. "You haven't answered my question."

Karrde resumed walking. "If I'm not interested in working for the Republic, I'm certainly not interested in working for the Empire. The Imperials have been coming here for the past few weeks to collect ysalamiri—sessile creatures, like the ones hanging on to the tree in the greatroom. I offered my assistance in helping them safely remove the ysalamiri from their trees."

"What did you get in return?"

"The privilege of watching them work," Karrde said. "Giving me that much extra information to try to figure out what they wanted with the things."

"And what *did* they want with them?"

Karrde glanced at Han. "Information costs money here, Solo. Actually, to be perfectly honest, we don't know what they're up to. We're working on it, though."

"I see. But you *do* know their commander personally."

Karrde smiled faintly. "That's information again."

Han was starting to get sick of this. "Have it your way. What'll this Grand Admiral's name cost me?"

"For the moment, the name's not for sale," he told Han. "Perhaps we'll talk about it later."

"Thanks, but I don't think there's going to be a later," Han growled, stopping. "If you don't mind, we'll just say our good-byes here and get back to the ship."

Karrde turned to him in mild surprise. "You're not going to finish our dinner? You hardly had a chance to get started."

Han looked him straight in the eye. "I don't especially like sitting on the ground like a practice target when there are stormtroopers wandering around," he said bluntly.

Karrde's face hardened. "At the moment, sitting on the ground is preferable to drawing attention in the air," he said coldly. "The Star Destroyer hasn't left orbit yet. Lifting off now would be an open invitation for them to swat you down."

"The *Falcon*'s outrun Star Destroyers before," Han countered. But Karrde had a point . . . and the fact that he hadn't turned the two of them over to the Imperials probably meant that he could be trusted, at least for now. Probably.

On the other hand, if they *did* stay . . . "But I suppose it wouldn't hurt us to stick around a little longer," he conceded. "All right, sure, we'll finish dinner."

"Good," Karrde said. "It will just take a few minutes to get things put back together."

"You took everything apart?" Lando asked.

"Everything that might have indicated we had guests," Karrde said. "The Grand Admiral is highly observant, and I wouldn't have put it past him to know exactly how many of my associates are staying here at the moment."

"Well, while you're getting things ready," Han said, "I want to go back to the ship and check on a couple of things."

Karrde's eyes narrowed slightly. "But you *will* be back."

Han gave him an innocent smile. "Trust me."

Karrde gazed at him a moment longer, then shrugged. "Very well. Watch yourselves, though. The local predators don't normally come this close in to our encampment, but there are exceptions."

"We'll be careful," Han promised. "Come on, Lando."

They headed back the way they'd come. "So what did we forget to do back at the *Falcon*?" Lando asked quietly as they reached the trees.

"Nothing," Han murmured back. "I just thought it'd be a good time to go check out Karrde's storage sheds. Particularly the one that was supposed to have a prisoner in it."

They went about five meters into the forest, then changed direction to circle the compound. A quarter of the way around the circle, they found a likely looking group of small buildings.

"Look for a door with a lock," Lando suggested as they came out among the sheds. "Either permanent or temporary."

"Right." Han peered through the darkness. "That one over there—the one with two doors?"

"Could be," Lando agreed. "Let's take a look."

The leftmost of the two doors did indeed have a lock. Or, rather, it had *had* a lock. "It's been shot off," Lando said, poking at it with a finger. "Strange."

"Maybe the prisoner had friends," Han suggested, glancing around. There was no one else in sight. "Let's go inside."

They slid the door open and went in, closing it behind them before turning on the light. The shed was less than half full, with most of the boxes piled against the right-hand wall. The exceptions to that rule . . .

Han stepped over for a closer look. "Well, well," he murmured, gazing at the removed power outlet plate and the wires poking through the gap. "Someone's been busy over here."

"Someone's been even busier over here," Lando commented from behind him. "Come have a look."

Lando was crouched down beside the door, peering into the inside of the door lock mechanism. Like the outside, half of its covering plate had been blasted off. "That must have been one beaut of a shot," Han frowned, coming over.

"It wasn't a single shot," Lando said, shaking his head. "The stuff in between is mostly intact." He pushed back the cover a little, poking at the electronics inside with his fingers. "Looks like our mysterious prisoner was tampering with the equipment."

"I wonder how he got it open." Han glanced back at the removed power plate. "I'm going to take a look next door," he told Lando, stepping back to the entrance and tapping the release.

The door didn't open. "Uh-oh," he muttered, trying again.

"Wait a second—I see the problem," Lando said, fiddling with something behind the plate. "There's a power supply been half spliced into the works . . ."

Abruptly, the door slid open. "Back in a second," Han told him, and slipped outside.

The shed's right-hand room wasn't much different from the other one. Except for one thing: in the center, in a space that had very obviously been cleared for the purpose, lay an open droid restraint collar.

Han frowned down at it. The collar hadn't been properly put away, or even closed again—hardly the way someone in an organization like Karrde's would be expected to take care of company equipment. Roughly in the center of the collar's open jaws were three faint marks on the floor. Skid marks, he decided, formed by the restrained droid's attempts to move or get free.

Behind him, the door whispered open. Han spun around, blaster in hand—

"You seem to have gotten lost," Karrde said calmly. His eyes flicked around the room. "And to have lost General Calrissian along the way."

Han lowered the blaster. "You need to tell your people to put their toys away when they're done," he said, nodding his head at the abandoned restraint collar. "You were holding a droid prisoner, too?"

Karrde smiled thinly. "I see Ghent was talking out of turn again. Amazing, isn't it, how so many expert slicers know everything about computers and droids and yet don't know when to keep their mouths shut."

"It's also amazing how so many expert smugglers don't

know when to leave a messy deal alone," Han shot back. "So what's your Grand Admiral got you doing? Formal slaving, or just random kidnappings?"

Karrde's eyes flashed. "I don't deal in slaves, Solo. Slaves *or* kidnapping. Never."

"What was this one, then? An accident?"

"I didn't ask for him to come into my life," Karrde countered. "Nor did I especially want him there."

Han snorted. "You're stretching, Karrde. What'd he do, drop in out of the sky on top of you?"

"As a matter of fact, that's very nearly the way it happened," Karrde said stiffly.

"Oh, well, that's a good reason to lock someone up," Han said sardonically. "Who was he?"

"That information's not for sale."

"Maybe we don't need to buy it," Lando said from behind him.

Karrde turned. "Ah," he said as Lando stepped past him into the room. "There you are. Exploring the other half of the shed, were you?"

"Yeah, we don't stay lost very long," Han assured him. "What'd you find, Lando?"

"This." Lando held up a tiny red cylinder with a pair of wires coming out of each end. "It's a micrel power supply—the kind used for low-draw applications. Our prisoner wired it into the door lock control after the power lines had been burned away—that's how he got out." He moved it a little closer. "The manufacturer's logo is small, but readable. Recognize it?"

Han squinted at it. The script was alien, but it seemed vaguely familiar. "I've seen it before, but I don't remember where."

"You saw it during the war," Lando told him, his gaze steady on Karrde. "It's the logo of the Sibha Habadeet."

Han stared at the tiny cylinder, a strange chill running through him. The Sibha Habadeet had been one of the Alliance's major suppliers of micrel equipment. And their specialty had been—"That's a bioelectronic power supply?"

"That's right," Lando said grimly. "Just like the kind that would have been put in, say, an artificial hand."

Slowly, the muzzle of Han's blaster came up again to point at Karrde's stomach. "There was a droid in here," he told Lando. "The skid marks on the floor look just about right for an R2 unit." He raised his eyebrows. "Feel free to join the conversation anytime, Karrde."

Karrde sighed, his face a mixture of annoyance and resignation. "What do you want me to say?—that Luke Skywalker was a prisoner here? All right—consider it said."

Han felt his jaw tighten. And he and Lando had been right here. Blissfully unaware . . . "Where is he now?" he demanded.

"I thought Ghent would have told you," Karrde said darkly. "He escaped in one of my Skipray blastboats." His lips twisted. "Crashing it in the process."

"He *what?*"

"He's all right," Karrde assured him. "Or at least he was a couple of hours ago. The stormtroopers who went to investigate said that both wrecks were deserted." His eyes seemed to flatten, just for a minute. "I hope that means they're working together to make their way out."

"You don't sound sure of that," Han prompted.

The eyes flattened a little more. "Mara Jade was the one who went after him. She has a certain—well, why mince words. In point of fact, she wants very much to kill him."

Han threw a startled glance at Lando. "Why?"

Karrde shook his head. "I don't know."

For a moment the room was silent. "How did he get here?" Lando asked.

"As I said, purely by accident," Karrde said. "No—I take that back. It wasn't an accident for Mara—she led us directly to his crippled starfighter."

"How?"

"Again, I don't know." He fixed Han with a hard look.

"And before you ask, we had nothing to do with the damage to his ship. He'd burned out both hyperdrive motivators tangling with one of the Empire's Star Destroyers. If we hadn't picked him up, he'd almost certainly be dead by now."

"Instead of roaming a forest with someone who still wants him that way," Han countered. "Yeah, you're a real hero."

The hard look hardened even further. "The Imperials want Skywalker, Solo. They want him very badly. If you look carefully, you'll notice that I *didn't* give him to them."

"Because he escaped first."

"He escaped because he was in this shed," Karrde retorted. "And he was in this shed because I didn't want the Imperials stumbling over him during their unannounced visit."

He paused. "You'll also notice," he added quietly, "that I didn't turn the two of *you* over to them, either."

Slowly, Han lowered the blaster. Anything said at the point of a gun was of course suspect; but the fact that Karrde had indeed not betrayed them to the Imperials was a strong argument in his favor.

Or rather, he hadn't betrayed them yet. That could always change. "I want to see Luke's X-wing," he told Karrde.

"Certainly," Karrde said. "I'd recommend not going there until tomorrow morning, though. We moved it somewhat farther into the forest than your ship; and there *will* be predators roaming around it in the darkness."

Han hesitated, then nodded. If Karrde had something subtle going here, he almost certainly would have already erased or altered the X-wing's computer log. A few more hours wouldn't make any difference. "All right. So what are we going to do about Luke?"

Karrde shook his head, his gaze not quite focused on Han. "There's nothing we can do for them tonight. Not with vornskrs roaming the forest and the Grand Admiral still in orbit. Tomorrow . . . We'll have to discuss it, see what we can come up with." His focus came back, and with it a slightly ironic smile. "In the meantime, dinner should be ready by now. If you'll follow me . . . ?"[1]

The dimly lit holographic art gallery had changed again, this time to a collection of remarkably similar flame-shaped works that seemed to pulsate and alter in form as Pellaeon moved carefully between the pedestals. He studied them as he walked, wondering where this batch had come from. "Have you found them, Captain?" Thrawn asked as Pellaeon reached the double display circle.

He braced himself. "I'm afraid not, sir. We'd hoped that with the arrival of local nightfall we'd be able to get some results from the infrared sensors. But they don't seem able to penetrate the tree canopy, either."

Thrawn nodded. "What about that pulse transmission we picked up just after sundown?"

"We were able to confirm that it originated from the approximate location of the crash site," Pellaeon told him. "But it was too brief for a precise location check. The encrypt on it is a very strange one—Decrypt thinks it might be a type of counterpart coding. They're still working on it."

"They've tried all the known Rebellion encrypts, I presume."

"Yes, sir, as per your orders."

Thrawn nodded thoughtfully. "It looks like we're at something of a stalemate, then, Captain. At least as long as they're in the forest. Have you calculated their likely emergence points?"

"There's really only one practical choice," Pellaeon said, wondering why they were making so much of a fuss over this. "A town called Hyllyard City, on the edge of the forest and almost directly along their path. It's the only popula-

1. In the original outline, it was Han and Leia, not Han and Lando, who went to see Karrde. In that version, Chewie and Lando did little after Nkllon except fly around the New Republic, pretending Leia was aboard their ship, in the hope of drawing away all the unwelcome Noghri attention she'd been receiving.

The final version is much better. While *Star Wars* can be seen as being the story of Luke Skywalker, it really is an ensemble cast. The final version of *Heir* gives each person in that ensemble more of a role, and more of a chance to shine.

—TZ

tion center anywhere for more than a hundred kilometers. With only the one survival pack between them, they almost have to come out there."

"Excellent." Thrawn nodded. "I want you to detail three squads of stormtroopers to set up an observation post there. They're to assemble and depart ship immediately."

Pellaeon blinked. "Stormtroopers, sir?"

"Stormtroopers," Thrawn repeated, turning his gaze to one of the flame sculptures. "Better add half a biker scout unit, too, and three Chariot light assault vehicles."

"Yes, sir," Pellaeon said cautiously. Stormtroopers were in critically short supply these days. To waste them like this, on something so utterly unimportant as a smuggler squabble . . .

"Karrde lied to us, you see," Thrawn continued, as if reading Pellaeon's mind. "Whatever that little drama was this afternoon, it was not the common pursuit of a common thief. I'd like to know what, in fact, it was."

"I . . . don't think I follow, sir."

"It's very simple, Captain," Thrawn said, in that tone of voice he always seemed to use when explaining the obvious. "The pilot of the chase vehicle never reported in during the pursuit. Nor did anyone from Karrde's base communicate with him. We know that—we'd have intercepted any such transmissions. No progress reports; no assistance requests; nothing but complete radio silence." He looked back at Pellaeon. "Speculation, Captain?"

"Whatever it was," Pellaeon said slowly, "it was something they didn't want us knowing about. Beyond that . . ." He shook his head. "I don't know, sir. There could be any number of things they wouldn't want outsiders to know about. They *are* smugglers, after all."

"Agreed." Thrawn's eyes seemed to glitter. "But now consider the additional fact that Karrde refused our invitation to join in the search for Skywalker . . . and the fact that this afternoon he implied the search was over." He raised an eyebrow. "What does *that* suggest to you, Captain?"

Pellaeon felt his jaw drop. "You mean . . . that was *Skywalker* in that Skipray?"

"An interesting speculation, isn't it." Thrawn agreed. "Unlikely, I'll admit. But likely enough to be worth following up on."

"Yes, sir." Pellaeon glanced at the chrono, did a quick calculation. "Though if we stay here more than another day or two, we may have to move back the Sluis Van attack."

"We're not moving Sluis Van," Thrawn said emphatically. "Our entire victory campaign against the Rebellion begins there, and I'll not have so complex and far-reaching a schedule altered. Not for Skywalker; not for anyone else." He nodded at the flame statues surrounding them. "Sluissi art clearly indicates a biannual cyclic pattern, and I want to hit them at their most sluggish point. We'll leave for our rendezvous with the *Inexorable* and the cloaking shield test as soon as the troops and vehicles have been dropped. Three squads of stormtroopers should be adequate to handle Skywalker, if he is indeed here."

His eyes bored into Pellaeon's face. "And to handle Karrde," he added softly, "if he turns out to be a traitor."

The last bits of dark blue had faded from the tiny gaps in the canopy overhead, leaving nothing but blackness above them. Turning the survival kit's worklight to its lowest setting, Mara set it down and sank gratefully to the ground against a large tree bole. Her right ankle, twisted somehow in the Skipray crash, had started to ache again, and it felt good to get the weight off it.

Skywalker was already stretched out a couple of meters on the other side of the worklight, his head pillowed on his tunic, his loyal droid standing at his side. She wondered if he'd guessed about the ankle, dismissed the question as irrelevant. She'd had worse injuries without being slowed down by them.

"Reminds me of Endor," Skywalker said quietly as Mara arranged her glow rod and blaster in her lap where they'd be accessible. "A forest always sounds so busy at night."

"Oh, it's busy, all right," Mara grunted. "A lot of the animals here are nocturnal. Including the vornskrs."

"Strange," he murmured. "Karrde's pet vornskrs seemed wide enough awake in late afternoon."

She looked across at him, mildly surprised he'd noticed that. "Actually, even in the wild they take small naps around the clock," she said. "I call them nocturnal because they do most of their hunting at night."

Skywalker mulled that over for a moment. "Maybe we ought to travel at night, then," he suggested. "They'll be hunting us either way—at least then we'd be awake and alert while they were on the prowl."

Mara shook her head. "It'd be more trouble than it's worth. We need to be able to see the terrain as far ahead of us as possible if we're going to avoid running into dead ends. Besides, this whole forest is dotted with small clearings."

"Through which a glow rod beam would show very clearly to an orbiting ship," he conceded. "Point. You seem to know a lot about this place."

"It wouldn't take more than an observant pilot flying over the forest to see that," she growled. But he was right, she knew, as she eased back against the rough bark. *Know your territory* was the first rule that had been drilled into her . . . and the first thing she'd done after establishing herself in Karrde's organization had been to do precisely that. She'd studied the aerial maps of the forest and surrounding territory; had taken long walks, in both daylight and at night, to familiarize herself with the sights and sounds; had sought out and killed several vornskrs and other predators to learn the fastest ways of taking them down; had even talked one of Karrde's people into running bio tests on a crateload of native plants to find out which were edible and which weren't. Outside the forest, she knew something about the settlers, understood the local politics, and had stashed a small but adequate part of her earnings out where she could get hold of it.

More than anyone else in Karrde's organization, she was equipped to survive outside the confines of his encampment. So why was she trying so hard to get back there?

It wasn't for Karrde's sake—that much she was sure of. All that he'd done for her—her job, her position, her promotions—she'd more than repaid with hard work and good service. She didn't owe him anything, any more than he owed her. Whatever the story was he'd concocted this afternoon to explain the Skipray chase to Thrawn, it would have been designed to protect his own neck, not hers; and if he saw that the Grand Admiral wasn't buying it, he was at perfect liberty to pull his group off Myrkr tonight and disappear down one of the other ratholes he had scattered throughout the galaxy.

Except that he wouldn't. He would sit there, sending out search party after search party, and wait for Mara to come out of the forest. Even if she never did.

Even if by doing so he overstayed Thrawn's patience.

Mara clenched her teeth, the unpleasant image of Karrde pinned against a cell wall by an interrogation droid dancing in front of her eyes. Because she knew Thrawn—knew the Grand Admiral's tenacity and the limits of his patience both. He would wait and watch, or set someone to do it for him, and follow through on Karrde's story.

And if neither she nor Skywalker ever reappeared from the forest, he would almost certainly jump to the wrong conclusion. At which point he would take Karrde in for a professional Imperial interrogation, and eventually would find out who the escaping prisoner had been.

And then he'd have Karrde put to death.

Across from her, the droid's dome rotated a few degrees and it gave a quietly insistent gurgle. "I think Artoo's picked up something," Skywalker said, hiking himself up on his elbows.

"No kidding," Mara said. She picked up her glow rod, pointed it at the shadow she'd already seen moving stealthily toward them, and flicked it on.

A vornskr stood framed in the circle of light, its front claws dug into the ground, its whip tail pointed stiffly back and waving slowly up and down. It paid no attention to the light, but continued moving slowly toward Skywalker.

Mara let it get another two paces, then shot it neatly through the head.

The beast collapsed to the ground, its tail giving one last spasmodic twitch before doing likewise. Mara gave the rest of the area a quick sweep with the glow rod, then flicked it off. "Awfully good thing we have your droid's sensors along," she said sarcastically into the relative darkness.

"Well, *I* wouldn't have known there was any danger without him," Skywalker came back wryly. "Thank you."

"Forget it," she grunted.

There was a short silence. "Are Karrde's pet vornskrs a different species?" Skywalker asked. "Or did he have their tails removed?"

Mara peered across the gloom at him, impressed in spite of herself. Most men staring down a vornskr's gullet wouldn't have noticed a detail like that. "The latter," she told him. "They use those tails as whips—pretty painful, and there's a mild poison in them, too. At first it was just that Karrde didn't want his people walking around with whip welts all over them; we found out later that removing the tails also kills a lot of their normal hunting aggression."

"They seemed pretty domestic," he agreed. "Even friendly."

Only they hadn't been friendly to Skywalker, she remembered. And here, the vornskr had ignored her and gone directly for him. Coincidence? "They are," she said aloud. "He's thought occasionally about offering them for sale as guard animals. Never gotten around to exploring the potential market."

"Well, you can tell him I'd be glad to serve as a reference," Skywalker said dryly. "Having looked a vornskr square in the teeth, I can tell you it's not something the average intruder would like to do twice."

Her lip twisted. "Get used to it," she advised him. "It's a long way to the edge of the forest."

"I know." Skywalker lay back down again. "Fortunately, you seem to be an excellent shot."

He fell silent. Getting ready to sleep . . . and probably assuming she was going to do the same.

Wish away, she thought sardonically at him. Reaching into her pocket, she pulled out the survival kit's tube of stimpills. A steady stream of the things could ruin one's health in short order, but going to sleep five meters away from an enemy would ruin it a lot faster.

She paused, tube in hand, and frowned at Skywalker. At his closed eyes and calm, apparently totally unworried face. Which seemed strange, because if anyone had ever had reason to be worried, it was he. Stripped of all his vaunted Jedi powers by a planetful of ysalamiri, trapped in a forest on a world whose name and location he didn't even know, with her, the Imperials, and the vornskrs lining up for the privilege of killing him—he should by rights be wide-eyed with pumping adrenaline by now.

Maybe he was just faking it, hoping she would lower her guard. It was probably something she would try, under reversed circumstances.

But then, maybe there was more to him than met the eye. More than just a family name, a political position, and a bag of Jedi tricks.

Her mouth tightened, and she ran her fingers along the side of the lightsaber hanging from her belt. Yes, of course there was more there. Whatever had happened at the end—at that terrible, confused, life-destroying end—it hadn't been his Jedi tricks that had saved him. It had been something else. Something she would make sure to find out from him before his own end came.

She thumbed a stimpill from the tube and swallowed it, a fresh determination surging through her as she did so. No, the vornskrs weren't going to get Luke Skywalker. And neither were the Imperials. When the time came, she would kill him herself. It was her right, and her privilege, and her duty.

Shifting to a more comfortable position against her tree, she settled in to wait out the night.

The nighttime sounds of the forest came faintly from the distance, mixed in with the faint sounds of civilization from the building at his back. Karrde sipped at his cup, gazing into the darkness, feeling fatigue tugging at him as he'd seldom felt it before.

In a single day, his whole life had just been turned over.

Beside him, Drang raised his head and turned it to the right. "Company?" Karrde asked him, looking in that direction. A shadowy figure, hardly visible in the starlight, was moving toward him. "Karrde?" Aves's voice called softly.

"Over here," Karrde told him. "Go get a chair and join me."

"This is okay," Aves said, coming over beside him and sitting down cross-legged on the ground. "I've got to get back to Central pretty soon, anyway."

"The mystery message?"

"Yeah. What in the worlds was Mara thinking of?"

"I don't know," Karrde admitted. "Something clever, though."

"Probably," Aves conceded. "I just hope we're going to be clever enough to decrypt it."

Karrde nodded. "Did Solo and Calrissian get bedded down all right?"

"They went back to their ship," Aves said, his voice scowling. "I don't think they trust us."

"Under the circumstances, you can hardly blame them." Karrde reached down to scratch Drang's head. "Maybe pulling Skywalker's computer logs tomorrow morning will help convince them we're on their side."

"Yeah. Are we?"

Karrde pursed his lips. "We don't really have a choice anymore, Aves. They're our guests."

Aves umphed. "The Grand Admiral isn't going to be happy."

Karrde shrugged. "They're our guests," he repeated.

In the darkness, he sensed Aves shrug back. He understood, Aves did—understood the requirements and duties of a host. Unlike Mara, who'd wanted him to send the *Millennium Falcon* away.

He wished now that he'd listened to her. Wished it very much indeed.

"I'll want you to organize a search party for tomorrow morning," he told Aves. "Probably futile, all things considered, but it has to be tried."

"Right. Do we defer to the Imperials in that regard?"

Karrde grimaced to himself. "I doubt if they'll be doing any more searching. That ship that sneaked out from the Star Destroyer an hour ago looked suspiciously like a stripped-down assault shuttle. My guess is that they'll set up in Hyllyard City and wait for Mara and Skywalker to come to them."

"Sounds reasonable," Aves said. "What if we don't get to them first?"

"We'll just have to take them away from the storm-troopers, I suppose. Think you can put a team together for the purpose?"

Aves snorted gently. "Easier done than said. I've sat in

on a couple of conversations since you made the announcement, and I can tell you that feelings in camp are running pretty strong. Hero of the Rebellion and all that aside, a bunch of our people figure they owe Skywalker big for getting them out of permanent hock to Jabba the Hutt."[2]

"I know," Karrde said grimly. "And all that warm enthusiasm could be a problem. Because if we can't get Skywalker free from the Imperials . . . well, we can't let them have him alive."

There was a long silence from the shadow beside him. "I see," Aves said at last, very quietly. "It probably won't make any difference, you know, in what Thrawn suspects."

"Suspicion is better than unequivocal proof," Karrde reminded him. "And if we can't intercept them while they're still in the forest, it may be the best we're going to get."

Aves shook his head. "I don't like it."

"Neither do I. But we need to be prepared for every eventuality."

"Understood." For another moment Aves sat there in silence. Then, with a grunted sigh, he stood up. "I'd better get back, see if Ghent's made any progress on Mara's message."

"And after that you'd better hit the sack," Karrde told him. "Tomorrow's going to be a busy day."

"Right. Good night."

Aves left, and once again the soft mixture of forest sounds filled the night air. Sounds that meant a great deal to the creatures who made them but nothing at all to him.

Meaningless sounds . . .

He shook his head tiredly. What *had* Mara been trying to do with that opaque message of hers? Was it something simple—something that he or someone else here ought to be able to decrypt with ease?

Or had the lady who always played the sabacc cards close to her chest finally outsmarted herself?

In the distance, a vornskr emitted its distinctive cackle/

2. In the real world, the repercussions of Jabba's death would ripple a long way outward.

Little details like that were what helped make the *Star Wars* movies feel genuine and realistic, and I tried to put some of those same touches into *Heir*.

—TZ

purr. Beside his chair, Drang lifted his head. "Friend of yours?" Karrde inquired mildly, listening as another vornskr echoed the first's cry. Sturm and Drang had been wild like that once, before they'd been domesticated.

Just like Mara had been, when he'd first taken her in. He wondered if she would ever be similarly tamed.

Wondered if she would solve this whole problem by killing Skywalker first.

The cackle/purr came again, closer this time. "Come on, Drang," he told the vornskr, getting to his feet. "Time to go inside."

He paused at the door to take one last look at the forest, a shiver of melancholy and something that felt disturbingly like fear running through him. No, the Grand Admiral wasn't going to be happy about this. Wasn't going to be happy at all.

And one way or the other, Karrde knew that his life here was at an end.

CHAPTER 25

THE ROOM WAS QUIET and dark, the faint nighttime sounds of Rwookrrorro floating in through the mesh window with the cool night breeze. Staring at the curtains, Leia gripped her blaster with a sweaty hand, and wondered what had awakened her.[1]

She lay there for several minutes, heart thudding in her chest. But there was nothing. No sounds, no movements, no threats that her limited Jedi senses could detect. Nothing but a creepy feeling in the back of her mind that she was no longer safe here.

She took a deep breath, let it out silently as she continued to listen. It wasn't any fault of her hosts, or at least nothing she could blame them for. The city's leaders had been on incredibly tight alert the first couple of days, providing her with over a dozen Wookiee bodyguards while other volunteers combed through the city like hairy Imperial Walkers, searching for the alien she'd spotted that first day here. The whole thing had been carried out with a

1. Though I tried to give each of the three main movie characters a fair share of the action in *Heir*, it was in the nature of this part of the story that Leia got a bit shortchanged.

Still, she has a few memorable moments, this being one of them. And of course, she'll have a much larger and more pivotal role later in *Dark Force Rising*.

—TZ

speed, efficiency, and thoroughness that Leia had seldom seen even in the top ranks of the Rebel Alliance.

But as the days passed without anyone finding a trace of the alien, the alert had gradually softened. By the time the negative reports also began coming in from other Kashyyyk cities, the number of searchers had dwindled to a handful and the dozen bodyguards had been reduced to three.

And now even those three were gone, returning to their regular jobs and lives. Leaving her with just Chewbacca, Ralrra, and Salporin to watch over her.

It was a classic strategy. Lying alone in the dark, with the advantage of hindsight, she could see that. Sentient beings, human and Wookiee alike, simply could not maintain a continual state of vigilance when there was no visible enemy to be vigilant toward. It was a tendency they'd had to fight hard against in the Alliance.

As they'd also had to fight against the too-often lethal inertia that seduced a person into staying too long in one place.

She winced, memories of the near disaster on the ice world of Hoth coming back to haunt her. She and Chewbacca should have left Rwookrrorro days ago, she knew. Probably should have left Kashyyyk entirely, for that matter. The place had become too comfortable, too familiar— her mind no longer really *saw* everything that went on around her, but merely saw some of it and filled in the rest from memory. It was the kind of psychological weakness that a clever enemy could easily exploit, simply by finding a way to fit himself into her normal routine.

It was time for that routine to be broken.

She peered over at the bedside chrono, did a quick calculation. About an hour until dawn. There was a repulsor-lift sled parked just outside; if she and Chewbacca got going now, they should be able to get the *Lady Luck* into space a little after sunrise. Sitting halfway up, she slid across the bed, set her blaster down on the nightstand, and picked up her comlink.

And in the darkness, a sinewy hand reached out to seize her wrist.

There was no time to think; but for that first half second there was no need. Even as her mind froze, stunned by the unexpectedness of the attack, old self-defense reflexes were already swinging into action. Falling away from her assailant, using the pull on her arm for balance, she swiveled on her hip, tucked her right leg under her, and kicked out with all her strength.

The edge of her foot thudded against something unyielding—body armor of some kind. Reaching back over her shoulder with her free hand, she grabbed the corner of her pillow and hurled it at the shadowy outline of his head.

Under the pillow was her lightsaber.

It was doubtful that he ever saw the blow coming. He was still in the process of scooping the pillow away from his face when the ignited lightsaber lit up the room. She got just a glimpse of huge black eyes and protruding jaw before the blazing blade sliced him almost in half.

The grip on her arm was abruptly gone. Closing down the lightsaber, she rolled out of bed and back to her feet, igniting the weapon again as she looked around—

And with a sudden, numbing blow to her wrist, the lightsaber was knocked across the room. It shut down in midflight, plunging the room again into darkness.

She dropped instantly into combat stance, but even as she did so she knew it was a useless gesture. The first alien had perhaps been lulled by the apparent helplessness of his victim; the second had obviously learned the lesson. She hadn't even turned all the way toward the attacker before her wrist was again captured and twisted around behind her. Another hand snaked around to cover her mouth, at the same time jamming her neck hard against the attacker's muzzle. One leg twined somehow around her knees, blocking any attempt she might make to kick him. She tried anyway, struggling to free at least one leg, while at the same time trying to get a clear shot at those eyes with her free hand. His breath was hot on her neck, and she could feel the shapes of needle teeth through the jaw skin pressing against her. The alien's body went abruptly rigid—

And suddenly, without any warning at all, she was free.

She spun around to face the alien, fighting to regain her balance in the sudden loss of anything solid to lean against and wondering what this new game was he was playing. Her eyes searched frantically in the dim light, trying to locate the weapon he was surely now bringing to bear on her—

But there was no weapon pointed at her. The alien just stood there, his back to the door, his empty hands splayed off to the sides as if preparing to protect himself from a backward fall. "*Mal'ary'ush,*" he hissed, his voice soft and gravelly. Leia took a step backward, wondering if she could get to the window before he launched his next attack.

The attack never came. Behind the alien, the door slammed open; and with a roar, Chewbacca boiled into the room.

The attacker didn't turn. He made no move at all, in fact, as the Wookiee leaped toward him, massive hands reaching for his neck—

"Don't kill him!" Leia snapped.

The words probably startled Chewbacca almost as much as they startled her. But the Wookiee's reflexes were equal to the task. Passing up the alien's throat, he swung a hand instead to cuff him solidly across the side of the head.

The blow sent the alien flying halfway across the room and up against the wall. He slid down and remained still.

"Come on," Leia said, rolling across her bed to retrieve her lightsaber. "There may be more of them."

[Not any morre,] a Wookiee voice rumbled, and she looked up to see Ralrra leaning against the doorway. [The otherr three have been dealt with.]

"Are you sure?" Leia asked, taking a step toward him. He was still leaning against the doorjamb—

Leaning *hard* against it, she suddenly realized. "You're hurt," she exclaimed, flicking on the room light and giving him a quick examination. There were no marks she could see. "Blaster?"

[Stun weapon,] he corrected. [A quieterr weapon, but it was set too low forr Wookiees. I am only a little weak. Chewbacca it is who is wounded.]

Startled, Leia looked over at Chewbacca . . . and for the first time saw the small patch of matted brown hair midway down his torso. "Chewie!" she breathed, starting toward him.

He waved her away with an impatient growl. [He is right,] Ralrra agreed. [We must get you away from herre, beforre the second attack comes.]

From somewhere outside a Wookiee began howling an alert. "There won't be a second attack," she told Ralrra. "They've been noticed—there'll be people converging on this house in minutes."

[Not on this house,] Ralrra rumbled, a strange grimness to his voice. [Therre is a firre fourr houses away.]

Leia stared at him, a chill running up her back. "A diversion," she murmured. "They set a house on fire to mask any alert you try to make."

Chewbacca growled an affirmative. [We must get you away from herre,] Ralrra repeated, easing himself carefully upright.

Leia glanced past him through the doorway to the darker hallway beyond, a strange dread suddenly twisting into her stomach. There had been *three* Wookiees in the house with her. "Where's Salporin?" she asked.

Ralrra hesitated, just long enough for her suspicions to become a terrible certainty. [He did not survive the attack,] the Wookiee said, almost too softly for her to hear.

Leia swallowed hard. "I'm sorry," she said, the words sounding painfully trite and meaningless in her ears.

[As arre we. But the time forr mourning is not now.]

Leia nodded, blinking back sudden tears as she turned to the window. She'd lost many friends and companions in the midst of battle through the years, and she knew that Ralrra was right. But all the logic in the universe didn't make it any easier.

There were no aliens visible outside. But they were there—that much she was sure of. Both of the previous teams she and Han had tangled with had consisted of considerably more than five members, and there was no reason to expect this one to be any different. Chances were that any attempt to escape overland would meet with a quick ambush.

Worse, as soon as the hue and cry over the burning house really got going, the aliens could likely launch a second attack with impunity, counting on the commotion down the street to cover up any noise they made in the process.

She glanced at the burning house, feeling a brief pang of guilt for the Wookiees who owned it. Resolutely, she forced the emotion out of her mind. There, too, there was nothing she could do for now. "The aliens seem to want me alive," she said, dropping the edge of the curtain and turning back to Chewbacca and Ralrra. "If we can get the sled into the sky, they probably won't try to shoot us down."

[Do you trust the sled?] Ralrra asked pointedly.

Leia stopped short, lips pressed tightly together in annoyance with herself. No, of course she didn't trust the sled—the first thing the aliens would have done would have been to disable any escape vehicle within reach. Disable it, or worse: they could have modified it to simply fly her directly into their arms.

She couldn't stay put; she couldn't go sideways; and she couldn't go up. Which left exactly one direction.

"I'll need some rope," she said, scooping up an armful of clothes and starting to get dressed. "Strong enough to hold my weight.[2] As much as you've got."

2. I was pleased, during this reread, to find very few things I would have edited differently now from the way I did twenty years ago. One exception appears here. It's been a while since we've seen Leia, and obviously some time has passed. Yet there's no mention of her advancing pregnancy. It's odd that I didn't request a sentence or two, especially as I was going through my own first pregnancy at the time and discovering that there is not a moment when that developing child escapes a mother's awareness. Yet Leia doesn't give a thought to her baby bump in this very exciting chapter. . . .

—BM

They were fast, all right. A quick glance between them—
[You cannot be serious,] Ralrra told her. [The dangerr
would be great even forr a Wookiee. Forr a human it would
be suicide.]

"I don't think so," Leia shook her head, pulling on her
boots. "I saw how the branches twist together, when we
looked at the bottom of the city. It should be possible for
me to climb along between them."

[You will neverr reach the landing platform alone,]
Ralrra objected. [We will come with you.]

"You're in no shape to travel down the street, let alone
underneath it," Leia countered bluntly. She picked up her
blaster, holstered it, and stepped to the doorway. "Neither
is Chewbacca. Get out of my way, please."

Ralrra didn't budge. [You do not fool us, Leiaorganasolo. You believe that if we stay herre the enemy will follow
you and leave us in peace.]

Leia grimaced. So much for the quiet, noble self-
sacrifice. "There's a good chance they will," she insisted.
"It's me they want. And they want me alive."

[Therre is no time to argue,] Ralrra said. [We will stay
togetherr. Herre, orr underr the city.]

Leia took a deep breath. She didn't like it, but it was
clear she wasn't going to be able to talk them out of it. "All
right, you win." She sighed. The alien Chewbacca had hit
was still lying unconscious, and for a moment she debated
whether or not they dared take the time to tie him up. The
need for haste won. "Let's find some rope and get moving."

And besides, a small voice in the back of her head reminded her, even if she went alone, the aliens might still
attack the house. And might prefer leaving no witnesses
behind.

The flat, somewhat spongy material that formed the
"ground" of Rwookrrorro was less than a meter thick.

Leia's lightsaber cut through both it and the house's floor with ease, dropping a roughly square chunk between the braided branches to vanish into the darkness below.

[I will go first,] Ralrra said, dropping into the hole before anyone could argue the point. He was still moving a little slowly, but at least the stun-induced dizzy spells seemed to have passed.

Leia looked up as Chewbacca stepped close to her and flipped Ralrra's baldric around her shoulders. "Last chance to change your mind about this arrangement," she warned him.

His answer was short and to the point. By the time Ralrra's quiet [All clearr] floated up, they were ready.

And with Leia strapped firmly to his torso, Chewbacca eased his way through the hole.

Leia had fully expected the experience to be unpleasant. She hadn't realized that it was going to be terrifying, as well. The Wookiees didn't crawl across the tops of the plaited branches, the way she'd anticipated doing. Instead, using the climbing claws she'd seen her first day here, they hung by all fours underneath the branches to travel.

And then they *traveled*.

The side of her face pressed against Chewbacca's hairy chest, Leia clenched her teeth tightly together, partly to keep them from chattering with the bouncing, but mostly to keep moans of fear from escaping. It was like the acrophobia she'd felt in the liftcar, multiplied by a thousand. Here, there wasn't even a relatively thick vine between her and the nothingness below—only Wookiee claws and the thin rope connecting them to another set of Wookiee claws. She wanted to say something—to plead that they stop and at least belay the end of their rope to something solid—but she was afraid to make even a sound lest it break Chewbacca's concentration. The sound of his breathing was like the roar of a waterfall in her ears, and she could feel the warm wetness of his blood seeping through the thin material of her undertunic. How badly had he been hurt? Huddled against him, listening to his heart pounding, she was afraid to ask.

Abruptly, he stopped.

She opened her eyes, unaware until that moment that she'd closed them. "What's wrong?" she asked, her voice trembling.

[The enemy has found us,] Ralrra growled softly from beside her.

Bracing herself, Leia turned her head as far as she could, searching the dark predawn gray behind them. There it was: a small patch of darker black set motionlessly against it. A repulsorlift airspeeder of some kind, staying well back out of bowcaster range. "It couldn't be a Wookiee rescue ship, I don't suppose," she offered hopefully.

Chewbacca growled the obvious flaw: the airspeeder wasn't showing even running lights. [Yet it does not approach,] Ralrra pointed out.

"They want me alive," Leia said, more to reassure herself than to remind them. "They don't want to spook us." She looked around, searching the void around them and the matted branches above them for inspiration.

And found it. "I need the rest of the rope," she told Ralrra, peering back at the hovering airspeeder. "All of it."

Steeling herself, she twisted partway around in her makeshift harness, taking the coil he gave her and tying one end securely to one of the smaller branches. Chewbacca growled an objection. "No, I'm not belaying us," she assured him. "So don't fall. I've got something else in mind. Okay, let's go."

They set off again, perhaps a shade faster than before . . . and as she bounced along against Chewbacca's torso, Leia realized with mild surprise that while she was still frightened, she was no longer terrified. Perhaps, she decided, because she was no longer simply a pawn or excess baggage, with her fate totally in the hands of Wookiees or gray-skinned aliens or the forces of gravity. *She* was now at least partially in control of what happened.

They continued on, Leia playing out the rope as they traveled. The dark airspeeder followed, still without lights, still keeping well back from them. She kept an eye on it as they bounced along, knowing that the timing and distance on this were going to be crucial. Just a little bit farther . . .

There were perhaps three meters of rope left in the coil. Quickly, she tied a firm knot and peered back at their pursuer. "Get ready," she said to Chewbacca. "Now . . . *stop.*"

Chewbacca came to a halt. Mentally crossing her fingers, Leia ignited her lightsaber beneath the Wookiee's back, locked it on, and let it drop.

And like a blazing chunk of wayward lightning, it fell away, swinging down and back on the end of the rope in a long pendulum arc. It reached bottom and swung back up the other direction—

And into the underside of the airspeeder.

There was a spectacular flash as the lightsaber blade sliced through the repulsorlift generator. An instant later the airspeeder was dropping like a stone, two separate blazes flaring from either side. The craft fell into the mists below, and for a long moment the fires were visible as first two, and then as a single diffuse spot of light. Then even that faded, leaving only the lightsaber swinging gently in the darkness.

Leia took a shuddering breath. "Let's go retrieve the lightsaber," she told Chewbacca. "After that, I think we can probably just cut our way back up. I doubt there are any of them left now."

[And then directly to yourr ship?] Ralrra asked as they headed back to the branch where she'd tied the rope.

Leia hesitated, the image of that second alien in her room coming back to mind. Standing there facing her, an unreadable emotion in face and body language, so stunned or enraptured or frightened that he didn't even notice

Chewbacca's entry . . . "Back to the ship," she answered Ralrra. "But not directly."

The alien was sitting motionless in a low seat in the tiny police interrogation room, a small bandage on the side of his head the only external evidence of Chewbacca's blow. His hands were resting in his lap, the fingers laced intricately together. Stripped of all clothing and equipment, he'd been given a loose Wookiee robe to wear. On someone else the effect of the outsized garment might have been comical. But not on him. Neither the robe nor his inactivity did anything to hide the aura of deadly competence that he wore like a second skin. He was—probably always would be—a member of a dangerous and persistent group of trained killing machines.[3]

And he'd asked specifically to see Leia. In person.

Towering beside her, Chewbacca growled one final objection. "I don't much like it either," Leia conceded, gazing at the monitor display and trying to screw up her courage. "But he let me go back at the house, before you came in. I want to know—I *need* to know—what that was all about."

Briefly, her conversation with Luke on the eve of the Battle of Endor flashed to mind. His quiet firmness, in the face of all her fears, that confronting Darth Vader was something he had to do. That decision had nearly killed him . . . and had ultimately brought them victory.

But Luke had felt some faint wisps of good still buried deep inside Vader. Did she feel something similar in this alien killer? Or was she driven merely by morbid curiosity?

Or perhaps by mercy?

"You can watch and listen from here," she told Chewbacca, handing him her blaster and stepping to the door. The lightsaber she left hooked onto her belt, though what use it would be in such close quarters she didn't know. "Don't come in unless I'm in trouble." Taking a deep breath, she unlocked the door and pressed the release.

3. I had a small problem with the Ewoks of *Return of the Jedi*. Not that they weren't effective as aliens, but they were just so darned *cute*—as they were of course meant to be—that it was hard for me to visualize them as real fighters.

The Noghri were sort of my answer to that. They were roughly the same size as Ewoks, with a similar family and village life and a sense of honor and commitment to those they've accepted as friends and allies.

Only they're true warriors, and extremely deadly. And they're not at *all* cute.

—TZ

The alien looked up as the door slid open, and it seemed to Leia that he sat up straighter as she stepped inside. The door slid shut behind her, and for a long moment they just eyed each other. "I'm Leia Organa Solo," she said at last. "You wanted to talk to me?"

He gazed at her for another moment. Then, slowly, he stood up and reached out a hand. "Your hand," he said, his voice gravelly and strangely accented. "May I have it?"

Leia took a step forward and offered him her hand, acutely aware that she had just committed an irrevocable act of trust. From here, if he so chose, he could pull her to him and snap her neck before anyone outside could possibly intervene.

He didn't pull her toward him. Leaning forward, holding her hand in an oddly gentle grip, he raised it to his snout and pressed it against two large nostrils half hidden beneath strands of hair.

And smelled it.

He smelled it again, and again, taking long, deep breaths. Leia found herself staring at his nostrils, noticing for the first time their size and the soft flexibility of the skin folds around them. Like those of a tracking animal, she realized. A memory flashed to mind: how, as he'd held her helpless back at the house, those same nostrils had been pressed into her neck.

And right after that was when he'd let her go . . .

Slowly, almost tenderly, the alien straightened up. "It is then true," he grated, releasing her hand and letting his own fall to his side. Those huge eyes stared at her, brimming with an emotion whose nature her Jedi skills could vaguely sense but couldn't begin to identify. "I was not mistaken before."

Abruptly, he dropped to both knees. "I seek forgiveness, Leia Organa Solo, for my actions," he said, ducking his head to the floor, his hands splayed out to the sides as they had been in that encounter back at the house. "Our orders did not identify you, but gave only your name."

"I understand." She nodded, wishing she did. "But now you know who I am?"

The alien's face dropped a couple of centimeters closer to the floor. "You are the *Mal'ary'ush*," he said. "The daughter and heir of the Lord Darth Vader.

"He who was our master."

Leia stared down at him, feeling her mouth fall open as she struggled to regain her mental balance. The right-angle turns were all coming too quickly. "Your master?" she repeated carefully.

"He who came to us in our desperate need," the alien said, his voice almost reverent. "Who lifted us from our despair, and gave us hope."

"I see," she managed. This whole thing was rapidly becoming unreal . . . but one fact already stood out. The alien prostrating himself before her was prepared to treat her as royalty.

And she knew how to behave like royalty.

"You may rise," she told him, feeling her voice and posture and manner settling into the almost-forgotten patterns of the Alderaanian court. "What is your name?"

"I am called Khabarakh by our lord," the alien said, getting to his feet. "In the language of the Noghri—" He made a long, convoluted roiling noise that Leia's vocal cords didn't have a hope of imitating.

"I'll call you Khabarakh," she said. "Your people are called the Noghri?"

"Yes." The first hint of uncertainty seemed to cross the dark eyes. "But you are the *Mal'ary'ush*," he added, with obvious question.

"My father had many secrets," she told him grimly. "You, obviously, were one of them. You said he brought you hope. Tell me how."

"He came to us," the Noghri said. "After the mighty battle. After the destruction."

"What battle?"

Khabarakh's eyes seemed to drift into memory. "Two

great starships met in the space over our world," he said, his gravelly voice low. "Perhaps more than two; we never knew for certain. They fought all the day and much of the night . . . and when the battle was over, our land was devastated."

Leia winced, a pang of sympathetic ache running through her. Of ache, and of guilt. "We never hurt non-Imperial forces or worlds on purpose," she said softly. "Whatever happened, it was an accident."

The dark eyes fixed again on her. "The Lord Vader did not think so. He believed it was done on purpose, to drive fear and terror into the souls of the Emperor's enemies."

"Then the Lord Vader was mistaken," Leia said, meeting that gaze firmly. "Our battle was with the Emperor, not his subjugated servants."

Khabarakh drew himself up stiffly. "We were not the Emperor's servants," he grated. "We were a simple people, content to live our lives without concern for the dealings of others."

"You serve the Empire now," Leia pointed out.

"In return for the Emperor's help," Khabarakh said, a hint of pride showing through his deference. "Only he came to our aid when we so desperately needed it. In his memory, we serve his designated heir—the man to whom the Lord Vader long ago entrusted us."

"I find it difficult to believe the Emperor ever really cared about you," Leia told him bluntly. "That's not the sort of man he was. All he cared about was obtaining your service against us."

"Only he came to our aid," Khabarakh repeated.

"Because we were unaware of your plight," Leia told him.

"So you say."

Leia raised her eyebrows. "Then give me a chance to prove it. Tell me where your world is."

Khabarakh jerked back. "That is impossible. You would seek us out and complete the destruction—"

"Khabarakh," Leia cut him off. "Who am I?"

The folds around the Noghri's nostrils seemed to flatten. "You are the Lady Vader. The *Mal'ary'ush.*"

"Did the Lord Vader ever lie to you?"

"You said he did."

"I said he was mistaken," Leia reminded him, perspiration starting to collect beneath her collar as she recognized the knife edge she was now walking along here. Her newfound status with Khabarakh rested solely on the Noghri's reverence for Darth Vader. Somehow, she had to attack Vader's words without simultaneously damaging that respect. "Even the Lord Vader could be deceived . . . and the Emperor was a master of deception."

"The Lord Vader served the Emperor," Khabarakh insisted. "The Emperor would not have lied to him."

Leia gritted her teeth. Stalemate. "Is your new lord equally honest with you?"

Khabarakh hesitated. "I don't know."

"Yes, you do—you said yourself he didn't tell you who it was you'd been sent to capture."

A strange sort of low moan rumbled in Khabarakh's throat. "I am only a soldier, my lady. These matters are far beyond my authority and ability. My duty is to obey my orders. *All* of my orders."

Leia frowned. Something about the way he'd said that . . . and abruptly, she knew what it was. For a captured commando facing interrogation, there could be only one order left to follow. "Yet you now know something none of your people are aware of," she said quickly. "You must live, to bring this information to them."

Khabarakh had brought his palms to face each other, as if preparing to clap them together. Now he froze, staring at her. "The Lord Vader could read the souls of the Noghri," he said softly. "You are indeed his *Mal'ary'ush.*"

"Your people need you, Khabarakh," she told him. "As do I. Your death now would only hurt those you seek to help."

Slowly, he lowered his hands. "How is it you need me?"

"Because I need your help if I'm to do anything for your people," she said. "You must tell me the location of your world."

"I cannot," he said firmly. "To do so could bring ultimate destruction upon my world. And upon me, if it were learned I had given you such information."

Leia pursed her lips. "Then take me there."

"I cannot!"

"Why not?"

"I . . . cannot."

She fixed him with her best regal stare. "I am the daughter—the *Mal'ary'ush*—of the Lord Darth Vader," she said firmly. "By your own admission, he was the hope of your world. Have matters improved since he delivered you to your new leader?"

He hesitated. "No. He has told us there is little more that he or anyone else can do."

"I would prefer to judge that for myself," she told him loftily. "Or would your people consider a single human to be such a threat?"

Khabarakh twitched. "You would come alone? To a people seeking your capture?"

Leia swallowed hard, a shiver running down her back. No, she hadn't meant to imply that. But then, she hadn't been sure of why she'd wanted to talk to Khabarakh in the first place. She could only hope that the Force was guiding her intuition in all this. "I trust your people to be honorable," she said quietly. "I trust them to grant me a hearing."

She turned and stepped to the door. "Consider my offer," she told him. "Discuss it with those whose counsel you value. Then, if you choose, meet me in orbit above the world of Endor in one month's time."

"You will come alone?" Khabarakh asked, apparently still not believing it.

She turned and looked him straight in that nightmare face. "I will come alone. Will you?"

He faced her stare without flinching. "If I come," he said, "I will come alone."

She held his gaze a moment longer, then nodded. "I hope to see you there. Farewell."

"Farewell . . . Lady Vader."

He was still staring at her as the door opened and she left.

The tiny ship shot upward through the clouds, vanishing quickly from the Rwookrrorro air-control visual monitor. Beside Leia, Chewbacca growled angrily. "I can't say I'm really happy with it, either," she confessed. "But we can't dodge them forever. If we have even a chance of getting them out from under Imperial control . . ." She shook her head.

Chewbacca growled again. "I know," she said softly, some of his pain finding its way into her own heart. "I wasn't as close to Salporin as you were, but he was still my friend."

The Wookiee turned away from the monitors and stomped across the room. Leia watched him, wishing there was something she could do to help. But there wasn't. Caught between conflicting demands of honor, he would have to work this out in the privacy of his own mind.

Behind her, someone stirred. [It is time,] Ralrra said. [The memorial period has begun. We must join the otherrs.]

Chewbacca growled an acknowledgment and went over to join him. Leia looked at Ralrra—[This period is forr Wookiees only,] he rumbled. [Laterr, you will be permitted to join us.]

"I understand," Leia said. "If you need me, I'll be on the landing platform, getting the *Lady Luck* ready to fly."

[If you truly feel it is safe to leave,] Ralrra said, still sounding doubtful.

"It is," Leia told him. And even if it wasn't, she added

silently to herself, she would still have no choice. She had a species name now—Noghri—and it was vital that she return to Coruscant and get another records search under-way.

[Very well. The mourning period will begin in two hourrs.]

Leia nodded, blinking back tears. "I'll be there," she promised.

And wondered if this war would ever truly be over.[4]

4. It would, in fact, be another ten years before the war with the Empire would end (in the Hand of Thrawn Duology).

And that brief period of peace would be quickly followed by the Yuuzhan Vong invasion, which would be followed by more trouble, and yet more trouble. Some galaxies never seem to catch a break . . .

—TZ

CHAPTER 26

THE MASS OF VINES hung twisted around and between half a dozen trees, looking like the web of a giant
spider gone berserk. Fingering Skywalker's lightsaber,
Mara studied the tangle, trying to figure out the fastest
way to clear the path.

Out of the corner of her eye, she saw Skywalker fidget-
ing. "Just keep your shirt on," she told him. "This'll only
take a minute."

"You really don't have to go for finesse, you know," he
offered. "It's not like the lightsaber's running low on
power."

"Yes, but *we're* running low on forest," she retorted.
"You have any idea how far the hum of a lightsaber can
carry in woods like this?"

"Not really."

"Me, neither. I'd like to keep it that way." She shifted her
blaster to her left hand, ignited the lightsaber with her
right, and made three quick cuts. The tangle of vines
dropped to the ground as she closed the weapon down.

"That wasn't so hard, now, was it?" she said, turning to face Skywalker and hooking the lightsaber back onto her belt. She started to turn away—

The droid's warning squeal came a fraction of a second before the sudden rustle of leaves. She whirled back, flipping her blaster into her right hand as the vornskr leaped toward Skywalker from a branch three trees away.

Even after two long days of travel, Skywalker's reflexes were still adequate to the task. He let go of the handles of the travois and dropped to the ground just ahead of the vornskr's trajectory. Four sets of claws and a whip tail took a concerted swipe at him as the predator shot by overhead. Mara waited until it had landed, and as it spun back around toward its intended prey, she shot it.

Cautiously, Skywalker got back to his feet and looked warily around. "I wish you'd change your mind about giving me back my lightsaber," he commented as he bent down to pick up the travois handles again. "You must be getting tired of shooting vornskrs off me."

"What, you afraid I'm going to miss?" she retorted, stepping over to prod the vornskr with her foot. It was dead, all right.

"You're an excellent shot," he conceded, dragging the travois toward the tangle of vines she'd just cleared out. "But you've also gone two nights without any sleep. That's going to catch up with you eventually."

"You just worry about yourself," she snapped. "Come on, get moving—we need to find someplace clear enough to send up the sonde balloon."

Skywalker headed off, the droid strapped to the travois behind him beeping softly to itself. Mara brought up the rear, watching to make sure the travois wasn't leaving too clear a trail and scowling hard at the back of Skywalker's head.

The really irritating part was that he was right. That pass from left to right hand a minute ago—a technique she'd done a thousand times before—she'd come within a hair of missing the catch completely. Her heart thudded constantly now, not quieting down even during rest. And there were long periods during their march where her mind simply drifted, instead of focusing on the task at hand.

Once, long ago, she'd gone six days without sleep. Now, after only two, she was already starting to fall apart.

She clenched her teeth and scowled a little harder. If he was hoping to see the collapse, he was going to be sorely disappointed. If for no other reason than professional pride, she was going to see this through.

Ahead, Skywalker stumbled slightly as he crossed a patch of rough ground. The right travois handle slipped out of his grip, nearly dumping the droid off the travois and eliciting a squeal of protest from the machine. "So who's getting tired now?" Mara growled as he stooped to pick up the stick again. "That's the third time in the past hour."

"It's just my hand," he replied calmly. "It seems to be permanently numb this afternoon."

"Sure," she said. Ahead, a small patch of blue sky winked down through the tree branches. "There's our hole," she said, nodding to it. "Put the droid in the middle."

Skywalker did as he was instructed, then went and sat down against one of the trees edging the tiny clearing. Mara got the small sonde balloon filled and sent it aloft on its antenna wire, running a line from the receiver into the socket where the droid's retrieval jack had once been. "All set," she said, glancing over at Skywalker.

Leaning back against his tree, he was sound asleep.

Mara snorted with contempt. *Jedi!* she threw the epithet at him as she turned back to the droid. "Come on, let's get going," she told it, sitting down carefully on the ground. Her twisted ankle seemed to be largely healed, but she knew better than to push it.

The droid beeped questioningly, its dome swiveling around to look briefly at Skywalker. "I said let's get going," she repeated harshly.

The droid beeped again, a resigned sort of sound. The

communicator's pulse indicator flashed once as the droid requested a message dump from the distant X-wing's computer; flashed again as the dump came back.

Abruptly the droid squealed in obvious excitement. "What?" Mara demanded, snatching out her blaster and giving the area a quick scan. Nothing seemed out of place. "What, there's finally a message?"

The droid beeped affirmatively, its dome again turning toward Skywalker. "Well, let's have it," Mara growled. "Come on—if there's anything in it he needs to hear, you can play it for him later."

Assuming—she didn't add—there wasn't anything in the message that suggested she needed to come out of the forest alone. If there was . . .

The droid bent forward slightly, and a holographic image appeared on the matted leaves.

But not an image of Karrde, as she'd expected. It was, instead, an image of a golden-skinned protocol droid. "Good day, Master Luke," the protocol droid said in a remarkably prissy voice. "I bring greetings to you from Captain Karrde—and, of course, to you as well, Mistress Mara," it added, almost as an afterthought. "He and Captain Solo are most pleased to hear you are both alive and well after your accident."

Captain Solo? Mara stared at the holograph, feeling totally stunned. What in the Empire did Karrde think he was doing?—he'd actually *told* Solo and Calrissian about Skywalker?

"I trust you'll be able to decrypt this message, Artoo," the protocol prissy continued. "Captain Karrde suggested that I be used to add a bit more confusion to the counterpart encrypt. According to him, there are Imperial stormtroopers waiting in Hyllyard City for you to make your appearance."

Mara clenched her teeth, throwing a look at her sleeping prisoner. So Thrawn hadn't been fooled. He knew Skywalker was here, and was waiting to take them both.

With a vicious effort, she stifled the fatigue-fed panic rising in her throat. No. Thrawn didn't *know*—at least, not for sure. He only suspected. If he'd known for sure, there wouldn't have been anyone left back at the camp to send her this message.

"The story Captain Karrde told the Imperials was that a former employee stole valuable merchandise and tried to escape, with a current employee named Jade in pursuit. He suggests that, since he never specified Jade as being a woman, that perhaps you and Mistress Mara could switch roles when you leave the forest."

"Right," Mara muttered under her breath. If Karrde thought she was going to cheerfully hand her blaster over for Skywalker to stick in her back, he'd better try thinking again.

"At any rate," the protocol droid continued, "he says he and Captain Solo are working out a plan to try to intercept you before the stormtroopers do. If not, they will do their best to rescue you from them. I'm afraid there's nothing more I can say at the moment—Captain Karrde has put a one-minute real-time limit on this message, to prevent anyone from locating the transmission point. He wishes you good luck. Take good care of Master Luke, Artoo . . . and yourself, too."

The image vanished and the droid's projector winked out. Mara shut down the communicator, setting the antenna spool to begin winding the balloon back down.

"It's a good idea," Skywalker murmured.

She looked sharply at him. His eyes were still closed. "I *thought* you were faking," she spat, not really truthfully.

"Not faking," he corrected her sleepily. "Drifting in and out. It's still a good idea."

She snorted. "Forget it. We'll try going a couple of kilometers north instead, circling out and back to Hyllyard from the plains." She glanced at her chrono, then up through the trees. Dark clouds had moved in over the past few minutes, covering the blue sky that had been there.

Not rain clouds, she decided, but they would still cut rather strongly into what was left of the available daylight. "We might as well save that for tomorrow," she said, favoring her ankle again as she got back to her feet. "You want to get—oh, never mind," she interrupted herself. If his breathing was anything to go by, he'd drifted off again.

Which left the task of putting camp together up to her. Terrific. "Stay put," she growled to the droid. She turned back to where she'd dropped the survival kit—

The droid's electronic shriek brought her spinning back around again, hand clawing for her blaster, eyes flicking around for the danger—

And then a heavy weight slammed full onto her shoulders and back, sending hot needles of pain into her skin and throwing her face-first to the ground.

Her last thought, before the darkness took her, was to wish desperately that she'd killed Skywalker when she'd had the chance.

Artoo's warbling alert jerked Luke out of his doze. His eyes snapped open, just as a blur of muscle and claw launched itself through space onto Mara's back.

He bounded to his feet, sleepiness abruptly gone. The vornskr was standing over Mara, its front claws planted on her shoulders, its head turned to the side as it prepared to sink its teeth into her neck. Mara herself lay unmoving, the back of her head toward Luke—dead or merely stunned, it was impossible to tell. Artoo, clearly too far away to reach her in time, was nevertheless moving in that direction as fast as his wheels could manage, his small electric arc welder extended as if for battle.

Taking a deep breath, Luke screamed.

Not an ordinary scream; but a shivering, booming, inhuman howl that seemed to fill the entire clearing and reverberate from the distant hills. It was the blood-freezing call of a krayt dragon, the same call Ben Kenobi had used to scare the sand people away from him all those years ago on Tatooine.

The vornskr wasn't scared away. But it was clearly startled, its prey temporarily forgotten. Shifting its weight partially off Mara's back, it turned, crouching, to stare toward the sound.

For a long moment Luke locked gazes with the creature, afraid to move lest he break the spell. If he could distract it long enough for Artoo to get there with his welder . . .

And then, still pinned to the ground, Mara twitched. Luke cupped his hands around his mouth and howled again. Again, the vornskr shifted its weight in response.

And with a sound that was half grunt and half combat yell, Mara twisted around onto her back beneath the predator, her hands snaking past the front claws to grip its throat.

It was the only opening Luke was going to get; and with a vornskr against an injured human, it wasn't going to last for long. Pushing off from the tree trunk behind him, Luke charged, aiming for the vornskr's flank.

He never got there. Even as he braced himself for the impact, the vornskr's whip tail whistled out of nowhere to catch him solidly along shoulder and face and send him sprawling sideways to the ground.

He was on his feet again in an instant, dimly aware of the line of fire burning across cheek and forehead. The vornskr hissed as he came toward it again, slashing razor-sharp claws at him to ward him back. Artoo reached the struggle and sent a spark into the predator's left front paw; almost casually, the vornskr swung at the welder, snapping it off and sending the pieces flying. Simultaneously, the tail whipped around, the impact lifting Artoo up on one set of wheels. It swung again and again, each time coming closer to knocking the droid over.

Luke gritted his teeth, mind searching furiously for a plan. Shadowboxing at the creature's head like this wasn't anything more than a delaying tactic; but the minute the distraction ceased, Mara was as good as dead. The vornskr would either slash her arms with its claws or else simply overwhelm her grip by brute force. With the loss of his welder, Artoo had no fighting capability left; and if the vornskr kept at him with that whip tail . . .

The tail. "Artoo!" Luke snapped. "Next time that tail hits you, try to grab it."

Artoo beeped a shaky acknowledgment and extended his heavy grasping arm. Luke watched out of the corner of his eye, still trying to keep the vornskr's head and front paws busy. The tail whipped around again, and with a warble of triumph, Artoo caught it.

A warble that turned quickly into a screech. Again with almost casual strength, the vornskr ripped its tail free, taking most of the grasping arm with it.

But it had been pinned out of action for a pair of heartbeats, and that was all the time Luke needed. Diving around Artoo's bulk and under the trapped whip tail, he darted his hand to Mara's side and snatched back his lightsaber.

The whip tail slashed toward him as he rolled back to his feet, but by the time it got there Luke was out of range around Artoo's side again. Igniting the lightsaber, he reached the blazing blade past the flailing claws and brushed the vornskr's nose.

The predator screamed, in anger or pain, shying back from this bizarre creature that had bit it. Luke tapped it again and again, trying to drive it away from Mara where he could safely deliver a killing blow.

Abruptly, in a single smooth motion, the vornskr leaped backward onto solid ground, then sprang straight at Luke. Also in a single smooth motion, Luke cut it in half.

"About time," a hoarse voice croaked from beneath his feet. He looked down to see Mara push half the dead vornskr off her chest and raise herself up on one elbow. "What in blazes was that stupid game you were playing?"

"I didn't think you'd like your hands cut off if I missed,"

Luke told her, breathing hard. He took a step back as she sat up and offered her a helping hand.

She waved the hand away. Rolling slowly onto hands and knees, she pushed herself tiredly to her feet and turned back to face him.

With her blaster back in her hand.

"Just drop the lightsaber and move back," she panted, gesturing with the weapon for emphasis.

Luke sighed, shaking his head. "I don't believe you," he said, shutting down the lightsaber and dropping it onto the ground. The adrenaline was receding from his system now, leaving both face and shoulder aching like fury. "Or didn't you notice that Artoo and I just saved your life?"

"I noticed. Thanks." Keeping her blaster trained on him, Mara stooped to retrieve the lightsaber. "I figure that's my reward for not shooting you two days ago. Get over there and sit down."

Luke looked over at Artoo, who was moaning softly to himself. "Do you mind if I look at Artoo first?"

Mara looked down at the droid, her lips compressed into a thin line. "Sure, go ahead." Moving clear of both of them, she picked up the survival pack and trudged off to one of the trees at the edge of the clearing.

Artoo wasn't in as bad a shape as Luke had feared. Both the welder and the grasping arm had broken off cleanly, leaving no trailing wires or partial components that might get caught on something else. Speaking quiet encouragement to the droid, Luke got the two compartments sealed.[1]

"Well?" Mara asked, sitting with her back to a tree and gingerly applying salve to the oozing claw marks on her arms.

"He's okay for now," Luke told her as he went back over to his own tree and sat down. "He's been damaged worse than this before."

"I'm so glad to hear it," she said sourly. She glanced at Luke, took a longer look. "He got you good, didn't he?"

1. Killing off a character, or even just lopping off one of his or her major body parts, can be highly traumatic, not only for the character but for the audience. Just ask Luke.

That's one of the handy things about droids. You can rip off any component you need to, and after a quick visit to the body shop everything will be fine.

Gilbert Gottfried, who voiced the parrot Iago in Disney's *Aladdin*, once commented that the screenwriters' philosophy seemed to be, "When in doubt, hurt the bird."

Not that I would ever deliberately think that way about R2. Of course not.

—TZ

Carefully, Luke touched the welt running across his cheek and forehead. "I'll be all right."

She snorted. "Sure you will," she said, her voice laced with sarcasm as she went back to treating her gashes. "I forgot—you're a hero, too."

For a long minute Luke watched her, trying once more to understand the complexities and contradictions of this strange woman. Even from three meters away he could see that her hand was shaking as she applied the salve: with reaction, perhaps, or muscle fatigue. Almost certainly with fear—she'd escaped a bloody death by a bare handful of centimeters, and she would have to be a fool not to recognize that.

And yet, whatever she was feeling inside, she was clearly determined not to let any of it out past that rock-hard surface she'd so carefully built up around herself. As if she was afraid to let weakness of any sort show through . . .

Abruptly, as if feeling his eyes on her, Mara looked up. "I said thanks already," she growled. "What do you want, a medal?"

Luke shook his head. "I just want to know what happened to you."

For a moment those green eyes flashed again with the old hatred. But only for a moment. The vornskr attack, coming on top of two days of laborious travel and no sleep, had taken a severe toll on her emotional strength. The anger faded from her eyes, leaving only a tired coldness behind. "*You* happened to me," she told him, her voice more fatigued than embittered. "You came out of a grubby sixth-rate farm on a tenth-rate planet, and destroyed my life."

"How?"

Contempt briefly filled her face. "You don't have the faintest idea who I am, do you?"

Luke shook his head. "I'm sure I'd remember you if we'd met."

"Oh, right," she said sardonically. "The great, omni-

2. Mara Jade's creation began with a simple idea and plan: to tie the opening section of *Return of the Jedi* more closely to the main story presented by the *Star Wars* movies.

To elaborate a bit. Han's rescue was, of course, a vital part of *Jedi*. But to me, it always felt a little disconnected from the main Rebellion plot line. (Which it was, of course. Rescuing Han was strictly personal, on everyone's part.)

As I mulled it over, it occurred to me that, after Vader's attempt to persuade Luke to join him in *The Empire Strikes Back*, the Emperor might very well have decided that Luke was more liability than potential asset and sent someone to take him out when he turned up at Jabba's palace.

What kind of person might Palpatine send? It would have to be someone competent, naturally. It would also have to be someone who could meet Luke's Jedi power head-on. Finally, it would have to be someone who was out of the normal chain of command, lest Vader get wind of the plan.

From all that came the idea of the Emperor's Hand, a shadowy agent

scient Jedi. See all, hear all, know all, understand all. No, we didn't actually meet; but I was there, if you'd bothered to notice me. I was a dancer at Jabba the Hutt's palace the day you came for Solo."

So that was it. She'd worked for Jabba; and when he'd killed Jabba, he'd ruined her life. . . .

Luke frowned at her. No. Her slim figure, her agility and grace—those certainly could belong to a professional dancer. But her piloting skills, her expert marksmanship, her inexplicable working knowledge of lightsabers—those most certainly did not.

Mara was still waiting, daring him with her expression to figure it out. "You weren't just a dancer, though," he told her. "That was only a cover."

Her lip twisted. "Very good. That vaunted Jedi insight, no doubt. Keep going; you're doing so well. What was I really doing there?"

Luke hesitated. There were all sorts of possibilities for this one: bounty hunter, smuggler, quiet bodyguard for Jabba, spy from some rival criminal organization . . .

No. Her knowledge of lightsabers . . . and suddenly, all the pieces fell together with a rush. "You were waiting for me," he said. "Vader knew I'd go there to try and rescue Han, and he sent you to capture me."

"Vader?" She all but spat the name. "Don't make me laugh. Vader was a fool, and skating on the edge of treason along with it. My master sent me to Jabba's to kill you, not recruit you."

Luke stared at her, an icy shiver running up his back. It couldn't be . . . but even as he gazed into that tortured face, he knew with sudden certainty that it was. "And your master," he said quietly, "was the Emperor."[2]

"Yes," she said, her voice a snake's hiss. "And you destroyed him."

Luke swallowed hard, the pounding of his own heart the only sound. He hadn't killed the Emperor—Darth

Vader had done that—but Mara didn't seem inclined to worry over such subtleties. "You're wrong, though," he said. "He *did* try to recruit me."

"Only because I failed," she ground out, her throat muscles tight. "And only when Vader had you standing right there in front of him. What, you don't think he knew Vader had offered to help you overthrow him?"

Unconsciously, Luke flexed the fingers of his numbed artificial hand. Yes, Vader had indeed suggested such an alliance during their Cloud City duel. "I don't think it was a serious offer," he murmured.

"The Emperor did," Mara said flatly. "He knew. And what he knew, I knew."

Her eyes filled with distant pain. "I was his hand, Skywalker," she said, her voice remembering. "That's how I was known to his inner court: as the Emperor's Hand. I served him all over the galaxy, doing jobs the Imperial Fleet and stormtroopers couldn't handle. That was my one great talent, you see—I could hear his call from anywhere in the Empire, and report back to him the same way. I exposed traitors for him, brought down his enemies, helped him keep the kind of control over the mindless bureaucracies that he needed. I had prestige, and power, and respect."

Slowly, her eyes came back from the past. "And you took it all away from me. If only for that, you deserve to die."

"What went wrong?" Luke forced himself to ask.

Her lip twisted. "Jabba wouldn't let me go with the execution party. That was it—pure and simple. I tried begging, cajoling, bargaining—I couldn't change his mind."

"No," Luke said soberly. "Jabba was highly resistant to the mind-controlling aspects of the Force."

But if she *had* been on the Sail Barge . . .

Luke shivered, seeing in his mind's eye that terrifying vision in the dark cave on Dagobah. The mysterious silhouetted woman standing there on the Sail Barge's upper

(cont.)
under Palpatine's sole command. And from *that*, ultimately, came Mara Jade.

And although her early history still remains mysterious, I've now had a chance to tell a few of the stories of her life as the Emperor's Hand, in *Star Wars: Allegiance* and the upcoming *Star Wars: Choices of One.*

—TZ

deck, laughing at him as she held his captured lightsaber high.

The first time, years ago, the cave had spun him an image of a possible future. This time, he knew now, it had shown him a possible past. "You would have succeeded," he said quietly.

Mara looked sharply at him. "I'm not asking for understanding or sympathy," she bit out. "You wanted to know. Fine; now you know."

He let her tend her wounds in silence for a moment. "So why are you here?" he asked. "Why not with the Empire?"

"What Empire?" she countered. "It's dying—you know that as well as I do."

"But while it's still there—"

She cut him off with a withering glare. "Who would I go to?" she demanded. "They didn't know me—none of them did. Not as the Emperor's Hand, anyway. I was a shadow, working outside the normal lines of command and protocol. There were no records kept of my activities. Those few I was formally introduced to thought of me as court-hanging froth, a minor bit of mobile decoration kept around the palace to amuse the Emperor."

Her eyes went distant again with memory. "There was nowhere for me to go after Endor," she said bitterly. "No contacts, no resources—I didn't even have a real identity anymore. I was on my own."

"And so you linked up with Karrde."

"Eventually. First I spent four and a half years sloshing around the rotten underfringes of the galaxy, doing whatever I could." Her eyes were steady on him, with a trace of hatred fire back in them. "I worked hard to get where I am, Skywalker. You're not going to ruin it for me. Not this time."

"I don't want to ruin anything for you," Luke told her evenly. "All I want is to get back to the New Republic."

"And I want the old Empire back," she retorted. "We don't always get what we want, do we?"

Luke shook his head. "No. We don't."

For a moment she glared at him. Then, abruptly, she scooped up a tube of salve and tossed it at him. "Here— get that welt fixed up. And get some sleep. Tomorrow's going to be a busy day."

CHAPTER 27

THE BATTERED A-CLASS bulk freighter drifted off the *Chimaera*'s[1] starboard side: a giant space-going box with a hyperdrive attached, its faded plating glistening dully in the glare of the Star Destroyer's floodlights. Sitting at his command station, Thrawn studied the sensor data and nodded. "It looks good, Captain," he said to Pellaeon. "Exactly the way it should. You may proceed with the test when ready."

"It'll be a few more minutes yet, sir," Pellaeon told him, studying the readouts on his console. "The technicians are still having some problems getting the cloaking shield tuned."

He held his breath, half afraid of a verbal explosion. The untested cloaking shield and the specially modified freighter it was mounted to had cost hideous amounts of money—money the Empire really didn't have to spare. For the technology to now suddenly come up finicky, particularly with the whole of the Sluis Van operation hanging squarely in the balance . . .

1. In Greek myth, the Chimaera was a fantastical fire-breathing beast that combined lion, goat, and snake. It was also held to be unconquerable, though it was eventually killed by Bellerophon.

Nowadays, the word refers to something made up of disparate parts (usually as a result of grafting or genetic manipulation), or something wildly and grotesquely imaginary.

All of those elements went into my decision to name Thrawn's flagship the *Chimaera*. Disparate elements (human plus Chiss), considered imaginary (and hence not taken seriously by others until Thrawn was ready to move), and unconquerable.

—TZ

But the Grand Admiral merely nodded. "There's time," he said calmly. "What word from Myrkr?"

"The last regular report came in two hours ago," Pellaeon told him. "Still negative."

Thrawn nodded again. "And the latest count from Sluis Van?"

"Uh . . ." Pellaeon checked the appropriate file. "A hundred twelve transient warships in all. Sixty-five being used as cargo carriers, the others on escort duty."

"Sixty-five," Thrawn repeated with obvious satisfaction. "Excellent. It means we get to pick and choose."

Pellaeon stirred uncomfortably. "Yes, sir."

Thrawn turned away from his contemplation of the freighter to look at Pellaeon. "You have a concern, Captain?"

Pellaeon nodded at the ship. "I don't like sending them into enemy territory without any communications."

"We don't have much choice in the matter," Thrawn reminded him dryly. "That's how a cloaking shield works— nothing gets out, nothing gets in." He cocked an eyebrow. "Assuming, of course, that it works at all,"[2] he added pointedly.

"Yes, sir. But . . ."

"But what, Captain?"

Pellaeon braced himself and took the plunge. "It seems to me, Admiral, that this is the sort of operation we ought to use C'baoth on."

Thrawn's gaze hardened, just a bit. "C'baoth?"

"Yes, sir. He could give us communications with—"

"We don't need communications, Captain," Thrawn cut him off. "Careful timing will be adequate for our purposes."

"I disagree, Admiral. Under normal circumstances, yes, careful timing would get them into position. But there's no way to anticipate how long it'll take to get clearance from Sluis Control."

"On the contrary," Thrawn countered coolly. "I've stud-

2. Cloaking shields are one of those SF gadgets that almost beg to be abused by the writer. A cloak of invisibility that lets you sneak up right beside your enemies and deliver lethal blows can make life way too easy for you, and way too easy for your characters.

I would probably not have used cloaking shields at all if it hadn't been for that comment in *The Empire Strikes Back*. Given that the Empire did have such a device, I couldn't very well ignore it, any more than I could ignore the existence of clones and cloning.

Fortunately, by the time I began writing *Heir*, West End Games had already come up with the kind of limiting factor that cloaking technology needs. Along with its expense, they also postulated that it was a two-way shield, with no light or signal getting out that your enemy could see, but also no sensor data getting in that *you* could see. A double-blind shield is automatically more difficult to use safely and effectively than the one-way type that

(cont.)
often shows up in science fiction.

Fortunately, coming up with inventive ways to use limited and otherwise questionable technology is one of Thrawn's specialties.

—TZ

ied the Sluissi very carefully. I can anticipate exactly how long it will take them to clear the freighter."

Pellaeon gritted his teeth. "If the controllers were all Sluissi, perhaps. But with the Rebellion funneling so much of their own material through the Sluis Van system, they're bound to have some of their own people in Control, as well."

"It's of no consequence," Thrawn told him. "The Sluissi will be in charge. *Their* timing will determine events."

Pellaeon exhaled and conceded defeat. "Yes, sir," he muttered.

Thrawn eyed him. "It's not a question of bravado, Captain. Or of proving that the Imperial Fleet can function without him. The simple fact of the matter is that we can't afford to use C'baoth too much or too often."

"Because we'll start depending on him," Pellaeon growled. "As if we were all borg-implanted into a combat computer."

Thrawn smiled. "That still bothers you, doesn't it? No matter. That's part of it, but only a very small part. What concerns me more is that we don't give Master C'baoth too much of a taste for this kind of power."

Pellaeon frowned at him. "He said he doesn't want power."

"Then he lies," Thrawn returned coldly. "All men want power. And the more they have, the more they want."

Pellaeon thought about that. "But if he's a threat to us . . ." He broke off, suddenly aware of the other officers and men working all around them.

The Grand Admiral had no such reticence. "Why not dispose of him?" he finished the question. "It's very simple. Because we'll soon have the ability to fill his taste for power to the fullest . . . and once we've done so, he'll be no more of a threat than any other tool."

"Leia Organa Solo and her twins?"

"Exactly." Thrawn nodded, his eyes glittering. "Once

C'baoth has them in his hand, these little excursions with the Fleet will be no more to him than distracting interludes that take him away from his *real* work."

Pellaeon found himself looking away from the intensity of that gaze. The theory seemed good enough; but in actual practice . . . "That assumes, of course, that the Noghri are ever able to connect with her."

"They will." Thrawn was quietly confident. "She and her guardians will eventually run out of tricks. Certainly long before we run out of Noghri."

In front of Pellaeon, the display cleared. "They're ready, sir," he said.

Thrawn turned back to the freighter. "At your convenience, Captain."

Pellaeon took a deep breath and tapped the comm switch. "Cloaking shield: *activate.*"

And outside the view window, the battered freighter—

Stayed exactly as it was.

Thrawn gazed hard at the freighter. Looked at his command displays, back at the freighter . . . and then turned to Pellaeon, a satisfied smile on his face. "Excellent, Captain. Precisely what I wanted. I congratulate you and your technicians."

"Thank you, sir," Pellaeon said, relaxing muscles he hadn't realized were tense. "Then I take it the light is green?"

The Grand Admiral's smile remained unchanged, his face hardening around it. "The light is green, Captain," he said grimly. "Alert the task force; prepare to move to the rendezvous point.

"The Sluis Van shipyards are ours."

Wedge Antilles looked up from the data pad with disbelief. "You've got to be kidding," he told the dispatcher. "*Escort duty?*"

The other gave him an innocent look. "What's the big deal?" he asked. "You guys are X-wings—you do escort all the time."

"We escort *people*," Wedge retorted. "We don't watchdog cargo ships."

The dispatcher's innocent look collapsed into thinly veiled disgust, and Wedge got the sudden impression that he'd gone through this same argument a lot lately. "Look, Commander, don't dump it on me," he growled back. "It's a standard Frigate escort—what's the difference whether the Frigate's got people or a break-down reactor aboard?"

Wedge looked back at the datapad. It was a matter of professional pride, that's what the difference was. "Sluis Van's a pretty long haul for X-wings," he said instead.

"Yeah, well, the spec line says you'll be staying aboard the Frigate until you actually hit the system," the dispatcher said, reaching over his desk to tap the paging key on Wedge's datapad. "You'll just ride him in from there."

Wedge scanned the rest of the spec line. They'd then have to sit there in the shipyards and wait for the rest of the convoy to assemble before finally taking the cargo on to Bpfassh. "We're going to be a long time away from Coruscant with this," he said.

"I'd look on that as a plus if I were you, Commander," the dispatcher said, lowering his voice. "Something here's coming to a head. I think Councilor Fey'lya and his people are about to make their move."

Wedge felt a chill run through him. "You don't mean . . . a *coup?*"

The dispatcher jumped as if scalded. "*No*, of course not. What do you think Fey'lya is—?"

He broke off, his eyes going wary. "Oh, I got it. You're one of Ackbar's diehards, huh? Face it, Commander; Ackbar's lost whatever touch he ever had with the common fighting man of the Alliance. Fey'lya's the only one on the Council who really cares about our welfare." He gestured at the datapad. "Case in point. All this garbage came down from Ackbar's office."

"Yeah, well, there's still an Empire out there," Wedge muttered, uncomfortably aware that the dispatcher's verbal attack on Ackbar had neatly shifted him to the other side of his own argument. He wondered if the other had done that on purpose . . . or whether he really was one of the growing number of Fey'lya supporters in the military.

And come to think of it, a little vacation away from Coruscant might not be such a bad idea, after all. At least it would get him away from all this crazy political stuff. "When do we leave?"

"Soon as you can get your people together and aboard," the dispatcher said. "They're already loading your fighters."

"Right." Wedge turned away from the desk and headed down the corridor toward the ready rooms. Yes, a quiet little run back out to Sluis Van and Bpfassh would be just the thing right now. Give him some breathing space to try to sort out just what was happening to this New Republic he'd risked so much to help build.

And if the Imperials took a poke at them along the way . . . well, at least *that* was a threat he could fight back against.

CHAPTER 28

IT WAS JUST BEFORE NOON when they began to notice the faint sounds wafting occasionally to them through the forest. It was another hour after that before they were close enough for Luke to finally identify them.

Speeder bikes.

"You're sure that's a military model?" Mara muttered as the whine/drone rose and fell twice more before fading again into the distance.

"I'm sure," Luke told her grimly. "I nearly ran one of them into a tree on Endor."

She didn't reply, and for a moment Luke wondered if the mention of Endor might not have been a good idea. But a glance at Mara's face relieved that fear. She was not brooding, but listening. "Sounds like they're off to the south, too," she said after a minute. "North . . . I don't hear anything from that direction."

Luke listened. "Neither do I," he said. "I wonder . . . Artoo, can you make up an audio map for us?"

There was an acknowledging beep. A moment later the

droid's holo projector came on and a two-color map appeared, hovering a few centimeters over the matted leaves underfoot.

"I was right," Mara said, pointing. "A few units directly ahead of us, the rest off to the south. Nothing at all north."

"Which means we must have veered to the north," Luke said.

Mara frowned at him. "How do you figure that?"

"Well, they must know we'll make for Hyllyard City," he said. "They're bound to center their search on the direct approach."

Mara smiled thinly. "Such wonderful Jedi naïveté," she said. "I don't suppose you considered the fact that just because we can't hear them doesn't mean they aren't there."

Luke frowned down at the holographic map. "Well, of course they *could* have a force lying in wait there," he agreed. "But what would it gain them?"

"Oh, come on, Skywalker—it's the oldest tactical trick in the book. If the perimeter looks impossible to crack, the quarry goes to ground and waits for a better opportunity. You don't want him to do that, so you give him what looks like a possible way through." She squatted down, ran a finger through the "quiet" section on the map. "In this case, they get a bonus: if we swing north to avoid the obvious speeder bikes, it's instant proof that we've got something to hide from them."

Luke grimaced. "Not that they really need any proof."

Mara shrugged and straightened up again. "Some officers are more legal-minded than others. The question is, what do we do now?"

Luke looked back down at the map. By Mara's reckoning, they were no more than four or five kilometers from the edge of the forest—two hours, more or less. If the Imperials had this much organization already set up in front of them . . . "They're probably going to try to ring us," he said slowly. "Move units around to the north and south, and eventually behind us."

"If they haven't done so already," Mara said. "No reason we would have heard them—they don't know exactly how fast we're moving, so they'll have made it a big circle. Probably using a wide ring of Chariot assault vehicles or hover-scouts with a group of speeder bikes working around each focal point. It's the standard stormtrooper format for a web."

Luke pursed his lips. But what the Imperials *didn't* know was that one of the quarry knew exactly what they were up to. "So how do we break out?" he asked.

Mara hissed between her teeth. "We don't," she said flatly. "Not without a lot more equipment and resources than we've got."

The faint whine/drone came again from somewhere ahead of them, rising and then fading as it passed by in the distance. "In that case," Luke said, "we might as well go straight up the middle. Call to them before they see us, maybe."

Mara snorted. "Like we were casual tourists out here with nothing to hide?"

"You have a better idea?"

She glared at him. But it was a reflexive glare, without any real argument behind it. "Not really," she conceded at last. "I suppose you're also going to want to do that role-switch thing Karrde suggested."

Luke shrugged. "We're not going to be able to blast our way through them," he reminded her. "And if you're right about that pincer movement, we're not going to sneak through them, either. All that's left is a bluff, and the better a bluff it is, the better chance we've got."

Mara's lip twisted. "I suppose so." With only a slight hesitation, she dropped the power pack from her blaster and handed it and the forearm holster to him.

Luke took them, hefted the blaster in his hand. "They may check to see if it's loaded," he pointed out mildly. "I would."

"Look, Skywalker, if you think I'm going to give you a loaded weapon—"

"And if another vornskr finds us before the Imperials do," Luke cut her off quietly, "you'll never get it reloaded fast enough."

"Maybe I don't care," she shot back.

Luke nodded. "Maybe you don't."

She glared at him again, but again, the glare lacked conviction. Teeth visibly grinding together, she slapped the power pack into his hand. "Thank you," Luke said, reloading the blaster and fastening it to his left forearm. "Now. Artoo?"

The droid understood. One of the trapezoidal sections at the top of his upper dome, indistinguishable from all the other segments, slid open to reveal a long, deep storage compartment beneath it. Turning back to Mara, Luke held out his hand.

She looked at the open hand, then at the storage compartment. "So that's how you did it," she commented sourly, unhooking his lightsaber and handing it over. "I always wondered how you smuggled that thing into Jabba's."

Luke dropped the lightsaber in, and Artoo slid the door shut behind it. "I'll call for it if I need it," he told the droid.

"Don't count on being very good with it," Mara warned. "The ysalamiri effect is supposed to extend several kilometers past the edge of the forest—none of those little attack-anticipation tricks will work anywhere near Hyllyard City."

"I understand," Luke nodded. "I guess we're ready to go, then."

"Not quite," Mara said, eyeing him. "There's still that face of yours."

Luke cocked an eyebrow. "I don't think Artoo's got anywhere to hide *that*."

"Funny. I had something else in mind." Mara glanced around, then headed off toward a stand of odd-looking bushes a few meters away. Reaching it, she pulled the end of her tunic sleeve down to cover her hand and carefully picked a few of the leaves. "Pull up your sleeve and hold out your arm," she ordered as she returned with them.

He did so, and she brushed his forearm lightly with the tip of one of the leaves. "Now. Let's see if this works."

"What exactly is it supposed to—*aah!*" The last of Luke's air came out in an explosive burst as a searing pain lanced through his forearm.

"Perfect," Mara said with grim satisfaction. "You're allergic as anything to them. Oh, relax—the pain will be gone in a few seconds."

"Oh, thanks," Luke gritted back. The pain was indeed receding. "Right. Now, what about this—mmm!—this blasted *itch?*"

"That'll hang on a little longer," she said, gesturing at his arm. "But never mind that. What do you think?"

Luke gritted his teeth. The itching was not-so-subtle torture . . . but she was right. Where she'd brushed the leaf the skin had turned dark and puffy, sprinkled with tiny pustules. "Looks disgusting," he said.

"Sure does," she agreed. "You want to do it yourself, or you want me to do it for you?"

Luke gritted his teeth. This was *not* going to be pleasant. "I can do it."

It was indeed unpleasant; but by the time he finished brushing his chin with the leaves the pain had already begun to recede from his forehead. "I hope I didn't get it too close to my eyes," he commented between clenched teeth, throwing the leaves away into the forest and fighting hard against the urge to dig into his face with both sets of fingernails. "It'd be handy to be able to see the rest of the afternoon."

"I think you'll be all right," Mara assured him, studying the result. "The rest of your face is pretty horrendous, though. You won't look anything like whatever pictures they have, that's for sure."

"Glad to hear it." Luke took a deep breath and ran through the Jedi pain suppression exercises. Without the Force they weren't all that effective, but they seemed to help a little. "How long will I look like this?"

"The puffiness should start going down in a few hours. It won't be completely gone until tomorrow."

"Good enough. We ready, then?"

"As ready as we'll ever be." Turning her back to Artoo, she took the travois handles and started walking. "Come on."

They made good time, despite the lingering tenderness of Mara's ankle and the distractions inherent in a faceful of itch. To Luke's relief, the itching began to fade after about half an hour, leaving only puffy numbness behind it.

Mara's ankle was another story, however, and as he walked behind her and Artoo he could see clearly how she was having to favor it. The added burden of Artoo's travois wasn't helping, and twice he almost suggested that they give up on the role switching. But he resisted the urge. It was their best chance of getting out of this, and they both knew it.

Besides which, she had far too much pride to agree.

They'd gone perhaps another kilometer, with the whine/drone of the speeder bikes rising and falling in the distance, when suddenly they were there.

There were two of them: biker scouts in glistening white armor, swooping up to them and braking to a halt almost before Luke's ears had registered the sound of their approach. Which meant a very short ride, with target position already known.

Which meant that the entire search party must have had them located and vectored for at least the past few minutes. It was just as well, Luke reflected, that he hadn't tried switching roles with Mara.

"Halt!" one of the scouts called unnecessarily as they

hovered there, both swivel blaster cannons trained and ready. "Identify yourselves, in the name of the Empire."

And it was performance time. "Boy, am I glad *you* showed up," Luke called back, putting as much relief into his voice as the puffy cheeks allowed. "You don't happen to have some sort of transport handy, do you? I'm about walked off my feet."

There was just the slightest flicker of hesitation. "Identify yourself," the scout repeated.

"My name's Jade," Luke told him. He gestured at Mara. "Got a gift here for Talon Karrde. I don't suppose *he* sent some transport, did he?"

There was a short pause. The scouts conferring privately between themselves, Luke decided, or else calling back to base for instructions. The fact that the prisoner was a woman did indeed seem to have thrown them. Whether it would be enough, of course, was another question entirely.

"You'll come with us," the scout ordered. "Our officer wants to talk to you. You—woman—put the droid down and move away from it."

"Fine with me," Luke said as the second scout maneuvered his speeder bike to a position in front of Artoo's travois. "But I want both of you to witness, for the record, that I had her fair and square before you showed up. Karrde weasels his way out of these capture fees too often; he's not going to weasel out of this one."

"You're a bounty hunter?" the scout asked, a clear note of disdain in his voice.

"That's right," Luke said, putting some professional dignity in his voice as a counter to the scout's contempt. Not that he minded their distaste. He was, in fact, counting on it. The more firmly the Imperials had the wrong image of him set in their minds, the longer it would take them to see through the deception.

Somewhere in the back of his mind, though, he couldn't help but wonder if this was the sort of trick a Jedi should use.

The second scout had dismounted and fastened the handles of Artoo's travois to the rear of his speeder bike. Remounting, he headed off at about the speed of a brisk walk. "You two follow him," the first scout ordered, swinging around to take up the rear. "Drop your blaster on the ground first, Jade."

Luke complied, and they set off. The first scout put down just long enough to scoop up the abandoned blaster and then followed.

It took another hour to reach the edge of the forest. The two speeder bikes stayed with them the whole time; but as they traveled, the party began to grow. More speeder bikes swept in from both sides, falling into close formation on either side of Luke and Mara or else joining up with the guards to both front and rear. As they neared the forest's edge, fully armored stormtroopers began to appear, too, moving in with blaster rifles held ready across their chests to take up positions around the two prisoners. As they did so, the scouts began drifting away, ranging farther out to form a kind of moving screen.

By the time they finally stepped out from under the forest canopy, their escort numbered no fewer than ten biker scouts and twenty stormtroopers. It was an impressive display of military power . . . and more even than the fact of the search itself, it drove home to Luke the seriousness with which the mysterious man in charge of the Empire was treating this incident. Even at the height of their power, the Imperials hadn't spent stormtroopers lightly.

Three more people were waiting for them in the fifty-meter strip of open land between the forest and the nearest structures of Hyllyard City: two more stormtroopers and a hard-faced man wearing a major's insignia on his dusty brown Imperial uniform. "About time," the latter muttered under his breath as Mara and Luke were nudged in his direction. "Who are they?"

"The male says his name is Jade," one of the stormtroopers in front reported in that slightly filtered voice they all seemed to have. "Bounty hunter; works for Karrde. He claims the female is his prisoner."

"*Was* his prisoner," the major corrected, looking at Mara. "What's your name, thief?"

"Senni Kiffu," Mara said, her voice surly. "And I'm not a thief. Talon Karrde owes me—he owes me big. I didn't take any more than I had coming."

The major looked at Luke, and Luke shrugged. "Karrde's other dealings aren't any of my business. He said bring her back. I brought her back."[1]

"And her theft, too, I see." He looked at Artoo, still tied to his travois and dragging behind the speeder bike. "Get that droid off your bike," he ordered the scout. "The ground's flat enough here, and I want you on perimeter. Put it with the prisoners. Cuff them, too—they're hardly likely to fall over tree roots out here."

"Wait a minute," Luke objected as one of the stormtroopers stepped toward him. "Me, too?"

The major raised his eyebrows slightly. "You got a problem with that, bounty hunter?" he asked, his voice challenging.

"Yeah, I got a problem with it," Luke shot back. "*She's* the prisoner here, not me."

"For the moment you're both prisoners," the other countered. "So shut up." He frowned at Luke's face. "What in the Empire happened to you, anyway?"

So they weren't going to be able to pass the puffiness off as Luke's natural features. "Ran into some kind of bush while I was chasing her," he growled as the stormtrooper roughly cuffed his hands in front of him. "It itched like blazes for a while."

The major smiled thinly. "How very inconvenient for you," he said dryly. "How fortunate that we have a fully qualified medic back at HQ. He should be able to bring that swelling down in no time." He held Luke's gaze a moment longer, then shifted his attention to the stormtrooper leader. "You disarmed him, of course."

1. From the very beginning it was clear that Luke and Mara worked well together.

At least, when Mara was willing to cooperate.

—TZ

The stormtrooper gestured, and the first of the biker scouts swooped close to hand Mara's blaster to the major. "Interesting weapon," the major murmured, turning it over in his hands before sliding it into his belt. From overhead came a soft hum, and Luke looked up to see a repulsorlift craft settle into place overhead. A Chariot assault vehicle, just as Mara had predicted. "Ah," the major said, glancing up at it. "All right, Commander. Let's go."

In many ways, Hyllyard City reminded Luke of Mos Eisley: small houses and commercial buildings crammed fairly tightly together, with relatively narrow streets running between them. The troop headed around the perimeter, clearly aiming for one of the wider avenues that seemed to radiate, spokelike, from the center of town. Looking into the city as they passed by the outer buildings, Luke was able to catch occasional glimpses of what seemed to be an open area a few blocks away. The town square, possibly, or else a spacecraft landing area.

The vanguard had just reached the target street when, in perfect synchronization, the stormtroopers abruptly changed formation. Those in the inner circle pulled in closer to Luke and Mara while those in the outer circle moved farther away, the whole crowd coming to a halt and gesturing to their prisoners to do the same. A moment later, the reason for the sudden maneuver came around the corner: four scruffy-looking men walking briskly toward them with a fifth man in the center of their square, his hands chained behind him.

They had barely emerged from the street when they were intercepted by a group of four stormtroopers. A short and inaudible conversation ensued, which concluded with the strangers handing their blasters over to the stormtroopers with obvious reluctance. Escorted now by the Imperials, they continued on toward the main group . . . and as they walked, Luke finally got a clear look at the prisoner.

It was Han Solo.

The stormtroopers opened their ranks slightly to let the

newcomers through. "What do you want?" the major demanded as they stopped in front of him.

"Name's Chin," one of them said. "We caught this ratch snooping around the forest—maybe looking for your prisoners there. Figured you might want to have a talk with him, hee?"

"Uncommonly generous of you," the major said sardonically, giving Han a quick, measuring glance. "You come to this conclusion all by yourself?"

Chin drew himself up. "Just because I don't live in a big flashy city doesn't mean I'm stupid," he said stiffly. "What hai—you think we don't know what it means when Imperial stormtroopers[2] start setting up a temporary garrison?"

The major gave him a long, cool look. "You'd best just hope that the garrison *is* temporary." He glanced at the stormtrooper beside him, jerked his head toward Han. "Check him for weapons."

"We already—" Chin began. The major looked at him, and he fell silent.

The frisking took only a minute, and came up empty. "Put him in the pocket with the others," the major ordered. "All right, Chin, you and your friends can go. If he turns out to be worth anything, I'll see you get a piece of it."

"Uncommonly generous of you," Chin said with an expression that was just short of a sneer. "Can we have our guns back now?"

The major's expression hardened. "You can pick them up later at our HQ," he said. "Hyllyard Hotel, straight across the square—but I'm sure a sophisticated citizen like yourself already knows where it is."

For a moment Chin seemed inclined to argue the point. But a glance at the stormtroopers clustered around evidently changed his mind for him. Without a word he turned, and he and his three companions strode back toward the city.

2. One of the unexpected complications with the *Heir* manuscript was that the copy editor evidently had never dealt with *Star Wars* before. When I got the manuscript, I discovered that this kind and thoughtful person had painstakingly changed all the *stormtroopers* to the more correct (at least for Earth usage) *storm troopers*.

I just as painstakingly changed all of them back again.

—TZ

"Move out," the major ordered, and they started up again.

"Well," Han muttered, falling into step beside Luke. "Together again, huh?"

"I wouldn't miss it," Luke muttered back. "Your friends there seem in a hurry to get away."

"Probably don't want to miss the party," Han told him. "A little something they threw together to celebrate my capture."

Luke threw him a sideways look. "Shame we weren't invited."

"Real shame," Han agreed with a straight face. "You never know, though."

They had turned into the avenue now, moving toward the center of town. Just visible over the heads of the stormtroopers, he could see something gray and rounded directly ahead of them. Craning his neck for a better view, he saw that the structure was in fact a freestanding archway, rising from the ground near the far end of the open village square he had noticed earlier.

A fairly impressive archway, too, especially for a city this far outside the mainstream of the galaxy. The upper part was composed of different types of fitted stone, the crown flaring outward like a cross between an umbrella and a section of sliced mushroom. The lower part curved in and downward, to end in a pair of meter-square supporting pillars on each side. The entire arch rose a good ten meters into the sky, with the distance between the pillars perhaps half that. Lying directly in front of it was the village square, a fifteen-meter expanse of empty ground.

The perfect place for an ambush.

Luke felt his stomach tighten. The perfect place for an ambush . . . except that if it was obvious to him, it must be obvious to the stormtroopers, as well.

And it was. The vanguard of the party had reached the square now, and as the stormtroopers moved out of the confines of the narrow avenue, each lifted his blaster rifle a little higher and moved a little farther apart from his fellows. They were expecting an ambush, all right. And they were expecting it right here.

Gritting his teeth, Luke focused again on the archway. "Is Threepio here?" he muttered to Han.

He sensed Han's frown, but the other didn't waste time with unnecessary questions. "He's with Lando, yeah."

Luke nodded and glanced down to his right. Beside him, Artoo was rolling along the bumpy street, trying hard to keep up. Bracing himself, Luke took a step in that direction—

And with a squeal, Artoo tripped over Luke's outstretched foot and fell flat with a crash.

Luke was crouched beside him in an instant, leaning over him as he struggled with his manacled hands to get the little droid upright again. He sensed some of the stormtroopers moving forward to assist, but for that single moment, there was no one else close enough to hear him. "Artoo, call to Threepio," he breathed into the droid's audio receptor. "Tell him to wait until we're at the archway to attack."

The droid complied instantly, its loud warble nearly deafening Luke as he crouched there beside him. Luke's head was still ringing when rough hands grabbed him under the arms and hauled him to his feet. He regained his balance—

To find the major standing in front of him, a suspicious scowl on his face. "What was that?" the other demanded.

"He fell over," Luke told him. "I think he tripped—"

"I meant that transmission," the major cut him off harshly. "What did he say?"

"He was probably telling me off for tripping him," Luke shot back. "How should *I* know what he said?"

For a long minute the major glared at him. "Move out, Commander," he said at last to the stormtrooper at his side. "Everyone stay alert."

He turned away, and they started walking again. "I

hope," Han murmured from beside him, "you know what you're doing."

Luke took a deep breath and fixed his eyes on the arch-way ahead. "So do I," he murmured back.

In a very few minutes, he knew, they would both find out.

CHAPTER 29

"OH, MY!" THREEPIO GASPED. "General Calrissian, I have—"

"Quiet, Threepio," Lando ordered, peering carefully
around the edge of the window at the minor commotion
going on across the square. "Did you see what happened,
Aves?"

Crouched down beneath the windowsill, Aves shook his
head. "Looked like Skywalker and his droid both fell over,"
he said. "Couldn't tell for sure—too many stormtroopers
in the way."

"General Calrissian—"

"Quiet, Threepio." Lando watched tensely as two stormtroopers pulled Luke to his feet, then righted Artoo. "Looks
like they're okay."

"Yeah." Aves reached down to the floor beside him,
picked up the small transmitter. "Here we go. Let's hope
everyone's ready."

"And that Chin and the others aren't still carrying their
blasters," Lando added under his breath.

Aves snorted. "They aren't. Don't worry—stormtroopers are always confiscating other people's weapons."

Lando nodded, adjusting his grip on his blaster, wishing they could get this over with. Across the way, the Imperials seemed to have gotten themselves sorted out and were starting to move again. As soon as they were all inside the square, away from any possible cover . . .

"General Calrissian, I *must* speak to you," Threepio insisted. "I have a message from Master Luke."

Lando blinked at him. "From *Luke?*"

—but even as he said it he suddenly remembered that electronic wail from Artoo just after he'd fallen over. Could that have been—? "What is it?"

"Master Luke wants you to hold off the attack," Threepio said, obviously relieved that someone was finally listening to him. "He says you're to wait until the stormtroopers are at the arch before firing."

Aves twisted around. "What? That's crazy. They outnumber us three to one—we give them any chance at all at cover and they'll cut us to pieces."

Lando looked out the window, grinding his teeth together. Aves was right—he knew enough of ground tactics to realize that. But on the other hand . . . "They're awfully spread out out there," he said. "Cover or no cover, they're going to be hard to take out. Especially with those speeder bikes on their perimeter."

Aves shook his head. "It's crazy," he repeated. "I'm not going to risk my people that way."

"Luke knows what he's doing," Lando insisted. "He's a Jedi."

"He's not a Jedi now," Aves snorted. "Didn't Karrde explain about the ysalamiri?"

"Whether he has Jedi powers or not, he's still a Jedi," Lando insisted. His blaster, he realized suddenly, was pointed at Aves. But that was okay, because Aves's blaster was pointed at him, too. "Anyway, his life is more on the line here than any of yours—you can always abort and pull back."

"Oh, sure," Aves snorted, throwing a glance out the window. The Imperials were nearing the middle of the square now, Lando saw, the stormtroopers looking wary and alert as anything. "Except that if we leave any of them alive, they'll seal off the city. And what about that Chariot up there?"

"What about it?" Lando countered. "I still haven't heard how you're planning to take it out."

"Well, we sure as blazes don't want it on the ground," Aves retorted. "And that's what'll happen if we let the stormtroopers get to the arch. The Chariot'll put down right across the front of it, right between us and them. That, plus the arch itself, will give them all the cover they need to sit back and take us out at their leisure." He shook his head and shifted his grip on the transmitter. "Anyway, it's too late to clue in the others to any plan changes."

"You don't have to clue them in," Lando said, feeling sweat collecting under his collar. Luke was counting on him. "No one's supposed to do anything until you trigger the booby-trapped weapons."

Aves shook his head again. "It's too risky." He turned back to the window, raised the transmitter.

And here, Lando realized—right here—was where it all came down to the wire. Where you decided who or what it was you trusted. Tactics and abstract logic . . . or people. Lowering his blaster, he gently rested the tip of the muzzle against Aves's neck. "We wait," he said quietly.

Aves didn't move; but suddenly there was something in the way he crouched there that reminded Lando of a hunting predator. "I won't forget this, Calrissian," he said, his voice icy soft.

"I wouldn't want you to," Lando said. He looked out at the stormtroopers . . . and hoped that Luke did indeed know what he was doing.[1]

1. In the original outline, which had Han and Leia coming to Myrkr instead of Han and Lando, this confrontation took place with the *Chimaera* still orbiting overhead. In that scenario, Chewie and Lando were scheduled to swoop in after the Imperials' defeat and pull Luke and the others off the planet before Thrawn could intervene.

As a matter of pure logic, not to mention reasonable storytelling, it's just as well that I came up with this version instead of having to use that one.

—TZ

The vanguard had already passed the archway, and the major was only a few steps away from it, when four of the stormtroopers abruptly blew up.

Quite spectacularly, too. The simultaneous flashes of yellow-white fire lit up the landscape to almost painful intensity; the thunderclap of the multiple detonations nearly knocked Luke over.

The sound was still ringing in his ears when the blasters opened up behind them.

The stormtroopers were good, all right. There was no panic that Luke could detect; no sudden freezing in astonishment or indecision. They were moving into combat position almost before the blaster fire had begun: those already at the archway hugging close to the stone pillars to return covering fire, the rest moving quickly to join them. Above the sound of the blasters, he could hear the increased whine of the speeder bikes kicking into high speed; overhead, he caught just a glimpse of the Chariot assault vehicle swiveling around to face the unseen attackers.

And then an armored hand caught him under each armpit, and suddenly he was being hauled toward the archway. A few seconds later he was dumped unceremoniously in the narrow gap between the two pillars supporting the north side of the arch. Mara was already crouched there; a second later, two more stormtroopers tossed Han in to join them. Four of the Imperials moved into position over them, using the pillars for cover as they began returning fire. Struggling to his knees, Luke leaned out for a look.

Out in the fire zone, looking small and helpless amid the deadly horizontal hail of blaster fire, Artoo was rolling toward them as fast as his little wheels would carry him.

"I think we're in trouble," Han muttered in his ear. "Not to mention Lando and the others."

"It's not over yet," Luke told him tightly. "Just stick close. How are you at causing distractions?"

"Terrific," Han said; and to Luke's surprise, he brought

his hands out from behind his back, the chain and manacles he'd been wearing hanging loosely from his left wrist. "Trick cuffs," he grunted, pulling a concealed strip of metal from the inside of the open cuff and probing at Luke's restraints. "I hope this thing—ah." The pressure on Luke's wrists was suddenly gone; the cuffs opened and dropped to the ground. "You ready for your distraction?" Han asked, taking the loose end of his chain in his free hand.

"Hang on a minute," Luke told him, looking up. Most of the speeder bikes had taken refuge under the arch, looking like some strange species of giant birds hiding from a storm as they hovered close to the stone, their laser cannon spitting toward the surrounding houses. In front of them and just below their line of fire, the Chariot had swiveled parallel to the arch and was coming down. Once it was on the ground . . .

A hand gripped Luke's arm, fingernails digging hard into the skin. "Whatever you're going to do, *do* it!" Mara hissed viciously. "If the Chariot gets down, you'll never get them out from cover."

"I know." Luke nodded. "I'm counting on it."

The Chariot settled smoothly to the ground directly in front of the arch, blocking the last of the attackers' firing vectors. Crouched at the window, Aves swore violently. "Well, there's your Jedi for you," he bit out. "You got any other great ideas, Calrissian?"

Lando swallowed hard. "We've just got to give him—"

He never finished the sentence. From the arch a blaster bolt glanced off the window frame, and suddenly Lando's upper arm flashed with pain. The shock sent him stumbling backward, just as a second shot blew apart that whole section of the frame, driving wooden splinters and chunks of masonry like shrapnel across his chest and arm.

He hit the floor, landing hard enough to see stars. Blinking, gritting his teeth against the pain, he looked up—

To find Aves leaning over him.

Lando looked up into the other's face. *I won't forget this,* Aves had said, no more than three minutes ago. And from the look on his face, he wasn't anticipating any need to hold that memory for much longer. "He'll come through," Lando whispered through the pain. "He will."

But he could tell that Aves wasn't listening . . . and, down deep, Lando couldn't blame him. Lando Calrissian, the professional gambler, had gambled one last time. And he'd lost.

And the debt from that gamble—the last in a long line of such debts—had come due.

The Chariot settled smoothly to the ground directly in front of the arch, and Luke got his feet under him. This was it. "All right, Han," he muttered. *"Go."*

Han nodded and surged to his feet, coming up right in the middle of the four stormtroopers standing over them. With a bellow, he swung his former shackles full across the faceplate of the nearest guard, then threw the looped chain around the neck of the next and pulled backward, away from the pillars. The other two reacted instantly, leaping after him and taking the whole group down in a tangle.

And for the next few seconds, Luke was free.

He stood up and leaned out to look around the pillar. Artoo was still in the middle of no-man's-land, hurrying to reach cover before he could be hit by a stray shot. He warbled plaintively as he saw Luke—

"Artoo!—*now!*" Luke shouted, holding out his hand and glancing across toward the southern end of the archway. Between the stone pillars and the grounded Chariot, the stormtroopers were indeed solidly entrenched. If this didn't work, Han was right: Lando and everyone else out there were dead. Gritting his teeth, hoping fervently that his counterattack wasn't already too late, he turned back to Artoo—

Just as, with a flicker of silver metal and perfect accuracy, his lightsaber dropped neatly into his outstretched hand.

Beside him, the guards had subdued Han's crazy attack and were getting back to their feet, leaving Han on his knees between them. Luke took them all in a single sweep, the blazing green lightsaber blade slicing through the glistening stormtrooper armor with hardly a tug to mark its passing. "Get behind me," he snapped to Han and Mara, stepping back to the gap between the two northern pillars and focusing on the mass of Imperials standing and crouching between him and the southern pillars. They were suddenly aware that they had an unexpected threat on their flank, and a few were already starting to bring their blasters to bear on him.

With the Force to guide his hand, he could have held out against them indefinitely, blocking their blaster shots with the lightsaber. Mara had been right, though: the ysalamiri effect did indeed extend this far outside the forest, and the Force was still silent.

But then, he'd never had any intention of fighting the stormtroopers anyway. Turning his back on the blasters tracking toward him, he slashed the lightsaber across and upward—

Neatly slicing one of the stone pillars in half.

There was a loud *crack* as suddenly released tension sent a shiver through the structure. Another stroke cut through the second pillar—

And the noise of the battle was abruptly drowned out by the awful grinding of stone on stone as the two fractured pillars began sliding apart.

Luke swung back around, peripherally aware of Han and Mara scrambling out from under the arch to safety behind him. The stormtroopers' expressions were hidden behind their masks, but the look of sudden horror on the major's face said it for all of them. Overhead, the mass of the arch creaked warningly; setting his teeth, Luke locked the lightsaber on and hurled it across the gap toward the pillars there. It cut through one of them and nicked the other—

And with a roar, the whole thing came crashing down.

Luke, standing at the edge, barely got out from under it in time. The stormtroopers, crouched in the center, didn't.

CHAPTER 30

KARRDE WALKED AROUND the mass of stone to where the crumpled nose of the Chariot assault vehicle poked out, a sense of slightly stunned disbelief coloring his vision. "One man," he murmured.

"Well, *we* helped some," Aves reminded him. But the sarcasm of the words faded beneath the grudging respect clearly there behind it.

"And without the Force, too," Karrde said.

He sensed Aves shrug uncomfortably. "That's what Mara said. Though of course Skywalker might have lied to her about it."

"Unlikely." A motion at the edge of the square caught his eye, and Karrde looked over to see Solo and Skywalker helping a distinctly shaky-looking Lando Calrissian to one of the airspeeders parked around the perimeter. "Took a shot, did he?"

Aves grunted. "Came close to taking one of mine, too," he said. "I thought he'd betrayed us—figured I'd make sure he didn't walk away from it."

"In retrospect, it's just as well you didn't." Karrde looked up, searching the skies. Wondering how long it would take the Imperials to respond to what had happened here today.

Aves looked up, too. "We might still be able to hunt down the other two Chariots before they get a chance to report," he suggested. "I don't think the headquarters people got any messages away before we took them out."

Karrde shook his head, feeling a deep surge of sadness rising through the sense of urgency within him. Not until now had he truly realized just how much he'd come to love this place—his base, the forest, the planet Myrkr itself. Now, when there was no choice but to abandon it. "No," he told Aves. "There's no way to cover up our part in what happened here. Not from a man like Thrawn."

"You're probably right," Aves said, his voice taking on a sense of urgency of its own. He understood the implications of that, all right. "You want me to head back and start the evacuation?"

"Yes. And take Mara with you. Make sure she keeps busy—somewhere away from the *Millennium Falcon* and Skywalker's X-wing."

He felt Aves's eyes on him. But if the other wondered, he kept his wonderings to himself. "Right. See you later."

He hurried away. The airspeeder with Calrissian aboard was lifting off now, heading back to where the *Falcon* was being prepped for flight. Solo and Skywalker were heading over toward a second airspeeder; with just a moment's hesitation, Karrde went over to intercept them.

They reached the craft at the same time, and for a moment eyed each other across its bow. "Karrde," Solo said at last. "I owe you one."

Karrde nodded. "Are you still going to get the *Etherway* out of impoundment for me?"

"I said I would," Solo told him. "Where do you want it delivered?"

"Just leave it on Abregado. Someone will pick it up." He turned his attention to Skywalker. "An interesting little trick," he commented, tilting his head back toward the mass of rubble. "Unorthodox, to say the least."

Skywalker shrugged. "It worked," he said simply.

"That it did," Karrde agreed. "Likely saving several of my people's lives in the bargain."

Skywalker looked him straight back in the eye. "Does that mean you've made your decision?"

Karrde gave him a slight smile. "I don't really see as I have much choice anymore." He looked back at Solo. "I presume you'll be leaving immediately?"

"As soon as we can get Luke's X-wing rigged for towing." Solo nodded. "Lando's doing okay, but he's going to need more specialized medical attention than the *Falcon* can handle."

"It could have been worse," Karrde said.

Solo gave him a knowing look. "A *lot* worse," he agreed, his voice hard.

"So could all of it," Karrde reminded him, putting an edge into his own voice. He could, after all, just as easily have turned the three of them over to the Imperials in the first place.

And Solo knew it. "Yeah," he conceded. "Well . . . so long."

Karrde watched as they got into the airspeeder. "One other thing," he said as they strapped in. "Obviously, we're going to have to pull out of here before the Imperials figure out what's happened. That means a lot of lifting capacity if we're going to do it quickly. You wouldn't happen to have any surplus cargo or stripped-down military ships lying around I could have, would you?"

Solo gave him a strange look. "We don't have enough cargo capacity for the New Republic's normal business," he said. "I think I might have mentioned that to you."

"Well, then, a loan, perhaps," Karrde persisted. "A stripped-down Mon Calamari Star Cruiser would do nicely."

STAR WARS: HEIR TO THE EMPIRE   379

"I'm sure it would," Solo returned with more than a hint of sarcasm. "I'll see what I can do."

The canopy dropped smoothly down over them and sealed in place. Karrde stepped back, and with a whine of repulsorlifts, the airspeeder rose into the sky. Orienting itself, it shot off toward the forest.

Karrde watched it go, wondering if that last suggestion had been too little too late. But perhaps not. Solo was the type to hold debts of honor sacred—something he'd probably picked up from his Wookiee friend somewhere along the line. If he could find a spare Star Cruiser, he'd likely send it along.

And once here, it would be easy enough to steal from whatever handlers Solo sent with it. Perhaps such a gift would help assuage Grand Admiral Thrawn's inevitable anger over what had happened here today.

But then, perhaps it wouldn't.

Karrde looked back at the ruins of the collapsed arch, a shiver running through him. No, a warship wasn't going to help. Not on this. Thrawn had lost too much here to simply shrug it off as the fortunes of war. He would be back . . . and he would be coming for blood.

And for perhaps the first time in his life, Karrde felt the unpleasant stirrings of genuine fear.

In the distance, the airspeeder disappeared over the forest canopy. Karrde turned and gave Hyllyard City one final, lingering look. One way or the other, he knew he would never see it again.[1]

Luke got Lando settled into one of the *Falcon*'s bunks while Han and a couple of Karrde's men busied themselves outside getting a tow cable attached to the X-wing. The *Falcon*'s medical package was fairly primitive, but it was up to the task of cleaning and bandaging a blaster burn. A complete healing job would have to wait until they could

1. This, plus the last bit of Chapter 32, was where I'd originally planned to end this book. But after reading the outline, Betsy told me I needed something even more slam-bang exciting to close off this first part of the trilogy. Hence, Sluis Van.

–TZ

get him to a bacta tank, but for the moment he seemed comfortable enough. Leaving Artoo and Threepio to watch over him—despite his protestations that he didn't need watching over and, furthermore, had had enough of Threepio—Luke returned to the cockpit just as the ship lifted off.

"Any problems with the tow cable?" he asked, sliding into the copilot's seat.

"Not so far," Han said, leaning forward and looking all around them as the *Falcon* cleared the trees. "The extra weight's not bothering us, anyway. We should be all right."

"Good. You expecting company?"

"You never know," Han said, giving the sky one last look before settling back into his seat and gunning the repulsorlifts. "Karrde said there were still a couple of Chariots and a few speeder bikes unaccounted for. One of them might have figured that a last-ditch suicide run was better than having to go back to the Grand Admiral and report."

Luke stared at him. "Grand Admiral?" he asked carefully.

Han's lip twisted. "Yeah. That's who seems to be running the show now for the Empire."

A cold chill ran up Luke's back. "I thought we'd accounted for all the Grand Admirals."

"Me, too. We must have missed one."

And abruptly, right in the middle of Han's last word, Luke felt a surge of awareness and strength fill him. As if he were waking up from a deep sleep, or stepping from a dark room into the light, or suddenly understanding the universe again.

The Force was again with him.

He took a deep breath, eyes flicking across the control board for the altimeter. Just over twelve kilometers. Karrde had been right—those ysalamiri did, indeed, reinforce one another. "I don't suppose you got a name," he murmured.

"Karrde wouldn't give it to me," Han said, throwing a

curious frown in Luke's direction. "Maybe we can bargain the use of that Star Cruiser he wants for it. You okay?"

"I'm fine," Luke assured him. "I just—it's like being able to see again after having been blind."

Han snorted under his breath. "Yeah, I know how that is," he said wryly.

"I guess you would." Luke looked at him. "I didn't get a chance to say this earlier . . . but thanks for coming after me."

Han waved it away. "No charge. And *I* didn't get a chance to say it earlier"—he glanced at Luke again—"but you look like something the proom dragged in."

"My wonderful disguise," Luke told him, touching his face gingerly. "Mara assures me it'll wear off in a few more hours."

"Yeah—Mara," Han said. "You and she seemed to be hitting it off pretty well there."

Luke grimaced. "Don't count on it," he said. "A matter of having a common enemy, that's all. First the forest, then the Imperials."

He could sense Han casting around for a way to ask the next question, decided to save him the trouble. "She wants to kill me," he told the other.

"Any idea why?"

Luke opened his mouth . . . and, to his own surprise, closed it again. There wasn't any particular reason not to tell Han what he knew about Mara's past—certainly no reason he could think of. And yet, somehow, he felt a strangely compelling reluctance to do so. "It's something personal," he said at last.

Han threw him an odd look. "Something *personal?* How personal can a death mark get?"

"It's not a death mark," Luke insisted. "It's something— well, *personal.*"

Han gazed at him a moment longer, then turned back to his piloting. "Oh," he said.

The *Falcon* had cleared the atmosphere now and was gunning for deep space. From this high up, Luke decided, the forest looked rather pleasant. "You know, I never did find out what planet this was," he commented.

"It's called Myrkr," Han told him. "And *I* just found out this morning. I think Karrde must have already decided to abandon the place, even before the battle—he had real tight security around it when Lando and I first got here."

A few minutes later a light flashed on the control board: the *Falcon* was far enough out of Myrkr's gravity well for the hyperdrive to function. "Good." Han nodded at it. "Course's already programmed in; let's get out of here." He wrapped his hand around the central levers and pulled; and with a burst of starlines, they were off.

"Where are we going?" Luke asked as the starlines faded into the familiar mottled sky. "Coruscant?"

"A little side trip first," Han said. "I want to swing by the Sluis Van shipyards, see if we can get Lando and your X-wing fixed up."

Luke threw him a sideways glance. "And maybe find a Star Cruiser to borrow for Karrde?"

"Maybe," Han said, a little defensively. "I mean, Ackbar's got a bunch of stripped-down warships ferrying stuff to the Sluis sector already. No reason why we can't borrow one of them for a couple of days, is there?"

"Probably not," Luke conceded with a sigh. Suddenly, it felt really good to just sit back and do nothing. "I suppose Coruscant can do without us for a few more days."

"I hope so," Han said, his voice abruptly grim. "But something's about to happen back there. If it hasn't happened already."

And his sense was as grim as his words. "Maybe we shouldn't bother with Sluis Van, then," Luke suggested, feeling a sympathetic shiver. "Lando's hurting, but he's not in any danger."

Han shook his head. "No. I want to get him taken care of—and *you*, buddy, need some downtime, too," he added, glancing at Luke. "I just wanted you to know that when we hit Coruscant, we're going to hit it running. So enjoy Sluis Van while you can. It'll probably be the last peace and quiet you'll get for a while."

In the blackness of deep space, three-thousandths of a light-year^2 but from the Sluis Van shipyards, the task force assembled for battle.

"The *Judicator* has just reported in, Captain," the communications officer told Pellaeon. "They confirm battle ready, and request order update."

"Inform Captain Brandei that there have been no changes," Pellaeon told him, standing at the starboard viewport and gazing out at the shadowy shapes gathered around the *Chimaera,* all but the closest identifiable only by the distinctive patterns of their running lights. It was an impressive task force, one worthy of the old days: five Imperial Star Destroyers, twelve *Strike*-class cruisers, twenty-two of the old *Carrack*-class light cruisers, and thirty full squadrons of TIE fighters standing ready in their hangar bays.

And riding there in the middle of all that awesome firepower, like someone's twisted idea of a joke, sat the battered old A-class bulk freighter.

The key to this whole operation.

"Status, Captain?" Thrawn's voice came quietly from behind him.

Pellaeon turned to face the Grand Admiral. "All ships are on line, sir," he reported. "The freighter's cloaking shield has been checked out and primed; all TIE fighters are prepped and manned. I think we're ready."

Thrawn nodded, his glowing eyes sweeping the field of running lights around them. "Excellent," he murmured. "What word from Myrkr?"

The question threw Pellaeon off stride—he hadn't thought about Myrkr for days. "I don't know, Admiral," he

2. For comparison, this is about 4.3 times the distance from our sun to Pluto. A nice, quiet neighborhood, perfect for this kind of gathering.

—TZ

confessed, looking over Thrawn's shoulder at the communications officer. "Lieutenant—the last report from the Myrkr landing force?"

The other was already calling up the record. "It was a routine report, sir," he said. "Time log . . . fourteen hours ten minutes ago."

Thrawn turned to face him. "Fourteen hours?" he repeated, his voice suddenly very quiet and very deadly. "I left orders for them to report every twelve."

"Yes, Admiral," the comm man said, starting to look a little nervous. "I have that order logged, right here on their file. They must have . . ." He trailed off, looking helplessly at Pellaeon.

They must have forgotten to report in, was Pellaeon's first, hopeful reaction. But it died stillborn. Stormtroopers didn't forget such things. Ever. "Perhaps they're having trouble with their transmitter," he suggested hesitantly.

For a handful of heartbeats Thrawn just stood there, silent. "No," he said at last. "They've been taken. Skywalker was indeed there."

Pellaeon hesitated, shook his head. "I can't believe that, sir," he said. "Skywalker couldn't have taken all of them. Not with all those ysalamiri blocking his Jedi power."

Thrawn turned those glittering eyes back on Pellaeon. "I agree," he said coldly. "Obviously, he had help."

Pellaeon forced himself to meet that gaze. "Karrde?"

"Who else was there?" Thrawn countered. "So much for his protestations of neutrality."

Pellaeon glanced at the status board. "Perhaps we should send someone to investigate. We could probably spare a Strike Cruiser; maybe even the *Stormhawk.*"

Thrawn took a deep breath, let it out slowly. "No," he said, his voice steady and controlled again. "The Sluis Van operation is our primary concern at the moment—and battles have been lost before on the presence or absence of a single ship. Karrde and his betrayal will keep for later."[3]

He turned back to the communications officer. "Signal

3. The fifth quality of a good commander: he keeps his priorities straight.

—TZ

the freighter," he ordered. "Have them activate the cloaking shield."

"Yes, sir."

Pellaeon turned back to the viewport. The freighter, bathed in the *Chimaera*'s lights, just sat there looking innocent. "Cloaking shield on, Admiral," the comm man reported.

Thrawn nodded. "Order them to proceed."

"Yes, sir." Moving rather sluggishly, the freighter maneuvered past the *Chimaera*, oriented itself toward the distant sun of the Sluis Van system, and with a flicker of pseudovelocity jumped to lightspeed.

"Time mark," Thrawn ordered.

"Time marked," one of the deck officers acknowledged.

Thrawn looked at Pellaeon. "Is my flagship ready, Captain?" he asked the formal question.

"The *Chimaera* is fully at your command, Admiral," Pellaeon gave the formal answer.

"Good. We follow the freighter in exactly six hours twenty minutes. I want a final check from all ships . . . and I want you to remind them one last time that our task is only to engage and pin down the system's defenses. There are to be no special heroics or risks taken. Make that clearly understood, Captain. We're here to gain ships, not lose them."

"Yes, sir." Pellaeon started toward his command station—

"And Captain . . . ?"

"Yes, Admiral?"

There was a tight smile on Thrawn's face. "Remind them, too," he added softly, "that our final victory over the Rebellion begins here."

CHAPTER 31

CAPTAIN AFYON of the Escort Frigate *Larkhess* shook his head with thinly disguised contempt, glaring at Wedge from the depths of his pilot's seat. "You X-wing hot-shots," he growled. "You've really got it made—you know that?"

Wedge shrugged, trying hard not to take offense. It wasn't easy; but then, he'd had lots of practice in the past few days. Afyon had started out from Coruscant with a planetary-mass chip on his shoulder, and he'd been nursing it the whole way.

And looking out the viewport at the confused mass of ships crowding the Sluis Van orbit-dock area, it wasn't hard to figure out why. "Yeah, well, we're stuck out here, too," he reminded the captain.

The other snorted. "Yeah. Big sacrifice. You lounge around my ship like overpriced trampers for a couple of days, then flit around for two hours while I try to dodge bulk freighters and get this thing into a docking station designed for scavenger pickers. And then you pull your snubbies back inside and go back to lounging again. Doesn't exactly qualify as earning your pay, in my book."

Wedge clamped his teeth firmly around his tongue and stirred his tea a little harder. It was considered bad form to mouth back at senior officers, after all—even senior officers who'd long since passed their prime. For probably the first time since he had been given command of Rogue Squadron, he regretted having passed up all the rest of the promotions he'd been offered. A higher rank would at least have entitled him to snarl back a little.

Lifting his cup for a cautious sip, he gazed out the viewport at the scene around them. No, he amended—he wasn't sorry at all that he'd stayed with his X-wing. If he hadn't, he'd probably be in exactly the same position as Afyon was right now: trying to run a 920-crew ship with just fifteen men, hauling cargo in a ship meant for war.

And, like as not, having to put up with hotshot X-wing pilots who sat around his bridge drinking tea and claiming with perfect justification that they were doing exactly what they'd been ordered to do.

He hid a smile behind his mug. Yes, in Afyon's place, he'd probably be ready to spit bulkhead shavings, too. Maybe he ought to go ahead and let the other drag him into an argument, in fact, let him drain off some of that excess nervous energy of his. Eventually—within the hour, even, if Sluis Control's latest departure estimate was anywhere close—it would finally be the *Larkhess*'s turn to get out of here and head for Bpfassh. It would be nice, when that time came, for Afyon to be calm enough to handle the ship.

Taking another sip of his tea, Wedge looked out the viewport. A couple of refitted passenger liners were making their own break for freedom now, he saw, accompanied by four Corellian Corvettes. Beyond them, just visible in the faint light of the space-lane marker buoys, was what looked like one of the slightly ovoid transports he used to escort during the height of the war, with a pair of B-wings following.

And off to the side, moving parallel to their departure vector, an A-class bulk freighter was coming into the docking pattern.

Without any escort at all.

Wedge watched it creep toward them, his smile fading as old combat senses began to tingle. Swiveling around in his seat, he reached over to the console beside him and punched for a sensor scan.

It looked innocent enough. An older freighter, probably a knockoff of the original Corellian Action IV design, with the kind of exterior that came from either a lifetime of honest work or else a short and spectacularly unsuccessful career of piracy. Its cargo bay registered completely empty, and there were no weapons emplacements that the *Larkhess*'s sensors could pick up.

A totally empty freighter. How long had it been, he wondered uneasily, since he'd run across a totally empty freighter?

"Trouble?"

Wedge focused on the captain in mild surprise. The other's frustrated anger of a minute ago was gone, replaced by something calm, alert, and battle-ready. Perhaps, the thought strayed through Wedge's mind, Afyon wasn't past his prime after all. "That incoming freighter," he told the other, setting his cup down on the edge of the console and keying for a comm channel. "There's something about it that doesn't feel right."

The captain peered out the viewport, then at the sensor scan data Wedge had pulled up. "I don't see anything," he said.

"Me, either," Wedge had to admit. "There's just something . . . Blast."

"What?"

"Control won't let me in," Wedge told him as he keyed off. "Too much traffic on the circuits already, they say."

"Allow me." Afyon turned to his own console. The freighter was shifting course now, the kind of slow and careful maneuver that usually indicated a full load. But the cargo bay was still registering empty . . .

"There we go," Afyon said, glancing at Wedge with grim satisfaction. "I've got a tap into their records computer. Little trick you never learn flitting around in an X-wing. Let's see now . . . freighter *Nartissteu,* out of Nellac Kram.[1] They were jumped by pirates, got their main drive damaged in the fight, and had to dump their cargo to get away. They're hoping to get some repair work done; Sluis Control's basically told them to get in line."

"I thought all this relief shipping had more or less taken over the whole place." Wedge frowned.

Afyon shrugged. "Theoretically. In practice . . . well, the Sluissi are easy enough to talk into bending that kind of rule. You just have to know how to phrase the request."

Reluctantly, Wedge nodded. It *did* all seem reasonable enough, he supposed. And a damaged, empty ship would probably handle something like an intact full one. And the freighter *was* empty—the *Larkhess*'s sensors said so.

But the tingles refused to go away.

Abruptly, he dug his comlink from his belt. "Rogue Squadron, this is Rogue Leader," he called. "Everyone to your ships."

He got acknowledgments, looked up to find Afyon's eyes steady on him. "You still think there's trouble?" the other asked quietly.

Wedge grimaced, throwing one last look out the viewport at the freighter. "Probably not. But it won't hurt to be ready. Anyway, I can't have my pilots sitting around drinking tea all day." He turned and left the bridge at a quick jog.

The other eleven members of Rogue Squadron were in their X-wings by the time he reached the *Larkhess*'s docking bay. Three minutes later, they launched.

The freighter hadn't made much headway, Wedge saw as they swung up over the *Larkhess*'s hull and pulled together into a loose patrol formation. Oddly enough, though, it had moved a considerable distance laterally,

1. Final Tuckerization of this book: Mark Callen, Florida fan.

—TZ

drifting away from the *Larkhess* and toward a pair of Calamari Star Cruisers orbiting together a few kilometers away.
"Spread out formation," Wedge ordered his pilots, shifting
to an asymptotic approach course. "Let's swing by and
take a nice, casual little look."

The others acknowledged. Wedge glanced down at his
nav scope, made a minor adjustment to his speed, looked
back up again—

And in the space of a single heartbeat, the whole thing
went straight to hell.

The freighter blew up. All at once, without any warning
from sensors, without any hint from previous visual observation, it just came apart.

Reflexively, Wedge jabbed for his comm control. "Emergency!" he barked. "Ship explosion near orbit-dock V-475.
Send rescue team."

For an instant, as chunks of the cargo bay flew outward,
he could see into the emptiness there . . . but even as his
eyes and brain registered the odd fact that he could see
into the disintegrating cargo bay but not *beyond* it—

The bay was suddenly no longer empty.

One of the X-wing pilots gasped. A tight-packed mass
of something was in there, totally filling the space where
the *Larkhess*'s sensors had read nothing. A mass that was
even now exploding outward like a hornet's nest behind
the pieces of the bay.

A mass that in seconds had resolved itself into a boiling
wave front of TIE fighters.

"Pull up!" Wedge snapped to his squadron, leaning his
X-wing into a tight turn to get out of the path of that
deadly surge. "Come around and re-form; S-foils in attack
position."

And as they swung around in response, he knew with a
sinking feeling that Captain Afyon had been wrong. Rogue
Squadron was indeed going to earn its pay today.

The battle for Sluis Van had begun.

They'd cleared the outer system defense network and the bureaucratic overload that passed for Control at Sluis Van these days, and Han was just getting a bearing on the slot they'd given him when the emergency call came through. "Luke!" he shouted back down the cockpit corridor. "Got a ship explosion. I'm going to go check it out." He glanced at the orbit-dock map to locate V-475, gave the ship a fractional turn to put them on the right vector—

And jerked in his seat as a laser bolt slapped the *Falcon* hard from behind.

He had them gunning into a full forward evasive maneuver before the second shot went sizzling past the cockpit. Over the roar of the engines he heard Luke's startled-sounding yelp; and as the third bolt went past he finally had a chance to check the aft sensors to see just what was going on.

He almost wished he hadn't. Directly behind them, batteries already engaging one of the Sluis Van perimeter battle stations, was an Imperial Star Destroyer.

He swore under his breath and kicked the engines a little harder. Beside him, Luke clawed his way forward against the not-quite-compensated acceleration and into the copilot's seat. "What's going on?" he asked.

"We just walked into an Imperial attack," Han growled, eyes flying over the readouts. "Got a Star Destroyer behind us—there's another one over to starboard—looks like some other ships with them."

"They've got the system bottled up," Luke said, his voice glacially calm. A far cry, Han thought, from the panicky kid he'd pulled off Tatooine out from under Star Destroyer fire all those years back. "I make it five Star Destroyers and something over twenty smaller ships."

Han grunted. "At least we know now why they hit Bpfassh and the others. Wanted to pull enough ships here to make an attack worth their while."

The words were barely out of his mouth when the emergency comm channel suddenly came to life again. "Emergency! Imperial TIE fighters in orbit-dock area. All ships to battle stations."

Luke started. "That sounded like Wedge," he said, punching for transmission. "Wedge? That you?"

"Luke?" the other came back. "We got trouble here—at least forty TIE fighters and fifty truncated-cone-shaped things I've never seen before—"

He broke off as a screech from the X-wing's etheric rudder came faintly over the speaker. "I hope you've brought a couple wings of fighters with you," he said. "We're going to be a little pressed here."

Luke glanced at Han. "Afraid it's just Han and me and the *Falcon*. But we're on our way."

"Make it fast."

Luke keyed off the speaker. "Is there any way to get me into my X-wing?" he asked.

"Not fast enough," Han shook his head. "We're going to have to drop it here and go in alone."

Luke nodded, getting out of his seat. "I'd better make sure Lando and the droids are strapped in and then get up into the gun well."

"Take the top one," Han called after him. The upper deflector shields were running stronger at the moment, and Luke would have more protection there.

If there was any protection to be had from forty TIE fighters and fifty truncated flying cones.

For a moment he frowned as a strange thought suddenly struck him. But no. They couldn't possibly be Lando's missing mole miners. Even a Grand Admiral wouldn't be crazy enough to try to use something like *that* in battle.

Boosting power to the forward deflectors, he took a deep breath and headed in.

"All ships, commence attack," Pellaeon[2] called. "Full engagement; maintain position and status."

He got confirmations, turned to Thrawn. "All ships report engaged, sir," he said.

But the Grand Admiral didn't seem to hear him. He just stood there at the viewport, gazing outward at the New Republic ships scrambling to meet them, his hands gripped tightly behind his back. "Admiral?" Pellaeon asked cautiously.

"That was them, Captain," Thrawn said, his voice unreadable. "That ship straight ahead. That was the *Millennium Falcon*. And it was towing an X-wing starfighter behind it."

Pellaeon frowned past the other. The glow of a drive was indeed barely visible past the flashing laser bolts of the battle, already pretty well out of combat range and trying hard to be even more so. But as to the design of the craft, much less its identity . . . "Yes, sir," he said, keeping his tone neutral. "Cloak Leader reports a successful breakout, and that the command section of the freighter is making its escape to the periphery. They're encountering some resistance from escort vehicles and a squadron of X-wings, but the general response has so far been weak and diffuse."

Thrawn took a deep breath and turned away from the viewport. "That will change," he told Pellaeon, back in control again. "Remind him not to push his envelope too far, or to waste excessive time in choosing his targets. Also that the spacetrooper mole miners should concentrate on Calamari Star Cruisers—they're likely to have the largest number of defenders aboard." The red eyes glittered. "And inform him that the *Millennium Falcon* is on its way in."

"Yes, sir," Pellaeon said. He glanced out the viewport again, at the distant fleeing ship. Towing an X-wing . . . ? "You don't think . . . Skywalker?"

2. Pellaeon, by the way, was named after Pelleas, an idealistic young knight in the King Arthur mythos.
  —TZ

Thrawn's face hardened. "We'll know soon," he said quietly. "And if so, Talon Karrde will have a great deal to answer for. A *great* deal."

"Watch it, Rogue Five," Wedge warned as a flash of laser fire from somewhere behind him shot past and nicked the wing of one of the X-wings ahead. "We've picked up a tail."

"I noticed," the other came back. "Pincer?"

"On my mark," Wedge confirmed as a second bolt shot past him. Directly ahead, a Calamari Star Cruiser was pulling sluggishly away, trying to get out of the battle zone. Perfect cover for this kind of maneuver. Together, he and Rogue Five dived underneath it—

"*Now.*" Leaning hard on his etheric rudder, he peeled off hard to the right. Rogue Five did the same thing to the left. The pursuing TIE fighter hesitated between his diverging targets a split second too long; and even as he swung around to follow Wedge, Rogue Five blew him out of the sky.

"Nice shooting," Wedge said, giving the area a quick scan. The TIE fighters still seemed to be everywhere, but for the moment, at least, none of them was close enough to give them any trouble.

Five noticed that, too. "We seem to be out of it, Rogue Leader," he commented.

"Easy enough to fix," Wedge told him. His momentum was taking him farther under the Star Cruiser they'd used for cover. Curving up and around it, he started to spiral back toward the main battle area.

He was just swinging up along the Star Cruiser's side when he noticed the small cone-shaped thing nestled up against the larger ship's hull.

He craned his neck for a better look as he shot past. It was one of the little craft that had come out with the TIE fighters, all right. Sitting pressed up against the Star Cruiser's bridge blister as if it were welded in place.

There was a battle going on nearby, a battle in which his people were fighting and very possibly dying. But something told Wedge that this was important. "Hang on a minute," he told Five. "I want to check this out."

His momentum had already taken him to the Star Cruiser's bow. He curved around in front of the ship, leaning back into a spiral again—

And suddenly his canopy lit up with laser fire, and his X-wing jolted like a startled animal beneath him.

The Star Cruiser had fired on him.

In his ear, he heard Five shout something. "Stay back," Wedge snapped, fighting against a sudden drop in power and giving his scopes a quick scan. "I'm hit, but not bad."

"They fired on you!"

"Yeah, I know," Wedge said, trying to maintain some kind of evasive maneuvering with what little control he had left. Fortunately, the systems were starting to come back on line as his R2 unit did some fast rerouting. Even more fortunately, the Star Cruiser didn't seem inclined to shoot at him again.

But why had it fired in the first place?

Unless . . .

His own R2 was too busy with rerouting chores to handle anything else at the moment. "Rogue Five, I need a fast sensor scan," he called. "Where are the rest of those cone things?"

"Hang on, I'll check," the other replied. "Scope shows . . . I don't find more than about fifteen of them. Nearest one's ten kilometers away—bearing one-one-eight mark four."

Wedge felt something hard settle into his stomach. Fifteen, out of the fifty that had been in that freighter with the TIE fighters. So where had the rest of them gone? "Let's go take a look," he said, turning into an intercept vector.

The cone thing was heading toward another Escort Frigate like the *Larkhess,* he saw, with four TIE fighters running interference for it. Not that there was much potential for interference—if the Frigate was manned anywhere near as sparsely as the *Larkhess*, it would have precious little chance of fighting back. "Let's see if we can take them before they notice us," he told Five as they closed the distance.

Abruptly, all four TIE fighters peeled off and came around. So much for surprise. "Take the two on the right, Rogue Five; I'll take the others."

"Copy."

Wedge waited until the last second before firing on the first of his targets, swinging around instantly to avoid collision with the other. It swept past beneath him, his X-wing shuddering as it took another hit. He leaned hard into the turn, catching a glimpse of the TIE fighter dropping into a pursuit slot as he did so—

And suddenly something shot past him, spitting laser fire and twisting back and around in some kind of insane variant on a drunkard's-walk evasive maneuver. The TIE fighter caught a direct hit and blew into a spectacular cloud of fiery gas. Wedge finished his turn, just as Rogue Five's second target fighter did likewise.

"All clear, Wedge," a familiar voice called into his ear. "You damaged?"

"I'm fine, Luke," Wedge assured him. "Thanks."

"Look—there it goes," Han's voice cut in. "Over by the Frigate. It's one of Lando's mole miners, all right."

"I see it," Luke said. "What's it doing out here?"

"I saw one stuck onto the Star Cruiser back there," Wedge told him, swinging back on course for the Frigate. "Looks like this one's trying to do the same thing. I don't know why."

"Whatever it's doing, let's stop it," Han said.

"Right."

It was, Wedge saw, going to be a close race; but it was quickly clear that the mole miner was going to win it. Already it had turned its base around toward the Frigate and was starting to nestle up against the hull.

And just before it closed the gap completely, he caught a glimpse of an acridly brilliant light.

"What was *that?*" Luke asked.

"I don't know," Wedge said, blinking away the afterimage. "It looked too bright for laser fire."

"It was a plasma jet," Han grunted as the *Falcon* came up alongside him. "Right on top of the bridge emergency escape hatch. That's what they wanted the mole miners for. They're using them to burn through the hulls—"

He broke off; and, abruptly, he swore. "Luke—we got it backwards. They're not here to wreck the fleet.

"They're here to *steal* it."[3]

For a long heartbeat Luke just stared at the Frigate . . . and then, like pieces clicking together in a puzzle, it all fell into place. The mole miners, the undermanned and underdefended capital ships that the New Republic had been forced to press into shipping service, the Imperial fleet out there that seemed to be making no real effort to push its way past the system's defenses—

And a New Republic Star Cruiser, mole miner planted firmly on its side, that had just fired on Wedge's X-wing.

He took a moment to scan the sky around him. Moving with deceptive slowness through the continuing starfighter battle, a number of warships were beginning to pull out. "We've got to stop them," he told the others.

"Good thinking," Han agreed. "How?"

"Is there any way we can get aboard them ourselves?" he asked. "Lando said the mole miners were two-man ships— the Imperials can't possibly have packed more than four or five stormtroopers in each one of them."

"The way those warships are manned at the moment, four stormtroopers would be plenty," Wedge pointed out.

"Yes, but I could take them," Luke said.

"On all fifty ships?" Han countered. "Besides, you blast

3. Tim reminds me that his original outline had the book end with Luke's escape but that I requested something bigger, saying his proposed finish wasn't exciting enough to close out a *Star Wars* adventure. The climactic clash at Sluis Van was the result. As well as being a space battle worthy of the giant screen, it also ties together a number of seemingly minor plot elements Tim had been setting in place throughout the book: the shortage of freighters that sent Han to the smugglers, the theft of the mole miners, Lando's presence on the scene, and more.

—BM

a hatch open to vacuum and you'll have pressure bulk-heads closing all over the ship. Take you forever to even get to the bridge."

Luke gritted his teeth; but Han was right. "Then we have to disable them," he said. "Knock out their engines or control systems or something. If they get out to the perim-eter and those Star Destroyers, we'll never see them again."

"Oh, we'll see them again," Han growled. "Pointed straight back at us. You're right—disabling as many as we can is our best shot. We're never going to stop all fifty, though."

"We don't have fifty to stop, at least not yet," Wedge put in. "There are still twelve mole miners that haven't at-tached themselves to ships."

"Good—let's take them out first," Han said. "You got vectors on them?"

"Feeding your computer now."

"Okay . . . okay, here we go." The *Falcon* twisted around and headed off in a new direction. "Luke, get on the comm and tell Sluis Control what's happening," he added. "Tell them not to let any ships out of the orbit-dock area."

"Right." Luke switched channels on the comm; and as he did so, he was suddenly aware of a slight change in sense from the *Falcon*'s cockpit. "Han? You all right?"

"Huh? Sure. Why?"

"I don't know. You seemed to change."

"I had half a grip on some idea," Han said. "But it's gone now. Come on, make that call. I want you back on the quads when we get there."

The call to Sluis Control was over well before they reached their target mole miner. "They thank us for the information," Luke reported to the others, "but they say they don't have anything to spare at the moment to help us."

"Probably don't," Han agreed. "Okay, I see two TIE fighters running escort. Wedge, you and Rogue Five take them out while Luke and I hit the mole miner."

"Got it," Wedge confirmed. The two X-wings shot past Luke's canopy, flaring apart into intercept mode as the TIE fighters broke formation and came around to meet the attack.

"Luke, try to blow it apart instead of disintegrating it," Han suggested. "Let's see how many people the Imperials have got stuffed inside."

"Got it," Luke said. The mole miner was in his sights now. Adjusting his power level down, he fired.

The truncated cone flared as the metal dead center of the shot boiled away into glowing gas. The rest of the craft seemed intact, though, and Luke was just lining up for a second shot when the hatch at the top abruptly popped open.

And through the opening, a monstrous, robotlike figure came charging out.

"What—?"

"It's a spacetrooper," Han snapped back. "A storm-trooper in zero-gee armor.[4] Hang on."

He spun the *Falcon* around away from the spacetrooper, but not before there was a flash from a protuberance atop the other's backpack and the hull around Luke slammed with a violent concussion. Han rolled the ship around, blocking Luke's view, as another concussion rocked them.

And then they were pulling away—pulling away, but with agonizing slowness. Luke swallowed hard, wondering what kind of damage they'd taken.

"Han, Luke—you all right?" Wedge's voice called anxiously.

"Yeah, for now," Han called back. "You get the TIE fighters?"

"Yes. I think the mole miner's still underway, though."

"Well, then, blast it," Han said. "Nothing cute; just blow it apart. But watch out for that spacetrooper—he's using miniature proton torpedoes or something. I'm trying to draw him away; I don't know if he'll fall for it."

"He's not," Wedge said grimly. "He's staying right on top

4. Spacetroopers were another cool invention from West End Games.
      —TZ

of the mole miner. They're heading for a passenger liner—
looks like they'll make it, too."

Han swore under his breath. "Probably got a few regular
stormtrooper buddies still in there. All right, I guess we do
this the hard way. Hang on, Luke—we're going to ram
him."

"We're *what?*"

Luke's last word was lost in the roar from the engines as
Han sent the *Falcon* flying straight out and then around in
a hard turn. The mole miner and spacetrooper came back
into Luke's line of sight—

Wedge had been wrong. The spacetrooper wasn't standing by the damaged mole miner; he was, in fact, sidling
quickly away from it. The twin protuberances on top of
his backpack began flashing again, and a couple of seconds later the *Falcon*'s hull began ringing with proton torpedo blasts. "Get ready," Han called.

Luke braced himself, trying not to think about what
would happen if one of those torpedoes hit his canopy—
and trying, too, not to wonder if Han could really ram the
spacetrooper without also plowing into the passenger
liner directly behind him. Ignoring the proton blasts, the
Falcon continued accelerating—

And without warning, Han dropped the ship beneath
the spacetrooper's line of fire. "Wedge: *go!*"

From beneath Luke's line of sight an X-wing flashed
upward, laser cannon blazing.

And the mole miner shattered into flaming dust.

"Good shot," Han told him, a note of satisfaction in his
voice as he veered underneath the liner, nearly taking the
Falcon's main sensor dish off in the process. "There you
go, hotshot—enjoy your view of the battle."

Belatedly, the light dawned. "He was listening in on our
channel," Luke said. "You just wanted to decoy him into
moving away from the mole miner."

"You got it," Han said. "I figured he'd tap in—Imperials
always do when they can . . ."

He trailed off. "What is it?" Luke asked.

"I don't know," Han said slowly. "There's something about this whole thing that keeps poking at me, but I can't figure out what it is. Never mind. Our hotshot space-trooper will keep for now—let's go hit some more mole miners."

It was just as well, Pellaeon thought, that they were only here to keep the enemy tied up. The Sluissi and their New Republic allies were putting up one terrific fight.

On his status board, a section of the *Chimaera*'s shield schematic went red. "Get that starboard shield back up," he ordered, giving the sky in that direction a quick scan. There were half a dozen warships out there, all of them firing like mad, with a battle station in backstop position behind them. If their sensors showed that the *Chimaera*'s starboard shields were starting to go—

"Starboard turbolasers: focus all fire on the Assault Frigate at thirty-two mark forty," Thrawn spoke up calmly. "Concentrate on the starboard side of the ship only."

The *Chimaera* gun crews responded with a withering hail of laser fire. The Assault Frigate tried to swerve away; but even as it turned, its entire starboard side seemed to flash with vaporized metal. The weapons from that section, which had been firing nonstop, went abruptly silent.

"Excellent," Thrawn said. "Starboard tractor crews: lock on and bring it in close. Try to keep it between the damaged shields and the enemy. And be sure to keep its starboard side facing toward us; the port side may still have active weapons and a crew to use them."

Clearly against its will, the Assault Frigate began to move inward. Pellaeon watched it for a moment, then returned his attention to the overall battle. He had no doubt the tractor crew would do the job right; they'd shown a remarkable increase in efficiency and competence lately.

"TIE Squadron Four, keep after that B-wing group," he instructed. "Port ion cannon: keep up the pressure on that command center." He looked at Thrawn. "Any specific orders, Admiral?"

Thrawn shook his head. "No, the battle seems to be progressing as planned." He turned his glowing eyes on Pellaeon. "What word from Cloak Leader?"

Pellaeon checked the proper display. "The TIE fighters are still engaging the various escort ships," he reported. "Forty-three of the mole miners have successfully attached to target ships. Of those, thirty-nine are secure and making for the perimeter. Four are still encountering internal resistance, though they anticipate a quick victory."

"And the other eight?"

"They've been destroyed," Pellaeon told him. "Including two of those with a spacetrooper aboard. One of those spacetroopers is failing to respond to comm, presumably killed with his craft; the other is still functional. Cloak Leader has ordered him to join the attack on the escort ships."

"Countermand that," Thrawn said. "I'm quite aware that stormtroopers have infinite confidence in themselves, but that sort of deep-space combat is not what spacetrooper suits were designed for. Have Cloak Leader detail a TIE fighter to bring him out. And also inform him that his wing is to begin pulling back to the perimeter."[5]

Pellaeon frowned. "You mean *now,* sir?"

"Certainly, now." Thrawn nodded toward the viewport. "The first of our new ships will begin arriving within fifteen minutes. As soon as they're all with us, the task force will be withdrawing."

"But . . ."

"The Rebel forces within the perimeter are of no further concern to us, Captain," Thrawn said with quiet satisfaction. "The captured ships are on their way. With or without TIE fighter cover, there's nothing the Rebels can do to stop them."

5. The sixth quality of a good leader: he doesn't waste his troops, but does what he can to get them to safety once their mission is complete or has been rendered impossible by the circumstances of the battle.

—TZ

Han brought the *Falcon* as close as he could to the Frigate's engines without risking a backwash, feeling the slight multiple dips in ship's power as Luke repeatedly fired the quads. "Anything?" he asked as they came up around the other side.

"Doesn't look like it," Luke said. "There's just too much armor over the coolant-feeder lines."

Han glanced along the Frigate's course, fighting back the urge to swear. They were already uncomfortably close to the perimeter battle, and getting closer all the time. "This isn't getting us anywhere. There's got to be *some* way to take out a capital ship."

"That's what other capital ships are for," Wedge put in. "But you're right—this isn't working."

Han pursed his lips. "Artoo?—you still on line back there?" he called.

The droid's beeping came faintly up the cockpit corridor. "Go through your schematics again," Han ordered. "See if you can find us another weak point."

Artoo beeped again in acknowledgment. But it wasn't a very optimistic beep. "He's not going to find anything better, Han," Luke said, echoing Han's own private assessment. "I don't think we've got any choice left. I'm going to have to go topside and use my lightsaber on it."

"That's crazy, and you know it," Han growled. "Without a proper pressure suit—and with engine coolant spraying all over you if it works—"

"How about using one of the droids?" Wedge suggested.

"Neither of them can do it," Luke told him. "Artoo hasn't got the manipulative ability, and I wouldn't trust Threepio with a weapon. Especially not with all the high-acceleration maneuvers we're making."

"What we need is a remote manipulator arm," Han said. "Something that Luke could use inside while . . ."

He broke off. In a flash of inspiration, there it was—the thing that had been bothering him ever since they'd walked into this crazy battle. "Lando," he called into the intercom. "*Lando!* Get up here."

"I've got him strapped in," Luke reminded him.

"Well, go *un*strap him and get him up here," Han snapped. "*Now.*"

Luke didn't waste time with questions. "Right," he said.

"What is it?" Wedge asked tensely.

Han clenched his teeth. "We were there on Nkllon when the Imperials stole these mole miners from Lando," he told the other. "We had to reroute our communications through some jamming."

"Okay. So?"

"So why were they jamming us?" Han asked. "To keep us from calling for help? From who? They're not jamming us *here,* you notice."

"I give up," Wedge said, starting to sound a little testy. "Why?"

"Because they had to. Because—"

"Because most of the mole miners on Nkllon were running on radio remote," came a tired voice from behind him.

Han turned around, to see Lando easing his way carefully into the cockpit, clearly running at half speed but just as clearly determined to make it. Luke was right behind him, a steadying hand on his elbow. "You heard all that?" Han asked him.

"Every part that mattered," Lando said, dropping into the copilot's seat. "I could kick myself for not seeing it long ago."

"Me, too. You remember any of the command codes?"

"Most of them," Lando said. "What do you need?"

"We don't have time for anything fancy." Han nodded toward the Frigate, now lying below them. "The mole miners are still attached to the ships. Just start 'em all running."

Lando looked at him in surprise. "Start them *running?*" he echoed.

"You got it," Han confirmed. "All of them are going to be near a bridge or control wing—if they can burn through enough equipment and wiring, it should knock out the whole lot of them."

Lando exhaled noisily, tilting his head sideways in a familiar gesture of reluctant acceptance. "You're the boss," he said, fingers moving over the comm keyboard. "I just hope you know what you're doing. Ready?"

Han braced himself. "Do it."

Lando keyed a final section of code . . . and beneath them, the Frigate twitched.

Not a big twitch, not at first. But as the seconds passed, it became increasingly clear that something down there was wrong. The main engines flickered a few times and then died, amid short bursts from the auxiliaries. Its drive toward the perimeter fighting faltered, its etheric control surfaces kicking in and then out again, striving to change course in random directions. The big ship floundered almost to a halt.

And suddenly, the side of the hull directly opposite the mole miner's position erupted in a brilliant burst of flame.

"It's cut all the way through!" Lando gasped, his tone not sure whether to be proud or dismayed by his handiwork. A TIE fighter, perhaps answering a distress call from the stormtroopers inside, swept directly into the stream of superheated plasma before it could maneuver away. It emerged from the other side, its solar panels blazing with fire, and exploded.

"It's working," Wedge called, sounding awed. "Look—it's working."

Han looked up from the Frigate. All around them—all throughout the orbit-dock area—ships that had been making for deep space were suddenly twisting around like metallic animals in the throes of death.

6. The final quality of a good commander: a willingness to retreat when the circumstances of battle make the objective no longer attainable.

Note that at the same time, he's maintaining the "glass half full" attitude vital to keeping up his troops' morale.

—TZ

7. So here at last we have all the pieces that went into the creation of Grand Admiral Thrawn.

He's competent and capable, enough so that his troops can be assured that they have the best possible chance of winning whatever battle they're being sent into.

He cares about his troops, and they know he won't sacrifice them for nothing.

And he's driven by logic and reason, not anger or ego or wounded pride.

Throw in the semi-mystical art thing (through which he can anticipate his enemies' moves), and make him an alien (because the Emperor disliked aliens, and would never give such a rank to one unless he was really, really good) . . . and when you've done all that, Grand Admiral Thrawn simply falls out of the equation.

All of them with tongues of flame shooting from their sides.

For a long minute Thrawn sat in silence, staring down at his status boards, apparently oblivious to the battle still raging on all around them. Pellaeon held his breath, waiting for the inevitable explosion of injured pride at the unexpected reversal. Wondering what form that explosion would take.

Abruptly, the Grand Admiral raised his eyes to the viewport. "Have all the remaining Cloak Force TIE fighters returned to our ships, Captain?" he asked calmly.

"Yes, sir," Pellaeon told him, still waiting.

Thrawn nodded. "Then order the task force to begin its withdrawal."

"Ah . . . withdrawal?" Pellaeon asked cautiously. It was not exactly the order he'd been anticipating.

Thrawn looked at him, a faint smile on his face. "You were expecting, perhaps, that I'd order an all-out attack?" he asked. "That I would seek to cover our defeat in a frenzy of false and futile heroics?"[6]

"Of course not," Pellaeon protested.

But he knew down deep that the other knew the truth. Thrawn's smile remained, but was suddenly cold. "We haven't been defeated, Captain," he said quietly. "Merely slowed down a bit. We have Wayland, and we have the treasures of the Emperor's storehouse. Sluis Van was to be merely a preliminary to the campaign, not the campaign itself. As long as we have Mount Tantiss, our ultimate victory is still assured."

He looked out the viewport, a thoughtful expression on his face. "We've lost this particular prize, Captain. But that's all we've lost. I will not waste ships and men trying to change that which cannot be changed. There will be many more opportunities to obtain the ships we need. Carry out your orders."

"Yes, Admiral," Pellaeon said, turning back to his status board, a surge of relief washing through him. So there would not be an explosion, after all . . . and with a twinge of guilt, he realized that he should have known better from the start. Thrawn was not merely a soldier, like so many others Pellaeon had served with. He was, instead, a true warrior, with his eye set on the final goal and not on his own personal glory.

Taking one last look out the viewport, Pellaeon issued the order to retreat. And wondered, once again, what the Battle of Endor would have been like if Thrawn had been in command.[7]

(cont.)

I think the greatest compliment Thrawn has ever received came from a U.S. serviceman. (I can't remember if he was a soldier or marine.) He told me he and his buddies had read the Thrawn Trilogy, and had agreed that they would unreservedly follow a commander like Thrawn.

Oh, and what would have happened if Thrawn had been in command at Endor? The Rebels, in my humble opinion, would almost certainly have lost.

—TZ

CHAPTER 32

IT TOOK A WHILE LONGER after the Imperial fleet pulled out for the battle to be officially over. But with the Star Destroyers gone, the outcome was never in doubt.

The regular stormtroopers were the easiest. Most of them were dead already, killed when Lando's activation of the mole miners had ruptured the airseals of their stolen ships and left them open to vacuum, and the rest were taken without much trouble. The eight remaining space-troopers, whose zero-gee suits had allowed them to keep fighting after their ships were disabled, were another story entirely. Ignoring all calls to surrender, they fanned out through the shipyards, clearly intent on causing as much damage as they could before the inevitable. Six were hunted down and destroyed; the other two eventually self-destructed, one managing to cripple a Corvette in the process.

He left behind him a shipyard and orbit-dock facility in an uproar ... and a great number of severely damaged major ships.

"Not exactly what you'd call a resounding victory," Captain Afyon grunted, surveying what was left of the *Larkhess*'s bridge through a pressure bulkhead viewport as he gingerly adjusted a battle dressing that had been applied to his forehead. "Going to take a couple months' work just to rewire all the control circuits."

"Would you rather the Imperials have gotten it whole?" Han demanded from behind him, trying to ignore his own mixed feelings about this whole thing. Yes, it had worked . . . but at what cost?

"Not at all," Afyon replied calmly. "You did what you had to—and I'd say that even if my own neck hadn't been on the line. I'm just saying what others will say: that destroying all these ships in order to save them was not exactly the optimal solution."

Han threw a look at Luke. "You sound like Councilor Fey'lya," he accused Afyon.

The other nodded. "Exactly."

"Well, fortunately, Fey'lya's only one voice," Luke offered.

"Yeah, but it's a loud one," Han said sourly.

"And one that a lot of people are starting to listen to," Wedge added. "Including important military people."

"He'll find some way to parlay this incident into his own political gain," Afyon rumbled. "You just watch him."

Han's rejoinder was interrupted by a trilling from the wall intercom. Afyon stepped over and tapped the switch. "Afyon here," he said.

"Sluis Control communications," a voice replied. "We have an incoming call from Coruscant for Captain Solo. Is he with you?"

"Right here," Han called, stepping over to the speaker. "Go ahead."

There was a slight pause; and then a familiar and sorely missed voice came on. "Han? It's Leia."

"Leia!" Han said, feeling a delighted and probably slightly foolish-looking grin spread across his face. A second later, though— "Wait a minute. What are you doing back on Coruscant?"

"I think I've taken care of our other problem," she said. Her voice, he noticed for the first time, sounded tense and more than a little ragged. "At least for the moment."

Han threw a frown across the room at Luke. "You *think?*"

"Look, that's not important right now," she insisted. "What's important is that you get back here right away."

Something cold and hard settled into Han's stomach. For Leia to be this upset . . . "What's wrong?"

He heard her take a deep breath. "Admiral Ackbar has been arrested and removed from command. On charges of treason."

The room abruptly filled with a brittle silence. Han looked in turn at Luke, at Afyon, at Wedge. But there didn't seem to be anything to say. "I'll be there as soon as I can," he told Leia. "Luke's here, too—you want me to bring him?"

"Yes, if he can manage it," she said. "Ackbar's going to need all the friends he can get."[1]

"Okay," Han said. "Call me in the *Falcon* if there's any more news. We're heading over there right now."

"I'll see you soon. I love you, Han."

"Me, too."

He broke the connection, turned back to the others. "Well," he said, to no one in particular. "There goes the hammer. You coming, Luke?"

Luke looked at Wedge. "Have your people had a chance to do anything with my X-wing yet?"

"Not yet," Wedge said, shaking his head. "But it's just been officially bumped to the top of the priority list. We'll have it ready to fly in two hours. Even if I have to take the motivators out of my own ship to do it."

Luke nodded and looked back at Han. "I'll fly into Coruscant on my own, then," he said. "Let me just come with you and get Artoo off the *Falcon.*"

1. Just as Tim is masterful at creating cliffhangers at the end of chapters, he brought this book to a close with so many compelling cliffhangers that readers came in droves to the next book. Ackbar's arrest is only one of them.
          —BM

"Right. Come on."

"Good luck," Afyon called softly after them.

And yes, Han thought as they hurried down the corridor toward the hatchway where the *Falcon* was docked; the hammer was indeed coming down. If Fey'lya and his faction pushed too hard and too fast—and knowing Fey'lya, he would almost certainly push too hard and too fast—

"We could be on the edge of a civil war here," Luke murmured his thought back at him.

"Yeah, well, we're not going to let that happen," Han told him with confidence he didn't feel. "We haven't gone through a war and back just to watch some overambitious Bothan wreck it."

"How are we going to stop him?"

Han grimaced. "We'll think of something."

To Be Continued . . .[2]

2. I always liked the way the *Back to the Future* movies did this: with a "To Be Continued" after the first movie (the later version of it, anyway), and a "To Be Concluded" at the end of the second, thus assuring the viewer that the saga would indeed be ending with part 3.

Little did we know at the time that the *Star Wars* Expanded Universe wasn't about to be concluded. In fact, it was just getting started.

—TZ

AFTERWORD

ABOUT THIS SAME TIME twenty years ago, I incorporated Lucasfilm's final corrections on *Heir to the Empire* and sent the manuscript to the production department, confident that Tim had delivered a terrific story but completely unaware of what an impact it would have on readers just a few months later. All of us at Bantam Spectra had loved the films, and we were honored that Lucasfilm would allow us to bring a new story to *Star Wars* fans. But would those fans want to *read* a new adventure rather than see it played out on the biggest screen possible? We had no way to know for sure.

I remember the day we sat in Lou Aronica's office to brainstorm which author might be best for the project. We'd made the deal with Lucasfilm, but no book would exist until a suitable author was found and an outline approved. First and foremost we wanted a writer who loved the films and would be excited to expand George Lucas's vision. We looked initially at people who were already being published at Bantam Spectra, wanting to give our own authors first shot.

Bantam published numerous popular writers at the time, so Tim's was not the first name to come up. I knew he'd be right for the job but was hesitant to mention him because we'd signed him up only a few months earlier and he was in the middle of writing the first of three novels we had under contract.

Still, I knew Tim was a huge fan. And from working with him previously at *Analog* magazine—where he'd won a Hugo Award for his story "Cascade Point"—and at Baen Books, where I'd been his editor on several novels including the Cobra trilogy and *The Backlash Mission,* I knew Tim had the writing skills to handle a big-picture *Star Wars* plot. Not only that, but he could also re-create the interplay among George Lucas's beloved characters as well as generate new ones who would capture readers' interest.

That trust was certainly borne out: In *Heir to the Empire,* Tim "gave birth" to the unforgettable Mara Jade, Grand Admiral Thrawn, and Joruus C'baoth and was already thinking of names for the twins Leia would bear later in the trilogy. *Heir to the Empire* hit number one on the *New York Times* hardcover bestseller list—almost unheard of for a science-fiction novel at that time—and went on to sell millions of copies. Tim and I were invited to Skywalker Ranch in San Rafael, California, and had the pleasure of meeting George Lucas, who thanked Tim for his contribution to the *Star Wars* universe. (Talk about somebody walking on air! I swear I could have swung a cat underneath Tim's boots during that encounter.)

It was the publishing experience of a lifetime, and it couldn't have happened to a nicer guy, or a better writer. Thank you, Tim!

—BETSY MITCHELL
November 2010

CRISIS OF FAITH

AN ORIGINAL Star Wars NOVELLA

TIMOTHY ZAHN

THE SKY LOOKED odd this morning, Trevik of the Midli of the Seventh of the Red thought as the Queen's entourage left the residence wing of the palace and began the short walk to the Dwelling of Guests. Perhaps it was clouds, he thought: clouds too high and too thin for his eyes to distinguish through the mists rising from the Dreaming Waters that lay to the north of the Red City.

But he'd seen the sky through thin clouds before. More likely it was something their guest had done, the chief of the thirty beings who had arrived a month ago, creatures with yellow eyes and hair the color of a storm cloud. Had their chief not said he would protect the Red City from the evil forces gathering among the stars over Quethold?

"Drink."

Quickly Trevik lifted the ornate bowl of nectar that he held clutched to his chest. The Queen leaned toward the bowl, her embroidered robes moving in time with the rhythmic swaying of her canopied litter, her long abdomen stretched out along the litter's couch—

"Higher," Borosiv of the Circling of the First of the Red growled tersely from his far less ornate litter behind the Queen's.

Wincing, Trevik stretched up his arms, raising the bowl as high as he could. The Queen drank deeply and then straightened up again, her mandibles shaking off the last drops of the rich liquid, her eyes flicking impassively across Trevik's face.

Trevik lowered the bowl again to his chest, feeling the thudding of his heart within his torso. Being selected to act as the Queen's bowlcarrier was the highest honor any Midli could achieve. It was as if all the Midlis on Quethold stood behind him, just as all the Circlings stood behind Borosiv. The last thing in the world he wanted was to fail, and through that failure to bring shame to his family.

"Straighten up," Borosiv continued in the same low, grouchy voice. "Watch the Workers. Duplicate their stance."

Trevik swallowed, a quick flush of shame flickering across his heart. He'd been told all this earlier, of course, but in the heat of the moment he'd forgotten.

Now he looked over at the line of Workers carrying the Queen's litter. There were eight of them, their torsos held nearly vertical despite the weight of the litter on their shoulders. Each Worker's abdomen stretched out behind him, perfectly level with the ground, with his four legs moving in precise lockstep rhythm.

Swallowing again, Trevik tried to match their stance and movement. The Queen, he'd heard, was willing to give a new bowlcarrier a certain degree of latitude on his first day. But that didn't mean he shouldn't try his very best.

Especially since Borosiv didn't seem inclined to give the new Midli any of that same slack.

The Dwelling of Guests was a circular building situated in the center of the courtyard. It was small, with only a modest central gathering area on the ground floor and ten small privacy rooms on the floor above. Two of the storm-haired aliens stood at the south entryway, their strange weapons held across their shoulders as they watched the Queen and her entourage approach.

It was the closest Trevik had ever been to these particular aliens, and he eyed them curiously as he and the litters drew near. They were upright beings, unlike the Quesoth but very similar to the Quesoth's allies, the Stromma. They had two legs, a torso with no separate abdomen, and a head topped with flowing black storm-cloud hair. Humanoid, he'd heard such beings called before.

But at least their eyes were proper, multifaceted like those of the Quesoth, though they were a bright yellow instead of Quesoth's pale blue. Perhaps their eyes were why the Queen had chosen to defy Quethold's old alliance with the Stromma and accept the Storm-hairs into the Red City as her guests.

Or perhaps it was because of the weapons the Storm-hairs had brought with them. Weapons more compact and powerful even than those of the Stromma.

Trevik focused on the Storm-hairs' weapons, feeling himself suddenly tensing. Along with the twelve Workers carrying the litters, the Queen's entourage also included twelve Soldiers, and if the Storm-hairs neglected the proper greeting the Queen might well order the aliens to be disciplined. Trevik hadn't seen the Storm-hairs' weapons in action, but he'd heard enough stories to know that he didn't especially want to. Especially not at close range.

Fortunately, the Storm-hairs knew the correct protocol. "Hail, O Queen of the Red," one of them intoned as the litter came within the prescribed five paces. "We live to serve, and die to serve."

The Queen remained silent as the aliens pulled open the doors and the group filed through. Under the circumstances, Trevik decided, her silence was probably a good thing.

The chief of the Storm-hairs was waiting in the center of the gathering area. It was the first time Trevik had seen the area since the Queen had granted them the Dwelling, and he was struck by how alien it had become. Changes in furniture were understandable—after all, the Storm-hairs weren't built anything like the Quesoth.

But the Storm-hairs had gone far beyond simple comfort and convenience. They had redone the entire room, from the hangings on the walls to the meditation sculptures about the walkways. In fact, even the pattern of the walkways had been changed. It was as if the Dwelling had been transformed into a part of the Storm-hairs' own world.

"Drink."

Trevik lifted the bowl, his heart again beginning to pound. Some of the sculptures the Storm-hairs had removed had been from the Queen's own meditation room. Would she take offense that those treasures had been taken out of sight?

Perhaps she already had. Lifting her face from the nectar bowl, she raised her voice in the high-pitched ululations of Soldier Speak.

Trevik tensed. But the two lines of Soldiers flanking the two litters didn't surge toward the chief Storm-hair. The commander replied in the same language, and all of the Soldiers spread out across the room toward the Dwelling's outer doors. They passed through and disappeared into the courtyard, closing the doors behind them.

"Down," the Queen ordered.

Trevik took a step to the side as the eight Workers carrying the litter lowered it to the floor and then knelt and curled themselves over into the Worker sign of homage. Behind the Queen's litter, Trevik heard a softer swishing of cloth as the four Workers in the rear likewise lowered Borosiv's litter.

The chief Storm-hair bowed low, his posture almost a caricature of the Workers' stance. "Hail, O Queen of the Red," he said.

Trevik frowned. Was that it? Did he not also live to serve and die to serve, as did the Quesoth and even the other Storm-hairs?

"Drink."

Hurriedly Trevik stepped back to the litter and offered the bowl. Apparently, the chief Storm-hair had indeed finished his greeting. Even more amazing, the Queen didn't seem offended by the lack of a death-pledge. It was almost as if she saw him as an equal, the way Trevik would see his brothers of the Seventh as equals.

But that was insane. The Queen *had* no equals.

The Queen finished her drink and waved Trevik away. "The threat remains, O Nuso Esva," she said, addressing the chief Storm-hair. "My Circlings have seen the flying cities, black against the stars."

"The threat remains, O Queen," the chief Storm-hair—Nuso Esva—agreed. "Let us take further counsel together as to how we may deal with our common enemy.

"Let us speak to the destruction of Grand Admiral Thrawn."

The other five members of the strategy session were already waiting in the bridge conference room of the Imperial Star Destroyer *Admonitor* when Senior Captain Voss Parck arrived. "My apologies, Admiral; gentles," he said as he circled the table to the empty chair at Grand Admiral Thrawn's right. "There was a last-minute report from the Tantsor system that I thought might be relevant to our discussion."

"Was it?" Stromma Council Liaison Nyama asked, his grasslike fur glinting in the room's lights, his heavy brow ridges angled over his pure black eyes, his normally snide tone even more insolent than usual.

"Yes," Parck said, long practice enabling him not to take offense at Nyama's manner. Loud belligerence was a universal—and highly prized—quality among the Stromma hierarchy, and the species' military professionals were no exception. "The rumored activity turned out to be nothing but a small smuggling group. The searchers found no connection between them and Nuso Esva, and no trace of actual warships."

"And in your vision this waste of effort constitutes *progress*?" Nyama scoffed.

"What Council Liaison Nyama means to ask," a younger Stromma at Nyama's side said in a more polite tone, "is whether clearing one system genuinely narrows the search for Nuso Esva's remaining forces, especially when so many other possibilities remain."

"Even negative information is useful," Thrawn said calmly, his glowing red eyes focused on Nyama. "Particularly since the probe droids we're leaving behind after each search ensure that Nuso Esva's forces don't move in behind us."

Nyama gave a throaty snort. "We *know* where he is," he said, jabbing a finger emphatically downward. "What do we care where his scattered remnant cowers?"

"Because as long as he lives, they remain a threat," Parck said. "You of all people should have learned that, Council Liaison. You were winning in the struggle against those forces until he returned to take personal command."

"The situation there was vastly different," Nyama growled. "The forces on Oristrom were well supplied and well entrenched. And there were a great deal more of them." He pointed down again. "Besides, Nuso Esva isn't going to be leaving Quethold. Not anymore. Certainly not alive."

"Liaison Nyama makes a valid point," Stormtrooper Commander Balkin said from the other end of the table. "Wherever his remnant is hiding, Nuso Esva surely has insufficient ships to break through our blockade."

"Agreed, Commander," Thrawn said. "Unfortunately, the blockade will very soon have to be lifted. There are other matters that urgently require my attention, other threats to this region and to those who have joined the Empire of the Hand."

"The admiral is correct," Parck seconded. "I can name at least ten such threats right now, and there will be more to come."

"Then make an end of him," Balkin said firmly. "The stormtroopers of the 501st stand ready to move in and bring you his head."

Nyama snorted again. "You have no idea what you're saying," he said scornfully. "You've never faced Quesoth Soldiers in battle. We, on the other hand, have dealt with them both as allies and as enemies. They're bigger even than the Workers—when they rear up they're nearly as tall as you or I—and immensely strong. They're also fiercely loyal to their Queen, obeying her orders unquestioningly and with no consideration for their own safety. And there are thousands of them within the Red City."

"We've faced loyal and numerous enemies before," Balkin said. "These will fall just as thoroughly."

"But at a severe cost," Nyama warned. "Are you ready to accept such losses, Grand Admiral Thrawn?"

"I don't accept unnecessary losses of any sort, Council Liaison," Thrawn said, his blue-skinned face impassive. "But I was unaware that you once fought against the Quesoth."

"It was long ago, during the foolish arrogance we called our Expansion Period, " Nyama said. For once, Parck noted with interest, the belligerent voice was almost introspective. "Even with the primitive ceremonial weapons they still use, we suffered greatly before we came to our senses and made peace with them." His nostrils flared. "As will you if you continue this path of foolishness."

"Perhaps someone on the council can talk to the Queen of the Red," Parck suggested. "If you could get her to see reason—"

"Queens of Quesoth make their own reason," Nyama said. "Whatever her logic for accepting Nuso Esva into her care, she will not be moved from it."

"Then she will suffer," Thrawn warned.

"We all suffer," Nyama said flatly. "Such is the way of life."

Parck grimaced. The Quesoth would suffer, all right, like the twenty and more species that had already suffered under Nuso Esva's reign of terror. Ever since the alien and his people—the warriors he proudly called his "Chosen"—had emerged from a still-unidentified planet in the Unknown Regions, they'd been cutting a deadly swath through peoples, worlds, and even small federations. Of all those attacked, only Thrawn had shown the skill and resolve necessary to block Nuso Esva's expansion and, eventually, to begin driving him back.

But victory had come with a terrible cost. The Chosen fought with fanatical zeal, and forced their client and subjugated peoples to fight alongside them with the same stubbornness.

Even worse, with every forced retreat the Chosen followed Nuso Esva's scorched-ground policy of destroying everything they couldn't take with them, not just weapons of war but also the means for the local populace to survive through the next winter or dry spell. Millions had died in Nuso Esva's conquests, and millions more in the aftermath of his retreats.

Including hundreds of thousands of Stromma who'd been caught in the crossfire and scorched ground when Thrawn finally succeeded in pushing Nuso Esva off their worlds. Which, for Parck, made Nyama's attitude that much more bewildering. Didn't he want to see his professed allies the Quesoth freed from Nuso Esva's bondage?

"Yet our job as civilized beings is to minimize that suffering as best we can," Thrawn said. If he was bothered by Nyama's apparent lack of compassion, it didn't show in his expression or voice. "I'd like to see the records of your wars against the Quesoth. With an insectoid species, even long-past battles may give us insight."

"Those records are old and fragmentary," Nyama said. "They would also be useless. Right now, it is Nuso Esva's strategy and tactics that they will use."

"He'll indeed be devising their overall strategy," Thrawn said, his tone thoughtful. "But as Quesoth Soldiers still use their ancient weapons, so may they also still hold to their ancient battlefield tactics."

Beside Balkin, TIE Squadron Commander Baron Soontir Fel stirred in his chair. "Those umbrella shields they've got over the central part of the city are hardly ancient weapons," he pointed out.

"True," Thrawn conceded. "Liaison Nyama may be right. We may indeed face a conflating of disparate tactics, a mixture that will be difficult to anticipate." He looked at Parck. "We need information, Captain. More information; better information. We're working blind."

"How quickly the indomitable Master Warrior stumbles," Nyama said sarcastically.

"What Council Liaison Nyama means"—the young conciliator spoke up again—"is that timely information is of course a necessary part of combat preparation." His eyes flicked briefly to Nyama. "He also suggests that there may be a way to obtain the information you seek."

Thrawn's eyes narrowed slightly. "Continue."

Nyama grimaced. "As I've already said, we've been allies with Quethold for many generations. As a result, we have contacts among the Quesoth of the Red. Perhaps I can speak to one of them for you."

"You already said they were unquestioningly loyal to their Queen," Balkin reminded him. "What good would talking to them do?"

"I said the *Soldiers* were loyal," Nyama shot back. "The Soldiers and Workers are barely even intelligent, let alone able to make their own decisions. I never said that was the case with the Circlings and Midlis."

"But they're still loyal, aren't they?" Balkin persisted.

"I *said* they can think for themselves," Nyama all but bellowed. "Are you deaf, you bald-skinned—"

"What Council Liaison Nyama means," the conciliator interrupted hurriedly, "is that there's a small but growing opposition to the Queen of the Red's alliance with Nuso Esva. If we can contact them, perhaps they can obtain the information you seek."

Nyama glared at the conciliator, but gave a reluctant nod. "Provided you want something within their capabilities," he growled.

"What *are* their capabilities?" Fel asked.

"Not much," Nyama said. "Circlings are the Queen's advisers and upper-tier breeders. They're the most intelligent Quesoth, but they deal in words and thoughts, not actions. Midlis are tasked with overseeing the Workers, so they're not *that* intelligent. But they can be reasoned with, and can handle equipment to a limited extent."

"The task should be easy enough," Thrawn assured him. "All I want is for one of them to smuggle a holocam into Nuso Esva's chambers."

"A *holocam*?" Nyama echoed disbelievingly.

"Nuso Esva had little of his own artwork with him when he fled to Quethold," Thrawn explained. "Most of what he has will be from the Queen's collection. I need to see which pieces he's chosen."

Nyama snorted and shook his head. "Your obsession with art, Grand Admiral Thrawn, is more unsettling than your obsession with Nuso Esva himself."

"His obsession with both is what drove Nuso Esva off Oristrom and gave you the freedom to be here today," Fel said.

Nyama glared at him. But he had no answer, and everyone in the room knew it. "You have this holocam with you?" he growled, turning back to Thrawn.

"It will be ready whenever you confirm that one of the disaffected Circlings or Midlis can get it into Nuso Esva's chambers," Thrawn said.

"And can then bring it out again, I suppose," Nyama growled. He stood up abruptly. "I return now to my ship and will attempt to communicate with the dissidents. How large will this holocam be?"

"Very small," Thrawn said, holding up his hand. "The size of one joint of my finger. We can disguise it in any way necessary to facilitate entry."

"Perhaps it could even be planted on one of the Workers or Soldiers who attend the Queen," Parck suggested. "I understand twelve of each accompany her wherever she goes."

"You understand correctly," Nyama said. "I'll inquire as to the best way to achieve this goal, and will communicate with you when I have more to say."

With a brisk nod to Thrawn, he turned and strode from the room, the young conciliator hurrying to keep up. The door slid shut behind them, and Thrawn looked around the table. "Comments?" he invited.

"It could work," Parck said cautiously. "The number of variables is still uncomfortably high, though."

"And if Nyama is typical of Stromma attitude," Fel added, "we'd better assume we'll be tackling Nuso Esva without them."

"They *are* allies with the Quesoth, after all," Balkin murmured. "It's not easy to make a stand against one's friends."

"Especially when they figure they can just stall down the chrono," Fel said. "Two years, isn't it, until Nuso Esva's time in Red City runs out?"

"Yes, if Nyama's numbers are accurate," Parck confirmed.

"His numbers are accurate, but his reasoning is flawed," Thrawn said. "Nuso Esva could do an enormous amount of damage to the people of the Red City in those two years. That's not a result I'm prepared to accept." He hesitated. "Bear in mind, too, that Liaison Nyama speaks for the Stromma council, and some of those members still blame us for the destruction their worlds suffered."

Fel muttered something under his breath. "I suppose they also blame their surgeons for damaging bits of good tissue when they're cutting out the poisoned rot?"

"I don't defend their opinions," Thrawn said mildly. "I merely state that those opinions exist. At any rate, we cannot allow the common people of the galaxy to suffer merely because their leaders sometimes refuse to face the universe's realities."

"Well, the reality here is that we can finally nail this son of a—that we can nail Nuso Esva," Fel amended hastily. "We've got him pinned, and there's no place he can run. *And* we understand how he works."

"True." Thrawn smiled faintly. "More important, he understands how *I* work."

"Hopefully, that will be enough," Parck said.

Thrawn inclined his head. "We shall see."

The sky still looked odd as Trevik left the palace at the half-darklight hour and set off down the gentle slope of the city hill and across the wide ring of Circling homes. Farther downslope, beyond the Circling ring, was the Midli area of the city where his own home was located.

The sky looked even stranger over the Circling area, he noted with interest as he walked. In places, it held the same strangely muted appearance as it did over the palace grounds. But in other, small places, the sky was as bright and blue as normal. He gazed at the wonder as he traveled, trying to figure out what it all meant.

Perhaps one of the Workers would know. They were the ones who built everything in the Red City. Trevik's brother Jirvin was overseer of one of the Worker groups that created and serviced the city's lighting equipment. Perhaps he would know what had happened to the sky.

A whiff of air stirred from beside him, bringing with it the scent of a Circling. Automatically, Trevik stepped to the side, out of the other's path—

A hand closed around his arm. "Walk," the Circling ordered quietly, steering Trevik off onto a different angle.

"Where do we go?" Trevik asked, fighting to keep up with the other's longer stride. "My home is in a different—"

"Walk in silence," the Circling said cutting him off.

They were well within the Midli circle when Trevik noticed that the sky had changed again. Now the areas of strangeness had become a patchwork of distinct circles, their edges almost touching, with proper sky in the gaps between them. Beyond the Midli area, Trevik could see that the strangeness ended completely across the wide expanse of Worker and Soldier homes.

He was still wondering at the sight when the Circling guided him to one of the Midli homes. The door opened as they approached, and with the Circling still urging him forward, Trevik stepped beneath the lintel.

There were three other Midlis awaiting them in the house's sharing room. Two were strangers; the third—

Trevik gasped. *"Jirvin?"*

"Hello, my brother," Jirvin of the Midli of the Seventh of the Red greeted him, his voice solemn. "Please forgive the manner of your coming. It was vital that we speak to you immediately."

"You could have simply called me on the farspeak when I reached my house," Trevik said.

"It was equally vital that we speak to you in a manner that the Storm-hairs could not overhear," Jirvin said. "Please; seat yourself."

For a long moment, Trevik thought about turning and walking out. But the Circling who had brought him here had planted himself beneath the lintel. With an unpleasant sensation twitching up his legs, Trevik slowly crossed to one of the couches and lowered himself gingerly onto it. "What is it you wish to say?" he asked.

He saw Jirvin brace himself. "We believe, my brother, that the Red City stands on the brink of destruction," he said. "We believe that the Queen of the Red has been led by deceit into allying herself with Nuso Esva."

"Impossible." The word burst from Trevik's mouth without conscious thought. "The Queen is all-knowing and capable of infinite depth of thought. No alien being could sway her mind to such an extent."

"Nevertheless, we believe that such has indeed occurred," Jirvin said. "We further believe that something must be done to prevent the imminent destruction of our city. Perhaps even our entire world."

Trevik stared at him. "What exactly are you saying, my brother?" he asked carefully.

"I'm saying that the being Thrawn of the First of the Chiss of the Empire of the Hand is not the great enemy that Nuso Esva has named him," Jirvin said. "We have spoken to one of the Stromma, who has revealed to us the true natures of Thrawn and Nuso Esva."

"And?"

"And we"—Jirvin waved a hand to encompass the entire sharing room—"have thus chosen to join ourselves with our Stromma friends. With them, and with Thrawn."

Furtively, Trevik looked again at the doorway. But the Circling was still standing beneath the lintel, blocking any chance of easy escape. "Why are you telling me all this?" he asked, turning back to his brother.

"Thrawn urgently needs information if we are to defeat Nuso Esva and free our Queen from his grasp," Jirvin said. "You, my brother, are the only one who can obtain that information."

"Impossible," Trevik repeated, the word again escaping his mouth without thought. "I'm a loyal Midli. More than that, I'm the Queen's own bowlcarrier."

"You've been bowlcarrier for a single day," one of the other Midlis scoffed. "Don't make it sound as if your entire past and family honor are at risk."

"My past may not be at risk, but my family honor surely is," Trevik insisted. "Regardless, I cannot betray my Queen in such a way."

"She is no longer your Queen," the Circling at the door rumbled. "She has become merely a hand tool of Nuso Esva."

"I cannot and will not believe that," Trevik shot back. "The Queen seeks only what is best for her people, and for all the people of Quethold." He leveled two fingers at the Circling. "It is this Thrawn who is the enemy. I have heard Nuso Esva say so."

"Have you heard the Queen herself say so?" Jirvin asked.

Trevik turned back to him, a quick and scathing response boiling up from within him.

Then he paused, the words unspoken. *Had* the Queen actually said such words in his presence? Now that he thought about it, he couldn't remember her doing so. "It doesn't matter," he said stubbornly. "Nuso Esva is here, and he is the Queen's guest."

"He is her captor, not her guest," the Circling said. "You would serve the Queen better by allying yourself with us than by standing idly by as he exploits her."

"You've offered no proof of that," Trevik insisted.

"You've offered no proof to the contrary."

Trevik hissed. "Your challenge is useless. How does one prove a negative?"

"By taking the holocam our Stromma friends have given us," Jirvin said, his voice low and earnest. "By taking pictures of the Queen, and of Nuso Esva, and of the artwork with which he has decorated the Dwelling of Guests, so that we may learn the truth."

Trevik blinked. "The *artwork*?"

"Thrawn is able to read the hidden hearts of people through their choice of artwork," Jirvin said. "Or so the Stromma claims."

"The pictures will also prove that the Queen is with Nuso Esva of her own free will," the Circling added. "If, indeed, she is."

"If she allies herself freely with him, then we shall cease our efforts here," Jirvin assured Trevik. "Like you, my brother, we seek only what is best for our Queen, our city, and our world."

Trevik lowered his gaze to the floor. The Queen had accepted Nuso Esva as her guest—he was sure of it. But there was no way to prove that to Jirvin and the others except by doing what they asked. "Very well," he said, the words stinging his throat. "Where is this holocam?"

Jirvin rose from his couch and pulled a small, flat object from one of his vest pockets. "Here," he said, laying it across Trevik's hand.

Trevik frowned. The device was smaller than even the smallest of his fingers. "This is a *cam*?"

"It is," Jirvin confirmed. "You'll note it has the same texture and color pattern as your official bowlcarrier vest. Once secured there, it will be invisible to even the most strong-eyed observer."

He was right on that one, at least, Trevik had to admit. The cam would blend in perfectly. Whoever this Stromma was, he knew precisely how a bowlcarrier's vest looked. "How do I operate it?"

"You touch the upper right corner as you arrive at the Dwelling of Guests," Jirvin said. "The cam itself will do the rest."

"And make certain that it faces each piece of Nuso Esva's artwork during the time you're in the dwelling," the Circling added.

"I will." Trevik drew himself up. "And I *will* bring proof that the Queen has indeed chosen Nuso Esva as our ally. Then will you cease this foolishness?"

"If you bring back such proof, we will cease," Jirvin promised. "But if the proof is of her captivity under Nuso Esva's strength of mind, then our opposition to his presence will continue."

Trevik grimaced. *How does one prove a negative?* But it was clear that this was the best he was going to get. "I will bring the cam back at this hour tomorrow," he said, rising from the couch. "And then you will cease."

"Agreed," the Circling said, finally stepping away from beneath the lintel. "Farewell. May you eat and sleep deeply."

"May you eat and sleep deeply," Trevik replied with a sinking heart.

A minute later he was once again walking beneath the strange sky, heading toward his home. Surely he was right. Surely the Queen had chosen Nuso Esva as her ally of her own free will and depth of thought.

But if she hadn't, what did that mean for her? What would it mean for the rest of the Quesoth?

More immediately, what would it mean to Trevik if he was caught spying for Thrawn?

He had no way of knowing. But he was certain that it would not be pleasant.

Trevik slept poorly that night, and his food was equally unsatisfying. He woke early, groomed himself with extra care, and made certain he was at the palace a few minutes earlier than required. The nectar bowl was waiting for him beside the Queen's litter in the welcoming chamber, along with the Workers who would carry the two litters and half of the Soldiers who would escort them. Borosiv arrived a few minutes later and without a word took his place on the smaller litter.

His timing was perfect, as was only proper for the Circling who was the chosen attendant to the Queen. Barely a minute after Borosiv had settled into place, the inner doors opened and the Queen strode into the welcoming chamber, flanked by the other six Soldiers of their guard. She climbed up onto her couch, and the Workers hoisted both litters to their shoulders.

And with Trevik trying not to look as nervous as he felt, the group headed out the door and across the courtyard to the Dwelling of Guests.

After all of the evening's worry and the night's fitful sleep, the day turned out to be a welcome anticlimax. No one spotted the cam, nestled into the pattern on Trevik's vest, and it was easier than he'd expected to surreptitiously take the pictures that Jirvin wanted. By the time the Queen recalled her Soldiers from their defensive ring outside the Dwelling and the group returned to the palace for her midday meal, he had managed to face the holocam toward every one of Nuso Esva's chosen artworks. After the meal, when they had returned to the Dwelling for more talk with Nuso Esva, he made sure to take a few more pictures.

There was one other big difference between Trevik's first and second days as the Queen's bowlcarrier. The day before, his mind had been fully occupied with keeping himself motionless and the bowl level. Today, after all those strange things Jirvin had said, he made an effort to listen to the conversation.

It was confusing. That didn't surprise Trevik—this was the Queen of the Red, after all, along with an alien she found intelligent enough to spend hours conversing with. Their talk was probably above even the wisdom and intelligence of a Circling, let alone a mere Midli like himself.

But the parts he did understand were disturbing. There was talk of shuttles, and of the building of fighter aircraft, and of weapons that were either hidden or soon would be. There was talk of umbrella shields, and traps, and more hidden weapons.

And there was a great deal of talk about death.

But none of that was important. What mattered was that the Queen was clearly not a prisoner of Nuso Esva and the rest of the Storm-hairs.

Later that evening, as he returned the cam to Jirvin, he told his brother exactly that. Jirvin said nothing, except to reaffirm his promise that he and the others would end their opposition to the Queen if the record bore out Trevik's own observations. His unexpected and unwanted mission finally ended, Trevik again made his way to his home.

And that night, he *did* eat and sleep deeply.

The recorder erupted with a bewildering cacophony of squeaks, clicks, and squealings. *"Go through the Dwelling doors,"* Nyama translated, his ears twitching with concentration as he listened to the recording their Circling contact had delivered an hour ago. *"Surround and protect the Guests."*

There was another squeal. *"We obey the Queen,"* Nyama translated. There was a faint scuffling of feet, then the sound of opening and closing doors. "And they're gone," Nyama added, leaning back in his seat. "Everything else from now on should be in Quesoth Common Speak. Which I presume you understand."

"We do," Parck said, looking at Thrawn at the head of the conference table. The Grand Admiral's glowing eyes were narrowed, his full attention apparently on the photos of the Dwelling of Guests artwork that the secret recorder had also provided. "What do you know about Soldier Speak, Liaison Nyama?" Parck asked as he keyed for a quick-search of the audio track.

The Stromma gave a snort. "Obviously, I can understand it," he said. "What else is there to know?"

"What Council Liaison Nyama means," the conciliator put in, "is that there is nothing more that anyone except a Quesoth Queen and Soldier *can* know. It is a highly secret language."

"Yet *you* know it," Parck pointed out. "So do several of our Stromma recruits."

"Including two of my stormtroopers," Balkin said.

"And will understanding gain you anything?" Nyama shot back. "I tell you right now that it will not. We've fought the Quesoth, Captain Parck. All that an understanding of Soldier Speak will gain you is the brief advantage of knowing which of your troops will be the next to die."

"Which can also be useful," Thrawn said, looking up from his data-pad. "More important, understanding a language is the first step toward speaking or otherwise reproducing it."

"No," Nyama said flatly. "There's no reproducing of Soldier Speak. Believe me, Admiral Thrawn, we tried."

"That was a long time ago," Thrawn reminded him. "We have re-sources that weren't available to you back then."

"There's no reproducing of Soldier Speak," Nyama repeated, his tone sharper this time. "Queens have a unique set of vocal cords and resonance cavities, which even Soldiers themselves don't have. Besides that, Soldier language utilizes at least five different resonances and pitch variants, not to mention an entirely different vocabulary from Common Speak. The fourteen loudspeakers they've set up beneath the umbrella shield zone have to be specially designed to handle that entire range."

"So they don't use comlinks in battle?" Fel asked.

"Weren't you listening?" Nyama ground out. "I *said* they needed special loudspeakers. No comlink ever built can even come close to handling the necessary frequency range. Their speakers are simply too small."

"Yes, we heard you," Fel said. "So if we can knock out the loudspeak-ers, we'll cut off all communication between the Queen and her troops."

"For all the gain that will bring you," Nyama said contemptuously. "They'll just continue to follow their previous orders. Most likely something simple like 'Kill all the attackers.'"

"There may be other ways to exploit that sort of communications system," Thrawn said.

Nyama snorted. "If you think that—"

"Wait—here comes more Soldier Speak," Parck interrupted as the computer caught the language keys. He turned up the volume, winc-ing as the squealing sounds again assaulted his ears.

The monologue was short. "Liaison Nyama?" Parck invited.

"Nothing useful," Nyama said. "*Soldiers: escort your Queen to the Palace.*"

"I thought all the Soldiers were outside," Fel said.

"There are air vents near the ceiling," Thrawn said, his eyes back on the pictures the holocam had taken. "They can hear her commands through those."

But now Parck could see that the tension lines in his commander's face had smoothed out. "You found something, Admiral?" he asked.

"I believe I may have found the solution," Thrawn said, laying the datapad aside. "From the artwork Nuso Esva has chosen to surround himself with, I anticipate he'll deploy most of his forces at the western edge of the city, clustered around Setting Sun Avenue."

Surreptitiously, Parck looked at Nyama. Thrawn's unique ability to read a species' deepest psychological core by studying its artwork was one of his greatest strengths, enabling him to anticipate his opponents' moves right down to their likely battlefield tactics. New allies seeing it demonstrated for the first time inevitably reacted with surprise, awe, or disbelief.

Nyama was apparently going for option three. "Brilliantly anticipated," the Stromma said sarcastically. "Of course he'll concentrate his forces there—that's the only spot on the perimeter where your juggernaut heavy tanks can enter the city. Everywhere else Nuso Esva's umbrella shields are angled at the edges to block vehicles of any size."

"Which suggests Setting Sun Avenue is the entrance to a trap," Balkin suggested.

"Indeed," Thrawn agreed calmly. "Because the area won't be guarded solely by Quesoth Soldiers. He'll also have a number of heavy-weapons emplacements concealed along the route, waiting for our juggernauts. As our forces enter the city, he'll angle the umbrella shields downward along the route, protecting the shields' generators from the juggernauts' fire, as well as preventing the tanks from straying off that path. Once the juggernauts have penetrated a predetermined distance into the city, he'll blast the first and last ones in line, thereby trapping all the others. At that point, he can destroy them at his leisure."

Parck nodded, a sour taste in his mouth. It was a tactic they'd seen Nuso Esva use to devastating effect in previous encounters against some of the Empire of the Hand's other allies. "So how do we counter it?" he asked.

"We first let him think his plan is working," Thrawn said. "That means sending the line of juggernauts in as he expects." His eyes glittered. "But before he can launch his attack, we destroy the trap."

"Allow me to guess," Nyama growled. "Squadron Commander Fel and his oh-so expert TIE pilots fly in through the gaps between the umbrella shields and blast the hidden guns."

"You scoff, but it's actually quite possible," Fel said. "The shields don't overlap nearly as well as they should. There are numerous gaps between them, including at least one along one of the steepest parts of the main city hill that's big enough to fly through if we come in at just the right angle. Once we're in and below the level of the shields, everything but the palace and palace grounds should be wide open to us."

"That assumes your pilots are able to insert at the necessary angle," Nyama countered. "In the heat and flurry of battle, such precision would be impossible."

Fel shrugged. "Impossible is Gray Squadron's specialty."

"And what of the laser cannons spread throughout the city?" Nyama persisted. "We gave them those cannons, Commander Fel, years before Nuso Esva's intrusion into this region. Each cannon is twin-barreled, with rapid-fire capabilities and enough power to take out one of your vaunted TIE fighters with a single shot. *And* they have massive forward shield plates, which makes them nearly impossible to destroy along their own fire-lines."

"But they have only manual targeting," Thrawn reminded them. "And the very shields that protect them also make them heavy and unwieldy. Even Nuso Esva's most expert gunners will have trouble with TIE attack speeds."

"Unless the TIE is coming straight at them, as is the case with Commander Fel's scenario," Nyama said acidly. "No, Admiral Thrawn. Trust me: your TIE fighters will be useless in this battle."

"Perhaps," Thrawn said. "We shall see."

"We shall *see*?" Nyama echoed. "Tell me, Admiral: if the *Admonitor*'s turbolasers are incapable of penetrating the shields, your TIEs certainly won't be able to do so. What then will you have them do? Destroy the homes of the Workers and Soldiers that lie outside the shield zone?"

"We do not make war on civilians, Liaison Nyama," Thrawn said, his voice suddenly cold and brittle. "A fact you well know."

For a second Nyama's antagonism seemed to waver. Then, his natural Stromma leadership attitude reasserted itself. "Then what *will* they do?" he demanded.

"As Commander Fel has already stated, there are gaps between the shields," Thrawn said. "While the juggernauts move into the city, the TIEs will be shooting through those gaps with the goal of demolishing one or more of the shield generators."

"Generators that are protected by the very shields they create?" Nyama scoffed. "You can't hit the generators unless you're already beneath the shields."

"Unless it happens that a gap between two shields opens up a targeting vector to a third," Thrawn pointed out. "I admit the probability is low, but as Commander Fel pointed out, the coverage is not as good as it would have been if Nuso Esva had had more shields available. And if such an attack succeeds, the TIEs will be in position to take full advantage of the situation. But no, the downfall of Nuso Esva's plan will not be our TIE fighters, but our stormtroopers."

"Your *stormtroopers*?"

Across the table, Balkin stirred at the implied slight against his forces. Thrawn's hand twitched a warning, and the other subsided.

"Nuso Esva will have instructed the Queen to array the bulk of her Soldiers along Setting Sun Avenue to prevent a sortie from the juggernauts," the admiral said. "We'll therefore send a small stormtrooper force into the city southwest of the main assault, angle up toward the juggernaut line's southern flank, and attack the avenue's shield generators from behind."

Nyama shook his head. "Nuso Esva will not sit idly by and let that happen. Nor will the Queen of the Red. The Soldiers lining the attack route will simply turn around and swarm against the stormtroopers."

"Of course they will," Thrawn said. "When that happens, the stormtroopers will retreat, drawing them still farther from the juggernauts and the shields." He smiled slightly. "And when they're too far back to respond, the stormtroopers inside the tanks will emerge, cut their way through the remaining Soldiers, and destroy the shields."

Nyama snorted. "And all this against Quesoth Soldiers? You have far too much confidence in your humans, Admiral Thrawn."

"The stormtroopers of the 501st consist of humans *and* nonhumans," Thrawn reminded him calmly. "Including a number of your own people."

"Not anymore." Abruptly, Nyama stood up. "I've heard enough. The Stromma council will not risk its warriors in this mad attack. Particularly not an attack against our allies. I hereby withdraw all of them from Imperial service, effective immediately."

Beside him, the conciliator's mouth dropped open in clear disbelief. "What Council Liaison Nyama means—"

"Council Liaison Nyama means exactly what he says," Nyama interrupted. "Give the orders, Admiral Thrawn. Or I will give them for you."

For a long moment, the room seemed to quiver with the silence of approaching death. Nyama loomed over the still-seated Thrawn like a grass-covered mountain, his black eyes hard, his mouth set at an angle that warned against argument.

Thrawn stirred. "Very well, Council Liaison," he said. "If you don't wish to assist in freeing your allies from bondage, your people will be ordered to your carriers."

"What I *don't* wish is for my people to die for nothing," Nyama ground out. "And it *will* be for nothing. In two years Nuso Esva and the remnant of his Chosen will find themselves masters of a deserted city. If at that time you still insist on having your vengeance, we will gladly march in alongside you and sing a song to your honor as you destroy him. But I won't waste my people in a useless and futile battle."

He glared at the conciliator, as if daring the younger Stromma to attempt to soften his words. But the conciliator had learned his lesson, and remained silent.

"Nuso Esva can do a great deal of damage in those two years," Parck said. It wasn't a particularly politic thing to do, he knew, speaking words of contradiction to a Stromma council liaison. But he had no intention of letting his commander take the full brunt of Nyama's contempt alone. "And there are manufacturing facilities below Red City that he might use to devastating effect. Are you willing to simply stand aside and watch all that happen?"

"The Queen of the Red invited Nuso Esva into her city," Nyama said, sending an acid-edged glare at Parck. "Whatever happens now is on her head, and upon the heads of her people."

He turned back to Thrawn. "I return to my shuttle, Admiral Thrawn. I expect all Stromma under your command to be assembled at the *Admonitor*'s hangar bay within the hour."

"I'll give the order," Thrawn said.

Nyama held the admiral's gaze another two seconds, then stepped away from the table and strode from the room.

The conciliator stood up, his face pained. "Admiral—"

"Go with your superior," Thrawn said, his face impassive.

The younger Stromma looked helplessly at the others around the table, then nodded and left without another word.

"Well," Fel said into the silence. "*That* went well."

"Hardly unexpected, though," Parck agreed heavily.

"True." Fel cocked an eyebrow at Thrawn. "You *do* know, Admiral, that I wasn't exaggerating about the size of that gap. You come in at the wrong angle and graze one of those shields, and it'll blow off that section of wing and give you enough spin to send you spiraling straight into the ground."

"I have full confidence that you and your pilots will make it work, Commander." Thrawn turned to Balkin. "As I also have confidence that you and your stormtroopers will do their part."

"We will, Admiral," Balkin said quietly.

"So the plan's still on?" Parck asked.

"It is," Thrawn confirmed.

Parck felt his lip twitch. "I *have* spoken to some of the other Stromma who understand Quesoth Soldier Speak," he said. "They say that even if we're able to record enough of the Queen's orders during the battle, it'll be impossible to pick-and-stitch the words together to create counter-orders of our own."

"My Stromma trainees say the same thing," Balkin confirmed. "There's some kind of pitch rhythm in the subharmonics that a set of randomly stitched words won't be able to match."

"We shall see," Thrawn said. "Are there any other thoughts or concerns?"

Parck looked around the table. No one seemed inclined to say anything more. "Then you're dismissed," Thrawn said formally. "Make your final preparations, then get your forces fed and to sleep."

His eyes glittered. "Tomorrow, at midmorning, we attack."

It was not in the nature of Imperial stormtroopers to hide themselves from view. Their entire attitude and training, not to mention their gleaming white armor, tended in exactly the opposite direction.

Nevertheless, stormtrooper Lhagva of the Stromma contingent was trying to stay out of everyone's sight.

For the first hour he succeeded, running a quiet path between the *Admonitor*'s main trooper kitchen area and the equipment storage facility, choosing a route senior officers seldom traveled unless they had a reason to be there. He kept an ear cocked as he strode silently along, listening for loud voices and stern, determined footsteps.

He was ten minutes into the second hour when his luck ran out. Rounding a stack of safety-webbed crates, he ran smack into Line Lieutenant Dramos Sanjin, perched casually on the saddle of a Mobquet reconnaissance swoop.

"Stormtrooper Lhagva," Sanjin said with an air of clearly artificial casualness. "You seem to have missed the order that all Stromma aboard the *Admonitor* were to report to the Number Three hangar deck for disembarkation."

"My apologies, Lieutenant," Lhagva said, striving for the right mix of surprise and chagrin. "I've been having trouble with my hearing lately."

"Really," Sanjin said. "You didn't seem to have any trouble with Commander Balkin's order to report to the practice range earlier this afternoon."

Lhagva grimaced. Sanjin had him, and there really was no point in carrying on the charade any longer. "I heard a rumor that all the Stromma were being taken off in advance of the attack," he said. "I wanted to stay."

"You feel entitled to ignore orders you don't feel like obeying?"

"You need me, Lieutenant," Lhagva said, painfully aware that he was walking on extremely thin stone here. "Puriv and I are the only ones in the assault force who understand Quesoth Soldier Speak. We're the only ones who can give you any advance warning of what the Queen of the Red is ordering her forces to do."

"Yet Puriv left the *Admonitor* as ordered," Sanjin said. "Are you saying he doesn't have the same loyalty to the unit that you do?"

"Puriv has a family, and a strong family honor that he must uphold," Lhagva said. "Disobeying his orders would shame them all."

"Whereas you're an orphan who has no one to shame?"

"I'm an orphan who will dishonor no one but myself," Lhagva corrected. "I'm willing to accept that shame."

"Stromma discipline can be harsh," Sanjin warned. "Imperial discipline can be even worse."

"I understand," Lhagva said. "Discipline or discharge me as you must, Lieutenant. But I beg you, don't do either until after tomorrow."

Sanjin studied Lhagva's face. "You feel that strongly about this battle?"

"The Quesoth are Stromma allies," Lhagva said. "More than that, I spent two years in the Stromma diplomatic enclave at the edge of the Black City. I like these people, and I don't want to see them destroyed."

"And you think that likely?"

"If Nuso Esva isn't stopped, it's the only possible outcome," Lhagva said. "If he succeeds in holding the Red City, it'll be only a matter of time before he also takes the White City, then the Black City, and then the entire planet."

"And you want to see him stopped."

"Yes, sir, I do."

"Even at the risk of your own life and honor?"

"I'm an Imperial stormtrooper, Lieutenant," Lhagva said. "I live or die at the pleasure of my superiors and my commander."

"And if it pleases those same superiors for you to sit this one out?"

Lhagva swallowed hard, wishing he could read Sanjin's face. But human expressions were always so hard for him to penetrate. "Then I will resign my commission and accompany my former unit to the surface as a civilian," he said. "Stowing away aboard the transport if need be."

For a dozen heartbeats Sanjin just gazed at him. "This hearing problem of yours," he said at last. "Comes and goes, does it?"

It took Lhagva a moment to figure out what Sanjin was talking about. And there was a strange look the human's eye ... "Yes, sir, it does," he said. "As I said earlier—"

"Sounds serious," Sanjin cut in. "You'd better report to the medical bay. I'll let the Stromma liaison officer know that you'll be remaining aboard until the diagnostic droids have come up with a reading and a course of treatment." He cocked his head. "I'm sure you'll be ordered to remain in the bay until the assault transports have all launched at midmorning tomorrow."

"Hopefully, my hearing will be functional when that order is given." Lhagva bowed his head. "Thank you, Lieutenant."

"Don't thank me yet," Sanjin warned. "Better yet, don't thank me at all. If we're both still alive this time tomorrow Captain Parck will probably flay both of us alive. That is, if Commander Balkin doesn't get to us first." He gestured. "Get to the medical bay, and then get some rest. One way or the other, tomorrow is likely to end badly."

It was midmorning, and Trevik was once again holding the nectar bowl at the Queen's side when one of the Storm-hairs came unexpectedly into the Dwelling of Guests with an urgent report.

The forces of Grand Admiral Thrawn had left the star caravan and were moving toward the edges of the Red City.

"Excellent," Nuso Esva said with an almost eager satisfaction in his voice. "All is prepared?"

"All is prepared," the other Storm-hair confirmed.

Nuso Esva turned to the Queen. "Your forces are also arrayed as I ordered, O Queen?"

Trevik's eyes flicked sideways to the Queen's litter. The Queen's Soldiers, as *Nuso Esva* had ordered? Had *ordered*?

Such blatant effrontery should have earned Nuso Esva words of sharp rebuke, possibly even death at the hands of the Soldiers standing their usual guard outside the Dwelling. But to Trevik's even greater surprise, the Queen made neither response. "They are so arrayed," she said instead. "You are certain your weapons can stop the invading forces?"

"They will do more than simply stop them, O Queen," Nuso Esva said with grim satisfaction. "Today is the beginning of your final dominion over this world."

Again, Trevik looked sideways at the Queen. But this time, his surreptitious glance was accompanied by a surge of unpleasantness that curled through him like a plume of black smoke. What did Nuso Esva mean by dominion? In two years the Queen of the White would arise, the air would change, and the Queen of the Red would die. The Circlings would go into hibernation in the lower citadel of the palace, where they would arise and breed a new Queen when their part of the cycle came again. Once the citadel had been sealed, the Midlis, Soldiers, and Workers would start the long journey to the White City; there, those who survived the ordeal would join in with the Queen of the White's offspring. Eighteen years later, the Queen of the Black would arise, and the cycle would begin anew.

But the Queen of the Red—the current Queen of the Red—would still be long dead. What could Nuso Esva possibly mean by speaking to her of dominion over Quethold?

Trevik had no idea. He also had no doubt that, whatever the meaning, he wasn't going to like it.

The eight transports put down at the edge of the Red City, landing in a widely spaced semicircle in the fields just outside the outermost ring of Worker homes. The arrangement of the semicircle was typically Thrawn, Fel saw as he and his three squadrons of TIE fighters flew cover over the landing site. Setting Sun Avenue, the road that led due east into the city, was the designated entry point, and Fel had known commanders who would have automatically centered the force on that vector so as to provide maximum flanking cover to the main thrust.

But Thrawn did things with a bit more subtlety. This semicircle was centered instead on a creek that flowed west-southwest across the city, crossing the line of transports about half a kilometer south of Setting Sun Avenue. The gently sloping banks of the creek offered another wide entry point, one that a clever and unconventional commander might choose to exploit. It was certainly a tactic Thrawn might use, and one Nuso Esva would surely anticipate.

Sure enough, Fel could see movement now in the inner parts of the city, the Midli and Circling areas protected by Nuso Esva's umbrella shields. Some of the Quesoth Soldiers who had been deployed there were leaving the center city and moving down the hill along the creekbed toward the handful of natural strongpoints on the banks.

Fel smiled tightly. Nuso Esva didn't know that most of the transports arrayed against him, including the one positioned along the streambed, were just for show.

"Commander Fel?" Thrawn's voice came through Fel's helmet comlink.

"No resistance so far, Admiral," Fel reported. "I have Soldiers redeploying to the stream, but so far everyone's staying well back inside the shield zone."

"Any of the laser cannons in evidence?"

Fel took a moment to glance at his fighter's compact tactical board, wishing briefly that he was in his usual TIE interceptor with its better instrument array. But of course, the newer, sleeker interceptor wouldn't have worked nearly so well with this particular mission. "Nothing visible," he said. "Shall I make a pass across the larger holes in the shield array and see if I can draw some fire?"

"Not yet, Commander," Thrawn said with that mixture of respect, patience, and amusement that Fel had noted the Grand Admiral always seemed to use with him. "Are we intercepting any of the Queen's orders yet?"

"Negative on that, too, sir," Fel said. "We're probably still too far out to pick up anything from the loudspeakers."

"Stay on it," Thrawn instructed him. "I want to know the minute you start hearing Soldier Speak. Armor Commander?"

"Armor Commander," said a flat nonhuman voice coming into the circuit.

"Are the juggernauts ready?"

"They are."

"Deploy juggernauts."

Fel turned his fighter into a tight curve back toward the transport that lay across Setting Sun Avenue. The access door slid up into the curved top of the vehicle and a juggernaut rolled into view, twenty-two meters' worth of weapons and heavy armor, moving a little awkwardly on its ten wheels as it maneuvered itself onto the road. It had stabilized itself and started toward the city when the second tank appeared, following in the track marks of the first. It, too, made it onto the road just as the one behind it emerged into view.

Fel nodded to himself and turned into another curve back toward the city. If the first three juggernauts had made it out all right, he had no doubt that the remaining six would do likewise.

Meanwhile, his TIEs had another job to do. "Gray Squadron, form up around me," Fel called into his comlink. "Blanket sweep over the city. Let's see what sort of holes we can find to shoot through."

The fourth of the nine juggernaut tanks had emerged in the distance when Lhagva's squad rolled out of their transport on the first of the attack force's three A-rack carriers.

The A-rack was a simple device, one that Lhagva was told had been adopted from one of Thrawn's other liberated worlds. It looked very much like an A-frame, fold-up clothing roller of the type he'd seen being pushed or pulled along busy walkways back in his own home city's garment district. The A-rack, though, was much sturdier than those, with oversized wheels, a top-mounted E-Web/M heavy repeating blaster, a center-mounted engine, and enough room on each side for five stormtroopers to stand facing outward. With the pair of cramped seats in the center section for the driver and gunner, the carrier could transport a full stormtrooper squad quickly and efficiently across medium-rough terrain.

The downside, which Lhagva always thought about when he rode one of the things, was that it also left the squad bunched close together and thus vulnerable to ambush.

But so far the enemy here hadn't made any such moves. The houses the three A-racks rolled past were showing no signs of life, not even the occasional furtive peek by a curious face at any of the windows. The Workers were apparently all out of the city as usual for this time of the morning, laboring in the fields, forests, and mines stretching out beyond the urban area.

As for the Soldiers, most of those Lhagva could see from his angle were gathered in clumps along the juggernauts' line of travel a few hundred meters to the north. Their backs were to the incoming A-racks, with no indication that they were even aware that three squads of stormtroopers were coming toward them from the south. It was as if Thrawn had completely blindsided Nuso Esva and the Queen of the Red.

Lhagva didn't believe it for a minute.

"Tighten it up, troopers," Sanjin called from the A-rack's gunner's seat. "Things are about to get hot."

Lhagva shot a quick look upward. They'd reached the outer circle of Midli houses, and the sky above them had gone dark and shimmery as they passed beneath the edge of the city's new patchwork of umbrella shields. From this point on, Commander Fel's TIEs would be unable to provide the stormtroopers with any cover fire.

Readjusting his grip on his BlasTech E-11 blaster rifle, Lhagva returned his attention to the houses and open areas on his side of the A-rack. Whatever Nuso Esva was planning, he knew, the battle was about to begin.

"Excellent," Nuso Esva said, his lips curled back, his faceted yellow eyes intent on the line of eight large monitors the other Storm-hairs had set up in the Dwelling of Guests gathering area. "Thrawn is nothing if not always precisely on schedule." He gestured to one of the monitors. "Observe, O Queen. Here come his soldiers."

The Queen leaned closer toward the image. Surreptitiously, Trevik did the same. The white-armored soldiers were heading northward through the southwestern part of the city, riding on three bouncy and fragile-looking metal frameworks. On one of the other monitors, larger, more substantial vehicles were rumbling into the city along Setting Sun Avenue.

And just like the soldiers, the large vehicles were moving in a straight line. Trevik didn't know much about tactics, but even to him that seemed foolish.

It apparently seemed that way to the Queen, as well. "I will order my Soldiers to attack," she said, picking up the special farspeak that rested beside her armrest, its wires snaking across the room to the connector in the wall. "They will make short work of them."

"Not yet," Nuso Esva said, holding out a hand. "Not yet."

Trevik flinched. The outstretched hand was a signal of command, a gesture Trevik had used many times when overseeing Workers and one that he'd received in turn from senior Midlis and occasional Circlings.

No one ever used such a gesture toward the Queen of the Red. Ever.

The very thought of such a blatant insult was both fantastic and outrageous.

Yet once again, the Queen gave no indication of such outrage. "Then when?" she simply asked.

"Be patient, O Queen," Nuso Esva said. To Trevik's relief, he lowered the discourteous hand again to his side. "The enemy fighter craft are about to make their first attempt to enter through my trap. When they do, my soldiers will open fire with the blaster cannons I set up in concealment—"

"The guns *my Workers* set up in concealment," the Queen corrected him.

Nuso Esva's eyes might have glittered with new fire. Trevik wasn't certain. "The cannons your Workers set up," he amended coolly. "Once they open fire, destroying or scattering the fighter craft, the cannons that I"—he inclined his head—"the cannons that your Workers set up along Setting Sun Avenue will destroy the first and last juggernauts in line. *Then* you will order your Soldiers to destroy the stormtroopers. All is as I predicted."

Nuso Esva turned his eyes on Trevik. "*Exactly* as I predicted," he added.

"Yes," the Queen said, and out of the corner of his eye Trevik saw her turn to him. Automatically, he lifted the bowl as he likewise turned to face her.

But to his surprise she didn't drink. To his even greater surprise, she continued to stare at him. "O Queen?" he asked, not knowing what else to say.

"Nuso Esva of the First of the Storm-hairs did indeed predict all," she said. "You, Trevik of the Midli of the Seventh of the Red, have betrayed me."

Trevik froze, a horrible flood of fear and shame exploding inside him. She knew. She knew about his brother Jirvin and the others who'd been in the house that evening. She knew about the cam Trevik had brought into the Dwelling of Guests. She knew that Trevik had given that cam to his brother, who had then given it to the enemy Thrawn.

And Trevik knew that he was dead. The Queen would call in her Soldiers from outside, and they would kill him—

"Calm yourself, O Queen," Nuso Esva said calmly. "You're frightening him. At any rate, it's hardly betrayal when his actions are a deliberate and necessary part of a plan."

"His actions may have been a part of *your* plan," the Queen said, still staring at Trevik. "But in his hidden heart, the Midli committed treason against his Queen."

"We thought he was controlling you," Trevik breathed, finally finding his voice. "I was told he was controlling you."

"No one controls a Queen of the Quesoth," the Queen said darkly. "It is *she* who controls."

"Which you should have realized from the beginning," Nuso Esva said. "How else do you think that Circling was actually willing to pretend to treason? He acted that way under his Queen's orders so that he could persuade you to take the pictures I wanted Thrawn to have."

Trevik tore his gaze away from the Queen's stare. "To persuade . . . ," he began weakly.

"Pictures of these," Nuso Esva said, waving a hand toward the walls of the gathering area. Even with his alien face and voice it was impossible for Trevik to miss his deep and malicious satisfaction. "Artwork carefully selected to lead our oh-so-clever Grand Admiral to exactly the wrong conclusions about my strategy."

Trevik could feel his breath coming in short, painful gasps. Jirvin had also said that about Thrawn, that in artwork he could read the hidden hearts of people. Trevik had accepted his brother's word, but he had never truly believed it.

Now, as he felt Nuso Esva's triumph wash over him, he knew that it was indeed true.

"You don't believe it, of course," Nuso Esva continued. "No one does. But rest assured, Thrawn is able to perform such magic. The Queen's own confidant and ally stayed aboard the star caravan long enough to confirm it." This time, his eyes definitely glittered. "Before he pulled all of your Stromma allies out of the battle."

"Which he would still have done without this Midli's betrayal," the Queen said.

"Calm yourself, O Queen," Nuso Esva said again. "Let us watch and savor the defeat of our enemy without these petty distractions. There will be plenty of time later to execute this Midli and his friends if you so choose." He turned back to the monitors. "Besides, I daresay Thrawn will have another trick or two waiting behind his back. Watch—and see how I anticipate and destroy each of them."

The sixth of the nine juggernauts had passed beneath the edge of the umbrella shields, and the stormtrooper force was nearly halfway to its target flank, when the order finally came. "Commander Fel, you may initiate your attack pattern," Thrawn said. "Let us see what exactly we have facing us."

"Acknowledged, Admiral," Fel said, turning his fighter into a smooth arc back toward the western part of the city. Thrawn's assumption had been that Nuso Esva would close off the entire umbrella shield array except in the western areas of the city. But even 90-percent-sure assumptions needed to be checked out, and Fel's TIEs were the logical ones to do it. Especially when they had nothing better to do anyway.

As usual, Thrawn had been right. Gray Squadron's sweep had confirmed that the rest of the city was completely covered, with gaps not even big enough to drop an MSE droid through. Only in the western sector, where Nuso Esva had set his traps, was there anything Fel could use.

With the juggernauts and stormtroopers now in harm's way, it was time for the TIEs to persuade Nuso Esva to start springing those traps.

As it turned out, the onetime warlord didn't need any persuading. Fel was passing over the lead juggernaut and starting to make his turn when the city below him erupted with laser cannon fire.

"Evasive!" Fel snapped, twisting his fighter around as a bolt came through one of the shield gaps and burned past his portside wing. Not that his pilots really needed the warning. "Target those lasers and destroy."

He was cutting dangerously low across the forest of umbrella shields when he spotted the swarm of Quesoth Soldiers appearing from concealment in the ring of Workers' houses directly behind Lieutenant Sanjin's stormtroopers.

◆◆◆

The first warning was a burst of Soldier Speak from a concealed loud-speaker a few blocks away. *"Soldiers in concealment,"* Lhagva called out in translation. *"Rise and attack the white-armored invaders."*

"Vec six!" one of the other stormtroopers snapped, pointing his E-11 back toward the edge of the umbrella shield zone. "Looks like—must be a hundred Soldiers, coming out of the Workers' houses."

Lhagva felt his mouth go dry. A hundred Soldiers, against thirty-six stormtroopers. Not good.

"Got another hundred fifty at vec three," someone else put in tautly. "I guess they don't want us heading toward the palace."

"Lucky we didn't want to go in that direction anyway," Sanjin said with his usual calm. "Here comes the vec-null contingent."

The words were barely out of his mouth when the western half of the city suddenly exploded with laserfire as a dozen concealed laser cannons opened up against the TIEs flying overhead.

"About time," Sanjin shouted over the noise. "A-racks, stop; gunners, grab the E-Webs. Kicker, find me some useful real estate."

Lhagva turned from the large insectoid beings closing on their rear, their short swords and heavy maces glinting in the shield-muted sunlight, and peered across the landscape in front of them. There was the vec-null contingent, just as Sanjin had said: another hundred or more Soldiers who had left their places along the juggernauts' insertion route and were heading toward the stormtroopers.

And that was a direction Sanjin's assault force *had* been hoping to go in.

Lhagva looked to the west. So far, that area was still clear of Quesoth. If Sanjin gave the order, and if they turned the A-racks and pushed them to the limit, they could probably get back out from under the umbrella shields and into TIE cover ahead of all three groups of Soldiers.

But that would mean running. And Imperial stormtroopers never ran. Not when they had a job to do.

Not even when they were outnumbered ten to one.

"Kicker?" Sanjin prompted.

"Yes, sir," a stormtrooper from one of the other squads called back, his eyes on the portable sensor looped over his shoulder. "One of the shield generators is in there." He pointed at a modest house just ahead and to the east. "Next nearest is over there," he added, pointing to another house to the northwest. "That enough, or do you want one more?"

"Two should do us," Sanjin said, looking back and forth among the incoming groups of Soldiers. "If we can wreck both generators, it should open the sky enough for the TIEs to get under the rest and access the whole city. Squad three, take the eastern house. Squads one and two, you're with me in the other one."

There was another burst of Soldier Speak from the nearby loudspeaker. "*North and east Soldiers, converge northeast at weapons site; defend and attack from there,*" Lhagva translated. "*South Soldiers, follow your current track.*"

"What does she mean, weapons site?" Sanjin asked. "A weapons cache, or one of those laser batteries?"

"I don't know," Lhagva said. "The term could apply to either."

"A laser battery would make more sense," Sanjin decided. "New plan: squad three to eastern house, squad two to northwest, squad one with me. We'll go to ground somewhere, wait for them to tag the weapons site for us, and try to get in. Smoke grenades; two per enemy force. Everyone ready? Grenades: go."

The grenades had just hit the ground when, in the distance, the rearmost juggernaut lumbering along through the city exploded.

In the dim light filling the *Admonitor*'s ground-tac center, a second display flared unnaturally bright and then went dark. "Juggernaut One has been hit," General Tasse reported. "Cam out; telemetry data . . . it's still moving, but just barely. Another hit like that and it'll be as dead in the mud as Juggernaut Nine."

"Acknowledged," Thrawn said.

Parck stole a sideways look at the admiral. Thrawn was standing in front of the tac board, his eyes sweeping methodically across the myriad displays and status readouts. To all outward appearances he seemed as calm as always.

But Parck knew better. The Grand Admiral's campaign against warlord Nuso Esva had been a long and bloody one, a road littered with betrayal and destruction, new allies and barely thwarted genocide. Now, at long last, Nuso Esva's end was finally in sight.

At least, all indicators pointed in that direction. The once-proud conqueror was trapped on Quethold, with limited resources, no more than thirty of his most loyal followers, and only a single medium-sized ship buried away out of easy reach in one of the mines north of the Red City. The remnants of his once-powerful battle fleet were scattered across probably a million cubic light-years of space, where they would, presumably, wither and die once Nuso Esva was no longer there to command.

And yet . . .

Parck ran his eyes over the tac board again. Preoccupied with the stream of reports from the scouts searching for Nuso Esva's remaining ships, he'd been somewhat out of the data loop for the planning of the Red City attack. There were undoubtedly a few pieces of Thrawn's plan that he didn't know.

But as he gazed at the turmoil being presented on the boards, he could feel an unpleasant sensation starting to tingle between his shoulder blades.

The *Admonitor* had six squadrons of TIEs aboard, yet Thrawn had chosen to deploy only three of them. He had over three thousand troopers available, not even counting allied forces, yet had sent only three squads of stormtroopers against the Red City's Soldiers. The line of juggernauts now under heavy attack was even more of a gamble.

And Liaison Nyama had been right about the number of Soldiers that Nuso Esva had available. The observers and sensors were registering at least four thousand of them, two thousand along the juggernauts' route, a few hundred attacking the stormtrooper squads, the rest arrayed in a defensive line between the palace and the transports. How could Thrawn have so badly underestimated his opponent's strength?

Or had he? Could it instead be that this long, wearying war against Nuso Esva had so blunted the Grand Admiral's tactical prudence that he was determined to defeat his enemy with the absolute minimum force possible?

Had this become personal?

The thought sent a fresh shiver up Parck's back. Four years earlier,

Emperor Palpatine had traveled to Endor burning with hatred for the Rebel Alliance. Four years before that, Grand Moff Tarkin had similarly made the attack on Yavin a matter of personal vengeance.

Both men had died at the scenes of their hoped-for triumphs, their certain victories snatched from their fingers. The Rebel Alliance had survived, and had gone on to turn much of their Empire into the so-called New Republic.

Parck had always assumed Thrawn knew better than to let emotion cloud his military judgment. Could he have been wrong?

"Patience, Captain."

Parck jerked out of his thoughts. "I'm sorry, Admiral?" he asked carefully.

"You're worried," Thrawn said, his voice low enough to assure that his words would be for the senior captain's ears only. "Worried about the operation"—he looked sideways at Parck—"and by extension, worried about me. But observe."

He pointed to one of the tac display's city overlays. Scattered amid the bright red spots marking Nuso Esva's laser cannon positions and the muted yellow dots of the umbrella shield generators were a dozen glowing blue lights. "The Queen's loudspeakers," he said identifying them. "The sensors in the TIEs, the juggernauts, and the stormtrooper A-racks are all listening for the distinctive sound of Soldier Speak. Every order she gives her troops brings us that much closer to our final thrust."

"Yes, sir," Parck said, trying to filter the doubt out of his voice.

Apparently, he hadn't filtered out *all* the doubt. "Patience, Captain," Thrawn said with a faint smile. "Patience."

"As I anticipated," Nuso Esva said, his voice brimming again with satisfaction. "You note, O Queen, that as the smoke clears the white-armored invaders are no longer anywhere to be seen?"

The Queen made a grotesque sound Trevik had never heard from her before. "True Soldiers would not flee a battle," she said.

"Nor have these," Nuso Esva said. "They've merely taken refuge in some of the homes, most likely the two or three nearest that contain shield generators. They no doubt hope to destroy or disable the generators before they're overwhelmed by the approaching Soldiers, thereby allowing the fighters overhead to enter your city. Hoping their deaths will not be useless." His eyes glittered. "But of course, they will."

Trevik gazed at the monitor, feeling an unexpected and discomfiting surge of sadness for the invading soldiers. From the earlier speech between the Queen and Nuso Esva he gathered that humans were like the Stromma, where each member had the same free choices that Quesoth Midlis and Circlings possessed. Unlike Quesoth Soldiers, the white-armored attackers were not bound irrevocably by their orders, and therefore could have retreated to safety when they saw the numbers arrayed against them.

Yet they had not. What kind of leader was this Thrawn, that his people willingly gave up their lives at his command?

"The shield generators must not be damaged," the Queen said, lifting her mike. "I will send more Soldiers."

"No need, O Queen," Nuso Esva said. "I have anticipated this move, and have prepared for it. No, keep your Soldiers where they are. The real battle will take place at the line of juggernaut vehicles. You see how the rearmost has already been disabled, blocking the rest from retreat? As soon as the one in the forefront has likewise been stopped, your Soldiers can move against the true prize."

"Yes, I see," the Queen said again. "You didn't say that two of the nine would be destroyed."

"I told you sacrifices would be necessary," Nuso Esva said. "In this case, the loss of two assures that we can capture the other seven intact."

"And seven will be enough?"

"More than enough," Nuso Esva said. "I've seen the strength of the Red City's lower citadel. I doubt that the White City's defenses will be any greater. Seven juggernauts will be more than sufficient to break through the barriers."

"The White City?" Trevik asked, the words coming out before he could stop them. "What? Break the *barriers*? What is this madness you speak of?"

"The old ways are at an end, Trevik of the Midli of the Seventh of the Red," the Queen said, her voice as calm as if she were asking for a drink of nectar. "Why should I accept death for myself and my city merely because the Queen of the White has arisen?"

"But—" Trevik stared at her. "But the old Queen always dies when the new Queen arises and the air changes. It's the way of the world."

"You're a naïve fool," Nuso Esva said scornfully. "A Queen—a *true* Queen—doesn't simply sit back and accept the way of the world." He held out his hand toward Trevik, his fingers closing into a fist. "A true Queen grasps the world by the throat and squeezes her own destiny from it. Understand?"

"No," Trevik said, the sheer shock of it draining all emotion from him as if a vein had been cut. "But I do understand one thing: the Queen of the White cannot arise if the Circlings of the White are dead." He looked at the Queen. "If they are murdered."

"It's a matter of survival," Nuso Esva said. "Survival of the strongest. That's how the universe operates, Midli. I have no doubt that the Queen of the White, if given this same choice, would take the same action."

"It will serve all of us," the Queen said. "Including you yourself, Trevik of the Midli of the Seventh of the Red. No more will you and the other Midlis and Circlings need to travel long distances to a new city, many of you dying along the way. You will remain here, in familiar surroundings, living out your lives in your own homes."

"And when you die?" Trevik asked.

The Queen smiled. "I will not die," she said, an unpleasant edge to her voice. "Without the changing of the air, I will live forever."

All living things die. Trevik wanted to say that.

But he couldn't. Not directly to her face.

Not to the Queen of the Red, who was supposed to be the leader of her city, and the steward of all the Quesoth.

She had betrayed them. She had betrayed them all.

But he couldn't say that, either.

"When will this happen?" he asked instead.

"When the battle is over and Thrawn has lost, he will leave," Nuso Esva said. "He'll have no choice. His defeat here by primitives will severely damage the reputation that holds his fragile coalition together, and he and his star caravan will need to travel to other conflicts to take personal charge of those battles. Once he's gone, we'll take our newly captured vehicles to the White City. The Queen of the Red will become the Queen of Quethold"—his eyes glittered—"and I will have free access to the industrial facilities beneath the White City. There I will construct vehicles in which I and my Chosen may leave this world and once again carry the war to my enemies."

Trevik nodded, his heart sickening within him. So that was what it came down to. Quethold was to be sacrificed, its stability and the lives of its people lost, so that the Storm-hairs could continue their thirst for conquest among the stars.

And there was nothing he could do to stop it. The Queen had revealed her own thirsts, and there was nothing a mere Midli could say that would change her mind. Nor was he a Soldier, who might fight the Storm-hairs on her behalf.

No, all Trevik could do was stand with his nectar bowl, and watch and listen.

And hope that, somehow, Grand Admiral Thrawn would be able to win.

Quesoth Soldiers were about as primitive a group of combatants as Lhagva had ever come across. They didn't wear armor, they didn't use blasters or even projectile weapons, and their tactics seemed limited to swarming their enemies in an attempt to overwhelm them with sheer numbers.

But their natural chitinous hides were tough enough to shrug off even a blaster bolt or two unless they were hit squarely in a vital organ, and they wielded their short swords and maces with incredible strength. And they definitely had the numbers for their chosen strategy.

It was also quickly clear that they weren't going to give up the laser cannon emplacement they'd been ordered to defend. Not while any of them was still able to fight.

"Flanking left," Sanjin called over the scream of the stormtroopers' blasterfire. "Lhagva, Shrinks—go."

"Right." Lhagva squeezed off one final shot through the sleeping room window of the house in which they'd taken refuge, then turned and sprinted out the door, down the hall, and into the gathering room, one of the other stormtroopers right behind him.

They were just in time. The Quesoth surge had overwhelmed the three stormtroopers guarding that approach, and a small knot of Sol-

diers had made it all the way up to the window. Even as Lhagva skidded to a halt and opened careful fire over his comrades' shoulders, one
of the Soldiers leaned in and slammed his mace hard across Bragger's
arm. The stormtrooper fell with a muffled curse, and the Soldier
started to climb in through the gap.

And fell backward out of sight as Shrinks opened fire from Lhagva's
side with the E-Web/M from their A-rack. Between the two of them,
they drove back the attackers.

Bragger was back on his feet by the time the two newcomers reached
him. "You all right?" Lhagva asked.

"Arm's probably broken," Bragger said calmly as he shifted his E-11
to his left hand and rested the muzzle on the windowsill. "I'll be fine."

Outside, the loudspeaker was blaring Soldier Speak again. "Lhagva?"
Sanjin called.

"*Soldiers of the Setting Sun and Soldiers of the defense: attack and
capture the armored vehicles*," Lhagva translated. "They must have gotten the lead juggernaut stopped."

"Sounds like it," Sanjin said. "I hope they like what they—"

"Hold on," Lhagva interrupted him as the Soldier Speak continued.
"*Kill the crews and all the white-armored invaders inside.*"

"Yeah, good luck with that," Sanjin said with a grunt. "Break time
over, troopers. Get back to work."

"Flanking right!" someone warned.

Lhagva fired one last shot through the window at the swarm of Soldiers and then turned back toward the doorway. "I'm on it," he called.

"There they go," General Tasse reported tightly, pointing at one of the
displays. "Coming out of concealment . . . must be two thousand of
them."

"The defensive line's on the move, too," one of the others said. "Another fifteen hundred at least. Looks like a few of Nuso Esva's personal
troops are in there with them."

Tasse grunted. "Looks like Nuso Esva's decided we don't have anything left in the transports we can throw at him, so he's retasked his
defense line," he said. "Figures the more bodies he throws against the
juggernauts, the faster he can batter his way in."

Parck winced. Nuso Esva was certainly right on that count. Thirty-five hundred Soldiers with maces would make quick work of even a juggernaut's hatch.

"Admiral, two of the umbrella shields are down," a lieutenant called from the tech board. "Southwest sector."

So Lieutenant Sanjin's stormtrooper contingent had come through.

"Can the TIEs get in through the breach?" Parck asked.

"No, sir," the lieutenant said. "The adjoining shields are angled downward like the ones at the city's outer edge. They're too low to permit any vehicle entry."

"As expected," Thrawn said calmly. "Nuso Esva is nothing if not thorough. What's Lieutenant Sanjin's status?"

"He reports two down," Commander Balkin reported. "The rest are holding for now."

"Order them to continue pressing on the laser cannon emplacement," Thrawn said. "The longer Nuso Esva thinks we're following his script, the longer it will take him to react to the genuine breach."

Parck frowned. "Following his *script*?"

"Of course," Thrawn said, frowning as if it was obvious. "Why else did you think I let him arrange the art in the Dwelling of Guests and then make it sound like I needed to see it? I wanted him to think that he'd manipulated our operation and had it under his control."

Parck felt a smile twitch at his lips. He should have known it was something like that. As Thrawn had said, Nuso Esva understood him. Or thought he did. "When do you plan to leave his script?"

"Right now." Thrawn pointed at the tac board. "The fourteenth loudspeaker has just been located." He keyed his comm. "Commander Fel, you may begin your run. Good luck."

"Acknowledged," Fel said, baring his teeth in a tight smile. Finally. "Gray Squadron, into your positions. Stent, on me."

He swung his TIE around, listening with half an ear to the chorus of acknowledgments from his pilots as he eyed the cityscape below. Considering some of the traps Nuso Esva had set in the past, he reflected, this one was almost simple. A single opening in the umbrella shield coverage, apparently there by accident, big enough for a TIE fighter to slip through if it came in at just the right vector. And on the same vector, a heavy twin-barreled laser cannon lurking in concealment, ready to blow apart an unwary pilot.

But as was also typical of Nuso Esva, the laser cannon wasn't there solely to seal the flytrap. The TIE pilots had had plenty of time to map the shields and weapons emplacements in that zone, and Fel had spotted at least eight other, smaller openings in the barrier nearby that the lasers could fire through. Even if an approaching pilot veered off the flytrap vector in time to survive the gunners' first shot, they would have several other chances to finish the job as he flew away. Assuming, that is, the gunners were fast enough and good enough.

Time to find out just how fast and good they were.

By the time Fel had brought his TIE onto the flytrap vector, Stent was in position, forming up fifty meters behind Fel off his starboard wing. Stent was a Chiss, one of Thrawn's people, who had severed ties with his homeworld in order to come out here and serve the Grand Admiral. He was also one of Fel's best pilots, which was why Fel had chosen him for this job.

And the two of them were going to get only one shot at this. Kicking his TIE to full power, jinking back and forth as much as he could while still maintaining his insertion vector, Fel headed in.

He'd closed to within a hundred meters of the flytrap opening when he spotted the telltale twitch of the laser barrels as they made their final targeting lock. Instantly, he did a final twitch of his own, jinking his fighter hard to starboard. The lasers flashed, the dual bolts sizzling past his canopy.

With a burst of fire and shattered metal, his portside wing burst into flame.

Twisting the yoke hard over, Fel spun away to starboard. His momentum was carrying him straight toward the unyielding patchwork of umbrella shields below; twisting around again, he pulled up sluggishly out of his dive.

And as he did so, he flew directly across one of the laser cannon's other firing gaps.

He tensed with anticipation. But Thrawn had been right. The gimmicked wing and its fake fire damage made Fel look fatally wounded, and Nuso Esva's gunners weren't going to bother with a fighter that would likely crash within seconds anyway. Certainly not when they had a much more interesting target coming their way.

Because while Fel had been fighting his burning craft, Stent had lined up onto the flytrap vector and was heading in.

Fel continued his turn, losing altitude and fighting to keep his wobble from getting out of control, all the while wending a twisting path toward the flytrap opening. He finally straightened out into a course more or less level over the city and perpendicular to Stent's own current vector. From Fel's new angle he could see that Stent was coming in at full power, with the same evasive maneuvering that Fel had been trying when the laser cannon opened up on him. Alternating his attention among Stent, the flytrap opening, and the ground, Fel flipped up the protective cover on the add-on section of his control board and braced himself.

For an instant he thought Stent had left it too late, and that Nuso Esva's gunners would nail him for sure. But at the very last second the Chiss pulled up, arcing off his approach vector just as the laser cannon fired. The bolts burned across his TIE's belly as he twisted up and away, clawing for altitude as he passed across one of the cannon's other firing gaps. The cannon spun around, firing through the gap, again just a shade too late, then swiveled to another angle as Stent continued past the emplacement and across another of its firing gaps.

And for the next three or four seconds, as the gunners furiously tracked Stent's apparently random-motion retreat, taking shot after shot through firing gap after firing gap, the flytrap opening was completely unprotected.

As usual, Nuso Esva had been clever. The size of the flytrap had been carefully tailored to allow insertion from but one direction.

Yet also as usual, he hadn't been clever enough . . . because he'd assumed that the intruder would be a *whole* TIE fighter, a cockpit/body equipped with the standard pair of large, hexagonal solar wings jutting out on both sides.

Smiling grimly, Fel pressed the button beneath the open safety cover.

And as the explosive bolts blew across the wing connectors, ejecting both wings to tumble to their destruction against the umbrella shields below, he deftly slid the cockpit section of his TIE sideways through the flytrap opening.

Nuso Esva's gunners must have instantly spotted their fatal error. But it was already too late. Even as they tried to bring the cannon around again, Fel rotated on his repulsorlifts and fired a close-in double burst from his own laser cannons. The bolts shattered the emplacement's rotational platform, leaving the weapons frozen in place, pointed uselessly at the sky.

Then, flying low over the houses, dipping and dodging where necessary to avoid the umbrella shields' edges, Fel began blasting the houses where those shield generators were located. The rest of Gray Squadron was right behind him, dropping through the ever-widening hole and joining in the task of systematically peeling open the nice secure lair that Nuso Esva had built for himself.

And as the rest of his squadron continued their destruction of the shield generators, Fel shifted to his own special assigned task. Flying widely across the edge of the city, he began eliminating the Queen's communication loudspeakers.

All of them, that is, except one. For that one, Grand Admiral Thrawn had something special planned.

"There is trouble," the Queen said.

For a few seconds Nuso Esva ignored her as he continued to jabber on his private farspeak in his incomprehensible alien language. Trevik braced himself, wondering what the Queen would say or do at this latest insult to her.

But she sat quietly on her litter, waiting with eerie patience for Nuso Esva to finish his other conversation. The alien talk ended, and Nuso Esva jammed the farspeak back into his belt. "There is trouble," the Queen repeated.

"Nothing that can't be handled," Nuso Esva growled, his voice barely within the limits of civility. "As soon as your Soldiers breach the juggernauts—"

"There is trouble," the Queen said again, much more emphatically. "Enemy aircraft fly free over my city, destroying the homes of Circlings and Midlis. You said that would not happen. You said that *could* not happen."

Nuso Esva seemed to gather himself together. "Calm yourself, O Queen," he said, more politely this time. "The fighters may have breached the outer parts of the city, but there's another angled rim to the shield array farther in. That edge will keep them out of the palace grounds and away from us."

"Yet they have entered my city," the Queen persisted. "You said they would not. You lied."

"They won't be there for long," Nuso Esva said. "Unlike the primitive cannons my Chosen have been forced to work with, the juggernauts' weaponry is equipped with computerized sensor targeting capabilities. Once we've gained control of them—"

One of the Storm-hairs by the monitors called something in the alien language. "The hatches are breached," Nuso Esva announced. "Now watch as I destroy the enemy fighters."

Trevik looked at the monitors. One of them showed an image that bounced dizzyingly while the Storm-hair carrying the holocam ran behind a group of Soldiers through the jagged metal edge where a hatch had once been. The Soldiers rushed inside, spreading aside out of the view of the cam.

Suddenly the image went still. Very still. For a pair of seconds it showed a view of a compact metal chamber, empty except for blinking lights, softly glowing displays, and some sort of small, round-topped metal object at the far end. Abruptly, the image spun around, paused, spun around again, paused again—

Nuso Esva spat something vile sounding. "No," he bit out as he snatched up his farspeak. "*No!*"

"What is it?" the Queen demanded. "What's happened?"

Nuso Esva ignored her, snarling more of his alien speech into his farspeak. The image on the monitor began bouncing again as the Storm-hair with the cam raced to the end of the metal chamber and stopped beside the round-topped metal object. There was a close-up view of the lights and monitors—

"*What has happened?*" the Queen bellowed.

Trevik shrank back in terror. Never in his life had he heard the Queen shout that way. Never had he realized she *could* shout that way.

Nuso Esva barely even took notice. He continued snarling into his farspeak, his free hand gripping the weapon belted at his side. Around the room, the other Storm-hairs also had their hands on their weapons. Trevik tensed, waiting for the Queen to shout again.

But she remained silent. A moment later, Nuso Esva lowered his farspeak, his yellow eyes glittering with fury. "The juggernauts have no crews," he bit out. "No crews, and no soldiers. Their drivers are nothing but droids. Mechanical Workers." He hissed something vicious sounding. "*And* there are no weapons. All have been removed."

For a long moment the gathering room was silent. Trevik kept his eyes on Nuso Esva, afraid to look at the Queen. "Then you have failed," she said at last.

"I haven't failed," Nuso Esva, turning his head back to the monitors. "The juggernauts are useless to us? Fine. There are other targets that will serve." He looked back at the Queen and gave the gesture of command. "Order your Soldiers to the transports waiting on the ground outside the city. They are to capture the vehicles and kill everyone aboard."

"Do the transports hold the weapons you claim will bring you victory?" the Queen countered. "Or do you simply seek a means of deserting Quethold and escaping back to the stars?"

"Don't waste precious time with foolish prattle," Nuso Esva spat. "Give the order."

"I cannot." The Queen pointed toward the monitors. "The loudspeakers have been silenced. There is no way for my voice to reach my Soldiers."

"What?" Once again, Nuso Esva twisted his head around toward the monitors. "So," he murmured bitterly. "We see now Thrawn's true strategy. He draws the majority of the Soldiers to the juggernauts, where they will be useless to me, then destroys the means by which they could be ordered elsewhere."

He turned back to the Queen. "But as always, his strategy is flawed. If your voice cannot travel to the Soldiers, then you, O Queen, must do the traveling." He gestured toward the Workers crouched beside the litter. "Order your Workers to their places. We travel at once to the juggernauts."

Trevik felt his eyes go wide. "You cannot order the Queen into battle," he objected.

"Silence, traitor," Nuso Esva said, not even bothering to look at him.

"Perhaps Trevik of the Midli of the Seventh of the Red is not the true traitor here," the Queen said darkly. "Perhaps it is *you* who are the traitor, Nuso Esva of the First of the Storm-hairs. You promised us victory. You promised me eternal life. You have broken faith on both."

"You wish eternal life?" Nuso Esva countered. "Then go to the juggernauts and order your Soldiers to attack the transports."

The Queen gestured in refusal. "No."

And then, suddenly, Nuso Esva's weapon was out of its sheath and pointed directly at the Queen. "Give your Workers the order," he said, his voice deathly quiet. "Or die."

The sole remaining loudspeaker was less than two hundred meters from the stalled juggernauts and the thirty-five-hundred Soldiers standing stiffly alongside them. Fel eyed them warily as he settled his TIE into a defensive hover above the support platform, wondering if they would decide they should take some action against the shuttle that was even now lowering a pair of techs onto the platform beside the loudspeaker array.

But they didn't. They'd been ordered to attack the juggernauts, they'd done that, and they were now waiting for further instructions.

"Patience," Fel murmured toward them.

There was movement by the crushed hatch of one of the juggernauts, and two of Nuso Esva's Chosen stepped outside, their yellow eyes glinting in the sunlight. One of them pointed at Fel, and they raised their blasters.

Fel nailed them both with a single shot. Again, the Quesoth Soldiers did nothing.

Fel gave the rest of the juggernaut hatches a quick check, then did another scan of the area to make sure more of the surviving Chosen weren't rushing to the attack. As Thrawn had ordered, he'd left this particular loudspeaker intact, merely severing the control, power, and communications cables that led to it. That meant the techs not only would have to set up the special Soldier Speak message Thrawn had prepared, but would also have to splice in power from the shuttle's generators.

With Sanjin's stormtroopers still battling for their lives against their own clump of Soldiers, Fel hoped the techs would hurry.

Two streets away, another pair of the Chosen were warily approaching. Fel rotated his TIE a few degrees in that direction and waited for them to come out of cover.

And then, abruptly, the loudspeakers came to life below him, filling the air with a volume and intensity that he could feel right through the lower hull of his TIE as Thrawn's message blared across this part of the city. The message ended and began to repeat.

For a moment nothing happened. Fel held his breath . . .

And then, all at once, the Soldiers by the juggernauts began to move. Flowing along the ground, more like a dark fluid than a collection of individual beings, they headed up the hill toward the palace.

The Soldiers had once again pressed their way to the house's windows, and Sanjin and the remaining stormtroopers had pulled back to one of the inner rooms to make their final stand when Lhagva heard the faint sound of the loudspeakers over the noise of blaster bolts and the thud of maces and swords. He frowned, wondering at the bizarre message—

And then, without a word, the Soldiers lowered their weapons. Turning, they filed quickly back through the doors and the holes they'd battered in the walls, heading out into the city.

Leaving the stormtroopers panting in the middle of an empty room.

Sanjin found his voice first. "What in the void was *that*?" he demanded.

With an effort, Lhagva worked some moisture into his battle-dried mouth. "You didn't hear the loudspeaker, did you?"

"No, I think I was getting clubbed with a mace at the time," Sanjin said, rubbing gingerly and ineffectually at the side of his helmet. "These things don't block that kind of blow nearly as well as I'd hoped. What happened? Did the Queen surrender?"

"I don't think so," Lhagva said. "It sounded like something Thrawn set up."

"I thought you couldn't fake Soldier Speak," one of the others said as he dropped to his knees beside a fallen stormtrooper, his field med-pac in hand.

"He didn't," Lhagva said. "It seemed to be just a straight recording, taken right from the Queen's mouth."

"Which said?" Sanjin prompted.

"*Go through the Dwelling doors,*" Lhagva translated. "*Surround and protect the Guests.*"

"But isn't that an order for the Soldiers to *protect* Nuso Esva?" one of the stormtroopers objected. "How's that going to help us?"

"Because," Sanjin said, and Lhagva could envision the other's grim smile behind his helmet, "Nuso Esva doesn't know that."

Nuso Esva was still pointing his weapon at the Queen when one of the other Storm-hairs suddenly chattered in their alien language. Nuso Esva barked something in return and took a step forward. "What did you tell them?" he demanded. "What orders did you give your Soldiers?"

"I gave no orders," the Queen said. "I cannot give any—"

"*Don't lie to me!*" Nuso Esva thundered, taking another step forward. "An order was given. You're the only one who can give such orders." He took another step toward her. "And now they're all coming here," he continued, his voice suddenly quiet. "*Why* are they coming here, Queen of the Red?"

"I don't know," the Queen said. "When they arrive, I will ask them."

Nuso Esva snorted. "No. You won't." Abruptly, his weapon spat a blaze of fire, and without a sound the Queen slumped over.

Dead.

Trevik gasped, his body stiffening as he stared in disbelief and horror at the Queen's lifeless form. This wasn't the way Queens of Quethold died. It was never the way Queens died. Dimly through the hiss of blood roaring through his ears and brain he heard the sound of more blasterfire . . .

"You. Traitor."

Trevik jerked his head around. Nuso Esva was staring at him, his weapon pointed directly at Trevik's face.

And only then did he realize that there were bodies of dead Quesoth all around him. The Workers, Borosiv of the Circling of the First of the Red—all of them were dead.

All of them had been murdered.

"You're going to take a message to Thrawn for me," Nuso Esva said, his voice grim and defiant.

And yet, beneath the alien warlord's determination, Trevik could somehow sense a bitter-edged melancholy. There were four thousand Soldiers marching on the palace, and he knew that his own death marched alongside them. "Tell Thrawn that he may think he's won," Nuso Esva continued. "But with my death, his own will not be far off. My followers are still out there, and they're more numerous than he can possibly imagine. No matter where he goes, no matter where he tries to hide, they *will* find him. You'll tell him that."

With a supreme effort, Trevik forced words into his mouth. "I will tell him," he promised.

For a moment Nuso Esva held his position. Then, at last, he lowered his weapon. "Go," he ordered.

Trevik was at the edge of the palace grounds, weaving his way through the lines of incoming Soldiers, when the Storm-hairs opened fire behind him.

He had reached the waiting group of white-armored humans when the Storm-hairs' firing came to an abrupt end.

Parck looked up from the report. "So that's it," he said.

"That's it," Thrawn confirmed. "One of the bodies in the Dwelling of Guests was positively identified as his."

Parck nodded, feeling a strange weariness stealing over him. After ten years of sporadic combat, slippery escapes, and unlikely victories across the Unknown Regions, warlord Nuso Esva was finally, finally dead. "What now?" he asked, setting the datapad aside.

Thrawn shrugged slightly. "There's little we can do for the Quesoth except aid in rebuilding the damage to the Red City," he said. "But they should be all right. Historically, there have been several instances when Queens have died prematurely. Sometimes that induces the next Queen to arise ahead of schedule; sometimes the affected city has to limp on alone until the regular time of arising. But whatever struggles the Red City ends up going through, the people of Quethold will survive. That's what's important."

"Yes," Parck agreed with a shiver. Especially considering what that Midli, Trevik, had told them about Nuso Esva's plans for the planet. He could have destroyed everything, and might even have gotten loose to spread more of his poison across the Unknown Regions.

But he hadn't. He was dead, and it really was over. "Actually, Admiral, I meant what were *we* going to do now," he said.

"You and the *Admonitor* will be heading back to the Chaos Triangle to begin cleaning up the legacy that Nuso Esva left behind," Thrawn said. "As for me, I can now finally turn my attention to an even more pressing problem than Nuso Esva. Namely, the restoration of the Empire."

Parck winced. Thrawn had returned only occasionally to Imperial space since Palpatine's death. Those trips had usually been short, had always been shrouded in secrecy, and had invariably left the Grand Admiral frustrated by the growing disorder there. Between the incompetence of its own leadership and the steady military pressure from the New Republic, the Empire had shrunk to barely a quarter of the size it had attained under Palpatine's rule. "You may have trouble persuading them to accept your help," he warned. "Some of their recent experience with Grand Admirals hasn't been all that positive."

"There's someone there I can contact," Thrawn assured him. "Captain Gilad Pellaeon, currently in command of the ISD *Chimaera*. I worked with him before, back when Nuso Esva made his one incursion into Imperial space."

"Yes, I remember," Parck said grimly. "Candoras sector. I also remember that it was shortly afterward that Nuso Esva launched the Braccio campaign and ended up nearly destroying half a dozen species."

"Your recollection is correct," Thrawn said, frowning slightly. "Your point?"

"That Nuso Esva was a vengeful son of a space slug," Parck said. "I don't expect his followers to be any less so. It may not be a good time for you to reintroduce yourself to Imperial politics."

Thrawn shook his head. "Don't worry, Captain. Whatever followers

Nuso Esva has left are few and scattered. Without his leadership, they'll slink back into the shadows where they belong."

"Perhaps," Parck said. "It still might not be a bad idea for you to take a few additional precautions out there."

"Your concern is touching," Thrawn said. "Again, you have no need to worry. Captain Pellaeon is a competent commander, and he's made the *Chimaera* into one of the finest warships in the fleet."

"What I meant—"

"And I've also made arrangements to have a bodyguard accompany me when I return to the Empire," Thrawn continued. "Whatever vengeance Nuso Esva had planned, or thought he had planned, it will never reach me."

"I hope not." Parck took a deep breath. He still didn't like this, but he knew better than to argue when Thrawn's mind was made up. "With your permission, Admiral, I'll go begin preparations to contact Captain Pellaeon and return you to the Empire." He smiled slightly. "To *your* Empire."

"Thank you, Captain," Thrawn said quietly. "And don't look so glum. This isn't just the end of Nuso Esva."

He smiled tightly. "It's also the beginning. The beginning of victory."

About the Author

Since 1978, TIMOTHY ZAHN has written nearly seventy short stories and novelettes, numerous novels, and three short fiction collections, and won the Hugo Award for best novella. Zahn is best known for his *Star Wars* novels *Heir to the Empire, Dark Force Rising, The Last Command, Specter of the Past, Vision of the Future, Survivor's Quest, Outbound Flight,* and *Allegiance,* and has more than four million copies of his books in print. His most recent publications have been the science-fiction Cobra series and the six-part young adult series Dragonback. He has a B.S. in physics from Michigan State University and an M.S. in physics from the University of Illinois. He lives with his family on the Oregon coast.

ABOUT THE TYPE

This book was set in Minion, a 1990 Adobe Originals typeface by Robert Slimbach. Minion is inspired by classical, old style typefaces of the late Renaissance, a period of elegant, beautiful, and highly readable type designs. Created primarily for text setting, Minion combines the aesthetic and functional qualities that make text type highly readable with the versatility of digital technology.